SINCE THE MARQUESS DEMANDS

ROGUE RULES
BOOK SIX

DARCY BURKE

Zealous Quill Press

SINCE THE MARQUESS DEMANDS

ROGUE RULES
When a young lady is ruined, her friends vow none of them
will ever be ensnared by a scoundrel again. They will resist
every gentleman's charms even—and especially—if it means
gaining a reputation for being impossible to woo. It will take
extraordinary rogues to break their rules...

Ellis Dangerfield has recently learned her life is a lie.
Desperate to start afresh, she applies for a position as secretary to a demanding, widowed marquess. Never mind that
she must pose as a man to get the job—Ellis is hiding far
worse secrets.

After losing his wife—and, perhaps more gutting, learning of
her unfaithfulness—Roman Garrick has sworn off human
connection. To avoid his pain, he buries himself in rebuilding
his family's ruined fortunes. When he discovers his brilliant

new secretary is actually a woman, he should dismiss her immediately. Instead, he's captivated.

Faced with an unwanted and dangerous attraction, Roman and Ellis struggle to maintain their professional relationship while also trying to resist their desires. Neither is willing to compromise the vows they've made to remain emotionally aloof. But when Ellis reveals the truth of her scandalous parentage and a shocking secret from the past surfaces, their chance at happiness hangs in the balance.

Don't miss the rest of the *Rogue Rules*!

Do you want to hear all the latest about me and my books? Sign up at Reader Club newsletter for members-only bonus content, advance notice of pre-orders, insider scoop, as well as contests and giveaways!

Care to share your love for my books with like-minded readers? Want to hang with me and see pictures of my cats (who doesn't!)? Join me on Facebook in Darcy's Duchesses!

Want more historical romance? Do you like your historical romance filled with passion and red hot chemistry? Join me and my author friends in the Facebook group, Historical Harlots, for exclusive giveaways, chat with amazing HistRom authors, and more!

THE ROGUE RULES

Never be alone with a rogue.
Never flirt with a rogue.
Never give a rogue a chance.
Never doubt a rogue's reputation.
Never believe a rogue's pledge of love or devotion.
Never trust a rogue to change.
Never allow a rogue to see your heart.
Ruin the rogue before he can ruin you.

CHAPTER 1

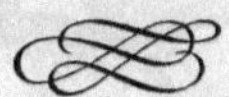

October 1816, London

"You look like a man to me!"

Ellis Dangerfield raised a brow at her giggling landlady, who'd helped assemble and don Ellis's disguise as a young man. Pivoting, Ellis regarded herself in the cracked glass that hung in her room. She could not see her entire body in the small oval, but viewing her face was enough. A dark brown beard and mustache masked her feminine features, particularly her mouth, and her blonde curls were tucked beneath a thick—and rather hot— wig of the same color.

"I don't know." Ellis chewed the inside of her lip as she faced Mrs. Palmer once more. "Perhaps this is too risky."

Mrs. Palmer cocked her head as she swept Ellis with her warm blue gaze. "Probably, but don't you have to try?"

Ellis was quickly losing her courage. Whilst she desperately needed employment, she ought to try for something suitable for a woman. Secretary to a marquess was not that. However, secretary to a marquess would pay far better than anything she would find as a woman. "Perhaps I should gain some sense and seek a more appropriate position."

Eyes narrowed, Mrs. Palmer tucked a wayward light brown lock into the cap she wore over her hair. "You've told me several times that you're capable of every single task a secretary to a marquess would need to complete. I don't even understand everything you said."

Ellis smiled at Mrs. Palmer, who was very smart. She just hadn't been offered the same level of education as Ellis, who, since the age of nine had lived in the household of the Duke of Henlow as companion to his daughter. She'd learned alongside Lady Minerva and had taken full advantage—with her own initiative—of His Grace's libraries, which he maintained at all his properties.

The duke had opened his home to Ellis after the death of her parents, who'd been friends of his. Indeed, her father's parents and the duke's parents had been dear friends. The family connection was strong, and he'd felt a responsibility to care for Ellis. He'd also had an affinity for her, which some had interpreted to mean that he was actually her real father —because Ellis had been adopted by the Dangerfields and then taken in by the duke after their deaths.

But the duke was not her father. She'd always known that because he'd told her so, and she believed him. He also didn't love Ellis the way her parents had done. Even after all this time, the thought of her mother and father and the end of the life she'd enjoyed as a cherished daughter cut sharp and deep. Especially now that she knew the truth of her parentage.

Learning that she was, in fact, illegitimate—though not because of the duke—had completely turned Ellis's life upside down. She now understood why the duchess had worked so hard to make her feel unworthy. Because she was. In the eyes of Society, Ellis would always be wanting due to the circumstances of her birth. *If* the truth were to become known.

But it didn't matter to Ellis. *She* knew—and knowing meant that everything she'd thought to be true was a lie.

She'd done the only thing that had made sense to her: she'd run from the truth and from the pain of the past seventeen years. Deciding that only she could choose her own path forward, she'd decided to seek independence. Why wait for the worst to happen when she could forge a new life? It was time for her to choose instead of having her story written by those around her who saw her as nothing more than a game piece to move about a board.

She needed this job as secretary to the marquess. And she was going to obtain it. Focusing on the coming interview, she regarded Mrs. Palmer, who was a dozen years older than Ellis's twenty-six years and an actual widow, unlike Ellis, who was merely pretending to be one. "What if the marquess immediately recognizes I'm a woman?"

"You beg his pardon and leave." Mrs. Palmer exhaled. "It's not as if he'll have you arrested for posing as a man in order to obtain employment at which you would excel and that would pay you enough money to live the life you want." Her eyes gleamed with determination, as if she were the one embarking on a plan to secure her own future. "The life you *deserve.*"

"That is kind of you to say." Ellis was glad for the woman's support, which buoyed her intent.

She'd come to stay at Mrs. Palmer's boarding house nearly a fortnight earlier when she'd quit the duke's household after learning of her illegitimacy. The duke had offered her money, but she'd only taken what she needed to travel to London from Bath, where she'd been staying with Min and the duchess—she and the duke did not care to reside together when they were not in London—and settle herself with lodgings. Ellis had refused an ongoing allowance. She didn't want any ties to the duke or his family, and she certainly didn't want to feel beholden.

The only problem was his daughter. Min was her dearest friend, and Ellis had left without speaking to her. Ellis wasn't ready to see her and didn't know when she would be. That was because Min was the reason Ellis had learned the truth.

Thinking of it now caused a tremor in Ellis's chest. She'd overheard Min fighting with her mother, the duchess. That hadn't been out of the ordinary as they often clashed, but this argument had been different. They'd been discussing Ellis, who was, shockingly, also the duchess's daughter.

To discover the horrid woman who'd treated Ellis like an ungrateful, unwanted servant of the lowest class—no, lower than that—was the woman who'd given her life had been devastating. The duchess loathed Ellis and had gone to great lengths to ensure Ellis had none of the luxuries of her other children, not that material items meant anything to Ellis. She'd only wanted the most precious thing of all—love. Or at least a sense of belonging. How could a woman treat her own flesh and blood so cruelly?

"Stop thinking about your past," Mrs. Palmer said sternly. Ellis had told her she was hiding from her deceased husband's terrible family. "You must put that behind you and move forward."

Ellis smiled. "You sound like me." Because she'd repeated those words a hundred times or more: *leave the past behind and move forward.*

"It is good advice after all you've been through."

"Thank you." Ellis had considered telling Mrs. Palmer the truth, for the desire to have a confidante was great. She was used to having Min by her side. Ellis could have her there again—she need only tell her.

But Ellis couldn't do that. Not yet. She understood that Min hadn't been part of the lifelong deception, that she had also been kept from knowing the truth. However, Min's life, her very identity, hadn't changed whilst Ellis's had. She would seek Min out once she was on the path that she'd chosen for herself.

Mrs. Palmer grabbed the hat and gloves from the table by the window and handed them to Ellis. "You should be on your way before you're late."

Ellis turned back to the glass and set the hat on her wig, then drew on the gloves.

"Don't you dare think you won't be hired," Mrs. Palmer warned. "I've spent far too much time putting together a wardrobe for you from my brothers' old things." She had two older brothers and had harvested their old clothing from crates in the attic. What she hadn't been able to find, she'd somehow acquired in other ways. "I'm still not finished, though I'm close to having a complete set of evening attire, should you need it."

"I won't," Ellis said, thinking this was all a far-fetched dream anyway.

"From now on, until you return here after your interview, you must lower your voice as you've practiced and speak as a man." Mrs. Palmer gave her an encouraging nod.

Ellis pitched her tone to a baritone, or what she hoped was a baritone. Thankfully, she had a deeper voice than most women, so that was already in her favor. "I should have been doing that the entire time. How's that?"

Mrs. Palmer beamed. "Perfect. Our practice has borne fruit. I shall ensure you won't encounter anyone." She left the chamber first, and Ellis followed, pulling the gloves on as they made their way to the stairs.

Leading her down two flights to the ground floor, Mrs. Palmer stayed far enough ahead so she could signal Ellis if she saw anyone, though that was unlikely. There were only two other lodgers, and they were typically gone by this time of the morning.

They hurried through the entrance hall and Mrs. Palmer opened the door to usher her outside. "I'll be anxious to hear about the interview. I know you'll do well!"

Ellis smiled at the landlady before embarking on her long walk to Mayfair from Wimpole Street in Marylebone. She dearly hoped she wouldn't encounter anyone she knew. Thankfully, the Marquess of Keele did not live on the same street or even very near Henlow House. And if she *did* see someone, they wouldn't recognize her anyway. Still, she kept her head down until she reached Keele's house.

She turned onto Bolton Street and approached the marquess's terrace, surprised at the narrow width. She'd expected something grander, but then she knew Keele, a widower, was rebuilding his family's fortune. He was a friend of Min's brother—Lord Shefford or Sheff as everyone called him—though Ellis had never met him. Keele didn't participate much in Society, but apparently frequented one of the clubs, which was where Sheff saw him on occasion.

The reason behind Keele's family's misfortunes was unknown to Ellis, nor did it matter to her except as it pertained to her potential position as his secretary. She certainly wasn't going to ask.

Her nervousness about the coming interview hadn't lessened as she'd walked through Mayfair. In fact, it had increased to where her stomach was in knots.

Ellis took a deep breath and approached the door. She tipped her head back to survey the red brick that covered the façade from the first floor up through the fourth. The ground floor was white stone, and a wrought-iron fence kept pedestrians from falling into the servants' access on the lower ground floor.

As she rapped on the door with her gloved hand, she was struck by the absurdity of what she was doing. Did she really expect to masquerade as a man whilst performing the duties of secretary for a marquess? One would think she'd lost her mind. Perhaps she had. The last several weeks had been the most trying of her life.

A butler opened the door. He was younger than she expected, perhaps in his middle thirties, with thick brown hair and deep-set gray-blue eyes. "Good afternoon. Are you Mr. Ellis?"

When Ellis had responded to Lord Keele's advertisement, she'd used the name Daniel Ellis. "Yes, I am," she replied in her deeper, hopefully masculine tone.

The butler inclined his head and invited her inside. "His Lordship is expecting you, of course. This way." He led her to the rear of the first floor, through the staircase hall.

The door to Lord Keele's study stood open, and the marquess rose from his desk, which was situated so he had a view of the small back garden. He came toward the door and extended his hand. "Welcome, Mr. Ellis. I'm pleased to meet you."

Ellis hadn't practiced shaking hands and hoped she would do so believably. Stepping into the office, she clasped his hand and was surprised at the strength of his grip. She should not have been, for the marquess was tall and powerfully built, with broad shoulders but a narrow waist. He appeared as though he could lift Ellis and hold her over his head. That was saying something, because Ellis was tall for a woman.

Keele released her hand and looked past her to the butler. "Thank you, Graham."

Ellis heard the door close followed by the muffled retreat of the butler's footsteps. Her gaze swept the marquess's study. It wasn't large, but then his house wasn't either. Aside from his oak desk, there was a chair near the hearth, a cabinet of drawers, two bookcases, and a second, much smaller desk situated in the corner, adjacent to the marquess's. The room wasn't crowded exactly, but it lacked the space and opulence of the Duke of Henlow's study.

"Let us sit." The marquess gestured to the chair by the grate. Covered in faded dark blue velvet, Ellis envisioned the marquess sitting there often as he reviewed documents or read an investment scheme.

Reminding herself that the marquess didn't need to wait for her to sit because he didn't know she was a woman, Ellis took the chair. Meanwhile, he sat behind his desk and pivoted his chair toward her.

The desk was cluttered, with an overflowing wooden box in one corner and several unkempt stacks of a variety of things that clearly needed to be sorted. The marquess appeared to be in dire need of assistance.

She eyed Keele's demeanor and copied him, situating herself against the back of the chair and resting one elbow on the arm. She did not worry about keeping her ankles together.

"I was glad to receive your letter," Keele began. "Your qualifications and education are excellent, but your letter of recommendation from the Duke of Henlow is extraordinary."

The recommendation from Henlow was the one thing Ellis had asked him for. He'd been eager to provide some kind of assistance and had offered the letter not just to Keele but to anyone else she wanted. "As he no doubt mentioned, my father worked for His Grace's steward collecting rents," Ellis said. That was the fib the duke had suggested.

Keele nodded. "He also said you worked for him temporarily when his secretary had to tend to a family matter for a fortnight. Most remarkably, he said your skill was exemplary and was tempted to replace his current secretary with you." The marquess possessed razor-sharp steel-gray eyes and a hawk-like nose that made him appear almost predatory. Indeed, the way he was regarding Ellis presently sparked the sensation that she was his prey.

She shifted her weight and again resisted the urge to cross her ankles. Sitting like this, without a skirt to cover her legs, made her feel incredibly vulnerable. Or perhaps it was more due to the intensity of his stare. Did he suspect she was not who she claimed to be? Did he doubt the duke's recommendation? Whilst Henlow had lied about how he knew her, the letter had been drafted by him without any contribution from her.

"That was kind of him to say," Ellis murmured. Too late, she realized such mild vocalization was likely too feminine. Men didn't murmur. They claimed space with their bodies, their actions, and their voices. "I enjoyed working for His Grace," she added in a stronger tone.

"As it happens, I know the duke's son very well. The Earl of Shefford is a friend of mine. Did you have occasion to meet him?"

Ellis was prepared for this question since she knew Keele and Sheff were friends. And Sheff was not aware of what she was doing. She preferred to have no contact at all with that family right now, except for the favor she'd requested of the duke. "I did not. I didn't meet anyone in the household."

"The duke mentioned you are excellent at shorthand," Keele noted. "I wonder if you might demonstrate?"

Henlow had asked for specific information about Ellis's

skills so he could include them in his recommendation. Ellis inclined her head in an authoritative manner, as a man would. "Certainly."

"You may sit at the secretary's desk there in the corner." Keele gestured to a small kneehole desk, the side of which nearly butted up to his.

Ellis stood, and as she drew closer to the desk, noted it was rather scuffed. Also, one of the drawers did not sit squarely. The chair was in similar condition and did not possess quite the same finish. They were not a matched set.

There was foolscap as well as a goose quill and an inkwell along with other writing implements. Thankfully, there was also a pencil, which was much more suited to shorthand. Ellis plucked up the pencil and poised her hand above the paper. "Whenever you're ready."

Keele stood and moved to his desk. He did not sit as he dictated a letter to his banker.

As he neared the end of the missive, Keele approached the secretary's desk. He stood over Ellis and looked down at her shorthand. She was keenly aware of his proximity and his interest. She didn't care for either. It made her feel scrutinized, which of course was the point of this interview. Still, she didn't like the sensation of being so intensely watched and judged.

When he was done, she tipped her head up and back to look at him. "Do you read shorthand?"

"A little, but not well enough to make sense of it. Yours seems very good, but I suppose the test is in the transcription. Please write the letter out now. I'll just work at my desk." He gave her a brief smile that made him look less like a hunter, then returned to sit behind his desk. His focus immediately turned to the papers before him.

Ellis watched him for a moment, thinking how scandalous it was for her to be in this office—with the door closed—alone with the Marquess of Keele. Instead of feeling anxious, she suppressed a laugh. She didn't give a fig about preserving her reputation as a woman, as she had no need of it. She only needed to establish her skill and worth as a male secretary.

Setting her mind to the task, Ellis wrote out the letter using the shorthand she'd taken. Satisfied she'd done a good job, she dusted the ink with the wooden sand shaker.

"Finished?" Keele asked, indicating that whilst he'd seemed engrossed in his task, he'd been listening, at least somewhat, to Ellis work.

"Yes." She was going to stand, but he extended his hand, and if she did the same, she realized, she only had to rise a short distance from the seat of her chair to present him with the letter.

Keele's gaze moved over the paper quickly. He appeared to be a fast reader. "Well done." He lifted his focus to her. "I hope you won't take offense, but your handwriting is quite nice. It's almost, dare I say, feminine."

Ellis's pulse started to pound. She'd worried about her handwriting and had taken pains to write less…pretty. It was too difficult, however, to completely change the way she wrote. So, she'd come up with an explanation. "I have four older sisters. I'm afraid their influence was rather heavy."

"Ah, I can only imagine what four older sisters might make their younger brother do." Keele's eyes glinted with amusement. "I do not have any siblings, so I was mercifully spared such torture. Though, one could argue I was also bereft of familial support." He said this in a purely matter-of-fact tone so that Ellis couldn't tell if he agreed with that sentiment or not.

Keele handed the letter back to her. "This is excellent. Prepare it for the Two Penny, and I'll have a footman take it."

"When I depart, I'd be happy to drop it at a receiving house, if you'd care to entrust me with the task," Ellis offered.

"I would, thank you." He gave her a slight nod as she set the paper on her desk. "Pre-paid. You may take the funds from the box in the top right drawer of the desk there. There is a notebook in which you'll record the withdrawal."

Ellis eyed the mess on his desk and the contents of the box that were spilling over the sides. "Is there anything I can do to help with organizing things for you?"

He sent her a sheepish look, but it was so brief that she doubted what she'd seen. "That would certainly demonstrate more of your skills." Keele scooped up several things and stood. He moved around his desk to deposit the pile on hers. "If you can sort through that, I'd be grateful."

"Do you have a preference for how it's organized?" she asked as she sat back down.

"Er, no." He appeared nonplussed before turning his attention back to the report—or whatever it was—that he was reading.

Ellis began reviewing what he'd given her. She set them in neat stacks—the household ledger, unpaid bills, and corre-spondence. The correspondence she further sorted into household and estate, social, and that which related to Lacey and Company Press. There were quite a few missives to do with the latter, and she wondered about Keele's business with the enterprise.

Once she'd separated everything, she did not start with the Lacey and Company correspondence, though that seemed the most interesting. Ellis had a habit of saving the tasks she liked best for last. Instead, she pulled the unpaid bills toward her and reviewed each one. When she was finished, she made notes on a piece of foolscap and put it atop the bills.

Taking the household ledger next, she reviewed the

contents and observed how the bills were recorded. There had been no entries for over a month, and she'd noticed that a few of the bills were past when they ought to have been paid. She tucked the ledger beneath the stack of unpaid bills, then moved on to the correspondence, starting with the stack regarding Lacey and Company.

"You've sorted through that already?" He stared, appearing awestruck, at the tidy stacks across the top of her desk with an expression of amazement.

"Yes." She picked up the bills with the note. "There are several unpaid bills that ought to be settled as soon as possible." She wondered if he wasn't able to and glanced away awkwardly. "I also found an error on one of them and drafted a note to the merchant that could be enclosed with the payment, the amount of which I adjusted to correct the mistake. I've summarized everything here." She held up the paper she'd put with the bills.

He blinked at her, his expression showing disbelief. "You did all that?"

"You doubt me?" Ellis couldn't help feeling a bit perturbed.

"No. I'm just...aghast. You work very quickly." He held out his hand. "May I see your note?"

"Of course." She also handed him the bills. "You can check my work if you like."

"I'm not sure I need to," he said quietly. It wasn't quite a murmur, but it was close.

Still, he flipped through the stack, stopping to read her note of correction to the fishmonger. Finishing, he exhaled and set everything down, then clasped his hands atop the pile. "I would like to hire you to start immediately, if you are able. However, there is one requirement to which you may not wish to agree. Whilst I am most eager to employ you, I'm afraid this point is non-negotiable."

Ellis frowned slightly, curious about the seriousness of his tone. "What is that?"

"As you can see, there is much to fix here. My last secretary drank too much, apparently, and created a rather large mess. I'm afraid you've only glimpsed a fraction of it." He grimaced. "I need my new secretary to reside here and be available to work every day, including Sundays. I will grant time off for church and any other necessary appointments, plus a half day off each week for respite. I would prefer this isn't always the same day, but that we agree upon which day it will be the following week. If that is acceptable to you, I'm offering one hundred guineas per annum paid quarterly. Plus, room and board, of course."

He wanted her to live here. That would mean maintaining this disguise far longer than she'd anticipated. She could only be Ellis in her chamber wherever that might be. And if she needed to be Ellis anywhere else, she'd have to leave the house as Daniel Ellis and change into her real self. How would she manage that?

For a hundred guineas, plus lodging and food, she would find a way. This would allow her to save much more quickly than she'd anticipated.

"Where would my room be located?" She dearly hoped it would be as far away from the main parts of the house as possible.

"On the first floor," he replied. "There's a bedchamber meant for guests. It should be sufficient for your needs."

Ellis wondered where Keele's bedchamber was located but wasn't going to ask. "Is there a desk? I'd like to be able to work there, if possible." That way she could have some relief from her disguise. Bathing would be a challenge, but hopefully the servants had a bathing chamber for their use. But how on earth would she wash her hair, then hide it as she returned to her room?

"I'll make sure there's a desk." His brow creased slightly. "Though, I prefer you work down here during the day—either at this desk when we're working together or at the desk in the front sitting room if I have meetings in here."

"Understood," she said gruffly, hoping she looked and sounded masculine. She needed to behave in that fashion as much as possible so that it became second-nature. Her femininity, indeed, her entire true self, must be hidden for the foreseeable future. Ellis didn't mind that. Being her true self had been rather awful of late. In fact, she wasn't at all sure who her "true" self was.

"May I ask about Lacey and Company?" Immediately, Ellis wanted to take back the question. Of course she could ask—she was now his employee. Actually, she hadn't officially agreed to the position. "I should say that I am pleased to accept your offer of employment, and your requirements are satisfactory to me." She would miss living at Mrs. Palmer's house.

"I'm both relieved and pleased, Mr. Ellis. I'm confident you will be an excellent addition to the household. And please understand that once things are better organized, you are free to take other lodgings. Though, you can stay here as long as you like." The marquess gave her an expectant look. "I don't suppose you can start working now and move in tomorrow?"

"I can, in fact." Ellis bit back a delighted smile. She had a job!

"Splendid," Keele said. "As for Lacey and Company, that is my father-in-law's company, in which I own a stake. He owns several subscription libraries and is a publisher."

"Of course," Ellis said, feeling a bit foolish. "I've been to Lacey's Library here in London."

"You have a subscription?" Keele seemed surprised, which he should be. Someone like Daniel Ellis would not have a subscription to Lacey's. The companion to the daughter of a duchess, however, would.

"I mean, I've been by it," she amended. "I've seen it."

"Well, you've no need for a subscription now. You may read any of the books you like. I have many of them in my library upstairs."

"You've a library?" Ellis was surprised, given the size of the house.

"I suppose it's really the drawing room, but since I do not entertain, I've no need for such a space." He shrugged. "It's far more useful as a library."

Nothing he could have said would have been more appealing to her. Books were her absolute favorite thing, and his preference for not hosting social events would make her disguise that much easier to maintain. She needn't worry about having to meet anyone she knew.

Ellis was quite glad she'd taken on the risk of living here. "I appreciate the invitation to use your library, my lord."

"Since you've a keen interest in books, perhaps I'll ask your opinion on some of the novels submitted to Lacey and Company."

"I'm not sure I possess the necessary knowledge and experience to make such judgments," Ellis said diplomatically, though the idea of assessing whether people might enjoy a book sounded rather appealing.

"If you are an avid reader, then you have precisely the knowledge and experience," Keele said. "Give me a few minutes to finish what I'm reading, and I'll review the Lacey and Company correspondence with you. I doubt it will take you long to grasp the nature of that business." He smiled. "I'm glad you accepted the position, Mr. Ellis. I anticipate a long and mutually satisfying association."

Ellis couldn't help smiling, for she was so very relieved—

and excited, actually. This job wasn't just what she needed. It was precisely what she wanted. "I hope so."

Keele's gaze narrowed slightly, and he seemed to focus on her mouth. Ellis froze, hoping she hadn't done or said something wrong. Or worse, that he'd somehow recognized that she was a woman.

He dropped his focus to the report on his desk and returned to reading. Ellis exhaled. In that moment, she decided it might be best if she didn't smile.

CHAPTER 2

$\mathcal{R}$oman Garrick, fourth Marquess of Keele, surreptitiously watched his new secretary as he transcribed a letter for which he'd just taken shorthand. Today was his fourth day working—the third since he'd moved in carrying only a modest valise. Upon learning his room was on the same floor as Roman's, in the opposite corner, Ellis had seemed slightly discomfited. Roman sensed he made the secretary nervous.

That wasn't terribly unusual since this was Ellis's first position as a secretary. Roman imagined he might feel overwhelmed to start in the employ of a marquess. Except Ellis had also worked, at least temporarily, for a duke.

No, that wasn't the reason behind the young man's... unease.

Roman couldn't quite determine the cause. Or if he was observing something that wasn't there. It wasn't as if he knew Ellis well yet. Nor did anyone else in the household, as Ellis didn't speak to them.

The household was rather small compared to others of Roman's rank. Aside from the coachman and groom in the mews, Roman employed a butler, a maid, a footman, a cook, and a scullery maid. They were a lean and, likely as a result, close crew. He'd heard from the butler, the cook, and the footman that the new secretary was aloof.

That made Roman think he wasn't imagining things when it came to Ellis being uncomfortable. He planned to ask the young man why just as soon as Roman's in-laws left. They would be here shortly and looked forward to meeting Roman's new secretary.

Seemingly unaware of Roman's covert regard, which was Roman's goal, Ellis continued his task. The man really did have rather feminine handwriting. Indeed, even watching the sweep of his hand across the parchment made Roman think he'd learned just about everything from women. Ellis's walk occasionally resembled that of a lady, and Roman had caught him crossing his ankles a time or two.

Roman had known other men who possessed a more feminine affect. But there was just something…different about his secretary.

Ellis's head turned, and his blue eyes, which had particularly long lashes for a man, fixed on Roman. They narrowed slightly, and vertical lines formed between his dark blond brows. "Is something amiss?"

Even Ellis's voice was odd. It was certainly deeper than a woman's, but there was a cadence to it that somehow also seemed feminine. Again, it was surely due to being raised in a household of women. Though, Ellis had to have had a father. Perhaps he'd died when Ellis was young. Roman had a mother, but he'd never known her.

"Not at all," Roman replied. "I'm only glad I hired you."

That was an understatement. In just four short days, Ellis had completely transformed Roman's desk and the entire study. He'd implemented systems for handling correspondence, managing the household accounts, and organizing business to do with the House of Lords. Though Parliament wasn't currently in session, there was still correspondence, and when it was in session, everything was already in order and Ellis would keep it that way. Roman could not have been more pleased.

"I'm glad to hear it, my lord."

Roman noticed that Ellis didn't smile. He'd done so that first day—just once. "Are you satisfied with your position?"

"Eminently." Ellis pressed his lips together, and his mouth curved up ever so slightly. It wasn't quite a smile. Rather, it appeared an approximation of one. Indeed, the secretary seemed to be trying very hard *not* to smile. Roman had the sense that most of what Ellis did was calculated, almost as if he were executing a performance. Perhaps he was simply putting forth great effort to make his best impression.

"I'm glad to hear it," Roman said. "I wondered if there was anything lacking, particularly with regard to your lodging."

"It's more than adequate," Ellis replied.

"Good. Has anyone in the household caused issue?" Roman asked with concern. "I notice you don't take meals with them, and you keep to yourself almost entirely."

"I'm the sort of person who prefers their own company," Ellis explained evenly. "With four sisters, our household was always busy. I find I like quiet and solitude."

"Did you not care for your sisters?"

"I did. I *do*," he amended. "I was merely offering an explanation as to why I keep to myself. I'm still very new here. I'm sure I will settle in the longer I am in residence."

"Of course." Roman hadn't meant to pressure the lad. "You've mentioned your sisters. What of your parents? Did you grow up with a mother and a father?"

"For a time, but we were all orphaned."

Before Roman could continue to satisfy his curiosity,

Graham stepped over the threshold. "My lord, the Laceys have arrived. I've escorted them to the library."

"Excellent." Roman bolted from the chair. "We'll be right up."

Graham nodded and left.

"Is it vital that I meet your in-laws?" Ellis asked, his quill still poised over the parchment. "I'd like to finish this letter."

"Yes, it is," Roman said. "Lacey and Company is my business as much as theirs. Whilst Josiah is my former father-in-law, he is also my business partner. Actually, partner is a strong word. He owns a much greater stake, and, so far, I've only contributed my efforts."

"Which have grown the company from what I can tell," Ellis said. "You oversee the libraries and have opened several in the past three years."

That was true. Roman had been surprised by how much he liked working for Lacey and Company. After the death of his wife, he'd immersed himself even more in the business as a means of distraction. Whilst theirs had not been a love match, Roman had developed feelings for her. Unfortunately, they had not been reciprocated, a fact he'd learned before she became ill and that had greatly tainted the remainder of their time together.

"That is precisely why you must meet them," Roman insisted. "You will be intrinsically involved in assisting me in my duties. You needn't stay for our meeting—unless you want to. This is our fortnightly discussion of the books we'd like to publish and those we will not. As an avid reader, I thought that might interest you."

Indeed, there was a light in Ellis's eyes as he'd discussed the books, now and at other times over the past several days. "I suppose I could attend for a short while. But I shouldn't be away from my desk for too long." He set down his quill and rose. His movements carried a fluid grace that was much more attributable to a female.

Why was Roman so bloody focused on that?

Ignoring the query in his mind, Roman preceded Ellis from the study and went upstairs to the library. The shelves were far from full, and there was plenty of room for more cases. The seating area was cozy but lacked polish as the furnishings were more than ten years old. At least they matched and were of a fine quality, even if the fabric on the settee was faded. It was a library in progress, evidence of a marquess whose finances were wanting.

The Laceys were already seated—Josiah in a chair and the ladies, his wife Harriet and his daughter Margot, on the settee. Margot had a sheaf of papers on her lap.

"Good afternoon," Roman said. "Allow me to introduce my new secretary, Daniel Ellis." He paused whilst Josiah inclined his head, which sported thick, light brown waves, with only a hint of gray. He appeared younger than his fifty years.

"Ellis, this is Mr. Josiah Lacey, Mrs. Lacey, and Miss Lacey," Roman continued. To him, they were family. Josiah had been a much kinder and overall better father than Roman's own, and his nurse, who'd been with him until the age of eight, was the closest he'd had to a female parent. Harriet Lacey was warm, loving, and thoughtful—precisely what one would want in a mother.

His gaze briefly settled on Margot. At twenty-one, she was five years younger than her sister, who'd been Roman's wife for two short years. With curly chestnut hair and dark-blue eyes like her mother, Margot was gregarious where Clarissa had been more quiet, even remote.

Clarissa was not at all the sort of woman Roman would have chosen to be his wife, but his duty demanded he wed an heiress, and she'd been the wealthiest choice with a dowry as well as an interest in her father's business. He'd also been drawn to her quiet demeanor and fierce intelligence.

"I'm pleased to make your acquaintance," Ellis said. He stood stiff straight with his hands clenched at his sides, making him appear nervous.

Josiah, a generally cheerful man, smiled at Ellis. His hazel eyes, that were so much like Roman's late wife's, lit with interest. "We're so glad Keele has found a worthy secretary." He was aware of the faults of Roman's former secretary. Indeed, it was Josiah who'd encouraged Roman to replace the man.

"Let us sit." Roman gestured Ellis toward an open chair near the one he moved to. The secretary moved tentatively, and when he sat, he did not sit against the back. Again, his posture reminded Roman of a woman.

"I'm quite keen to discuss our potential acquisitions," Margot said enthusiastically. Her eyes sparked with anticipation as she looked from her parents to Roman.

"All in good time, dear." Josiah chuckled as he looked toward Roman. "Margot is excited about a particular novel she read. In fact, she's set a meeting with the author tomorrow. But I am moving ahead." He waved his hand. "First, I want to discuss the next book from M.E. Tremaine. *The Captain's Daughter* was a great success, and I believe the next one will be too."

"Tremaine has written another book?" Ellis asked.

Everyone's attention shifted to the secretary.

"Yes, *The Heiress of Tidehaven*."

Ellis was suddenly quite engaged, and his apparent nervousness disappeared. "Another coastal romance?"

"Indeed," Josiah replied. "The heiress inherits a manor and is beset by suitors."

Roman met Ellis's gaze, which was rather animated. "Have you read *The Captain's Daughter*?"

"I have," he replied with enthusiasm. "I found the story most riveting. Tremaine's style is both familiar and somehow singular. Charlotte was very well-written. I—that is, my sisters said they identified with her greatly. I appreciated Lieutenant Moreton's honor and quiet dignity." He glanced toward Josiah. "I didn't realize you were the publisher."

Josiah's features gleamed with pride. "I'm pleased to hear your sisters enjoyed the novel. They are the readers we hope to reach."

"The description snared their interest immediately," Ellis said.

Josiah's dark brows arched. "Did it? Margot wrote that." He sent a proud look toward his daughter.

"It was very well done," Ellis noted with a nod at Margot. "I tried to help someone write something similar for a novel they wrote, and it's more difficult than one would think."

"Thank you," Margot replied with a gleeful smile. "It can be challenging. Though I think writing a novel would be much harder. In fact, I'm struggling with writing something for Tremaine's next story." She turned her focus to her father. "Perhaps Mr. Ellis should read *The Heiress of Tidehaven*. Then he could assist me with writing a description. It certainly sounds as though he shares our appreciation for Miss Tremaine." She grimaced briefly. "Oh dear, now I've exposed our author's gender, and she'd hoped her identity would remain secret."

"I won't say a word," Ellis vowed sincerely. "Not even to my sisters."

"Thank you," Margot replied with an expression of relief. "What do you think, Papa?"

"If Mr. Ellis has the time to read *The Heiress of Tidehaven*, his observations may be most helpful. However, he may be too busy with his current role."

"I'd be happy to read it when I am not working," Ellis offered eagerly.

Though Roman didn't yet know him well, he could see how keen the young man was to read the novel. He could also see just how passionately he felt about the first book. Furthermore, Roman had noted which books Ellis had removed from the library since taking up residence, and they were—to a one—novels that were written primarily for a female audience. "I've no issue with Ellis reading *Tidehaven* and participating in our discussions. In fact, I would like him to so that he may take a record. His shorthand skills are excellent."

"Excellent idea," Josiah said. "It's wonderful to find someone who is so enthusiastic about Tremaine's work. Perhaps you'd even like to meet her. She is unwed and around your age, I would guess." He chuckled and gave Ellis a meaningful look.

Ellis's brows briefly shot up, and Roman could have sworn he saw a bit of pink in the secretary's cheek above his beard. Then Ellis chuckled. The sound was a bit higher in tone than his voice. The two didn't go together.

Roman interpreted Ellis's reaction as discomfort. Perhaps he already had a betrothed. Or didn't want to marry. Or wasn't attracted to women.

Harriet pursed her lips at her husband. "Do not say such things to Mr. Ellis, dear. Perhaps he is already engaged."

"I am far too busy to bother with marriage," Ellis said gruffly. He turned his attention to Roman. "Should I fetch a notebook and pencil?"

"Yes, thank you," Roman replied.

Ellis stood, and as soon as he was gone from the library, Harriet sat forward slightly and shifted her gaze toward Margot then Roman. "Now that your secretary is absent for a few minutes, may we speak of your engagement?"

Roman schooled his features lest he reveal anything. Whilst he wasn't entirely opposed to marrying his former sister-in-law, he also hadn't decided if they would suit. Margot was vivacious and…young. It wasn't that she was immature, for she wasn't. She just felt a bit like a younger sister, even though Roman hadn't come to know her very well until after his wife had died. Whilst they were married, Margot had spent most of her time with family near Cambridge. Harriet's older brother was a vicar with a substantial living, and he'd taken on educating both Clarissa and Margot.

Roman would certainly benefit from marrying another heiress, though he wondered if he ought to find a bride from another family, as mercenary as that sounded. Margot had the same cash dowry as her sister, but the business interest, which was quite valuable, had only been for Josiah's firstborn daughter. He could likely obtain an overall higher dowry if he married someone else. Furthermore, if he could marry within the peerage, it would only bolster his family's standing, particularly after its near bankruptcy thanks to Roman's father.

Still, marrying Margot would be easy. Roman already knew her, he liked her, and he loved her parents as his own. These were compelling arguments for agreeing to the union that both Harriet and Josiah hoped to secure.

What of Margot? She had been curiously quiet on the subject. In fact, she typically endeavored to change the topic of conversation. Roman eyed her now to see her reaction, but, like his, it was nonexistent. Perhaps she was also trying to mask her true feelings. Did that mean she was conflicted, as he was?

"Is now the right time to discuss this, Mama?" Margot asked finally. "This is a business meeting."

"One might argue that your marriage is business," Josiah

said with a faint shrug. "It certainly was with your sister. Until it wasn't." A nostalgic expression passed over Josiah's features as he glanced at Roman.

"I would prefer my marriage not be included with business," Margot said firmly.

Roman had noted a faint twitch at the side of her mouth as her father had spoken. He didn't want her to be uncomfortable. "We can discuss it next time we have dinner." They dined together frequently, usually once a week.

Harriet smiled warmly. "Wonderful. We'll talk about it on Sunday then. I'd like to announce the betrothal before Christmas."

Ellis returned, and his arrival stopped any further discussion. Roman flicked a glance toward Margot and thought she seemed relieved. She also tossed a furtive, perhaps perturbed, look at her mother. Perhaps he and Margot should have a conversation soon. Shouldn't two people who were contemplating marriage have some idea of what the other thought? Roman would prioritize speaking with her.

Retaking his seat, Ellis opened the notebook and began writing with the pencil. He was likely recording the date and those present. He was incredibly efficient.

They spent the next while discussing the performance of works recently published and those that were forthcoming. Then it was time to review submissions, which went entirely through Margot now. She'd begun reading them a year or so ago to amuse herself. But she'd had incisive observations about the writing and stories, so much so that her father had asked her to assume evaluation of everything they received.

"Tomorrow is our appointment with the author of *A Season in Shadow*," Margot said. "I'm most eager to meet them."

Harriet's brow creased. "I'm still not sure this story is right for Lacey and Company."

Roman had started the novel last night, and whilst the author had clearly read—and been influenced by—Wollstonecraft, he didn't see that as negative. However, he knew Harriet wouldn't agree. She could be conservative in some of her thoughts about a woman's place.

"Mama, it's an exceptional story. We *must* publish it," Margot asserted. "If someone else does, we'll regret it. I'm sure of that."

"Perhaps we can decide after Keele finishes it," Harriet said diplomatically.

Josiah sent his wife a discerning glance. "You don't typically offer your opinions."

"That's because I usually agree with Margot—and with you," Harriet replied. "However, I'm concerned the conclusion of this story will be disappointing and even shocking to some."

"Given Margot's enthusiasm, if Keele also likes it, I'm inclined to support the book's publication," Josiah said.

"Though I haven't yet finished the novel, I already support it. That said, I haven't completed it, so I can't speak to the conclusion." He met Harriet's gaze. "I'll finish reading it tonight."

"Thank you. Do try to consider how the ladies of Society will react," she added.

"I will." Roman was now keen to see what gave Harriet pause.

"Perhaps Mr. Ellis should also read the novel," Margot said. "He seems well-versed in this genre, which is remarkable for a man." She laughed good-naturedly. "You will make someone a splendid husband, I think."

"Well, I'm afraid I have the only copy right now," Roman said. "But perhaps he should attend the meeting to take notes." He looked to Ellis. "I know you're busy putting things in order since you took on this position, but you can manage to come, I'm sure."

"I don't suppose the meeting is here?" Ellis asked. "I shouldn't want to lose much time going somewhere."

"We are meeting at Lacey and Company on Paternoster Row," Roman replied. "You've worked very hard this week. I'm sure you can spare the time. In fact, I insist. I would like you to see the offices, as you may work there on occasion."

Ellis's brows drew together sharply, but he quickly smoothed his expression. Even so, it was hard to miss that his initial reaction had been disdain—or even alarm. "Then of course I shall attend."

"Splendid!" Margot exclaimed. She grinned at Ellis. "It's so refreshing to meet a gentleman who appreciates romantic novels."

Whilst Ellis inclined his head in response, there was a sheepish cast to his gaze as he glanced away from the seating area.

"We should be on our way," Josiah announced.

The ladies stood; Ellis bolted to his feet. In his haste, he dropped his notebook to the floor. Pivoting away from Roman, the secretary quickly bent. The tails of his coat split with his movements, and Roman had a very distinct view of Ellis's backside. The truth, which Roman had begun to suspect, was unmistakable to his eyes now.

The Laceys took their leave a few moments later. Ellis started to turn. "I should return to work."

"Just one moment," Roman said. "I'd like to speak with you about something." He moved past the secretary and closed the door to the library with alacrity. Turning, he rejoined Ellis, whose expression had turned wary.

"Should I sit?" Ellis asked with the barest edge of apprehension.

"I don't think so, though it depends on the length of your explanation." Roman crossed his arms over his chest.

Now Ellis's blue eyes took on a sheen of fear. "My explanation about what?" The secretary's tone was higher than normal, and Roman assumed it was closer to Ellis's real voice.

"It's clear to me you are not who you purport to be. I've felt something was off since I hired you, but now I'm certain. You're a woman masquerading as a man." He pierced the secretary, who looked more and more to him like a bearded lady, making him wonder how he'd ever been fooled in the first place, with an expectant stare. "Why?"

CHAPTER 3

*E*llis worked to maintain her composure as she stood in front of Keele. It was difficult. She wanted to flee.

He didn't seem angry exactly, but he also didn't appear pleased. And why would he be? She'd completely misrepresented herself.

Compounding her humiliation was the fact that she'd actually thought she'd been successful in her endeavors. With each day that passed since she'd taken the position, she believed she could maintain her disguise and conceal her true identity, that she'd fooled her employer and everyone else.

But she had not. She would have to come up with another way to earn money. She didn't think she could attempt this sort of arrangement again, nor did she want to. It had been a huge risk, and she'd failed.

"How did you know?" she asked softly, abandoning the effort to lower her voice.

"Something about you just wasn't quite right," Keele replied, uncrossing his arms. His features were enigmatic.

She still couldn't tell precisely how he felt. "You have feminine mannerisms, and there's your feminine handwriting. And you like books with a feminine bent. In addition to having read *The Captain's Daughter*, I noted you took novels from the library this week that are of the same romantic nature." He gestured toward the cases where such books were kept. "I believed you when you said these things were due to having four sisters, but—and this isn't something a gentleman should say—when you bent to retrieve your notebook a short while ago, it became blatantly obvious that you are, in fact, a female."

Heat flamed Ellis's cheeks. Could he see her embarrassment behind her beard? She hoped not.

"I didn't think of that," she said, wondering how she could have disguised her backside, if that was indeed to what he was referring. She narrowed her eyes at him as she sought to confirm what he meant. "Are you saying my posterior is too feminine?"

"I don't know that it can be *too* feminine," he replied. "But it is not the backside of a young man. That much I know for certain." His gaze found hers for a brief but rather heated moment, then he quickly looked away. "We should not continue discussing that. I didn't mean to cause offense, but I had to call you out. You understand?"

Ellis exhaled. Her shoulders drooped slightly, but she worked to straighten her spine. "I knew this was a terrible risk, and I probably shouldn't have taken it. However, I am in need of employment, and I knew I could do this job."

"In fact, you can," he said. "You do it incredibly well."

"Thank you." Pride helped to lift her shoulders and her spirits.

He surveyed her as if she were a puzzle he needed to work out. "I'm confounded as to why you would take such a risk. Why disguise yourself as a man to be secretary to a marquess?"

"Because I possess the skills to do the job, and being a woman with those skills would not allow me to obtain such a position and, more importantly, the salary that comes with it."

"You've a valid point." He went quiet for a moment, and Ellis's insides churned. Whilst he didn't seem angry, she wasn't sure what to expect. "Was the letter from the Duke of Henlow real? The seal on the envelope appeared to be his."

"Yes," she replied evenly, though her heart was pounding. "My family is acquainted with his."

"Did you actually work for him?" Keele asked with more than a hint of skepticism.

"His Grace offered to write me a letter of recommendation. It is not my place to quarrel with what he wrote." Ellis was skirting the truth and might earn the marquess's ire, but she wasn't going to admit that she hadn't worked for Henlow. Keele could deduce what he liked.

He regarded her somewhat dubiously, and Ellis became certain that was the end of things. As it should be. How could he trust her to work for him now?

She took a deep breath to try to calm her racing pulse. "I'm sorry I lied to you. I will pack my things and be on my way." She took a step toward the door, but he held his hand up in front of her.

"I didn't ask you to go. Just because you're a woman doesn't mean you can't work for me."

Ellis stared at him. "That would be highly irregular and unacceptable. Furthermore, I lied to you. I wouldn't blame you for not being able to trust me in your employ."

Keele cocked his head and lifted a shoulder. "It *would* be irregular, and whilst many would not find it acceptable, it is acceptable to me. What is your real name?"

Ellis' breath snagged in her lungs. It was one thing for him to know she was a woman, but if he learned she was also the former companion to Lady Minerva Halifax—rather, Lady Minerva Pierce now—she would be completely exposed. He would certainly tell his friend, Sheff, and Sheff would tell Min. Ellis was trying to forge a new path away from her past. She didn't want to see any of them yet. She also didn't want to chance the duchess discovering where she was or what she was doing. There was every reason to believe she would do her best to ruin things for Ellis, as she'd done since she'd been forced to accept Ellis into her household.

"Would you mind if I didn't say?" she asked. "I'm no one important."

"I should at least like to know what to call you," he said.

"Ellis is fine. It's an old family name." That much was true. Well, it was an adopted family name, anyway.

She studied him a moment, surprised at how easily he accepted her gender and that he wanted her to remain in the position. "You really want me to stay on? I'd prefer to continue my disguise."

He nodded. "I won't tell anyone. Though, I imagine it's difficult keeping yourself in disguise all the time." He grimaced. "I'm surprised you agreed to live here. You can't ever be who you really are."

Ellis smiled and saw the flicker of surprise in his gaze. "It's actually wonderful. Just now, it's quite nice to be someone else."

His brows drew together as he contemplated her with sympathy. "You're in hiding, then."

That was precisely what she was doing. "I suppose I am."

"Perhaps that's why you don't want me to know your real name." Keele exhaled. "Very well. You may hide here for as long as you need, provided you continue to excel at your job.

My retainers would keep your secret, but I agree it's probably best if you just maintain your disguise. And I won't tell the Laceys, of course. Is that why you looked distressed when you were invited to the meeting tomorrow? You didn't want to leave the house and risk being seen for who you really are?"

"You noticed that bothered me?" Ellis shook her head. "You are far too astute, my lord. I believe it is best for my disguise if I encounter as few people as possible. I actually welcomed your offer to live here. Not only does it save me money, it's simpler not to have to go back and forth between dressing as a man and a woman."

"I'm glad to have helped inadvertently," he said with one of his rare smiles. Ellis found herself staring at him, thinking he was remarkably handsome in a dark and predatory way. It was his nose and the rough planes of his face. His features were strong and commanding, and his eyes were an impenetrable steel.

"So you'll continue as my secretary?" he asked.

She noted that he hadn't addressed her lying to him. "You don't care that I misrepresented myself?"

"Without knowing the details that are motivating you to hide, I still accept that you were trying to find the best possible position for yourself and that you were induced to present yourself as a man to achieve that end. I actually admire your courage. Have you lied about anything else?"

She shook her head. "Nor will I."

"Good. I am more than satisfied with your work, and I would like you to continue," he replied firmly. "I will do what I can to help keep your secret, because I have a vested interest."

"Thank you." At last, her pulse began to move at a normal pace. "I won't disappoint you."

"How are you bathing?" he blurted.

Warmth flooded her face once more. Why had he thought of that? "I haven't yet taken a proper bath," she admitted. "I know of the bathing chamber on the lower ground floor, off the servants' hall. I thought I would use that."

He cocked his head. "How will that work? You'll go downstairs in your disguise, remove the hair from your face to wash, then replace it to go upstairs? I can't imagine you sleep with the fake beard. That sounds very inefficient. And how will you wash your hair? I assume you're wearing a wig."

She was surprised at how thoroughly he'd thought about her disguise and the problems she would encounter here. "I am. I thought about cutting my hair, but if this didn't work out and I had to be a woman again, I decided that would be bad. I've been pondering how I will wash my hair," she admitted. "I'm sure I'll think of something."

"No need," Keele said, lifting his hand. "You shall use my bath chamber. I'll arrange it with Alvin. Are you already fetching your own water to wash?"

"I am," she replied.

He shook his head. "That won't do."

Ellis was surprised at his strong reaction. "Why? Because I'm a woman?"

He stopped and stared at her, his features blank. "Yes." His brow creased as if he realized how absurd that sounded.

"I'm already doing a man's job," she reminded him.

"And better than most men," he muttered. "Your point is well taken. You may continue to fetch your own water. However, filling a tub is too much. I will instruct Alvin to prepare a bath for you."

Ellis could imagine the young footman, as well as the rest of the retainers, wondering why the secretary was permitted to bathe in the lord's bath chamber. "Don't you think your household will find this arrangement strange?"

"I'll tell them you're painfully shy, which won't be hard for them to believe, since you don't spend time with them. Indeed, they find you aloof. But now I understand why you take your meals in your room or in the study."

She didn't like being thought of as aloof, but it was for the best in this situation. "Telling them I'm shy is a good excuse."

"Are you shy?" he asked.

"Not really," she replied.

His gaze softened. "Are you lonely, then?"

This question stabbed into her chest like a well-aimed arrow. She *was* lonely. More specifically, she missed Min and the household that had become her home for more than fifteen years. But that emotion had not eclipsed the hurt and anger of discovering the duchess was her mother. Perhaps when that happened, Ellis would be ready to face Min and Sheff.

Though she didn't answer, he seemed to understand. "Then we shall dine together sometimes. I insist."

Ellis continued to be astonished by his acceptance and, more importantly, his kindness. "Why are you being so understanding?"

"I told you—you're excellent at your job." He shrugged as if her disguising herself as a man and lying to him were of little consequence. "Indeed, you've already become invaluable to me, and I cannot imagine you leaving. It's purely selfish on my part."

"I appreciate you allowing me to stay." And everything else he'd agreed to and offered. Ellis could hardly believe her fortune, but perhaps she was due after all that had happened. She was glad to feel that she was wanted somewhere.

"I can't promise you won't be found out," he said. "If that happens, you'll have to leave, and I'll pretend I didn't know either. Otherwise, it might reflect poorly on you."

"If I'm discovered, it most definitely will," she said without hesitation." But I don't want it to reflect poorly on *you*. If at any time you change your mind and want me to leave, you must say so. I do not want to put you at risk."

"How would I be at risk?" he asked. "My reputation won't be harmed. It will be yours."

"My reputation doesn't matter." She was no longer companion to the daughter of a duke. "As I said, I'm no one."

"That's not true," he said softly. "You *are* someone. You are worthy, and you are needed here. Now, let's get back to work."

Ellis's throat felt tight. "Thank you, my lord."

Keele stepped aside and gestured for her to precede him from the library. She opened the door and exhaled, realizing she'd been holding her breath.

When she reached the top of the stairs, she wasn't sure if Keele was following her. She turned her head and saw that he stood outside the doorway to the library, his gaze fixed on her. Specifically, on her backside.

Ellis knew what it looked like when a man was attracted to a woman. She'd felt that attraction on a few occasions. And she knew without question that Keele found her desirable.

She whipped her head around and hastened down the stairs. Was that why he'd invited her to stay? Did he hope to take advantage?

Though she didn't know him well, she couldn't see him doing that. Everything she'd observed over the past four days had indicated he was a man of integrity and honor—at least in business. She didn't know much about his personal reputation, whether he'd been a rogue before he was married, or even during his marriage.

She thought of the Rogue Rules that she and her friends

had drafted two years ago after one of them, Pandora Barclay, had been ruined when she'd been caught in the arms of the Earl of Banemore. Rather than marry her, Bane had fled to marry someone else, leaving Pandora's reputation in tatters.

Thinking of the rules they'd come up with, Ellis realized Pandora had broken almost every one of them with Bane, not that they'd existed before she'd met him. Ellis didn't blame Pandora, for Bane had led her to believe he cared for her and that he wanted to marry her. Yes, Pandora had been naïve, but she hadn't deserved to have her life destroyed. Thus, the rules were born and the rest of them strove to follow them.

Except Ellis. She didn't need to preserve her reputation for marriage, not like the rest of them did. As a companion, Ellis wasn't particularly marriageable, especially since, at twenty-six, she was firmly on the shelf. But as the illegitimate daughter of a duchess and her lover, Ellis was completely *un*marriageable.

Not that she cared. Because of her station, she'd never entertained fantasies of marriage and motherhood, and certainly not of love. Which wasn't to say she hadn't wanted to experience physical satisfaction. She had, and she'd done that years ago—twice. Once with a boy when they'd both been seventeen and a few years later with a young gentleman who had no doubt been a rogue.

Clearly, she had no problem with rakish males. Indeed, she didn't particularly care if Keele possessed a roguish reputation. But if he was keeping her in his employ so that he could entice her to his bed, she wanted to know.

She'd have to come up with a way to determine what sort of man he was. If he were a rogue, she'd have to decide whether she should stay.

Shockingly, she thought she just might.

he following afternoon, Roman's coachman drove them to the Lacey and Company offices in Paternoster Row. It was strange to be riding alone in a coach with a young lady, though for all Roman knew, Ellis was married or even widowed. But he didn't think so. He estimated her to be in her middle twenties. It was more likely that she was either nearing or had entered spinster territory.

He was very curious about why she was hiding. Perhaps she was married and was avoiding a violent husband. Whatever the reason, Roman was glad to provide her shelter.

As they stopped in front of the offices, he looked across the coach at Ellis. She clutched her notebook, and Roman knew she'd stashed a pencil in her pocket.

"Are you nervous?" he asked.

"A bit," she replied, glancing in his direction. "I just need to remember that you will leave the coach before I do." A faint smile lifted one side of her mouth.

When they'd departed his house, she'd moved toward the coach as if she would step inside first, and she should have, since she was a lady. But in her disguise as the secretary Daniel Ellis, she would not enter the coach until after her employer, the Marquess of Keele.

"I will endeavor to keep you from slipping up," Roman said.

"Thank you."

As the coachman opened the door, Roman stepped out first and stood on the pavement as he waited for Ellis to climb down. Church bells tolled nearby, adding to the bustle of the busy, narrow street.

"Are those the bells of St. Paul's?" she asked.

"Indeed they are." Roman turned and gestured across the

street over the tops of the buildings. "You can see the spire there. The cathedral is very close."

Ellis had pivoted with him. "I see it."

He heard the excitement in her voice. "Have you been there?"

She nodded. "Many times. It's beautiful."

"You can see more of the cathedral from the first floor," Roman said. "Come, I'll show you." He resisted the urge to put his hand behind her back as if he were guiding a woman into the building.

A plaque with gold lettering that read "Lacey and Company, Publishers and Booksellers" was affixed to the front of the four-storey brick-faced building. The main entrance led directly into the bookshop.

They moved inside, and Roman took a deep breath. He loved the smell of paper, print, and leather bindings. Shelves lined the left wall and displayed many works, mostly three-deckers, such as *The Captain's Daughter*.

Ellis immediately gravitated toward the shelves. Roman let her browse for a moment.

"Afternoon, my lord," the clerk said from behind the counter on the right side of the shop. The young man, Samuel Briggs, had been in the position for over a year now. He was friendly and efficient, with bright light-blue eyes and blond hair. "The Laceys are already upstairs."

"Thank you," Roman said. "Has the author arrived?"

Briggs shook his head. "Not yet."

Moving to where Ellis stood perusing the latest three-deckers, Roman followed her gaze. "See anything you want to read?"

"Nothing you don't already have in your library and that I've already taken." She gave him a sheepish look.

"That's what I thought, but I wanted to ask anyway, in

case you missed something in my library. But I should know better—you don't miss a thing."

"It's wonderful to see so many books fresh and new." She turned toward him. "What a strange thing for a marquess to be involved with. What do people think of that?"

"Mostly, they find it odd or downright awful," he said with a smirk. "I'm in trade, you know. Utterly scandalous."

She suppressed a smile, and he wished she wouldn't. It was hard to see how a smile would change her face because of the fake hair she had covering it, but he imagined she was quite pretty.

"Have you always been scandalous?" she asked.

In fact, he'd been somewhat of a scoundrel before his father had died, but Roman hadn't known about the devastation his father had wrought on their family fortune. He'd learned the extent of his father's financial mismanagement after his death, and that had changed the course of Roman's life forever. Desperate to avoid bankruptcy, he'd immediately set about finding an heiress as quickly as possible. He'd been unable to secure a wife from the peerage due to the reputation he'd built, so he'd settled for marrying Clarissa Lacey.

He didn't regret it, for he enjoyed his work with Lacey and Company, and he loved her family. However, if he had it to do over again, he would have chosen differently.

That wasn't the same as regret, was it?

"I desperately want to read *A Season in Shadow* after the discussion yesterday," Ellis said. "Will I be able to now that you're finished?"

"Certainly. I look forward to hearing what you think."

"And what was your final opinion?" She regarded him with great interest.

Knowing the ending was perhaps "shocking," Roman hadn't been able to turn the pages fast enough last night. He'd been disappointed actually, for he'd expected something momentous. Then he'd remembered what Harriet had said. "I imagine there will be Society ladies who don't care for it, but I think the controversy will ensure it finds great popularity."

"You are in favor of publishing it then?"

"I am." Roman hoped Harriet wouldn't be upset. He wouldn't know today because she didn't come to these kinds of meetings.

Roman guided Ellis from the shop into the counting room at the back, where another clerk was recording receipts in the ledger. Charles Appleby was nearing forty and had worked for Josiah Lacey for nearly a decade. He oversaw the shop, and Briggs and lived upstairs in the top floor with his wife. Mrs. Appleby kept the shop and offices tidy.

Roman led Ellis up a narrow flight of creaky stairs to the first floor and onto a landing. He gestured toward the front of the building. "Josiah's office is this way. That's where we'll be meeting."

Motioning for Ellis to precede him into the office, Roman noted her reaction as she surveyed the room. Josiah's office was far grander than Roman's study. The polished oak of the wainscoting and the bookcases gleamed in the afternoon light streaming through the tall windows that looked over Paternoster Row. A seating area with dark green velvet chairs and a matching settee that easily held three or even four people was situated before the hearth. Josiah's large French desk was situated near the windows, and there was a rectangular table with six chairs. It was usually covered with proofs and folios, but it was completely clean today, save the second copy of *A Season in Shadow*.

Roman inclined his head toward the windows. "There, you can see St. Paul's again," he whispered.

She glanced at him, and the edge of her mouth ticked up. "I do."

He caught another glimpse of the woman behind the beard and found himself enchanted.

"Come in," Josiah said, standing from behind the desk and breaking Roman's trance. "We're just awaiting Miss Brightly."

"Is that the author's name?" Ellis asked almost sharply.

Margot had been perched on a small chair beside the desk and also stood. "It is." She looked toward Roman. "Keele, what is your decision about acquiring *A Season in Shadow*?"

Roman could see that Margot was most eager to hear his opinion. "I agree with you—if we don't publish it, we'll regret not doing so."

"Then it's settled," Josiah said. "I plan to offer Miss Brightly one hundred and fifty pounds for the copyright."

"That is a very attractive offer." Roman hoped the author was open to selling the copyright. Some were not.

The sound of the stairs creaking carried to the office. Everyone's attention darted to the doorway.

"That must be the author now," Josiah said.

A moment later, a surprisingly young woman swept into the office. She wore a military-style blue spencer over a blue and white striped gown with minimal decoration on the hem. Roman thought she looked stylish, but he did not keep up on current fashions, particularly women's.

Ellis drew in a sharp but soft breath. Roman snapped his head toward his secretary. The sound she'd made was not loud enough to carry to anyone else, and the flicker of recognition in her gaze was gone as quickly as he detected it. Perhaps he was mistaken.

He shifted his focus to Miss Brightly and could have sworn he saw the same flash of recognition in her expression, but it was quickly replaced with confusion.

"Miss Euphemia Brightly?" Roman asked. "I am Lord Keele."

Miss Brightly dipped a curtsy. "I'm pleased to make your acquaintance, my lord."

Roman caught Ellis's expression. She had her lips pressed together as if she were trying not to laugh or smile, but that didn't make sense. What was going on between her and Miss Brightly?

He looked back to the author, but she still appeared perplexed. "This is Mr. Lacey and his daughter, Miss Lacey."

Miss Brightly walked over to the desk and held out her hand to Margot. "I've enjoyed our correspondence."

"I have too," Margot said warmly.

Roman noted that Miss Brightly went to Margot first instead of Josiah. She ought to have addressed him first, but perhaps she didn't know that. Except her clothing and demeanor gave him the impression she was Quality. Why was she writing novels? She was of a marriageable age and very beautiful, with blonde hair and wide, blue-green eyes that reminded him of the sea on a summer day. Indeed, she was an ideal English beauty.

Miss Brightly turned her attention to Josiah. "Mr. Lacey, I do appreciate you meeting with me today. It is my honor to have your interest in my book."

"I'm delighted to meet you," Josiah said. "My daughter cannot stop raving about your novel. I confess I found it rather provocative. It's sure to generate a great deal of conversation."

Roman agreed. Miss Brightly had penned a story that would surely set Society on its ear, for the protagonist of the novel, Miss Dinah Peabody, does not end up wed despite having two very different suitors. Instead of choosing either of them, she chooses herself. Rather, she chooses to be an independent woman, which her aunt's wealth will allow.

"I hope that means you enjoyed it," Miss Brightly said coyly.

"I did, in fact," Josiah replied, though Roman didn't think his enthusiasm for the content matched his daughter's. Instead, Josiah almost certainly saw the potential for great sales because of the novel's controversial ending.

"I liked it immensely," Roman said, drawing Miss Brightly's regard. "I found it very interesting and unique."

"I should like to read it," Ellis said.

Roman realized he'd been remiss in introducing her. "Miss Brightly, this is my secretary, Mr. Ellis. He'll be recording notes from our meeting day."

That look of recognition flashed—very briefly—again in Miss Brightly's gaze. One of her sculpted blonde brows arched. "Mr. Ellis?"

Ellis nodded. "Pleased to make your acquaintance, Miss Brightly."

"Likewise," the author murmured with the faintest hint of a smile.

Once again, Roman had the sense there was something going on. In fact, he was almost certain of it. Did the author know Ellis? More accurately, did Miss Brightly know Ellis as a woman? She would have to. Roman didn't think Ellis had masqueraded as a man in any other situation.

"Shall we sit?" Josiah extended his arm toward the table and moved toward the chair at the head. "Come sit beside me, Miss Brightly." Josiah indicated the seat to his left.

Margot went to take the chair on her father's right, and Roman hastened to hold it for her. He nearly did the same for Ellis before recalling that she was a man. He needed to stop thinking of her as a woman, but that had become difficult since he'd made out the distinct feminine curve of her backside. He'd also noticed that she let her voice pitch upward when they were alone. He assumed that her natural voice, which, while deeper than most women, was still deliciously feminine.

Delicious?

Yes. He found the lower timbre of her tone utterly alluring.

"I don't see any point in prevaricating," Josiah began. "Miss Brightly, we would like to publish your novel. I'm prepared to offer one hundred and fifty pounds to purchase the copyright."

Miss Brightly smiled, but right away, Roman could see this was not what she wanted. Whilst she appeared pleased, her expression lacked satisfaction along with her joy.

"I'm so glad you're interested in publishing *A Season in Shadow*, however, I have been advised by my solicitor not to sell the copyright. In fact, I would prefer you negotiate the terms of a commission-style arrangement with him directly, if you are amenable to that."

"Are you sure you want a commission arrangement?" Josiah asked. "If the novel isn't successful, you won't make nearly as much as you would if you sold the copyright."

"And if it *is* successful, I stand to earn much more," she said slyly. "Forgive me, but I do think this novel has the potential to be in high demand."

"I do too," Margot said. "We'll do a commission if that's what you prefer." She glanced toward her father, whose brows had shot up as soon as she revised the offer.

Margot had never done that before, and it wasn't really her place. Still, Roman couldn't see Josiah being angry with her. He allowed Margot ample participation in Lacey and Company with regard to the publishing side of the business. As their sole remaining child, he and Harriet didn't deny her anything, as far as Roman could tell.

"I'd also support a commission arrangement," Roman said, and Margot sent him a grateful smile. He focused on the author. "You're a shrewd businesswoman, Miss Brightly."

She met his gaze with a fiery stare. "I've nothing to lose, my lord."

"Now I really can't wait to read the book," Ellis said.

It seemed to Roman that his secretary could scarcely keep from smiling. Her eyes were aglow as she regarded Miss Brightly with something akin to…pride? It could be that Ellis was simply happy to see another woman's success, but Roman was certain there was more to it than that. He looked forward to discovering what that was.

"How shall I contact your solicitor?" Josiah asked.

"He's actually downstairs," Miss Brightly said as a touch of pink colored her cheeks. "I brought him—and my aunt—along in case you made an offer of publication."

Josiah chuckled. "Well, I admire your confidence, Miss Brightly. And I can't say I'm surprised by it. I expected the author of *A Season in Shadow* to be a singular person. Your writing is as astute as it is enchanting."

"Thank you." Miss Brightly's expression now held satisfaction—and pride—along with her substantial joy. "I'll just go downstairs and fetch my solicitor and aunt." She started to stand, but Margot waved her down.

"I need to be on my way shortly, and I'd be happy to send them up," Margot said. "My mother will be arriving to fetch me. We've a shopping excursion planned." She rose.

Roman stood with Josiah and noted that Ellis didn't move from her chair. She was focused on Miss Brightly. Roman made a sound in his throat. Ellis snapped her gaze toward him and bolted to her feet.

Josiah glanced at Margot. "I'll walk you downstairs." He transferred his attention to Miss Brightly. "I'll invite your aunt and solicitor to come back up with me."

Miss Brightly smiled. "Thank you, Mr. Lacey." She looked to Margot. "It really was lovely to meet you."

"I do hope we will see each other again whilst you're in

London," Margot said. "Perhaps we can meet at the library on New Bond Street."

"Perhaps," Miss Brightly replied in a noncommittal tone. Roman wondered why she was being evasive.

As soon as the Laceys departed the office, Roman strode quickly to the door and mostly closed it, leaving just an inch of space. He positioned himself there so he could see when Josiah returned with the others, but he speared a stare toward the women sitting together at the table.

"Quickly, how do you two know one another?"

CHAPTER 4

*E*llis should have realized that Keele had seen the connection between her and her dear friend, Pandora Barclay. Euphemia Brightly wasn't just her assumed author name; it was the one Ellis and Min had chosen for their unserious plans to someday pen horrid novels together when they were spinsters sharing a cottage by the sea. As soon as Ellis had heard the name, she'd become apprehensive.

"Did you think I was Min because of the name I used?" Pandora asked softly.

Anxiety tore through Ellis once more. Keele had no idea who Ellis really was, and the name Min was a clue she couldn't afford. "I wasn't sure what to think," Ellis said. Hoping to divert the conversation before Pandora could reveal anything else, she turned toward her employer. "Miss Brightly is a friend of mine."

"You recognized her name," Keele said.

"I did recognize the name, but I didn't know who the author was until she walked in," Ellis explained.

Keele appeared nonplussed.

"Euphemia Brightly is not my real name," Pandora said with a chuckle.

"She does not care to use her real name," Ellis added.

"I do not." Pandora regarded Ellis with unchecked curiosity. "Nor do I imagine you want anyone knowing you're a woman, though clearly Lord Keele does."

"He knows I'm a woman seeking to…avoid notice."

"He's keeping your secret and providing you with employment?" Pandora asked in surprise. She sent an approving look toward the marquess. "Thank you."

"I respect Ellis's wishes."

Pandora's brows shot up. "You call her by her first name?"

Ellis tried not to grimace, especially since Keele was now surveying her. "Ellis is your Christian name?" he asked.

She nodded and then sent a pleading glance toward Pandora, hoping she would realize she shouldn't say anything more. Pandora answered with the barest apologetic nod.

"I shan't pry," Keele said. "For the moment." He looked at Pandora with sympathy. "I understand why you would prefer to remain anonymous. You've written a novel that has the potential to be rather controversial."

Pandora smiled in that self-effacing way she'd developed over the past two years. "It's more than that. If people knew the true identity of the author of *A Season in Shadow*, they would never buy or borrow it, no matter how badly they might want to read it."

Ellis nearly laughed, but from cynicism not humor. "I don't know if that's true. I think people might be *more* interested if they knew who wrote it."

"You are likely right," Pandora said with a light snort.

The sound reminded Ellis of Pandora's older sister, Persephone, as well as of Min. They were close friends and had a shared habit of unladylike snorting.

"You've utterly lost me," Keele said in bewilderment.

"I was involved in a ruinous scandal a couple of years ago," Pandora said. "Ellis can tell you more about it since I'm sure we're about to be interrupted."

"How are the two of you friends, exactly?"

Ellis and Pandora exchanged a long look. Pandora pressed her lips together, clearly indicating she would let Ellis respond since she was the one hiding in a men's costume. "We've known each other several years," Ellis replied. "As it happens, we met in a seaside resort."

Keele laughed, surprising Ellis. "Then it's no wonder the protagonist of your novel hails from one," he said to Pandora.

"Does she?" Ellis asked. "I need to read this book."

"You really should." Pandora's lips stretched in a vaguely apologetic smile as she fixed her gaze on Keele. "Would you mind excusing us before we are set upon by the others?" Without waiting for his reply, she gently clasped Ellis's arm and steered to the corner, turning her back on Keele. "*What are you doing?*"

"Working as secretary to the Marquess of Keele."

Pandora let out an exasperated breath. "I can see that. But why?"

"Don't you know what happened? I thought perhaps you might have attended Min's wedding since you're in town."

"I did, in fact. I was shocked to learn you weren't there —and Min told me why. To the best of her ability. She doesn't really understand why you aren't responding to her letters." Deep creases pleated Pandora's brow. "She's very upset, Ellis. Particularly because you didn't attend the wedding."

Ellis hated missing Min's wedding, but she couldn't risk the duchess being present. "I'm upset too. Please don't tell them you've seen me or what I'm doing. I just can't face any of them. Not yet." She was still waiting for her emotions to shift—if they even would.

"Well, that is unfortunate because I was hoping to convince you to visit me at Wellesbourne House whilst I'm in town. Persey and Acton have gone to the country, so it's just me and Aunt Lucinda. We could invite Iona since she's in town—and perhaps Min and Jo?"

"Ahem." Keele had moved toward them, but Ellis hadn't noticed because her back was also partially turned to the door and she'd been too engrossed in her conversation with Pandora. "They are coming."

Pandora quickly embraced Ellis. "Please come to visit."

Ellis was shaken. She'd successfully insulated herself from the pain of discovering the truth about her blood parents, specifically her mother. Which also meant she'd pushed away the people who meant the most to her—Min and Sheff, and her friends. What of her father, Rowland Harker, who didn't even know she existed? Unless Min, or Sheff, or his wife, Jo, had told him. It would make sense for Jo to do so since Harker was also her father. Ellis, who had thought she had no family, had suddenly gained several half-siblings as well as two parents, one of whom she despised and the other she'd briefly and barely recalled.

The idea of a family, siblings and perhaps a father, dangled before her like a tempting sweet. Still, the pain of that family having been denied her for so long cut through her extinguishing the longing she felt for familial connection. In the end, she had to rely on herself, especially if her illegitimacy ever became publicly known.

Stepping back, Ellis went to stand behind her chair. She kept her head down in case Pandora's aunt recognized her, though she doubted that would happen. Aunt Lucinda did not know Ellis as well as Pandora did, and Ellis was confident in her disguise, at least in this element. She wouldn't mistakenly do something that might be viewed as feminine, which had led to Keele's finding her out. Although the retainers at his house hadn't done that, nor had the Laceys—so far. It occurred to her, however, that perhaps none of them paid as close attention to her as Keele did.

That realization sent a tiny, not-unpleasant shiver up her spine.

Josiah Lacey entered the office with Lucinda Barclay-Fiennes and the solicitor. Introductions were made, and Pandora's real name was revealed with the express requirement that it not be disclosed to anyone outside the room, except for Margot.

They set to negotiating the agreement for Pandora's book. She also agreed to provide them with the first evaluation of her next manuscript whenever it was ready. Ellis was delighted to hear she was going to write another book.

Ellis did her best to take notes during the discussion, but her mind was still churning with thoughts of Min and her other friends. She would love to see them all, including Min and Jo, but she was safe in her current situation.

What did safe mean? It meant she couldn't be hurt again.

Ellis refocused her attention on the meeting and was grateful when it ended. Pandora left with her aunt and the solicitor, and Ellis and Keele departed soon after that. Ellis expected he would query her about Pandora when they were in the coach, and she was not wrong.

"Is Ellis really a family name?" he asked, surprising her with that question instead of something about Pandora or their friendship.

"Yes."

"I don't suppose you'll tell me your surname?"

She shook her head.

Keele exhaled. "Once I heard Miss Barclay's real name, I

vaguely recalled the scandal about her. It involved Banemore, didn't it?"

"Yes. He led her to believe that he cared for her and wanted to marry." Ellis struggled to keep the derision from her voice. Bane had utterly ruined Pandora, who'd made the mistake of falling in love and tossing her sense out the window. "When they were caught in a compromising position, he fled and married someone else."

"Ah, yes," Keele said with a grimace. "I remember now. He is no longer married."

There was a sadness in his voice as he said that. "I know he is widowed," Ellis said. Was Keele thinking of his own widowed state? Did he miss his wife? "Are you and he friendly?"

"Not anymore. We used to be somewhat close." His gaze was focused on the window, and his shoulder twitched. Ellis sensed a discomfort within him. "That was before I became the marquess." He turned his attention to her, his gray eyes smoldering in the afternoon light that cut through the coach from the window. "I overheard what Miss Barclay said to you about visiting her at Wellesbourne House. My ears pricked because I wondered what her association with Wellesbourne could be, but once I learned her real name, it made sense. Wellesbourne is her brother-in-law. Why don't you want to visit her and your friends?"

"Because I'm in hiding, or did you forget?" Ellis snapped. She realized she sounded waspish, but she didn't care. She didn't need or want him meddling in her personal affairs.

"I'm sure we could find a way to keep your visit secret. Unless you're hiding from them?"

"Just because I've shared a secret with you doesn't mean I'm going to divulge all of them. I don't want to see anyone. Besides, I don't have time," she added firmly. "I have a job with little time to myself, remember?"

"I would give you more time," he offered in a quiet but steely tone. "It's becoming clear to me that you are far from 'no one.' You have connections to some very influential people."

"I don't want more time. I want to work. Please stop prying into my personal life. None of this is your business." Ellis turned her head away and even angled her body toward the window. She fixed her gaze outside but didn't really see anything.

She could feel him looking at her, probably judging her and thinking she was silly to be hiding herself away from such "influential" people. But he didn't know the truth. He didn't know that she'd been lied to her entire life and that she'd been subjected to the cruelty of her own mother, who felt nothing but contempt for Ellis.

Someday, she would accept that and be able to move on. At least, she hoped so. She still had so much anger. And hurt. She truly did just want to focus on her work. It was challenging and kept her mind occupied. That was far preferable to what she was doing now—thinking too much about things she couldn't control.

Except she could try to regain some happiness or release some of her fury. She could do that by seeing and spending time with people who cared for her. Min. Pandora. Their other friends.

Keele.

Ellis blinked. He was not one of those people. He scarcely knew her. He didn't even know her full name. And yet, he'd demonstrated his support for her disguise and had pledged to keep her secret. He'd also offered to help her see her friends. If that wasn't someone who cared for her, what was it?

Had she been too hurt that she could no longer see the goodness in people? She hoped that wasn't the case. Her mother had done enough damage. Perhaps Ellis shouldn't allow her to inflict any more.

She glanced toward Keele. He'd leaned his head back against the squab and closed his eyes. She doubted he was sleeping, but he appeared relaxed. He seemed far less intense without the steel gray of his eyes flashing with intensity. Part of the reason she enjoyed her work so much was his passion for it. She'd never met anyone who worked as hard or as diligently as he did. He'd made astonishing progress in improving his family's fortunes in a relatively short time. But she could see he was driven to keep pushing for more.

She recalled what he'd said about being closer to Bane before he'd become marquess and decided she could ask him questions since he'd poked his nose into her business. She knew he'd inherited the marquessate about five years ago. "You said you knew Bane before. Were you part of that group of rogues?"

Keele's lids parted and revealed his storm-gray eyes. They pierced into Ellis with an intensity that sent another shiver up her spine. It was still pleasant. Perhaps even exciting.

"*Rogues?*" he asked.

"Bane's reputation is that of a scoundrel, as were those of his friends."

"You're referring to Shefford, Wellesbourne, and Somerton," he said flatly. "They were the core members of that group, but I, along with a few others, joined in their debauchery more than I care to admit in retrospect."

"So you were a rogue, but you're not anymore?"

"I gained a need to be serious when my father died." He arched a dark brow at her. "You're aware of the state my finances were in at that time."

"I am. I'm also aware of how you've improved them. It's admirable. Was your marriage part of your financial strategy?"

He narrowed his eyes at her, but he didn't seem angry. "Now *you're* being intrusive. I suppose I deserve that. Yes, I married Clarissa Lacey because she had a massive dowry, and her father was keen to let me invest in his company—with my time and status instead of with money since I had precious little of that."

"You've been a great asset to Lacey and Company," she said. "And you have a decent fortune now." He wasn't as wealthy as the Duke of Henlow or even Wellesbourne or Somerton, but he certainly wasn't "poor."

"We have different opinions of *decent*," he replied blandly. "I've plenty more work to do in order to achieve what I would like."

Ellis was thoroughly interested. She sat slightly forward, caught up in his fierce commitment to restoring his family. "And what's that?"

"To never be at risk of bankruptcy again." His eyes glittered with promise. "Not in this generation or any other."

"Well, I shall do what I can to help you," Ellis said.

He crossed his arms over his chest and stretched out his legs. His body overwhelmed the interior of the coach. Ellis was increasingly aware of him as a man and not just her employer.

His gaze locked with hers. "I continue to be thrilled that I hired you. I hope that never stops."

Thrilled.

Yes, that was an excellent word to describe how Ellis felt at the current moment as she shared this small space with him. Perhaps it would be best if she didn't ride anywhere with him again.

*A*s the final course was laid at dinner on Sunday evening at the Laceys' home in the new and very fashionable Bryanston Square, Roman marveled at how his father-in-law's house and household was much closer to what one might expect from a marquess than Roman's own house and household. The Laceys had moved into this five-bayed house a year ago. It was both large and most elegantly furnished.

Though there were only four of them this evening, they ate in the grand dining room that would easily seat probably eight times their number if the mahogany table was at its full extension. They were clustered at one end with Josiah at the head, Harriet to his right, and Margot on his left. Roman sat beside her.

Roman's dining room did not have an Axminster carpet nor Sevres china, but he supposed it did have the Keele crest embellishing the silver that had, thankfully, not been sold.

Margot was particularly animated this evening, but then she often was due to her overtly charming and convivial personality. She was so unlike her sister, whose demeanor had been more enigmatic, as if she were a puzzle that needed solving. Roman had been intrigued by her. He thought they might have shared something in common with regard to buried emotions or inner secrets. He'd been terribly wrong.

Harriet smiled at him and Margot from across the table, the diamonds at her throat and dangling from her ears sparkling in the candlelight from the John Blades cut-glass chandelier that was also reflected in the massive gilt mirror hanging above the hearth. "We did say we would discuss your engagement this evening," she said, finally bringing up the topic that Roman had been expecting.

Margot's enthusiasm immediately dimmed.

Josiah inclined his head in agreement before he took a bite of apple tart. "Yes, we should discuss it."

"Am I allowed to say that I'm not quite ready for courtship?" Margot asked. She sent Roman an apologetic glance.

He was not upset by her comment. In fact, he was relieved whilst still torn. Though he didn't particularly wish to marry her, he loved her parents and very much enjoyed evenings like this, where he felt part of a family. It was a sensation he hadn't known until he'd married Clarissa.

Harriet's brows gathered as she regarded her daughter with concern. "You are of a marriageable age, dear."

Margot frowned slightly. "Why is there a predetermined age when women are required to wed? Men don't seem to be held to the same standard."

Josiah chuckled. "They are not. If you need a little more time, we understand. But Keele may wish to wed sooner than later. He does need an heir." He ate another mouthful of tart.

"I am not in a rush," Roman said. Though Josiah was right. He did need to wed and do his duty by providing an heir, and Margot would not be a poor choice. Marrying her would ensure he remained a part of this family in the same way he was now.

He tried to imagine Margot as his wife. She was pretty and far more interested in Lacey and Company than Clarissa had ever been, so they would have that in common. But Roman didn't love Margot, nor would he ever. He wouldn't love anyone after what Clarissa had done to him.

She'd pretended to be eager to wed, all whilst already being in love with another man. Roman hadn't known that until much later, of course. The early days of their marriage had been pleasant and even sweet. Clarissa had behaved somewhat shyly and had asked for time to become acclimated to marriage before they became intimate.

Roman had understood her reticence and had worked to gain her trust and her affection. Though, when she'd finally shared his bed, she hadn't seemed to enjoy it despite Roman's best efforts. He'd bloody well tried to make a good marriage with her, but she'd always had a reason for remaining remote. She was shy. She was nervous. She suffered pain.

Roman had felt awful. Until he'd learned that she'd not only been unfaithful to him but had been in love with this other man since before they'd even wed. She'd fabricated all the tender feelings she'd shown toward him, both before and after the wedding, and she'd made it clear that she'd never tried or even wanted to love Roman. She'd left him hurt and angry. In some ways, she'd ruined him.

Margot deserved better than someone like him and the marriage of convenience he now sought. Unless of course, she didn't care about love and just wanted to be a marchioness and gain status in society. He knew her parents hoped for that—it was the entire reason Josiah had originally approached Roman with an offer to wed Clarissa. He'd known that Roman was in need of funds, and he'd wanted to have friends—or family—in lofty places.

However, Roman and Clarissa's marriage hadn't worked out the way anyone had intended. Clarissa had gone along with her parents' wishes despite already having given her heart to another. Josiah and Harriet believed she'd been a willing participant, but it turned out she was increasingly unhappy. They did not know about her love affair, and Roman planned never to tell them.

"Will you at least spend more time together if you won't yet enter into a formal courtship?" Harriet asked hopefully. "I feel confident you will form a close bond. I do realize I'm being a bit selfish, because I would like grandchildren."

Margot met her mother's gaze. "I know, Mama. We will

endeavor to spend more time together." She looked over at Roman, who nodded in agreement.

They finished the course, and the ladies withdrew, leaving Roman and Josiah to their port.

Josiah swirled the wine in his glass. "I hope Harriet isn't being too forceful with her talk of marriage."

"Not at all," Roman said politely. "She cares for Margot and wants to see her settled."

"She does indeed." Josiah sipped his port and sent a sideways glance toward Roman. "Are you truly interested in marrying Margot? I would understand if you're hesitant. I know your union with Clarissa was not what we had all hoped it would be. Were you happy at all?" Josiah asked, his features creased with deep and, what seemed to Roman, heartfelt concern.

"I was," Roman replied, and it wasn't entirely untrue. He *had* been happy at the start. When he had believed that both he and Clarissa had entered into the marriage in good faith.

"I'm glad to hear that," Josiah said. "I do think you're perhaps better suited to Margot, particularly given her interest and passion for her work with Lacey and Company. She would make you an excellent partner in home and in business."

"That is appealing," Roman agreed. "But I do hope you'll let her decide without any undue pressure."

"That is what happened with Clarissa, isn't it?" Josiah posed the question in a whisper that was difficult to hear. "I know it is," he added more loudly with a confident nod. "She once told me, before you were wed, that she hoped she wasn't making a mistake. I thought she was worried about being a marchioness. She sometimes lacked confidence. As I said, Margot is likely a better match for you." Grief and regret briefly shadowed his features.

"I hope you don't blame yourself for Clarissa's death," Roman said earnestly.

Josiah didn't hesitate. "No, nor do I blame you. She was deeply unhappy and hid it from all of us. Harriet and I wish we knew why."

Roman knew, of course, but would never tell them. He'd suspected she was unfaithful and confronted her about it. She'd tried to lie, but Roman had seen the truth. Furious and hurt, he'd demanded that she end the affair and reveal the man's identity. She refused to do either, saying she was deeply in love. Roman had considered hiring someone to follow her, to discover her lover, but had decided against revealing his wife's infidelity to anyone. Instead, he told her what a disappointment she would be to her parents. That had bothered her, but it still hadn't been enough to persuade her to terminate the liaison.

As Roman continued to question her about her lover, she began taking laudanum. After several weeks of persistent arguing and turmoil, she'd flown into a rage one night and admitted that her paramour had grown tired of her. She'd furiously lamented that she'd ruined her life for nothing. Roman hadn't known how to respond, so he'd simply left her to her ravings.

The next morning, she didn't wake. She'd ingested too much laudanum. Whether she'd imbibed too much on purpose or by accident could never be known, and to Roman it made no difference.

Roman and Josiah hadn't ever discussed Clarissa's death and whether it was intentional. "I hope you know that I tried to make her happy," Roman said.

"Of course I do. I should not have pushed her to wed. She was too reserved for you, but I didn't know you well then." His features darkened again. "It was a tragedy for which there is no one at fault."

That wasn't true. Clarissa's lover carried the blame. What kind of man pursued a young, unwed lady and continued to do so after she became another's wife? And how depraved was he to turn away from her then, not from a fit of conscience but because he was weary of her? If Roman ever discovered his identity, he'd ensure the man suffered. His careless behavior had destroyed Clarissa and ravaged her family.

Josiah somehow brightened, his lips curling into a smile. "Harriet and I are so grateful to have you in our lives. You eased the pain of Clarissa's passing as we shared our grief. Like my wife, I have selfish reasons for wanting you to marry Margot, but it isn't about grandchildren. I very much like having you as part of our family." He blinked, then looked toward his port, but Roman had seen the man's emotion.

"I feel the same. You are the father I wish I'd had." Roman lifted his glass, and Josiah did the same.

"To family," Josiah said. "You shall always be a part of ours."

"Thank you." Roman's throat felt oddly tight, and he had to wait a moment before he could drink his port.

"Are you still pleased with Mr. Ellis?" Josiah asked after a moment.

Roman was glad for the easier topic. "Exceedingly. He is everything I need in a secretary."

"How do you like having him live with you? Do you expect him to work all the time?" Josiah asked with a chuckle.

"He does work quite a bit, but I try not to be too demanding. He's made great progress in fixing everything my former secretary bungled."

"I'm sure that is a great relief to you."

"It is." Roman took another sip of his port.

Josiah did the same, and as he set his glass down, his brow furrowed. "Forgive me for saying so, but is Ellis a bit odd?"

Roman tensed. He worried that someone else might deduce what he had—that Ellis was really a woman. But he'd convinced himself that nobody spent as much time with her as he did, so they would likely not come to the same conclusion. Perhaps he'd been wrong in thinking that.

"In what way?" Roman asked in the most nonchalant tone he could manage.

Josiah waved his hand. "Oh, I don't know. I suppose I find his reading habits unusual."

"That is definitely true," Roman said cautiously. "He has four older sisters who have influenced him greatly. I would say Ellis has a keen understanding of the female mind. His future wife will be quite fortunate."

Josiah laughed. "How fortuitous for him. I do have one piece of business I wish to discuss with you. What are your thoughts on the Oxford library?"

Roman oversaw all the libraries, while Josiah focused most of his attention on the publishing. "Aside from New Bond Street, it's our best-performing branch. I credit Mr. Pritchard. He's an excellent librarian."

"Agreed." Josiah sipped more port. "Honestly, Pritchard is the best we have. I've been thinking about bringing him to New Bond Street to replace Mr. Inman, but I should hate to push him out. It isn't that Inman isn't a good librarian. Pritchard is just…better. He has more energy and enthusiasm for growing the subscription base. He also entices ladies to visit, and they are often our best customers," he added with a pointed smile.

That was true. Pritchard was a young, unmarried man who also happened to be quite handsome, with dark blonde waves crowning his sculptured, aristocratic features. He was the youngest son of a baron who'd planned to enter the clergy but found he preferred being in a library. "I'm not sure Pritchard would be interested in coming to London, even if we had a plan for Inman." Roman did not want to see Inman displaced. He'd been at the New Bond Street branch since it opened and was truly a fixture after more than a decade.

"Find out," Josiah said. "No sense retiring Inman if Pritchard isn't interested in taking over New Bond Street."

"I'll write to him and ask," Roman said.

"Excellent." Josiah finished his port. "Shall we join the ladies?"

Roman tossed back the remainder of his wine and stood. The word *ladies* brought Ellis to mind, but of course she wasn't here. He realized it was dangerous to think of her as a woman. Yesterday, he'd caught himself as he'd nearly referred to her as "she" in front of his butler.

He wished she were present—as a woman. He found himself more and more curious about her, especially since learning of her friendship with Pandora Barclay and what seemed to be several members of Society, including the Duchess of Wellesbourne.

What was Ellis hiding from? Or who?

Roman cautioned himself. The last time a woman had intrigued him, he'd come away deeply damaged. It was probably best if he kept his distance from his secretary and whatever secrets she was keeping.

CHAPTER 5

$\mathcal{E}$llis sat at her small desk transcribing a letter from the shorthand she'd taken earlier. Keele had dictated several letters, and she'd finally reached the last one.

This second week had been as busy as the first, but they'd settled into a now-familiar routine. Most mornings, Keele went to the Lacey and Company office on Paternoster Row or to one of the subscription libraries in London. New Bond Street was the main branch, but there were smaller ones in the Strand, Bloomsbury, and Marylebone. Apparently, he sometimes ventured to libraries in other cities and towns, but he did not have any current plans to do so.

He spent the afternoons here in the study. Ellis usually worked alongside him—each of them busy at their own desks, which were in close proximity.

His solicitor had come one day last week, and another peer from the House of Lords had visited for a meeting. He'd seemed rather put out because Keele rarely went to clubs where government business was often discussed. Ellis had learned that Keele only visited the Phoenix Club—perhaps once or twice a week—and that this noble was not a member there.

Keele was unlike any peer she'd met, not that she knew a great many. Still, she was acquainted with several because of her former position as the companion to Lady Minerva, daughter of the Duke of Henlow and sister of the Earl of Shefford. Furthermore, several of their friends were now wedded to peers. Pandora's sister, Persephone—or Persey as they called her—was married to the Duke of Wellesbourne, whilst another was the Baroness Droxton. Min's new sister-in-law had become the Viscountess Somerton earlier this year.

All those peers, save Droxton, who was terribly serious, had past reputations as rogues and scoundrels. They were the very reason Ellis and her friends had come up with the rogue rules—to stay clear of men like them. And yet, several of their number had broken their own rules and married precisely the blackguards they'd planned to avoid.

Ellis had never imagined the rules were for her, because she wasn't in their position. No one was trying to arrange an advantageous marriage for her, nor was any rogue hoping to gain her hand for wealth or position. One might, however, attempt to lure her into his bed. And one *had* been successful —but that was years ago, long before the Rogue Rules had been devised.

Recently, Ellis had begun to wonder if she might ever consider another such liaison.

Keele sat at his desk to her left. She was always aware of his presence. He worked very hard, and she found industriousness attractive, apparently.

She also couldn't deny that he was exceptionally handsome. He looked as though he'd been carved from rough stone and could weather anything. Yes, that was incredibly appealing to her.

Which was why she kept stealing glances at him. Thankfully, he had yet to catch her surreptitious perusals. Pausing in her writing, she darted her gaze to the left.

Bloody hell. He was staring right at her.

Her pulse picked up speed. She hoped he couldn't see she was flustered.

"Pritchard responded to my letter," he said, gesturing with a piece of parchment.

Ellis straightened and angled herself slightly toward him, relieved he seemed not to be aware of her notice. On Monday, they'd dispatched a letter to Oliver Pritchard, the librarian they employed in Oxford. Keele and Mr. Lacey had discussed making him the head librarian on New Bond Street but first wanted to ascertain whether he was interested.

"What does he say?" Ellis asked.

"He's quite enthusiastic about the prospect." Keele set the letter on the desk, grimacing faintly. Then he pressed his hand against his forehead before wiping it down over his eyes. "Unfortunately, that means I have to determine what to do with Mr. Inman, the librarian at New Bond Street."

Ellis knew Mr. Inman from when she'd visited the library with Min, but she hadn't told Keele that. She didn't want him to know anything so specific about the life she'd led before coming to work for him. He already knew too much, since he was aware of her friendship with Pandora and other *influential*—as he called them—people.

"I assumed Inman was retiring, and that was why you were seeking a replacement," she said. "Is that not the case?"

Keele shook his head. "Pritchard is an exceptionally good librarian—he's grown the subscriptions at Oxford exponentially. We'd like to see him in charge at our largest branch." He frowned. "But I hate to displace Inman. He's been with the New Bond Street branch since Josiah opened it over a decade ago."

"That is a dilemma," she said softly.

Roman sat forward in his chair and leaned toward her over the desk. "Do you have any suggestions for how I might deal with this situation? Inman is past sixty. Shouldn't he want to retire?"

As it happened, Ellis knew Mr. Inman wished to spend more time with his children and grandchildren, particularly after his wife had died last year. However, she couldn't tell Keele any of that without revealing how she knew. "He may. I would say that people like to feel valued, especially at the end of their service. Perhaps if you made his retirement seem like an honor that he's earned, he might embrace it."

"I know he's widowed," Keele said. "I'm concerned he appreciates having this job to fill his days."

"Perhaps you could give him something to do that takes less time," Ellis suggested.

"That's a good idea. Inman has been an extraordinary asset to Lacey and Company. I would truly hate to lose him entirely." He thought for a moment before meeting her gaze once more. "Do you have any thoughts as to what he could do?"

Ellis lifted a shoulder. "Perhaps he can be a consulting librarian. He could host literary discussions in one of the reading rooms. You could even name the room after him. I imagine he would feel very honored."

Keele grinned, and Ellis felt as though she were floating. The room around them disappeared, leaving her in just the glorious warmth of his smile.

"You are a genius, Ellis."

"Thank you." She liked his compliments more than she should, and now she was back to thinking about how attracted she was to him. Perhaps that was because he was staring at her mouth.

He suddenly stood and leaned further over the desk. What was he doing? Had he somehow read her thoughts, felt the same attraction, and decided to act upon it?

Reaching out, he nearly put his thumb to her lower lip. But he froze just before he made contact with her flesh. Their eyes met and held. Her breath caught.

Again, the room stilled and faded. Ellis felt a pull toward Keele, like a magnet drawing her. She parted her lips.

He blinked. The spell dissipated, and the study returned. Ellis took a breath.

"Forgive me." He withdrew his hand and sat back down. "You've ink on your lip. At least, I think it's ink."

Oh. "That happens sometimes when I'm writing." She turned her body toward her desk once more and shifted her focus to her work. "I'll tidy it when I'm finished with this letter. I've only a few lines left."

"Should I get you a mirror to keep in your desk?" he asked. "So that you can ensure you don't have ink on your face in future?"

"No," she replied quickly, self-conscious that her appearance was lacking, which was ridiculous, because she didn't even look like herself. He'd never even seen her as a woman. What did it matter if his secretary had ink on his lip?

She hurriedly finished the letter, then practically jumped to her feet. "Please excuse me for a few minutes."

"Please don't worry about the ink," he said. "I didn't mean to make you feel uncomfortable."

She couldn't meet his gaze. "I'm quite comfortable." How asinine that sounded.

Her heart had not slowed to a regular pace since he'd nearly touched her, and she realized it had nothing to do with the ink on her face and everything to do with how much she *wanted* him to touch her. The reason she needed to leave right now was not to clean her face, though she would, but to calm herself and cool the heat rising within her. This attraction she felt for her employer was dangerous, and she could not afford to lose her job. She simply had to stop thinking of him as an alluring gentleman.

That would be much easier if he could just stop being one.

~

This was the first night Roman had taken dinner in his study with Ellis. He'd wanted to suggest it a couple of days ago, but they'd shared that awkward moment when he tried to wipe the ink from her lip, and he didn't extend the invitation.

He didn't know what he'd been thinking trying to touch her like that. Noting the ink on her lower lip, he'd tried to ignore it. Except he was often drawn to her mouth anyway, and the presence of the ink only attracted his attention more fiercely. Could one be jealous of an ink smudge?

Ultimately, he'd leaned forward to wipe it away with his thumb. Thankfully, he'd stopped himself a moment before committing the indiscretion. Even so, there had been a long, rather charged moment between them as he realized what he'd done—and she had too. What he couldn't decide was whether she was horrified at his behavior or, and this seemed unlikely, that she was disappointed that he'd stopped.

He was foolish even to think that, let alone hope for it. They had a professional relationship, and though he had a clear and persistent attraction to her, he had to assume it was one-sided. Even if it wasn't, what were they to do about it? He was her employer. He was not the sort of man who took advantage of those who worked for him in any role.

"*Blast,*" Ellis muttered. She'd turned her chair toward his desk so that they were sitting across from each other, using his desktop as their dining table.

"Is something wrong?" he asked.

She set her fork down and lifted her gaze to his. Her features were lined with frustration. "I find the facial hair intrusive when I eat. I don't know how men with beards and mustaches tolerate them. But then I also don't know how men can put up with shaving all this every day." She waved her hand in front of the lower half of her face.

He chuckled. "We either shave, or we deal with food in our beards."

"Have you ever grown a beard?"

"Briefly. I lost a wager when I was at Oxford."

"How long was the beard?" she asked, narrowing one eye at him, as if she were trying to imagine him with facial hair.

"Longer than yours as I had to grow it over the summer holiday and return to school so everyone could see how wild I'd become." He rolled his eyes as he smiled. "The dean immediately instructed me to shave it off. He said I looked as though I ought to be living in some folly at a far-flung estate."

"As a hermit?" she asked.

"Yes." He'd assumed she would know what a hermit was when he mentioned the folly. With friends like the Duchess of Wellesbourne, it seemed more than likely that she was familiar with such things.

"I think I might enjoy being a hermit," she mused.

"Why?" He set his utensils down and leaned back in his chair.

Ellis had just forked a few peas into her mouth. After she swallowed, she put her utensils on the desk. "Being a hermit in a folly on a far-flung estate is the ultimate hiding place, isn't it?" She gave him a sly smile.

He laughed. "Whatever or whomever you are trying to

avoid must be truly horrible if you would consider such a thing."

"On second thought, I don't think I'd like it," she said. "Whilst being alone is appealing sometimes, I'm not sure I would care for it all the time, unless there was a never-ending supply of books."

"If you could be a hermit in a library, you'd be quite satisfied?"

She nodded. "I think so. Anyway, I'm not sure I'll agree to further meals here with you. It's too irritating. Not you, the beard," she quickly added.

"Is that why you haven't had any meals outside your room in the past week and a half?" he asked.

"Yes," she replied. "I prefer to eat with a bare face."

"Understandable." Though, Roman was disappointed she wouldn't be dining with him again. "What about the attire? Do you prefer men's clothing? I imagine it's less constricting than what you wear as a woman."

"I suppose it can be, though it's not as though my costume is entirely made for your gender. I'm still a woman under-neath. In fact, I had to mask that by—" She abruptly stopped as a blush crept up her face. "Forgive me. I should not discuss such matters."

He laughed and took a sip of wine. "It's quite all right. I'm enjoying our conversation. It's a pity you weren't able to get rid of your corset, if that is what you're referring to."

"Some men wear corsets," she noted. "Though I'm sure you don't."

Their eyes met and held. This dialogue was treading perilously close to flirting. Roman didn't think he cared, but he absolutely should. Except he was enjoying her company far too much. He couldn't remember the last time he'd spoken this way with a woman—certainly never with

Clarissa. And he'd shared very little female company in the pair of years since her death.

"I do *not* wear a corset," Roman confirmed. "I'm curious why you would wear one. I assume that was what you meant. Why would you need a corset beneath your clothing?"

The blue of her eyes darkened, and he sensed a sudden heat between them. "It's not just a corset. I had to augment it in order to disguise myself."

He still wasn't entirely clear on her undergarments, but he understood that she would need to hide her curves, and that would include her breasts. Now he was imagining their size and shape. Bloody hell, this was beyond inappropriate.

Thankfully, they were interrupted before Roman could make a complete arse of himself. The footman pushed the door, which had been ajar, open all the way and stepped inside carrying a tray. "I brought the last of the peaches along with Bakewell tart. Cook hopes you will enjoy it." He set the dishes down on the desk. "Shall I take your dinner plates?" he asked.

"Yes, please," Ellis replied. "I'm finished."

"I am as well," Roman said.

The footman gathered up their dishes but left the wine and departed.

Ellis stood. "I think I'll go upstairs now." She kept her head bowed, and he feared he'd gone too far with their almost-flirting.

"Must you?" he asked. "Surely you want the tart?"

"I do, but I would prefer to eat it with my own face." She arched a brow at him, and there was a sauciness that led him to believe she wasn't upset, just eager to put aside her disguise.

Roman understood, though he was still disappointed. "Of course. Please enjoy your tart."

She sent him a furtive glance, and he caught the lingering

smolder in her gaze before she swept up her dish and strode from the room.

He exhaled, but his pulse, which had kicked up as they regarded one another, was still moving too quickly. Indeed, his entire body was thrumming with an urgent desire. He even had a bloody erection.

This would not do.

He'd enjoyed their first dinner together, but it was perhaps best that it was also their last. He brought the tart before him and picked up the fork.

Hopefully, his lust would diminish quickly. If not, a cool bath would be required.

More than likely, he'd have to satisfy himself in ways his alluring secretary could not. But the rogue in him would almost certainly imagine her doing just that.

~

After finishing his tart, Roman remained in his office for quite some time. He recalled that Ellis would be using the bathing chamber this evening and didn't want to go upstairs until she was finished. Because the bathing room adjoined his bedchamber, he'd been able to hear her moving about in there. It was most distracting—in a delightfully sensual way.

Truthfully, it had been a terrible idea to allow her use of his bath. But he didn't regret it.

Since she'd been due to be done half an hour ago, Roman decided it was safe to go up. Tonight, he'd had the sense she might be attracted to him in the same way he was to her. It was decidedly best if they didn't tempt that attraction.

He was still in a heightened state of desire as he climbed the stairs. The slightest thought of Ellis hardened his cock again. Past time for that cool bath.

He'd have to ring for water if he wanted a true bath, but the footman had likely left a basin of water for him to wash his face. It was possible Ellis's bathwater might still be in the tub. No, he wasn't even going to *think* about her and her bath.

He stripped his clothes away until only his pantaloons remained, though he unbuttoned the top of the fall. Opening the door to the bathing chamber, he walked inside.

Just as Ellis stepped out of the bathtub.

He froze as she grabbed a length of toweling from a hook. At last, he saw her as a woman. She had long hair. Though it was wet, he could tell it was blonde. The rest of her was completely bare—from the gentle slope of her shoulder to the plane of her back, down her spine, to the graceful curve of her backside, leading to the long elegance of her legs.

Roman's throat went dry as he stared at her. The erection he'd fought to keep at bay came roaring back as primal lust coursed through him.

She turned, clutching the toweling to her breast, and stared at him, her eyes wide. Her face was bare like the rest of her—no beard or mustache to disguise her unparalleled beauty. Roman had simply never seen a more stunning woman. It wasn't possible she could ever despise her faux facial hair as much as he did.

Her lips parted. "My lord," she managed in a strained, dark whisper. Her gaze flicked down his body, lingering on his bare chest, then pausing even longer where his fall was unbuttoned and his cock had lengthened.

He quickly spun around, depriving himself of the glorious view of her. "I didn't realize you were still in here. I thought you would be finished by nine."

"That was when I told the footman I would *start* my bath."

Damn. He'd utterly cocked that up. "I misunderstood. I'll not make the same mistake again."

"Perhaps the footman was mistaken and communicated the wrong time," she said.

"That could be. I'll speak to him. Was your bath all right? Let me know if the water temperature wasn't adequate. I can speak to him about that as well." Roman realized he was babbling when he should just leave.

"It was lovely," she replied, her already unusually deep feminine voice even huskier—and more seductive—than usual. "I'll hurry. I didn't realize you wanted to take a bath tonight."

"I don't. I was just going to wash up."

"There isn't any warm water."

"I prefer cold at the moment." He really needed to stop talking.

"I see," she murmured. Something about her tone—the way the word *see* had climbed—made him think she was not completely innocent. Perhaps she understood what it meant if a man was specifically seeking cold water.

Roman could not allow his mind to chase those thoughts. "I truly am sorry. About this...and about earlier. I hope I didn't drive you away." He knew he hadn't, or so she said. She'd just wanted to eat the tart without hair on her face. "The tart was quite good," he added, apparently unable to keep from talking to hide the incredible tautness of the encounter.

"It was delicious." The way she said that last word sent a tantalizing shiver across his flesh. "I took it with me, if you recall."

"Yes, I knew that." He forced out a breath. "I'm very distracted."

The sound of her laughter danced along his spine. It relaxed him and made him smile. Without thinking, he looked back over his shoulder at her. Their eyes locked. She sobered. The heat filled her gaze once more.

With great effort, Roman turned away from her. "I'll leave you to it." He started toward the door.

"Be careful. There's a bit of water on the—"

Roman cut off her speech by finding the puddle of water on the floor to which she referred. His bare foot slipped, and his leg went forward. He reached and barely caught the doorframe. Still, he stretched himself in a rather awful way and was certain he appeared a complete fool. He pulled himself up with a grunt, his hand still holding the door jamb.

"Are you all right?" she asked. Her voice was much too close. And far too full of concern. She touched his bare arm, sending a jolt of desperate heat straight through Roman. He turned his head toward her, but she quickly snatched her hand back.

Roman was filled with regret in that moment—that he hadn't wiped the ink from her lip, that he hadn't asked her to stay and eat the tart with him, that he was going to leave the bathing chamber without taking advantage of their distinct lack of clothing and potential mutual interest in exploring that state.

The edge of her mouth ticked up in a sultry smile that made him want to groan. "We have to stop doing this." She was definitely aware of the sparks between them.

"I'll be honest, I don't mind if we *don't* stop doing this. I mean—" He still couldn't help sounding like a complete idiot. He ought to be plainer. "I wouldn't mind if we took it further."

She sucked in a breath and looked away.

He'd surprised her. And perhaps not in a pleasing manner. "I can't seem to stop causing problems. Please forget what I just said. It was highly inappropriate. Good night, Ellis."

Turning from her, he stepped quickly into his bedchamber and pulled the door closed behind him—probably too forcefully. He leaned back, grateful for the cool wood as it soothed his heated flesh. He worked on taking deep breaths.

He told himself to move away, but he couldn't stop listening to her finish her toilet. The entire time, his body raged with want for her. Without thought, he slipped his hand into his open fall and withdrew his hardened cock. He stroked himself, and he could no longer hear Ellis's movements due to his blood storming through his veins. He could see her, however, in his mind's eye—her gorgeous back and enchanting backside, her naked, feminine face. He could've stared at her all night. He never wanted to see her with facial hair again.

Closing his eyes, he leaned his head back as he moved his hand faster over his rigid flesh. This was madness. His heart was racing, and he was nearly panting with want as his body tumbled toward release. He should stop.

He slowed his movements, but then he heard the distinct sound of the other door to the bathing chamber creaking open then closing. She was gone. He gripped himself more tightly and worked his cock until he came with a grunt that she would have certainly heard if she hadn't left. It was many moments before he could catch his breath.

A flurry of sensations washed over him, but regret wasn't one of them. Damn, if that hadn't been the finest orgasm he'd had in many years. Perhaps in his entire life.

Opening his eyes, Roman swore. He shouldn't lust after his secretary. He didn't even know her real surname.

If he couldn't find a way to stop thinking of Ellis as anything other than an exemplary employee, he was going to have to let her go. Anything else wasn't fair to her, and it certainly wasn't right for him to continue wanting her.

He was a better man than this, rutting after someone who worked for him, who trusted him, wasn't he? He hoped so, but he'd been too long without a woman and even longer without a woman who truly wanted him.

That was the real danger. He saw his own desire reflected in Ellis's eyes, felt it in the touch of her hand—which she'd immediately withdrawn. He wouldn't impose himself on her, employee or not.

But if she invited his attentions?

Roman didn't think he could resist.

CHAPTER 6

$\mathcal{E}$llis reread the note she'd just received from Pandora, delivered by one of Wellesbourne House's footmen. She hoped the delivery to the Marquess of Keele's *secretary* from such a prominent household hadn't drawn Keele's butler's attention. But how could it not? She would have to mention the delivery to Keele so he could extinguish any curiosity. Particularly since it was the second time in the past week that such a note had arrived.

Exhaling, she set the parchment to the side of her desk. Ellis didn't blame Pandora for trying to persuade her to visit. This note and the prior one asked her to come to Wellesbourne House. The first note had again mentioned including their friends who were in town—Iona, Jo, and Min. Ellis had responded to decline.

Today's note invited Ellis to dine with Pandora this evening to celebrate Bonfire Night. Pandora specifically stated it would be just the two of them. Aunt Lucinda planned to dine elsewhere with friends.

The invitation was tempting. How lovely it would be to wear a gown and be herself again. Ellis missed being a woman. That realization had surfaced the night before last when Keele had walked into the bathing chamber as she'd stepped from the bath.

His reaction to seeing her was forever imprinted on her mind—and her body. She still tingled when she thought of his thorough and passionate regard, not to mention his frank invitation to take their mutual attraction to the next step.

Ellis had no doubt their desire was mutual. It felt so wonderful to be not just a woman, but a woman who was *wanted*. After learning that her mother hadn't ever wanted her and never would, Ellis had wondered if she would ever feel as though she had value—at least to another person—again.

Even so, in her head, she knew that was silly. She *knew* Min and Jo and her other friends valued her. Pandora was demonstrating that presently.

Perhaps Keele's interest in her was so appealing because he was new to her life. He didn't know her, wasn't aware of her situation, and he didn't feel sorry for her. To think she could be intimate with someone, even just physically, was incredibly appealing. Just as she was mulling Pandora's invitation to dinner, she couldn't help pondering Keele's offer of seduction.

Which was *terrible* since she was his employee. He'd been right when he'd said it was inappropriate, and it was good that he'd left because Ellis had been quite vulnerable. She had almost asked him to stay.

It was torture knowing he was just on the other side of the door in his bedchamber. She'd hurried to dry herself and leave the bathing chamber as soon as possible.

In her haste, she'd left her hairbrush behind and had to go back to fetch it. It was then that she'd heard something moving against the door to Keele's chamber. She'd crept towards it, listening intently.

She'd frozen as an unmistakable groan carried from the other side of the door. Ellis had pressed her ear to the wood and could hear Keele panting. Images of what he'd almost certainly been doing had filled her mind, and she'd fled the bathing chamber to do precisely what he'd done in the privacy of her own bed.

"Afternoon." Keele's voice jolted Ellis from her reverie. She didn't turn her head, for she knew her cheeks were flaming. And she was slightly breathless from thinking of him pleasuring himself.

"Afternoon," she murmured.

Keele went to stand behind his desk and gestured toward Pandora's note. "Is that for me?"

Ellis plucked it up and folded the parchment in half. "No, it's a note from Pandora Barclay inviting me to dinner this evening." Satisfied that her face was no longer scarlet, she pivoted toward him. "A footman from Wellesbourne House delivered it. Unfortunately, he did not stay to receive a reply as he did the first time."

"This is not her first message to you?"

"Yes. I take it Graham didn't mention anything to you about the first note. That gives me some comfort, as I hoped his curiosity wasn't piqued that your secretary is receiving correspondence from Wellesbourne House. But now it's happened again…" She frowned.

"Graham is incredibly discreet. That said, it's possible he will mention it to me since it happened a second time." Keele waved his hand. "Do not concern yourself. I will manage the situation."

"I *will* concern myself as the matter concerns *me*," Ellis said. "But I do thank you for helping to maintain my privacy."

"That is part of our agreement, and I will not renege, even if I disagree with your reasoning." He arched a brow at her, and her breath caught at how devilishly handsome he was. "Which I don't because I have no idea what it is."

Ellis heard the question in his voice but didn't address it. She wasn't going to explain who she was or why she was hiding.

"Are you going to dine with her?" he asked.

"I'd planned to bathe." That was the truth, but she hadn't meant to say that out loud. Not after what happened. Surely that simple word—*bathe*—aroused the same thoughts and sensations in him as it did in her. Ellis avoided the temptation to look at him, but it took supreme effort.

"During dinner?" His voice carried a hitch. He coughed.

She kept her gaze on the desk in front of her. "I thought that would be the best time, so as not to have another misunderstanding as we did the other night."

"I can't ask Alvin to ready a bath during dinner," Keele said. "He is otherwise engaged."

"I can heat and carry my own water—even to fill an entire tub," Ellis said. "I'm perfectly capable." She'd been doing that at the boarding house where she'd been living, and it wasn't too difficult. Granted, she hadn't been carrying it upstairs, but she was strong.

She was answered with a lengthening silence. Curious about his reaction, she turned her head and saw him moving around his desk. He came to stand behind her chair, and she pivoted to look up at him.

He narrowed his beguiling gray eyes at her. "You are friends with a duchess, take excellent shorthand, are apparently capable of drawing your own bath, and you're the finest secretary I've ever encountered." He searched her face as bewilderment furrowed his brow. "Who the hell are you?"

Ellis pushed her chair back from the desk, forcing him to edge backward slightly. She stood and faced him, thinking it would be best if she retreated for a while, since the air in the room had seemed to electrify.

"I have told you repeatedly: I am no one." She held his gaze for a long moment.

He shook his head slowly. "I don't believe you. Is someone searching for you? Am I going to have trouble when someone *finds* you?"

"No one is going to find me." Ellis couldn't promise that. Since Pandora knew she worked for Keele, there was a distinct possibility that someone *would* find her. And if her identity were exposed, she'd be ruined, not that she had a reputation or standing that would suffer. However, she ought to think of Keele. It might not reflect well on him if he were found to have employed the former companion to Lady Minerva, daughter of the Duke of Henlow—and that mattered to Ellis, for she'd come to care for him.

How could she not? He'd demonstrated genuine concern by allowing her to keep her secrets, even though that clearly frustrated him. At every turn, he'd been kind, understanding, and incredibly generous, particularly with his trust. There was also the undeniable sensual pull they felt toward one another.

His eyes were dark, and Ellis couldn't tell what he was feeling. The longer he went without saying anything, the thicker the air became and the more persistent Ellis's desire.

This kept happening. The attraction simmering between them was growing hotter each time they had an interaction like this. They became acutely aware of each other as a man and a woman and clung to that moment, even knowing they should not.

"Here we are again," she whispered.

"Yes, here we are, desiring each other." When she opened her mouth to refute him, to lie, he leaned toward her, his gaze smoldering with intensity. "Tell me that isn't true."

Ellis tried to form the words, but they wouldn't come. He wouldn't have believed her anyway. "I can't."

"Tell me who you really are." He spoke softly, but it wasn't a question. It was a command.

"I can't do that either."

His nostrils flared the slightest bit, and she could see he was growing agitated but tamping that down. She'd observed his mastery of controlling his emotions whilst they worked together. He neither lashed out at bad news or with frustration nor rejoiced with excitement when he found success or learned of a positive outcome.

"You *won't*." He edged closer to her until there was barely any space between them at all. "That is very different from being unable to deny what is happening here between us."

Ellis notched her chin up. It was the only defense she could find in their current position. She was pinned between her desk, his desk, the wall—and him. "Fine. I *won't* tell you who I really am."

"What if I demand to know?" he asked, his voice low and edged with steel. "Tell me, or I'll turn you out."

Her heart was pounding so loud, she could hear the rhythm in her ears. She wasn't afraid. Her reaction was entirely due to the need sweltering between them. Because she was certain he felt it too, she arched her brow in challenge. "Then turn me out."

He bent his head toward hers. "I'd much rather kiss you instead." His wanting was plainly etched in the hard, impassioned lines of his face and the slight parting of his lips.

Ellis couldn't remember a time she'd felt more remarkable, more…alive. Because she hadn't. No one had regarded her as if she were the center of everything. She never wanted to lose this sensation, and she would do everything in her power to sear it into her memory. "Then kiss me."

A dark, fiery lust lit his eyes. "Don't tempt me if you don't mean to."

Ellis put her hands on his chest. "I will never say something to you I don't mean."

Keele's mouth captured hers. Ellis slid her hands up his chest and around his neck, where she clutched his nape. She stood on her toes and kissed him with an urgent desire she'd never before experienced.

He grasped her waist and held her against him as he parted his lips against hers. She did the same and touched her tongue to his. With a tortured groan, he accepted her invitation to deepen the kiss. She dug her fingers into his flesh as he moved his hands down over her backside, cupping her and bringing her flush to his groin.

Kissing in men's clothing allowed her to feel far more than the layers of a woman's garments did. Ellis was keenly aware of his erection. A desperate ache bloomed in her sex.

She was also annoyingly conscious of her facial hair, and the impediment it caused to kissing. She did not like the feel of it between them and could only imagine what Keele thought of the nuisance.

He brought one hand around her waist and slid it up beneath her coat to cup her breast. Only they were flattened because she bound them beneath her corset before dressing as a man. Keele lifted his head briefly. "Well, that is disappointing."

"Quite," Ellis agreed.

Keele continued his ascent and cupped her neck, which forced her to move her arm down. She mimicked him and slipped her hand between his coat and waistcoat, pressing her palm against his ribs as he ravaged her mouth with an onslaught of deepening kisses.

She dug her fingertips into him again, eager for more. Soft whimpers escaped her between kisses. He slid his hand from her backside to the back of her thigh and applied pressure for her to lift her leg. As soon as she did, he clasped the space just above her knee and brought her leg around his hip.

Ellis gasped into his mouth as her sex became more accessible. He held her against him as he thrust his hips forward. A thrilling ecstasy shot through her, and she didn't think it would take much effort for her to fully climax.

Keele dragged his mouth from hers and kissed over her beard to her throat, where his thumb rested against her pulse.

"I'm sorry about the hair," she murmured.

"I don't care about it. I assume you have hair down below, and I believe I'll quite enjoy kissing that area." He snagged his teeth on her earlobe.

A rush of heat made her sex throb. "We can't do this here," Ellis rasped. Though she was powerless to stop him. She wanted to tear off their clothing and beg him to kiss her everywhere.

"I know. Just one more minute." He lifted his head and kissed her again, thrusting his tongue into her mouth as he caressed her thigh. His hand moved higher, and she kept her leg wrapped around him. Her breath caught when his fingers pressed against her sex.

A distant sound broke into Ellis's fevered state. Was that the door?

"What are you doing?"

~

*R*oman withdrew his hand from between Ellis's thighs at the same moment she slid her leg from his hip. He lifted his head and stood back from her, painfully aware that the outline of his hardened cock was likely unmistakable if anyone looked at his groin.

Margot stood in the doorway, gaping at them.

Ellis put her hand to her mouth as her face flushed scarlet. She angled herself away from Margot.

"Come in and close the door," Roman said, his voice gruff as he worked to quell his lust.

Margot did as he asked, quickly closing the door and standing in front of it. "Well, this makes the reason for my visit much easier."

Roman moved to stand behind his desk. It didn't cover his erection, but moving helped pull him from his impassioned state. "What's that?"

"I came to talk with you about our engagement," Margot said primly.

Ellis darted her gaze to Roman. "You're *betrothed?*" She sounded shocked and perhaps even angry. He noted that she did not bother to disguise her voice.

"Not yet," Margot replied. "And not ever, I hope, particularly after what I've just witnessed."

"Let me explain," Roman said.

Margot held up her hand. "There's no need. I'm actually relieved it appears you have other interests." She stared at him, her eyes rounding slightly. "Is that why you were hoping for a marriage of convenience with me? Because you don't care for women, and that is the only kind of marriage you can have?"

"I am *not* a man." Ellis exhaled as she briefly closed her eyes.

Roman was surprised Ellis had so quickly revealed herself to Margot. Although Roman wasn't sure how else he would have convinced Margot that she'd misread the situation. But had she? Though Ellis wasn't a man, she was someone to whom he was clearly attracted. That seemed to also support a marriage of convenience, or at least a marriage that wasn't destined to be a love match or perhaps even happy. Roman would never do such a thing, since that was precisely what Clarissa had done.

Margot's brow creased. "You aren't—"

"Look closely," Roman said. "The disguise is good, but it's not perfect."

Margot stepped toward Ellis and narrowed her eyes slightly as she scrutinized Ellis' face. After a moment, she gasped. "You *are* a woman. Why are you dressed as a man?"

"Because I wanted to work as a secretary," Ellis replied wryly.

"Why?" Margot blinked at her in disbelief.

"I needed employment, and I thought I would be good at this."

"She's an exceptional secretary," Roman declared. "I expect you to keep her secret, as I don't want to lose her."

"Just because she's an *exceptional secretary*?" Margot asked dubiously.

"What you witnessed was a regrettable lapse in judgment," Ellis said. "Please try to put it from your mind. I know I'm going to." She did not look at Roman, and he couldn't help feeling incredibly slighted. He didn't regret their kissing one bit. But he supposed she was right that it had been a lapse in judgment since they were in his office in the middle of the afternoon. The door had been closed but not locked. Still, Roman hadn't thought anyone would just walk in without knocking.

Margot nodded. "I will happily do that." She cocked her head. "Why can't you just be a woman since Keele doesn't seem to mind and is quite happy with your performance?"

"I don't wish my true identity to be known," Ellis replied. "I am...hiding from my family. I can't explain why."

"You poor thing," Margot said, instantly sympathetic. "Your reasons must be truly terrible if you've taken such drastic measures."

"You must tell no one about Ellis," Roman repeated.

Margot pressed her hand to her heart. "I promise I will not."

Roman crossed his arms over his chest, relieved that his lust had cooled and his pelvic area was no longer an embarrassment. "What was the purpose in coming to speak with me about our potential engagement?"

"I came to tell you I don't wish to marry you. It's nothing to do with you," Margot said diplomatically. "I actually like you very much, but I honestly think of you in more of a brotherly sense because you were married to my sister." She wrinkled her nose faintly as she referred to him as a sibling.

"That is understandable. I confess I typically think of you in the same way and wondered if that would be an obstacle for us." Roman was surprised at the surfeit of relief he felt.

Margot's dark blue eyes sparkled with a hint of mischief. "There's also the fact that I am already in love with someone else." Her face beamed with joy, and Roman felt a small stab of envy. He didn't think he'd ever known that kind of happiness and never expected to.

Roman was also keenly aware that her sister had been in the same situation—already in love with someone else. Only Clarissa hadn't told Roman. She'd gone through with their marriage anyway. Roman gave Margot a great deal of credit.

"Who is the lucky gentleman?" he asked.

"You may be surprised to learn it's Oliver Pritchard, the librarian at our Oxford branch."

"That is *quite* surprising." Roman wondered how they even knew one another. "I imagine you will be equally surprised to learn that your father wants to bring Pritchard to London and have him oversee the New Bond Street branch."

Margot gasped again, but this time with excitement. "That would be wonderful! I was hoping for a way he could move to London and continue to work for Lacey and Company so that we could live here after we are wed."

"I think you're getting ahead of yourself," Roman said evenly. "You're going to have to convince your parents that Pritchard is a worthy husband." They'd been very clear about wanting both their daughters to marry titles if possible. Whilst Pritchard was the third son of a baron, he had little possibility of inheriting as his older brothers already had offspring. Roman wasn't aware of his having any sort of measurable wealth, either.

"I know." Margot clasped her hands and twisted them. "I've been nervous about telling my parents."

"How do you even know Pritchard?" Roman asked.

A faint grimace creased Margot's brow. "We've been secretly writing to one another for several months."

"Is that why his letters to you come here?" Ellis asked.

Margot's eyes rounded briefly with surprise. "You noticed that?"

"It's hard not to when I receive one every other day," she replied with a smile.

"I was not aware of this," Roman said, trying not to scowl. He would speak to Ellis about informing him of any odd correspondence patterns. And why? Was there anything wrong with Pritchard and Margot writing to one another?

Ellis shrugged. "I found it curious but not notable. Now it makes sense."

Margot blushed. "His letters have increased in frequency this past week. I do appreciate your receiving them and forwarding them to me. He couldn't send them to me at home or to Paternoster Row, as we didn't want my parents to notice."

"I don't understand," Ellis said with a slight frown. "Is Pritchard not an acceptable suitor?" She glanced at Roman. "You mentioned the Laceys may not find him worthy." She turned her attention to Margot. "And you're nervous about telling them."

"He doesn't have a title. My parents were very much hoping I would wed a peer, especially since my sister became a marchioness and then, well, you know." Margot mumbled the last as she studied the floor briefly.

Roman wasn't sure if Margot was sad about losing her sister or something else. They'd never seemed particularly close, at least as far as he could tell.

"That is why they were hoping the two of you would marry," Ellis concluded. "Arranged marriages or those made for some kind of personal gain are rarely successful, in my opinion."

"I agree," Margot said with great enthusiasm. "I have always wanted to marry for love, and my parents said I could after Clarissa married Keele. Now I have that chance. I know my parents will come to see how well-suited Oliver and I are. I can't wait to see him again!"

Roman stared at her. "*Again?*"

Margot's cheeks flamed. "He visited a fortnight ago. Please don't tell my parents."

"I absolutely will *not*. And I don't want to know the details. I will happily endorse your courtship with Pritchard. He's a good and highly intelligent man. Your father is very much looking forward to having him at the New Bond Street Library to increase the subscription base there, as he's done in Oxford."

"He will do an excellent job," Margot assured him. "But what about Mr. Inman? He's such a dear man, and he's been a wonderful asset to the library."

"Don't fret about Mr. Inman," Roman said. "Ellis and I have a plan for him. We will ensure he's not cast aside."

Margot exhaled with relief. "I'm glad to hear it. When is Oliver coming to town?"

"We haven't yet set a date for his visit, but my thought was to invite him to come this week, perhaps on Thursday, if that's convenient for him. We'll show him the New Bond Street Library, and he can converse with Inman about the position."

"Could you arrange for him to stay a few days, at least?" Margot asked.

"I wonder if you could engage in some social events together," Ellis suggested. "You could pretend to have an instant romantic connection, and Mr. Pritchard could ask to court you before he returns to Oxford. Your parents need never know you already engaged in an epistolary attachment."

"You're brilliant!" Margot grinned. "I could hug you."

Ellis smiled. "You can if you like, though I understand if you would prefer not to in my current garb."

Margot leapt forward and embraced Ellis anyway. "Thank you."

Roman couldn't see Ellis's face until they broke apart. He caught the remnants of her smile before it disappeared completely. Then he looked toward Margot. "I do think you could be honest with your parents if you wanted to try. They only want you to be happy."

At least, that's what Roman hoped, particularly after his recent conversation with Josiah about his marriage to Clarissa and the fact that they weren't happy. Roman wanted to believe that Josiah would be delighted to learn his younger daughter had fallen in love, even if he wasn't the type of husband they were hoping for.

Roman could persuade him—and Harriet—that it was better for Margot to wed a man of character and integrity instead of just hoping for a title. Roman's father had been titled, and he'd been an absolute blackguard.

"Where will Oliver stay?" Margot asked. "Perhaps he could come to our house. We have plenty of room."

Roman narrowed his gaze at her. "I don't think that's wise. He can stay here. I'll arrange for you to visit with him—under supervision."

Margot pursed her lips. "Just as you and Ellis are supervised?"

"I am not a marriageable young lady," Ellis said. "You must protect your reputation."

"But I'm going to marry Oliver," Margot argued.

Ellis shook her head. "That doesn't matter. Even if you're betrothed, you must behave above reproach. If any compromising behavior were to be rumored, any potential place you had in Society would be gone."

Margot blinked. "Truly?"

"Yes," Roman said. "Trust me as someone raised in Society with its double standards and ridiculous expectations, as well as its penchant for gossip."

"We will be careful," Margot vowed. "I appreciate your facilitating our time together." She looked at Roman. "You're truly not disappointed about us not marrying?"

"Not at all," he assured her. A marriage of convenience would have been extremely awkward, especially right now, when the only woman he could think about was Ellis. Roman would have to marry at some point, for he needed an heir, but he had plenty of time.

"Thank you both. My maid is waiting in the hall, so I must go." Margot moved to open the door and glanced back over her shoulder. "Should I close this again?"

"That isn't necessary," Ellis said.

Margot nodded and slipped away, leaving the door ajar.

Ellis turned and shuffled papers on her desk. "I think it may be best if I worked somewhere else in the house."

"Why?" Roman wanted to step around his desk to be closer to her but decided she might not want that after the way they'd been interrupted, which had necessitated her exposing herself as a woman.

Ellis gaped at him as if he'd gone daft.

"I don't regret what happened before," he said. "I'm sorry Margot walked in, but nobody else would do so without knocking."

"You don't know that." She went back to needlessly moving papers. "We can't continue in that manner. I'm your employee."

She was right. She was his employee, and he knew it was wrong to take advantage of that situation. Even if she was interested or *eager* to engage in a physical relationship, he should not overstep. "I apologize for kissing you," he said softly.

She did not look at him, and he hated that. "The blame lies with both of us. We should move on."

"Agreed." Except Roman knew he wouldn't be able to forget what happened, and setting aside the almost incoherent passion he felt for her would be extremely difficult. The best he could do would be to avoid temptation. "We could work more at the offices in Paternoster Row," he suggested. "Or you could work in your room if you have sufficient space there."

"The desk in my room is fine. In fact, I'll go there now." She picked up some things and took a step toward the door.

"What about your dinner with Miss Barclay?"

Ellis turned to face him. "I don't want to go, but I don't have a way to send a note back to her. I do think she might have told the footman not to wait for a reply on purpose."

"You should go."

"How do you propose I do that? The only way I can is in

this disguise, and you know I don't like eating with this nest of hair on my face."

"You can take my coach," he offered. "And a gown. You can change from your disguise into your regular clothing on the way there. I'll make sure my coachman doesn't say a word."

She goggled at him as if he'd suggested she impersonate the queen. "First of all, I don't have any of my own outer garments."

He found that surprising. Unless she'd fled without any of her belongings. He suddenly wondered where she'd obtained her men's clothing. "Where is it?"

"That doesn't matter right now," she said. "I will not change my clothing in your coach. That would be impossible in such a space."

"I could at least deliver a message to Miss Barclay for you," he offered.

Ellis exhaled. "No, I don't want you doing that either. I'll just go like this. And I'll take a hack."

"The hell you will," Roman said with a surprising amount of heat. "I don't want you going out alone like that after dark. You'll take my coach. In fact, I'll go with you, and I'll wait while you're inside."

"That is completely unnecessary," Ellis said with an equal dose of vigor. "No one is going to bother an unaccompanied young man going out in the evening. Furthermore, you don't get to decide what I do or how I do it."

"You are my employee, and I will ensure your safety. You either agree to my demands, or I will go to Wellesbourne House now and tell Miss Barclay you aren't coming."

Ellis glowered at him. "Fine." She pivoted on her heel and stalked out the door.

Roman tried not to stare at her backside and completely

failed. He then vowed to himself that he wouldn't obsess over their kisses.

It took approximately two minutes for that resolution to go entirely up in flames.

CHAPTER 7

*E*llis strode quickly into the entrance hall a few minutes before she was due to meet Keele for the trip to Wellesbourne House. She hoped to escape the house before Graham or anyone else saw her.

Fortunately, Graham was absent. *Unfortunately,* Keele was early.

His gaze locked on her and swept her from head to toe, with a very distinct pause in her pelvic area. Why didn't men's coats cover that region? Earlier, Keele had been a victim of this lapse in fashion sense when his erection had been clearly outlined behind his fall. Ellis didn't think Margot had noticed, but Ellis had struggled not to admire it.

"You look splendid," he said. "I didn't realize you had evening garments." He couldn't seem to stop surveying her—with great interest.

"I wanted to be prepared for anything." Ellis was now grateful that Mrs. Palmer had finished assembling an evening ensemble. She glanced down at herself. "Is there something wrong with my costume?"

"No, but I think there must be something wrong with me,

because I'm finding it incredibly arousing, and I've never before been aroused by men's clothing." His voice sounded rough and irritatingly provocative. "Then again, I've never seen a woman wearing men's evening wear." Now, his tone held unmistakable appreciation.

Ellis opened the door and walked outside. The cold evening air soothed her heated face. The coach was waiting with the coachman standing at the open door. Belatedly, she realized she should not have preceded Keele from the house. She paused and waited for him.

Catching up to her, Keele gestured to the coach. "After you."

Wordlessly, she climbed into the coach and sat on the rear-facing seat. Keele sat opposite her, and the door closed.

"I shouldn't have left the house before you, and you shouldn't have indicated I enter the coach first," Ellis said. "Did you forget I'm supposed to be a man?"

"I did actually." His focus was trained on the window, and she had the sense he was trying not to look at her.

"How can you forget I'm a man, given the way I'm dressed?"

"The breeches are rather tight." He sounded somewhat strained. "I noticed when you were climbing into the coach in front of me." He turned his head, and their gazes met in the shadowy, seductive light of the lantern affixed to the side of the coach.

Ellis bit the inside of her lip as heat swelled through her. No good could come of this conversation when they were alone together in a small, dark place. She reached up and began to peel the hair from her face. The removal was always a rather unpleasant experience, and her skin would be red for a while. Hopefully, it would diminish by the time they arrived at Wellesbourne House.

"What are you doing?" Keele asked.

"Since I have to go as a man, I decided I don't want to wear the facial hair whilst I'm eating. I can only hope no one notices my features are rather feminine." She tucked the fake hair into the upper fob pocket of her breeches.

His features creased with concern. "I hate to dampen your spirits, but I think that's an unrealistic expectation. Just keep your head down as much as possible, and instruct the footman to leave the dining room, which I imagine you would do anyway, so that you can speak about things that would surely reveal you as a woman."

Ellis swore under her breath.

"Did you just curse?" he asked.

"This was a terrible idea." Ellis crossed her arms over her chest, and the fabric of the coat pulled across her shoulders. Damn, it was also too tight. "I should have allowed you to go and tell her I couldn't come."

"Why didn't you?"

She unfolded her arms and rolled her shoulders to readjust the coat. "Because you would have pressed her for information about me."

"I wouldn't have," he said. "And something tells me Miss Barclay would not have revealed your secrets, even if I had."

"Well, it's too late now," she said. "I'll just go inside and speak to her for a short while then leave. I won't stay for dinner." She scowled. "There was no reason for me to take the blasted facial hair off."

Keele sent her a cautious glance. "You *could* trust me with your secret. Haven't I demonstrated my intention to keep you hidden and protect your safety? Indeed, I was willing to let Margot believe you're a man."

She snapped her gaze to his. The lamp in the coach offered enough light for her to see the sincerity in his expression.

"I can't believe you would have done that, but you seem

earnest." After a long moment, she dragged her focus from him and looked toward the window. "I have nothing I want to share at the moment. I should think you would understand that, since you didn't see fit to share that you were on the cusp of becoming betrothed to Margot."

"You sound irritated about that. Why should you care?" he asked.

Ellis had not meant to sound that way. She didn't want him thinking she was bothered by him being engaged to someone else, except she realized suddenly that she was. She shoved that thought from her head and lifted a shoulder. "I just found it rich that you would press me to reveal my secrets yet keep your own."

"You make a valid point," he said with an edge of discomfort. "There are things I do not disclose about myself. I will not ask about your secret anymore. However, I would like us to become better acquainted, if possible. What can you tell me about yourself that wouldn't give anything away? Perhaps how you learned shorthand?"

Ellis thought of how she'd seen her mother using shorthand to keep the household accounts and to quickly draft letters for her father, who'd been a solicitor. One day, Ellis copied the ink strokes having no idea what they'd meant. She'd just wanted to be like her mother. Laughing warmly, her mother had promised to teach Ellis one day. But that had never happened because her mother had died when Ellis was just nine.

At Beacon Park, the Duke of Henlow's seat where Ellis had spent much time, along with Henlow House in London, the steward had used shorthand. Ellis had tried to learn by reading his ledgers, but then he'd offered to teach her instead. "A very kind man taught me, and that is all I can say about that."

"What about your love of books?" Keele asked. "Where did that come from?"

That had also come from her mother. They'd read together every night for as long as Ellis could remember. In fact, her very first memory was of sitting next to her mother on her bed, reading *Original Stories from Real Life* by Mary Wollstonecraft. Ellis still had that book. In fact, it was one of the few things she'd taken with her when she'd left the Henlow household. It was upstairs in her room at Keele's house.

"My mother taught me to read, and she is why I love books," Ellis said. "Please don't ask me anything else. Both she and my father are dead."

"I see," he said quietly. "Mine are too, but I never knew my mother. She died in childbirth."

Ellis felt a rush of sympathy and had to fight the urge to touch him. At least she'd had a mother for nine years. Poor Keele hadn't ever known his. "Did your father remarry?" she asked softly.

"No. I always wished he would, because I wanted a mother. He wasn't a very good father."

"I'm sorry to hear that." Ellis was curious but wouldn't press, not when she didn't want to share her own past. Best to keep the conversation lighter—if possible, since they'd already tread near melancholy. "Who taught you to read?"

"My nurse," he replied. "She was the closest thing to a parent I had."

"And is she still a part of your life?" Ellis hoped so.

Keele shook his head. "My father sent her away when I was eight. He thought I was too dependent on her." He blew out a breath as he crossed his arms. "After that, I was assigned a valet and a tutor."

"You had a valet at the age of eight?"

"A rather stodgy one too. But Lester possessed a kind

heart that he hid from my father," Keele said with a faint smile. "When I went away to Eton, my father dismissed him."

Keele's experience showed that Ellis was not the first person who had suffered at the hands of a cruel parent, nor would she be the last. In fact, Min had suffered too. Ellis suddenly felt selfish for turning away from her dearest friend. No, Min was her sister, both in emotion and in truth.

She was inching closer to overcoming the bitterness she'd felt at discovering her mother's identity and the manner in which she'd learned it. She'd begun forging a solid path for herself and was starting to feel...safe. Her anger was finally dissipating. Only anger wasn't entirely right. Ellis realized she felt a bit of jealousy too. Not for what Min had, but for what she *was*—legitimate.

The coach arrived at Wellesbourne House, which Ellis had visited on several occasions. It was one of the largest on Brook Street, if not *the* largest. White pilasters framed the brick doorway of the five-bayed terrace.

Keele scooted to the far side of the seat so she could easily depart the coach. "I'll just wait here until you're finished. Take your time."

She cast him a slightly scolding glance. "Don't stare at my backside when I leave."

He arched a brow at her, his expression utterly wicked. "How will you know?"

Ellis stifled a smile as she climbed out of the coach. They ought not flirt, but she couldn't deny his attention made her feel good. It made her feel...wanted.

The coachman was apparently already aware that Keele would not be accompanying her inside. She kept her face averted as she walked past him to the front door. She put her hand to her face, lightly covering the bottom half.

The butler, resplendent in his dark blue livery, regarded her expectantly. Hopefully, he would not recognize her from her prior visits as Ellis Dangerfield, companion to Lady Minerva.

"I am Mr. Ellis," she said in her deepest, most authoritative tone. "For Miss Barclay." She had moved her hand to speak and now turned her head slightly as the butler opened the door and invited her inside.

"Miss Barclay is awaiting you in the drawing room. If you'll follow me." He led her up the staircase, and Ellis recalled her other visits to see her friend Persephone, the Duchess of Wellesbourne, always in Min's company. Fleetingly, Ellis wondered if those women were only her friends because of Min, but that seemed silly. She was seeing Pandora on her own without Min. Surely that meant Ellis was their friend.

Ellis stopped cold as the butler moved into the drawing room. What if Min *was* there? What if Pandora had tricked Ellis into coming so that Min could see her?

"Mr. Ellis?"

The sound of the butler saying her name drew Ellis to blink and move forward. He gestured for her to precede him, then followed her over the threshold. "Mr. Ellis has arrived," he announced.

Pandora jumped up from a chair, smiling broadly. "Thank you, Ralston."

He departed, and Ellis walked toward Pandora, who kept grinning. "You're not wearing the beard."

"I despise it," Ellis said. "I find it difficult to eat with it on. However, I've decided I don't think it's wise for me to stay for dinner. You'd have to ask the footman to leave, and I don't want to draw attention to myself or how I look." It had been bad enough when Keele had figured out almost immediately that she was a woman, and now Margot knew as well. But Ellis wasn't going to tell Pandora any of that.

"I understand," Pandora said, though she appeared a bit

disappointed. "I'm just glad you're here. You'll stay for a while?"

Ellis smiled. "I would like that."

They moved to a settee and sat down, angling themselves so they faced one another.

"Are you thrilled to have your book published?" Ellis asked.

"I think I'm still in shock," Pandora replied. "But yes. I wasn't sure anyone would like it."

"It's brilliant," Ellis said. "I've read it twice."

Pandora glowed. "Have you?"

"Eagerly. I know what really happened to you two years ago with Bane, and there are many parallels in this book. I was not at all surprised when Dinah chose herself over either of the men who claimed to love her."

"I assumed you and our other friends would not be surprised. Persey said the same thing after she read it."

"You're a skilled writer," Ellis said. "I hope you plan to continue."

"I do," Pandora replied. "Writing *A Season in Shadow* was challenging, but it also healed me, I think. I hope the next book will be a bit more enjoyable to write," she added with a laugh.

"I hope so too, but drawing on your personal experience is undoubtedly what has made *A Season in Shadow* such a compelling story." Ellis paused as she studied her friend. "Does this mean you've chosen yourself forever?"

"I didn't intend to." Pandora shook her head with regret. "When he said he loved me and that he wanted to marry me, I believed him. I don't think I could ever trust a man again, nor do I want to. Everyone knows how devastated I was, but I've come to accept my spinsterhood. Indeed, I'm quite comfortable in it. Now I have my writing and an income. I feel surprisingly satisfied overall." She clasped her hands in her lap and smiled benignly, looking more than satisfied if Ellis had to describe her.

Ellis couldn't help feeling a bit of envy. "I'm so happy for you. Will you continue to live with your aunt, or do you plan to set up your own household?"

"I'm quite content living with Aunt Lucinda. She's the mother I always wished I'd had."

Much to Ellis's chagrin, her envy intensified. "That's lovely," she murmured.

"Someday, I imagine I'll have my own household, but I don't know when that will be. What about you?" Pandora asked.

"Like you, I'm quite satisfied with my work for now." Though, Ellis would enjoy it more if she could be herself and stop sticking fake hair to her face.

"As a secretary in which you have to dress as a man," Pandora noted wryly. It was as if she'd read Ellis's thoughts. "I'm glad you're happy for now, but I can't think this is a permanent situation. I do hope you've been able to work through some of your—well, I don't know what emotions you were feeling when you found out the truth about your parents. Are you still struggling with it?"

"How could I not?" Ellis replied. She'd known this subject would come up, of course, but that didn't mean she wanted to talk about it. "By the way, I wanted to thank you for ensuring I had to come tonight by telling your footman not to stay for a reply. I'm assuming you did that on purpose."

Pandora pressed her lips together with what seemed like guilt. "My apologies, but I needed to make sure you're all right and that you're truly in a situation that you chose and are happy with. You can always come live with me and Lucinda. That was her idea, by the way," she added. "She's at a party this evening, which is why I invited you tonight, so that you wouldn't have to see her if you didn't want to."

"I appreciate that," Ellis said softly. "Though I like your aunt very much. Please thank her for the kind offer."

"We would give you much more than a roof over your head, though I daresay having that would be help enough so you don't have to pay for lodging."

"I don't pay for lodging since I'm living in Keele's house." Too late, Ellis realized Pandora hadn't known that. She'd only been aware that Ellis was his employee.

Pandora's eyes widened. "You're *living* at his house? Secretaries don't typically live with their employers."

"No, but he wanted someone who could work a great deal and who would be available at all hours." She sounded almost defensive. Perhaps because their relationship had gone beyond employer and employee, at least briefly.

"And he knows you're a woman?" Pandora didn't wait for an answer, for she already knew he did. "This seems nearly scandalous. Is it?"

"No, because nobody else is aware that I'm a woman." Except that wasn't true anymore.

Shockingly, Ellis found she would rather discuss her parentage than her living situation with Keele. After their kisses earlier, she could not banish him from her mind for more than a few moments. Riding in the coach with him had been torture, particularly knowing her clothing aroused him.

This could easily become a scandalous situation unless they were very careful to avoid temptation. It seemed they would try after their discussion about where Ellis would work, but tonight, the attraction between them felt even more insurmountable.

"Let me assure you, I am well and content," Ellis said.

"Whilst I'm glad to hear that, what about Min and Jo?" Pandora stared at her with an almost pleading expression. "They both care for you, especially Min. She was devastated that you didn't come to her wedding."

Ellis's throat constricted. She hadn't turned her back on them—at least not permanently. "I couldn't risk the duchess being there," she said weakly.

"She wasn't there," Pandora said. "In fact, she's been banished from both Henlow House and Beacon Park, including the dowager house. She remains at her house in Bath, as far as anyone knows, for she has nowhere else to go."

Ellis was glad to hear that she'd been ostracized. Now she needn't worry that she would encounter her here in London. However, her presence in Bath meant living with Pandora and her aunt would be unacceptable. Ellis didn't care to inhabit the same city as the duchess. "I do want to see Min—soon," Ellis said carefully. "When you speak with her, please tell her I'm well and that I miss her."

Pandora frowned. "Are you angry with her?"

"*No*," Ellis replied without hesitation. "My feelings are… complicated. I've been at everyone's mercy for so long, and I'm not who I thought I was. I'm not even legitimate." She tried to keep the bitterness from her voice and failed. "Working for Keele and becoming independent is helping me to move forward, to determine my own fate instead of having it decided by others."

"I think I understand," Pandora said gently. "What about meeting your father? Jo is hoping to introduce you. As father and daughter, that is. She said you met him at her and Sheff's engagement ball."

That was true, though Ellis remembered little about him. He had blond hair like hers and was incredibly gregarious. She recalled him laughing and smiling, and he seemed to know everyone. "Does he know about me?"

"I don't believe so. Would you consider speaking to Jo?"

"I would like to meet my father." Ellis couldn't resist the potential of having one parent who might care for her. "Perhaps it would be best if Jo coordinated that."

"I know she would love to arrange that meeting *and* go with you." Pandora smiled encouragingly. "Can I arrange for you to speak with her?"

"Yes, but not at Henlow House. I would certainly be recognized." The more people who knew of her disguise and whom she worked for, the higher the risk she would be discovered. She just wasn't ready to face Min or Sheff—and definitely not their mother. "I also can't meet with Jo as a woman because I don't have my clothing. It's at the boarding house where I was living before."

"I could fetch it for you," Pandora offered.

"I would have to leave Keele's house as a man, change my clothes, meet with Jo, then change back into my secretary clothing to return to Keele's house." She blew out a breath in frustration. "That sounds far too difficult."

"What if you met Jo at the Siren's Call? You already look as if you might be going there later," Pandora added with a chuckle.

The Siren's Call was a gentlemen's gaming club owned by Jo's mother, Jewel Harker, and where Jo had worked before she'd married Sheff. All the employees were women, which appealed to the almost exclusively male clientele. It was perfect—Ellis could arrive as a man, meet with Jo, and leave as a man.

"All right." Ellis turned back to face Pandora. She was both excited to see Jo and worried she'd been selfish in avoiding them.

Pandora grinned. "Excellent. Do you mind if I tell Min this is happening? She just wants you to be happy, and if that means not seeing her for a while, she'll accept that."

That tore at Ellis's heart. "I would rather wait. I want to see Min too, but perhaps after I meet my father."

Pandora nodded.

"In the meantime, I expect you won't reveal to anyone

that I'm working for Keele. I need that to continue to be our secret." She gave Pandora a wry look. "I don't want anyone else sending me messages at his house."

"Apologies," Pandora said softly. "Come, I'll walk you downstairs."

"Thank you." Ellis stood.

Pandora rose and linked arms with her as they walked to the door, then reluctantly let her go. "I'll be much happier when you're fully Ellis again."

"I will too." Except Ellis wasn't sure who that was.

She thought about what Pandora had said, that Ellis's current situation wasn't permanent. Ellis knew that, of course, but she hadn't really thought too much about what she would do after she saved the money she needed to live independently somewhere in a sleepy village. Perhaps she could be a librarian for a new Lacey and Company branch.

But that was in the distant future. For now, she would continue in her disguise and hope no one else discovered she was a woman. And she would see Jo and meet her father. The idea of having a living parent who might actually care for her was wonderful. It was silly, but Ellis had just felt so *alone* after learning the truth about her parentage. She'd felt as if she didn't belong anywhere.

Strangely, she'd found a place in Keele's household. She felt both useful and valued. And *wanted*, even if it was in a purely physical manner.

As Ellis said good night to Pandora and walked to Keele's coach, she decided that being wanted in any fashion was intoxicating. She feared in that moment she would cling to that feeling with everything she had, regardless of the consequences.

~

"How was your visit?" Roman asked as Ellis situated herself on the seat opposite him in the coach.

"Why did you move to the rear-facing seat?" she asked.

Instead of answering her question, Roman shrugged. "I wanted to let you ride facing forward."

"That's kind of you," she said, sounding wary. "But I don't mind which way I face."

He cocked his head. "Do you typically ride on this seat?" He moved his hand over the cushion and realized the action could be interpreted as an invitation. If she had taken it that way, he would not have minded.

"Occasionally."

Did she realize he was able to glean bits of information about her from their conversations? He wasn't doing it on purpose. It was just a natural result of the small things she revealed.

For instance, he knew she was quite comfortable riding in a coach, and now he knew she spent at least a fair amount of time on the rear-facing seat, which meant somebody else was on the forward-facing seat.

"How was your visit?" he repeated. "I hope it went well."

"It was very nice, thank you. I appreciate your providing transportation."

"I'm happy to and will do so whenever you require."

Ellis straightened against the squab and clasped her hands in her lap. Her posture was very feminine.

"You're sitting like a woman," he said.

She swore under her breath again, and Roman had to stifle a smile.

"Do you do that often?" he asked. "Curse like that, I mean."

She sent him a perturbed glance. "Not before I started working for you."

Roman couldn't contain his bark of laughter. "I will try to be less irritating."

Ellis unclasped her hands and rested one on her thigh whilst she braced the other on the seat beside her. Then she widened her legs to a more masculine pose that drew Roman's attention to her shapely thighs as well as the distinct lack of a male organ behind her fall. He forced himself to look away.

She was copying his posture. As he thought back over her time with him, he wondered what else he'd done that she'd imitated. Perhaps kissing? She was arrestingly good at it, and he would wager she had experience. However, she may have just been quickly learning from him.

"I thought we could discuss Oliver Pritchard's visit to town," Ellis said.

That was not only a good idea; it would keep him from trying to flirt with her.

That afternoon, they'd dispatched a letter inviting him to arrive on Thursday. "I thought we would have dinner here on Thursday evening," he suggested. "That allows Pritchard and Margot to meet for the 'first' time."

Ellis inclined her head, and Roman continued. "On Friday, we can visit the library on New Bond Street and introduce Pritchard to Inman as well as discuss the timing of the transition."

"That means we must speak with Mr. Inman as soon as possible," Ellis said.

"We should do that tomorrow," Roman replied. "We will present the idea of the reading room in his name."

"*We?*" Ellis asked, her eyebrows raised. "You want me to accompany you?"

"Of course. You're the one who came up with the brilliant

ideas on how to keep him involved. I thought you'd want to take part in telling him. I would very much like you to be there."

Ellis's features softened, and her lips curved into a slight smile. "Thank you for your confidence in me, truly, but this will be a difficult conversation. Would it be best if you spoke with him alone?"

"I want you to come with me," he said. "I insist."

He wondered if that was because he felt she was vital to the conversation, or whether he wanted to make sure Inman knew she was to credit for the reading room in his name. In truth, it was probably mostly because he enjoyed spending time with her, but he wasn't going to say that.

Ellis glanced out the window. "We're nearly home."

As she pulled her facial hair from her pocket and tried to stick it to her face, Roman was struck by her use of the word *home* to describe her lodgings at his house. He found it surprisingly pleasing.

She blew out a frustrated breath, pulling him from his increasingly Ellis-obsessed thoughts. "Damn, I can't get this to stick without more adhesive, and I'm running low on it."

"Where do you get adhesive?" Roman asked. "I can have some delivered tomorrow."

Her expression turned dubious. "I don't think it's wise to have this sort of thing delivered to your house. It may raise questions."

Roman scoffed. "I highly doubt anyone would notice. Graham or Alvin will receive the delivery, and they won't ask about it."

"They won't ask *you* about it. But it will surely pique their curiosity, and they may discuss it downstairs."

"I suppose." Roman found her knowledge of servants' gossip noteworthy.

"Don't worry about it." Ellis gave up on trying to press the hair to her face and exhaled with resignation. "I'll purchase some as soon as I can."

"What shall we do about dinner?" Roman asked. "I'm assuming you didn't eat, since you planned not to, and you weren't inside long enough to have done."

"I don't want to dine together if that's what you're suggesting." She tucked her facial hair back into her breeches pocket. "I can't get my beard back on, so I'll have to go straight to my room. And we can't take dinner in there alone together."

They *could*, but he understood why they *shouldn't*. "Just keep your head down when we go inside, and I'll provide cover as you race for the stairs. I'll have dinner sent up to your room."

She met his gaze. "You are very kind. I appreciate the effort you take to guard my secret."

"I don't want to lose you as my secretary." He relied on her. He enjoyed her. He couldn't stop thinking about her. "It's quite selfish of me."

The air between them crackled with energy. Stark lust flashed through Roman, and he had a powerful urge to leap across the coach and kiss her. Then he envisioned a great many sordid things involving the removal of her clothing. His cock hardened.

The coach came to a stop in front of the house, and Roman took a deep breath to calm his racing pulse. "It's good we arrived, or I think we'd be in trouble," he whispered.

Ellis's attention flicked to his erection. "I agree."

"You must precede me from the coach," he said. "I need a moment."

She nodded. "Understood."

The coachman opened the door, and Ellis cast him a darkly brazen stare. Then, as she descended, she flipped the tail of her coat in such a way that he had a clear and thoroughly arousing view of her backside in the too-tight breeches.

Roman groaned softly. "Minx."

He sat in the coach for a long moment before departing. She was already inside, and he realized he'd failed to provide her cover while she dashed upstairs, but that was her fault. She'd taunted him, and she bloody well knew it.

Roman needed to have dinner, but first he would have hers sent up. Then he needed to frig himself.

They were playing a dangerous game, and Roman didn't want to stop.

CHAPTER 8

The following afternoon, they climbed into the carriage once more to go to the New Bond Street library branch to meet with Mr. Inman. This time, Roman preceded Ellis into the coach, and he sat on the forward-facing seat. He was trying to behave as he ought, which was as her employer and treating her as though she were male.

Ellis set her notebook on her lap, then almost immediately transferred it to the seat and adopted more of a sprawl. She wasn't copying Roman just then, but he knew she was trying to affect a more masculine posture.

Once they were moving, she glanced at him. "If it's acceptable to you, I should like to have this evening off."

"Are you going to fetch adhesive?" he asked. "I could accompany you."

"That is not what I'm doing," she said. "And before you ask, it's none of your affair."

"Will you at least tell me where you're going and how you plan to get there?"

"Regardless of what you think, my lord, I am not your responsibility. I appreciate your concern, but what I do in my free time is my business." She arched a brow at him. "Do you ask other members of your household what they do and how they do it?"

Roman flinched inwardly. He did *not* do that, but other members of his household were not masquerading as the opposite sex, nor were they hiding from people. Nor had he taken a *particular* interest in them as he had with Ellis.

"I'm happy to escort you wherever you need to go," he said. "Or I will simply give you the use of my coach. I assume wherever you're going, you'll be dressed as you currently are."

"I can't leave your house any other way." She hesitated before adding, "It would be convenient to use your coach, but I don't think I want your coachman speculating about my destination." She grimaced faintly, then turned her head toward the window.

Now Roman was concerned about her plans. "Why would he speculate about your destination? Where are you going?"

She arched a brow at him but said nothing, her mildly irritated expression conveying that it was none of his affair.

"I think I may follow you," Roman said. "I would feel terrible if something happened to you."

"Nothing's going to happen to me. I'm going to a perfectly respectable establishment. It is orderly and safe." She exhaled, sounding impatient. "I'm going to the Siren's Call. You can't be worried about me going to a place that is owned and run entirely by women."

Roman sat up and leaned forward slightly. "That's a *gaming hell*. Why are you going to a gaming hell? Is part of the reason you're hiding because you need funds?"

She gave him a bland look. "If it were, I would have asked you to advance my pay, wouldn't I?"

"I don't know." He regarded her intently. She was an enigma. He would wager a large sum that she was some kind of Quality, and yet she was also perfectly comfortable in her role as a lesser member of his household. She understood coaches, men's evening wear, and household hierarchy. She also seemed comfortable in Mayfair. He was incredibly curious as to why she was going to the Siren's Call if she was not going to gamble.

"I'm familiar with the Siren's Call," Roman said. "May I please escort you? I'll tell the coachman we're going for an evening out."

She did not appear impressed or convinced. "Isn't that strange for you to seek entertainment with your secretary?"

Roman lifted a shoulder. "Perhaps, but I doubt it. They're aware that you and I work closely together. They know I'm pleased with your performance and happy to have you working for me. If I tell them I want to reward your hard work by taking you to the Siren's Call this evening, I don't think anyone would find that strange."

She pursed her lips. "All right, you may accompany me, but at the club, I must be your friend, not your secretary. I appreciate your not asking why I'm going."

"I know better." Roman flashed her a quick grin.

They arrived on New Bond Street a moment later and quickly departed outside the library, a three-storey, brick-fronted terrace. A bow-shaped window on the first floor gave the façade a distinctive character from its neighbors, as did the black-painted pilasters framing the door and ground-floor window. "Lacey's Library" was emblazoned in gold lettering across the entablature over the door and window.

Roman stopped himself from holding the door for Ellis. He felt strange walking in before her, almost uncomfortable even.

The scent of polished wood, leather bindings, and paper welcomed them. A counter stretched along the right wall of the reception room, behind which stood one of the two clerks the library employed. Two racks stood against the back wall—one stocked with new works and the other with Lacey and Company titles. A third rack next to the hearth on the left wall held copies of current newspapers and magazines. There were several chairs where one could sit and browse near the fireplace or in front of the window. A doorway at the back next to the counter opened to the lending room, whilst another archway in the opposite corner led to a staircase.

The librarian, Mr. Inman, a short, slender, and immaculately garbed gentleman in his late sixties, greeted them. He adjusted his gold-rimmed glasses on his nose. "Good afternoon, my lord. What a pleasure to see you."

"Good to see you too, Inman." Roman gestured to Ellis. "Allow me to introduce my new secretary, Mr. Daniel Ellis."

Ellis gave the librarian a slight bow. "Good afternoon, Mr. Inman. I'm pleased to make your acquaintance." Her voice was pitched low, and, to Roman at least, she appeared and sounded masculine.

"I'm delighted to meet you." Inman stared at Ellis a moment longer than seemed appropriate, then quickly looked away. Doubt crept into Roman's thoughts, and he hoped Inman hadn't detected she was a female.

"I wonder if we could remove to your office to have a conversation," Roman said.

"Certainly." Inman led them toward the stairs, glancing back over his shoulder at Roman as they walked. "I hope there's nothing amiss."

"Not at all," Roman replied with a smile. "I continue to be impressed by your work, as is Mr. Lacey, and we know our patrons value you immensely, just as we do."

Inman glanced back at him as they started up the stairs. "I appreciate the praise, my lord, though it is unnecessary."

On the landing, the librarian turned to the left toward the

back of the building, and they shortly entered his office. It wasn't terribly large, but there was a cozy seating area with more than enough places for them to sit.

"Shall we sit?" Inman moved toward a chair.

There was a narrow settee that Roman would love to share with Ellis, for the space would have necessitated that their thighs touched. However, he feared he wouldn't be able to concentrate on the conversation he needed to have. It was best they not sit together. Setting his incessant attraction to Ellis aside, he took another one of the chairs whilst Ellis situated herself on the settee in a, thankfully, masculine pose.

"What is it you wish to speak about?" Inman asked.

Roman had thought about what he would say and hoped it came out the way he'd planned. Ellis gave him a subtle nod of support, which he greatly appreciated. He realized he'd come to rely on her in many ways.

"As I said before, we greatly value your work here at the library," Roman said. "I do wonder, however, if you would like more time to yourself. Forgive me, this is a delicate thing to say, but I suspect you're reaching an age where you may even wish to retire from this work."

"I don't think I'll ever retire from the library," Inman said. "Unless I'm forced," he added with a perhaps nervous chuckle.

Roman feared he'd botched things. He sent a worried glance toward Ellis.

"No one would force you from the library," Ellis assured him in her deeper voice. She was very good at maintaining a masculine tone.

Inman smiled. "That is nice to hear. However, I confess I wouldn't mind having more time to spend with my children and grandchildren. As you may recall, my wife died last year, and I find I crave more time with my family."

"That's completely understandable." Roman felt a slight

envy that Inman had a family with whom he wanted to spend time. "We would like to rename the reading room after you and hope you might be interested in hosting literary events, perhaps fortnightly or monthly."

Inman drew in a sharp breath, and his eyes rounded slightly. "That is quite an honor, my lord."

"In addition to hosting these events, we hope you might assist in coordinating them," Roman said. "That would mean inviting authors to speak, as well as occasions where readers discuss certain works. Obviously, we would prefer to focus on the authors and publications from Lacey and Company."

"Certainly, my lord, and that would be my preference as well." His eyes gleamed with pride. "Lacey and Company publishes the very best."

Roman caught the smile that passed briefly across Ellis's mouth. She was so damn pretty when she smiled. He wished he could make her do it more often, but it would probably increase the likelihood of her being exposed as a woman.

He couldn't remotely see her as a man at this point. The facial hair was a nuisance, but to him, it did not disguise her feminine beauty in the least.

"This is all so very splendid," Inman said. "However, I wouldn't know who to invite aside from our customers. I imagine you're hoping to grow the subscription base, and I'm afraid that has never been my strength. Furthermore, this would add to my duties, not allow me more time with my family."

"You are correct." Roman smiled faintly as it was time to reveal the true goal. "We would bring a new librarian to the branch. That would give you more time to spend with your family, and your focus here could be on the events in the reading room."

Inman's gaze turned wary. "Who is this new librarian?"

"Oliver Pritchard from our Oxford branch," Roman

replied. "He's expanded the subscription base at Oxford so much that we need to find new premises. You will like him immensely, I'm sure."

"I see," Inman said, and Roman had the sense that he did indeed understand. Thankfully, he didn't seem upset. Inman continued, "It would be beneficial, I think, to invite some notable admirers of literature to these reading room events, but I'm uncertain who those people are outside of our customers."

"I'm not sure I know who those people are either." If Roman had spent more time in Society and paid heed to something besides rebuilding his fortune, perhaps he would be more helpful.

"I believe the new Countess of Shefford would be interested in participating," Ellis suggested. "She has attended many literary gatherings."

Roman snapped his attention to Ellis. How on earth did she know Lady Shefford? Was she another one of Ellis's high-placed friends, like the Duchess of Wellesbourne?

"I didn't realize you knew Lady Shefford," he said, though perhaps he should have waited to point that out until they returned to the coach.

"Only vaguely," Ellis replied with a quick glance toward him, but she did not make eye contact.

"You are correct," Inman said to Ellis. "Lady Shefford has been here a few times recently. She's an enthusiastic reader. I shall speak with her. Lord Keele, when do you plan to bring Mr. Pritchard to London?"

"I don't know exactly, but he'll be visiting later this week."

"We'll bring him here to introduce you," Ellis said. "That way you can give us your assessment."

Inman straightened, and he smiled, appearing very pleased. "I will do my best."

Roman looked at Ellis appreciatively. She wasn't just

telling Inman he was valuable; she was showing him too. Even though the decision to bring Pritchard to London had already been made, Roman would be glad to hear Inman's opinion. "We will rely on you to train him. The patrons in London are much different from those in Oxford."

"I'm certain of that," Inman agreed with a chuckle.

They spoke for a while longer before standing to take their leave. Again, Inman's gaze locked on Ellis for a long moment. "You must pardon me, Mr. Ellis, but you look familiar. I just can't place how. Have we met before?"

"No, we have not," Ellis said firmly. "Perhaps I remind you of someone."

Inman nodded vaguely. "That must be it. Well, it was nice to make your acquaintance. I will see you both later in the week."

Roman thanked him, then he and Ellis returned to the coach.

As Roman climbed inside, it occurred to him that Lady Shefford used to manage the Siren's Call before she married. Ellis was going there tonight. That couldn't be a coincidence. Did Ellis know Lady Shefford? She'd seemed to.

Once the coach had started forward, Roman studied Ellis, noting the lines between her eyes. "Were you worried Inman was trying to discern whether you were a woman?"

"Weren't you?" she replied before wiping her hand over her face. "This is very stressful. I don't think I want to accompany you to any such meetings in the future."

"It's very hard for you to be my secretary and not ever accompany me anywhere," he said.

She blinked at him. "I don't think so. I've known secretaries who don't accompany their employers anywhere."

"You have?"

Ellis pressed her lips together, obviously realizing she'd

once again shared something informative. Roman was desperate to ask her how she knew Lady Shefford but didn't.

Roman watched Ellis's face bloom pink then red. She appeared quite flustered.

"Ellis, are you all right?" he asked with genuine concern.

"I'm a little agitated, is all. I don't know what I would have done if Inman had recognized me."

Did she mean recognized her as a woman, or recognized who she was? Roman suspected she'd been to the library before and had actually met Inman—as a woman.

"Did you know he was going to be so accepting of relinquishing his position?" Roman asked. "Perhaps you were aware of his family?"

"Please stop." Ellis held up her hand. "You keep pressing me for more, and I don't want to share any of that with you. You must stop trying to determine who I am."

Roman moved from his seat to join her on hers. She gasped softly and scooted away from him.

"I'm not actively trying to discover who you are, but I can't help wanting to know you. I'm incredibly drawn to you —surely you know that. I like you. I like spending time with you. I like learning things about you. In fact, the more time I spend with you, the more I hate not knowing things about you. I want to learn everything." He paused a moment as her wariness became almost…curiosity. "You have this underlying darkness, and I can't tell if it's fear or anger or something else. I would help you if you would let me."

She turned her head toward him. "I can't," she whispered. "Anyway, this won't be forever."

"What do you mean?" he asked.

"My position with you. I'd hoped it would last at least a year, but I don't think that's going to be possible, given the way my disguise is going."

"If you need to stay hidden for a year, I'll help you find

another way," he said, surprising himself with how strongly he felt about protecting her. "I hate thinking you might be afraid."

"I'm not afraid," she said, meeting his gaze with a surprising warmth. "Well, perhaps I am a little, but that isn't to do with why I'm hiding, and everything to do with this situation between us. I should probably leave your employ as soon as possible, because our efforts to avoid temptation seem to be failing rather spectacularly."

Roman chuckled softly. He lifted his hand and caressed her cheek. The coarseness of her fake beard scratched his fingertip.

"And you see, I would rather you stay so that we can consider surrendering to temptation." Her nostrils flared, and he sensed her arousal. "I know I shouldn't want that, but I can't help myself. If you tell me to stop or to leave you alone, I will."

"I don't want you to." Her voice was a low rasp, and it enflamed Roman's desire.

He clasped the side of her face as he leaned forward and captured her mouth in a searing kiss. Rapture sang through him as his body thrummed with a desperate, driving need.

She moved toward him and wrapped her arms around his neck as their tongues met in a fierce collision of want. They clutched at one another, their hands moving and seeking. The interior temperature of the coach increased with each kiss. She tugged at his hair as he grazed his teeth along her lip.

Too late, he realized the coach had stopped moving. He pulled away from her just as the coach door opened. She twisted from him and turned her head toward the opposite side of the coach.

He heard her ragged breathing, and it matched his own. *Bloody hell.*

Roman sprang from the seat and jumped from the coach. He hoped the coachman hadn't seen that they were sitting together, let alone embracing.

Ellis spent the afternoon working in her chamber, which Roman understood. He did not bother her, but she consumed his thoughts. How was he going to escort her to the Siren's Call that evening and keep his hands to himself in the coach?

What's more, did she even want him to?

CHAPTER 9

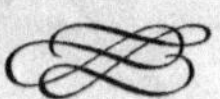

Garbed once more in her too-tight evening costume, Ellis made her way downstairs after taking a light repast in her chamber, where she'd been hiding to avoid Keele. Not hiding—she'd been working. Mostly. When she hadn't been thinking of her employer and his tantalizing kisses.

It was more than that. She couldn't stop thinking of the way he valued and respected her. Remarkably, he'd allowed her to retain her position after discovering she was a woman, and he'd continued to display an astonishing amount of concern—and trust—by allowing her to keep her secrets, even though that clearly frustrated him. At every turn, he'd been kind, understanding, and generous, such as involving her in Lacey and Company and insisting she participate in speaking with Mr. Inman.

There'd been a moment in the coach earlier when he'd demonstrated a clear desire to help her without even knowing why she might need that. He'd said he hated thinking she was afraid. The depth of care he'd revealed touched her deeply.

This deepening connection was not what she needed in her life right now. She'd been through great turmoil and wanted a new direction for the future. Keele was not part of that except for providing the financial foundation for whatever she chose to do next. The problem was that she didn't know what that would be, especially since she truly couldn't rely on staying in this position as long as she'd hoped. Every day she spent with Keele endangered her disguise.

He was waiting for her in the entrance hall again. Graham held the door for them as they departed the house and made their way silently to the coach. Keele climbed in first and took the forward-facing seat. Ellis sat opposite and watched him warily.

As soon as the door closed and she heard the coachman climb onto his seat, she spoke. "You must promise to stay on your side of the coach."

"I will. My apologies for earlier."

"Don't apologize. It's not as if I minded. But it isn't wise, and we both know that."

He exhaled, and there was no mistaking his disappointment. "Yes." He brushed something from his thigh. He was also dressed in evening clothes, and Ellis was having difficulty not staring at him.

Keele cut an exceedingly handsome figure, and unlike her costume, his clothing was expertly tailored. The black wool somehow accentuated the breadth of his shoulders, and the cut revealed his trim waist, confirming what she'd already suspected—that he had no need of corsets or any other sort of body-shaping undergarment.

His dark hair was styled more severely this evening, with the waves of his hair more contained. Ellis preferred his slightly tousled look. It gave him an air of irreverence that she found appealing.

It was somewhat roguish, she realized. Apparently, she

liked roguish. She was relatively certain she was going to fail at adhering to the Rogue Rules where Keele was concerned. And she didn't think she cared.

She mentally chastised herself for thinking such thoughts, as they were not helpful. However, dwelling on her attraction to Keele kept her from being nervous about seeing Jo. Lady Josephine Halifax was not only Ellis's half-sister and married to Min's brother, she was, like Ellis, not from the same class as the others in their group.

In fact, Jo's background was rather scandalous, largely due to her parents' public separation. They were not divorced, but they had not lived together perhaps ever, and Jo's mother had a long-time lover with whom she now resided. Jo's father, on the other hand, had not settled down with any one person and possessed a roguish reputation. And, of course, he was also Ellis's father, which meant her background was now scandalous too—if anyone ever learned she was Rowland Harker's daughter. Never mind that she was the illegitimate daughter of a duchess as well.

Hopefully, no one would learn the truth about her parentage. Ellis didn't want Harker to claim her, nor did she want anyone to know the Duchess of Henlow was her mother. The duke and duchess were even more famously separated than Jo's parents, simply because of their rank. The marriage of the owner of a gaming hell and a cheerful scoundrel who sometimes worked as an artist or a writer was not as interesting to the gossips of the *ton*.

Ellis didn't mind becoming acquainted with Harker, though. In fact, she would be pleased to have some kind of relationship since she didn't have any parents. She glanced across the coach at Keele. He didn't have parents either.

"Do you miss not having a mother or father?" she blurted without thinking and immediately wished she hadn't.

"A mother, because I never knew one. I don't miss having *my* father, but if I could choose another, I would."

"Why was your father so awful?" she asked quietly. "You don't have to answer."

"I'm happy to share things about myself," he replied. "Perhaps you'll even do the same someday." He winked at her, likely to ensure she knew he was teasing. Even so, she didn't think his curiosity about her had vanished.

Keele met her gaze as he crossed his arms over his chest. "My father was, in a word, a blackguard. He gambled incessantly, drank spirits from the moment he woke until he fell unconscious, cheated vendors, treated his retainers poorly, and frequented the bawdiest of houses. In fact, sometimes he didn't even go to houses. He found women—or men—on the street. I saw him once, with a young man. We'd attended the theatre when I was home from Oxford, and he left me in the coach whilst he stopped for some 'air.' I could see him receiving the young man's attentions from the window."

The former marquess seemed even more debauched than the Duke of Henlow, whose reputation with women was renowned. The duke, however, did not cheat anyone, nor did he treat his employees with anything other than kindness and appreciation, at least as far as Ellis had witnessed. "How old were you?"

"Fourteen, I think."

"That must have been shocking.

He nodded. "I told him not to do that again when I was with him. He laughed, and I knew he would, so I simply never accompanied him anywhere ever again."

"Not once?"

"No. And I was much happier for it."

Now Ellis's curiosity about him was beginning to match his about her. "You said you'd been a rogue before you inherited the title. Were you…like your father?"

"God, no." He unfolded his arms and shifted on the seat, bringing his knees up. "I did gamble far more than I should have done, but I didn't know our coffers were dwindling. I no longer wager, and not just because I can't afford to. I've seen how it can ruin a person." He pursed his lips for a moment, and she sensed he was lost in the memory of his father. She waited to see if he would continue and was glad when he did.

"I also frequented a particular bawdyhouse, but it was, I think, respectable. I certainly never caught any diseases, because I was quite consistent in wearing a French letter. After seeing the ravages of my father's behavior—he died from his indiscretions—I knew better than to leave myself exposed."

Ellis was fascinated to hear about his sexual experiences. In fact, she wanted to ask more about them but decided that was a bad idea.

"You don't gamble, and yet you're familiar with the Siren's Call. What will you do tonight whilst I'm...busy?" She'd almost said meeting with Jo, but he didn't know why she was going.

His brows shot up. "What do you mean you'll be busy? I thought you were going to play games of chance and wager."

"I might," she lied. "However, the primary reason for my visit is to meet with someone—privately. Don't bother asking with whom."

He studied her a moment, and she wondered what he was thinking. "I would never pry. Again," he added with a brief smile.

She couldn't help smiling in return. "I appreciate your sharing some of your past. I'll try to do the same. Soon."

"Don't worry about me. I can be patient." His eyes glittered like steel in moonlight in the light of the coach. "I'll wait for you in the common room, if you don't mind. I hope that won't interfere with your plans."

"Not at all." When Ellis arrived, she was to find an employee with bright red hair. Her name was Becky, and she would take Ellis to Jo.

They arrived at the Siren's Call and departed the coach. Ellis reminded herself to open the door and not wait for Keele to do it for her. But he moved ahead of her and opened it anyway, then gestured for her to precede him.

Ellis gave him a slight shake of her head before walking into the club. She'd never been there, of course, and realized she was a trifle excited along with feeling anxious. There was something temptingly forbidden about being here dressed as a man. She slid a peek at Keele. It was a similar sensation to what she felt about him, but not as intense.

A woman in a beautiful purple velvet gown greeted them. "Lord Keele, it's been some time since we've seen you," she said in a sultry tone. She sounded like the velvet of her gown, if the fabric could speak, which was absurd.

"Hannah, aren't you usually serving in the common room?"

"Not tonight." She gave him a flirtatious look. "Does that disappoint you, love?" A full, rich laugh floated from her, and Ellis didn't think she could ever master such effortless flirtation, not that she needed to.

Keele flashed a heart-stopping grin that made Ellis's toes curl in her slippers that were, unlike her costume, slightly too large. "Mayhap a little." Why was he flirting back?

Because that was what men did, even former rogues. However, what if he wasn't a *former* rogue, but one that had simply been hibernating? Ellis's pulse thrummed. She might prefer that he were a rogue. It wasn't as though she was considering him for a husband. Her interest was entirely to do with bedding him.

Did she really want that?

A combustive lust swept through her and provided the definitive answer: *yes.*

Hannah's gaze fell on Ellis. "Who's that with you?"

"My friend, Mr. Ellis."

"You're a pretty thing," Hannah said as she surveyed Ellis's face. "I mean that as a compliment. You've delicate features, which some find very appealing."

"Thank you." Ellis glanced toward Keele. "I'm going inside." She didn't have time to stand around and watch him flirt with Hannah, who was about to accurately guess that Ellis wasn't a man at all.

"Good to see you, Hannah," Keele said before looking to Ellis and gesturing faintly with his head that she should go on into the common room.

Ellis walked down a few steps into the large, well-appointed space. There were more than a dozen tables and a few seating areas, all decorated in rich mahogany, deep purple similar to Hannah's gown and accented with gilt. Many gentlemen were in attendance around the room, and several ladies were serving them, all dressed in a rather provocative manner. Ellis knew that was to attract the men to come to the Siren's Call over any other gaming club. It wasn't to offer anything else—this was not a brothel. In fact, Jo had told her that employees who dallied with patrons were dismissed.

She didn't see anyone with red hair. Hopefully, Becky would turn up so Ellis wouldn't have to ask for her.

"Where are the games?" Ellis whispered.

Keele gestured briefly toward an arched doorway at the back of the room. "Through there. This area is for dining and drinking. The food is quite good, actually. If I had known how long you planned to be, I might have chosen to dine here."

"I can't say, but if you'd like to have a meal, you should do so. I can always wait in the coach after I'm finished."

He shook his head. "I don't want you to do that. Besides, the coachman has moved away from the door, and he'll be watching for me to leave to come back 'round and fetch us. You'd have to go out and search for him. I'll just wait for you here and have a glass of port."

A tall server with bright red hair entered from another doorway at the back, carrying a tray with glasses, which she delivered to a table. That had to be Becky.

Ellis sent Keele a brief look. "Please excuse me." She didn't wait for his response before hurrying to the redhead. Becky stood at the table and flirted with the occupants in much the same way that Hannah had done with Keele.

At length, Becky finally turned to Ellis. "I ken I know who ye are. Come with me." She had the thick Scottish brogue Pandora had told her to expect.

Becky, serving tray tucked under her arm, led Ellis to the right side of the common room up the same number of stairs Ellis had walked down from the vestibule. They walked through the split in a pair of heavy purple drapes, and Becky pointed toward a staircase. "Go upstairs and knock. That's the private residence. Jo—I mean, Lady Shefford is there."

"How did you know who I was?" Ellis asked.

"Jo—Lady Shefford—" Becky made a quick face. "I can never remember to call 'er that. She's always been Jo to me. She told me ye were a woman dressed as a man."

Ellis exhaled in defeat. "Is it that obvious I'm not of the masculine gender?"

Becky shrugged. "Ye don't look like any o' the gentlemen who come in here. Ye lack swagger."

"Perhaps I should practice." She would ask Keele for his assistance. "Thank you, Becky." Ellis summoned a smile before turning to ascend the stairs. On the landing, she knocked as instructed and a moment later, Jo answered the door. With dark hair and sharp hazel eyes, Jo possessed an arresting beauty. She had a rich laugh and a dry wit.

Jo's dark, naturally arched brows drew together. "Ellis? I think that's you, but it's difficult to tell for certain with that beard."

Ellis wasn't prepared for the rush of emotion upon seeing her friend—nor the size of Jo's belly. "I didn't think you'd be so big!"

Jo laughed as Ellis clapped her hand to her mouth in horror. "My mother keeps saying I'm having twins, but I hope not. I fear she may be right, for I've still a couple of months to grow even larger yet."

"I'm sorry." Ellis threw her arms around Jo and embraced her tightly. Seeing her was somehow more affecting than seeing Pandora. Perhaps it was because she'd never greeted Jo knowing they were related until now.

They clung to each other for several moments before Jo finally pulled away. She wiped at her eyes. "I'm a blithering water pot since I've been carrying." She closed the door behind Ellis. Turning, she swept her gaze over Ellis. "I forgot you were dressing as a man. Your disguise is rather convincing."

"Is it?" Ellis was glad to hear that someone she knew well was persuaded. "Becky said I lack swagger."

Jo laughed. "How typically Becky." She turned and moved to the seating area. Again, Ellis was struck by how much she'd missed her friends.

"I'm sorry," Ellis blurted.

"What about?" Jo dropped rather heavily into a chair.

Ellis sat on a settee as close to Jo as she could get. "For calling you big... And for pushing you and everyone else away. Especially Min. I'm sorry I missed her wedding. I was certain Her Grace would be there, and I don't ever want to see her again."

Jo wrinkled her nose. "I don't think any of us do."

"She hasn't been very kind to you," Ellis said.

"No, but she's been far worse to you, especially considering she is your *blood*. You are completely justified in your anger and hurt. I think I would have wanted to disappear too." She gave Ellis such a warm, sympathetic regard that Ellis feared she would become a watering pot too. "I can only imagine what you're feeling."

"Angry and hurt, as you said." Ellis's shoulders relaxed. "But also grateful that I have not one, but two sisters."

Jo smiled broadly. "That made me very happy. I have always wanted a sibling."

Ellis sniffed and blinked away the tears that threatened. "I'm especially happy that Min is my sister in blood and not just in my heart."

"You should tell her," Jo said softly.

"I will. I suppose I've been waiting for something inside me to change, to give me a signal that I'm ready to accept everything I've learned and find my new place. But that hasn't happened yet. Probably because I've no idea what or where my new place should be." Ellis's plan to earn money so she could establish herself independently in some quiet village seemed farther away than ever. Her brilliant plan to mask as a male secretary wasn't turning out the way she'd hoped. Whilst she still had a job, she wasn't sure how long it would last, particularly since the relationship between her and her employer appeared to be growing more complicated.

"I imagine you feel as though you don't belong. I feel that way nearly every day now that I'm a countess. I worry I'll do something wrong or embarrass Sheff."

"You could never," Ellis said firmly. She knew Sheff, and his love for Jo was deep and unparalleled. "But I understand feeling like an imposter. I have always felt that I don't belong, and now I know I really don't—I'm not even legitimate."

Jo's features creased. "I honestly hadn't considered that. I suppose because it doesn't matter to me. Truly," she added with a deep gravity.

Ellis voiced her greatest fear. "I don't want anyone to find out I'm the illegitimate daughter of the Duchess of Henlow." She let out a short, humorless laugh. "It's funny because there used to be rumors that I was Henlow's daughter, and that never bothered me. That was because I knew it wasn't true. But the truth is that I am illegitimate—just not in the way anyone thought."

"I can hear how much that pains you," Jo said with great sympathy. "I'm sorry. I wish things were different. How were you certain Henlow wasn't your father?"

"Because he told me so," Ellis said simply.

"And you just believed him?" Jo sounded surprised and perhaps a bit stunned.

Ellis shrugged. "Despite his many indiscretions and mistakes, he's always been kind and generous to me. When he welcomed me into the household, he promised he would always take care of me and ensure I had a home. I didn't realize at the time that he was making it clear to everyone, particularly Her Grace, that I was safe and protected. I know now that he's the only reason she didn't toss me out." She voiced another of her fears. "Since learning the truth, I've wondered if I would have been better off if she had."

Jo stared at her. "How can you say that? Where would you have gone? What would you have done?"

"I could have gone to live with my adoptive mother's cousins in Wales. They offered to take me in." Ellis's mother had corresponded with them regularly, and Ellis had continued to do so after her death, even now. The duke was kind enough to forward their letters since he knew where

Ellis was living. She hadn't told them anything about the duchess or Rowland Harker. "It would have been a very different life."

"But would you have wanted that?" Jo asked.

Ellis lifted a shoulder. "How can I know?"

She did wonder if that life would have allowed her to marry and have a family of her own, something she never expected as Min's companion and certainly couldn't hope for now as the illegitimate daughter of a duchess. Unless she was able to keep it secret.

Except Ellis knew the truth, and it made her feel unworthy. All the years of the duchess's harsh comments and snide remarks hadn't beaten her down, but the revelation of the truth had succeeded where Her Grace hadn't.

"I suppose we mustn't discount things with which we have no experience," Jo said. "I didn't think I ever wanted to be a mother, and look at me now." She smiled as she gently caressed the roundness of her belly.

Shockingly, Ellis felt a stab of envy. Why? She'd never wanted—or at least expected—to be a mother. Did she want that? She'd honestly never allowed herself to imagine it, and she wasn't going to start now.

Setting those thoughts aside and hopefully never contemplating them again, Ellis fixed her full attention on Jo. "Tell me about our father. He still doesn't know about me, does he?"

Jo shook her head. "I didn't want him to know until you were ready. After the way you found out about your parents, I think you more than deserve to manage what happens next."

"*Nothing* is going to happen with the duchess." Ellis allowed her lip to curl, for she could not hide her loathing for the woman. "I do appreciate you thinking of me, but don't you think our father deserves to know the truth?"

"I'm not sure, actually. I'm rather angry with him about the timing of it all. You know you're only three months younger than me?"

Ellis drew in a sharp breath. She hadn't realized that. "Our mothers were carrying at the same time? Was your mother aware?"

Jo pursed her lips as she nodded. "Yes, which is why I have never lived with my father. My mother turned him out. He didn't particularly mind, for he'd decided—obviously— that monogamy was not for him."

"He's the worst sort of rogue," Ellis said.

Jo smirked. "Yes. Perhaps if my mother had been presented a copy of the Rogue Rules before marrying my father, she might have reconsidered. I do love him, and I think you will too. He's not like your mother. He's amusing and charming, but also frivolous and hedonistic. He's a wonderful writer and an even better painter, and he loves scientific experimentation. However, he's also distractable, so he's never worked at anything hard or long enough to make a name for himself."

"I like to paint," Ellis said. "Perhaps I inherited that from him."

"He will be ecstatic," Jo replied before adopting a serious expression. "I hope you aren't expecting his financial support because he has little money. He had a small inheritance from a distant uncle that he mostly frittered away. Mama took from him what was left several years ago and invested it. She now gives him an allowance from the interest it earns and augments the payments with some of her own money, though he doesn't know that. She still cares for him as someone she once loved and the father of her only child, but she'd deny it."

Ellis hadn't known what to expect from Rowland Harker, but it wasn't financial support. She simply wanted a parent.

"I suppose I would just like to know that I have a father and that he might care for me."

Jo gave her an encouraging smile. "I think he will, though he really isn't much of a father. He's more like a friend with whom you'd like to walk in the park or meet at Gunter's for ice cream. He's great fun, but not remotely dependable. And he has ridiculous expectations. He was over the moon when I was betrothed to the heir to a *duke*."

"He didn't know the betrothal was fake in the beginning, did he?" Ellis asked.

"No, we didn't trust him with the secret. Which is why we haven't told him about you. He would have run straight to you and declared himself your father."

Honestly, that might have been better than the way Ellis had actually found out—overhearing Min arguing with their mother. "So, I will be the one to tell him?"

"If you want. Or someone else can if that's your preference. As I said, it should be up to you what happens next."

Ellis wasn't sure what she wanted. Not yet. "May I think about it?"

"Of course!" Jo assured her. "There's certainly no hurry. Though, I do hope you'll want to see Min sooner than later."

"Does she know you're seeing me today?" Ellis asked softly.

Jo shook her head. "I didn't want her to be hurt. And I don't say that to be cruel. It's simply the truth. She misses you terribly and feels awful about what happened—how you overheard her."

"I know. I just wish she'd told me." Ellis had thought through that conversation she'd overheard a thousand times, and whilst the pain had lessened, she didn't think she'd ever forget the shock and devastation she'd felt in that moment. It had been a horrible, life-changing event, and Ellis had simply run away. "I suppose I understand why you were hesitant, but it does hurt to know that Min knew something so important about me and didn't tell me. But I'm not angry with her. Not anymore."

"Perhaps I will tell her I saw you," Jo said.

"You should if you want to. I want her to know I'm well and that I miss her. Please tell her I love her and I'll see her soon."

"I will. But what are you doing now? Where are you lodging? Pandora says she's sworn to secrecy. Min and I are aware that the duke knows where you're living."

"I'd rather not say." Ellis didn't want anyone trying to communicate with her while she was in Keele's employ. She probably shouldn't have taken a position with someone who moved in the same circle as the very people she was trying to avoid.

But as complicated as her job was turning out to be, she didn't regret it. After so many years of being made to believe she was a burden and wondering what would happen to her when Min wed, it was wonderful to make her own choices, to have a chance to map her own future.

She also couldn't deny that the growing attraction between her and Keele gave her a thrilling excitement she'd never experienced. It was clear they wanted each other and that it would take very little to push them into the other's arms. Ellis wasn't sure how much longer she could resist the inexorable pull she felt not just when she was with him, but at every waking moment. Even now, she could scarcely wait to return downstairs and see if the coach ride home would lead to more kissing.

"I won't press you," Jo said. "You know how to reach me. Us. We will wait to hear from you. Can Pandora forward messages to you from us?"

"I'd prefer you went through the duke, as you've been doing." Ellis didn't have to worry that he would raise suspicion. When he sent missives to her, he did so through the regular post and not via a liveried footman. He also didn't use anything signifying his title or name on the envelope.

"Certainly." Jo nodded. "I'm not sure how much longer Pandora will be in London anyway. It sounds as though she's finalized her publishing contract. It's so exciting! I wish I could host a literary soiree for her, but she's to remain anonymous, of course."

Ellis had to bite her tongue—not in reality—to keep from telling Jo that she was involved, at least in a small way, with the publication of *A Season in Shadow*. Indeed, she should be on her way lest she reveal too much overall. She also didn't want to keep Keele waiting too long.

"I should be going." Ellis stood, and Jo pushed herself up. "You don't have to stand."

"I need to go too," Jo said. "Sheff will be here soon to fetch me."

"He's coming here?" Ellis didn't mean to sound panicked, but she wasn't ready to see Sheff either. He was her half-brother now—an earl. She wanted to laugh at the absurdity of being a bastard whilst also being related to nobility. Though Sheff wasn't some arrogant peer. He'd always been the older brother who teased Min. Ellis realized he'd never done that to her, but then he hadn't known they were siblings.

"Yes." Jo grimaced. "Are you worried about running into him? I didn't think of it. I'm sorry."

Ellis was more concerned that Sheff would run into Keele downstairs in the club. She'd need to gain Keele's attention without Sheff seeing her. Though her disguise had convinced Jo, Ellis wasn't sure it would fool Sheff, not after years of living in the same household together.

"He doesn't know I'm here, does he?" Ellis asked.

"No, and I won't tell him."

"I hate asking you to be secretive." Ellis also missed Sheff nearly as much as she missed Min. "Please tell him you saw me and that I'll see him soon too."

They embraced once more before Ellis departed.

On the way down to the club she tried to think of when and how she would see Min. Regardless, she needed to tell Min—and Pandora and Jo and anyone else who wanted her to return to her old life—that she was now on her own path and she wasn't yet sure where it would lead. She didn't want to sever her ties with them completely, but they were the past, the lie that Ellis had been living for over a decade and a half.

Ellis didn't want that life anymore. She wanted something new, something she chose and in which she had power.

She just had to determine what that was.

CHAPTER 10

Roman was on his second tankard of porter as he sat in the common room waiting for Ellis. He vaguely knew some of the other patrons but hadn't said more than a few words in passing to any of them whilst he'd been there. He wondered how much longer Ellis would be and hoped her meeting was going well, whatever she was doing.

A new arrival came down the steps into the common room, and since Roman was relatively close to the vestibule, he made eye contact with the man. It was Lord Shefford, who everyone called Sheff, and whom Roman had known for some time. They were the same age and had been at Oxford at the same time but had not attended the same college. They had, however, been part of a set of rakish young men. When they'd finished at Oxford, there had been many house parties and hunts and a rather debauched London Season or three.

When Roman reflected back on that time, he didn't recognize the young man he'd been. He now knew that most of what he'd done had been to try to draw his father's attention, but nothing he did accomplished that. His father had been far too involved in his own life and troubles.

"Keele," Sheff said warmly as he came toward the table. "I'm surprised to see you here. I can't think of the last time you were at the Siren's Call."

"I'm surprised to see you here as well," Roman replied. "Aren't you about to become a father?"

Sheff nodded. "After the new year. Jo and I will be removing to the country in a few weeks. Shockingly, I'm looking forward to it."

"To the country or becoming a father?" Roman asked.

"Both, but especially the latter." Sheff chuckled. "I know what you're going to say. It's what everyone says—'*what the hell has happened to you?*'"

Roman smiled. "Yes, it was some version of that. But I'm glad to see you so happy. You're completely gone for your wife and the baby you're expecting, aren't you?"

"Absolutely," Sheff confirmed with pride. "And I wouldn't have it any other way."

A surprising sense of longing swept through Roman briefly. First, he'd envied Margot falling in love, and now he was thrown by Sheff's unadulterated joy. He shouldn't be moved by their romantic happiness, not when he'd sworn not to risk love again. "This is an astounding change from the young rogue with whom I caused havoc after Oxford."

Whilst Roman's behavior had been less than exemplary, Sheff and Banemore had been the worst of their set. To see Sheff now, besotted and eager to be a father, was proof that people could change—or perhaps that one should be open to the unexpected. "If you're so eager to be in the country, why not leave now? Is there anything keeping you here?"

Sheff lifted his shoulder. "There's some family strife at the moment. Jo and Min don't want to leave London right now.

It's to do with my sister's former companion." He waved his hand. "Doesn't matter. None of that is of interest to you."

"I'm sorry to hear there's difficulty. I hope it will be resolved soon."

"I don't know if that can happen. It's just an unpleasant time. That sounds incredibly cryptic," Sheff said with a laugh.

"It's quite all right," Roman said. "You don't need to explain. You've had a great deal of excitement this year with your marrying, and your sister was recently wed. I imagine your parents are thrilled."

"My father is," Sheff replied with a smirk. "Our mother is horribly disappointed that we both married beneath our rank. That we are madly in love and happy is of no consequence."

Though Sheff spoke rather lightly, Roman heard the underlying anger he held toward his mother. "I can appreciate having a difficult parent," Roman said in commiseration. He briefly wondered what was worse—having a parent you didn't like, and perhaps didn't like you, or having none at all.

Just then, Roman saw Ellis come back into the common room. Her gaze immediately found him but then moved to Sheff. She abruptly angled herself away and put her head down, skirting the edge of the room toward the vestibule. It was clear to Roman that she'd had a reaction to seeing Sheff.

Roman jumped up from his chair. "Forgive me, Sheff. I must be on my way. Sorry I can't keep you company."

"It's all right, I'm here to pick up my wife." Sheff gestured with his head toward the archway where Ellis had gone and recently returned. "She's upstairs visiting with her mother."

Was she?

Ellis was acquainted with Lady Shefford, and Lady Shefford was here. Furthermore, Ellis had perhaps gone upstairs for whatever business she had here this evening. Was she simply speaking with the countess about the literary events Inman would oversee at the library? If so, why wouldn't she tell Roman the reason for her visit tonight? There was no reason for her to hide that from him.

Roman bid Sheff good evening then hastened to join Ellis in the vestibule. She was already stepping outside. As Roman caught up with her on the pavement, he looked down the street and saw his coach. He waved his hand at the coachman.

"Are you all right?" Roman asked.

"I'm fine." She didn't sound fine. She sounded tense, and her shoulders were hunched up.

"Did you recognize the man I was speaking with?" Roman asked casually as the coach pulled toward them.

She glanced at him. "No."

Though he was still coming to know her well, Roman didn't think she was telling the truth. He recalled what Sheff had said about there being trouble in his family to do with his sister's former companion.

Former companion.

Before Roman had agreed to marry Clarissa, he'd been hunting for an heiress. He'd considered making a play for Lady Minerva and her sizable dowry but decided he didn't want a marriage of convenience with his friend's sister. Still, he'd danced with her a time or two at a ball, and he recalled that she'd had a companion.

Roman summoned whatever memories he could find of the elusive figure and remembered the woman was tall and blonde. He didn't think they'd ever spoken, but her name suddenly leapt into his mind: Miss Dangerfield. She'd lived in the Henlow household since childhood, if he was remembering correctly, and for several years, there were rumors that she was actually the duke's by-blow.

What had happened to the companion now that Lady

Minerva was married? Was that why she was a *former* companion? He couldn't imagine Lady Minerva, who he'd found to be charming and kind, would simply turn her out. But what was the strife then?

Roman looked at Ellis.

The coach stopped, and the coachman jumped down to open the door. Ellis waited for Roman to move into the coach and glanced back at the door to the club nervously. He could see that she was eager to be away from the club.

"Go ahead," he said, ushering her into the coach ahead of him.

Ellis sat ramrod straight on the rear-facing seat, her face paler than usual in the light from the lantern. Roman sat down and contemplated her agitated state as they started moving.

"You seem upset," he said. "If you'd like to unburden yourself, I'd be glad to listen. Or if you'd simply like to sit with me and rest your head on my shoulder, I can provide that too."

She shifted her gaze to the window. Her jaw was pulled tight as if she were clenching her teeth, perhaps. He didn't think he'd ever seen her this distraught.

Roman decided to just say what he was thinking. "I believe you were meeting with Lady Shefford. Sheff was there to fetch her. And who else would you be seeing at the Siren's Call? I know you're acquainted based on what you told Inman earlier." He paused before asking the next question, but then he didn't have to.

She met his gaze, her expression surprisingly flat, given the tension in her body. "You know who I am, don't you? Did you tell Sheff?"

She *was* Lady Minerva's companion. "No, I didn't tell him. I didn't puzzle it out until we came outside. I vaguely remember Lady Minerva having a tall blonde companion. I wasn't entirely certain it was you. But I am now."

Apprehension darkened her features. "*Will* you tell Sheff?"

"No. I told you that your secret is safe with me. Knowing who you are now doesn't change anything. I will keep you safe. Do you trust me?"

"I do." She took a deep, shaky breath. "Is your shoulder still on offer?"

"Absolutely." He scooted to the side of his seat, and she moved over to join him.

After briefly making eye contact, she leaned against him and removed her hat before laying her head on his shoulder. Roman would have rather put his arm around her and held her in that position, but he savored this.

"Why do you care about me?" she asked softly.

"I don't know exactly." He took her hand and stroked his thumb along the back. He wished they weren't wearing gloves. "I sense you're clinging to something—your pride or your independence. And I know you're fighting to survive on your own without assistance. I wish I knew why, but I still don't need you to tell me." Sheff had said there was strife. Had something happened with Ellis? He couldn't see her being the cause of any trouble.

A horrible thought stole into his mind. He was well aware of the Duke of Henlow's reputation for debauchery, and he knew from Sheff that most of it was true. Fear and fury curled through him. "Are you hiding from them because someone did something to you?" he whispered.

She turned her head and looked up at him. Her blue eyes were the color of the sky as the sun began to set, vibrant and dusky at the same time. "What do you mean?"

"Did the duke…" Roman didn't want to say it out loud, but he must. "Did Henlow abuse you in any way?"

"Heavens, no." Her reply came so fast and so strong that Roman didn't doubt its veracity. "He has been nothing but kind to me since my parents died. He even wrote me a recommendation for this position, if you recall."

"Yes, but perhaps he did it out of guilt."

"He did not," she said vehemently. "He has lived a sordid life, but it's not what you think. He's done what he could to survive an extremely unhappy marriage."

"Yes, I am aware that he and the duchess do not care for one another. I believe all of London knows that."

"But something *did* happen," she said quietly. "Nothing that physically hurt me," she added. "I still don't wish to discuss it. I would rather not think of it at all right now." She held his gaze, and there was no mistaking her desire—or her invitation.

Roman moved his hand up above her glove and found her bare wrist. He stroked his thumb along the underside, feeling the rapid beat of her pulse beneath her warm flesh. "Is there a way I could assist in distracting you?"

"Yes." She pivoted on the seat and sat straighter before pressing her mouth to his.

He angled toward her and cupped the back of her head with his free hand as he returned her kiss with fierce demand. Her beard scratched his face, and he longed to kiss her without it.

Their positioning was awkward. He wanted to feel her against him. She must have felt the same, for she threw her leg over his lap and straddled him.

Groaning, Roman kept hold of her nape and clasped her waist with his other hand. She splayed one hand against his upper chest whilst the other slid along his neck. She rose up, so he had to tip his head back to kiss her. Using her advantage, she speared her tongue into his mouth, ravishing him with a brazen rapture that sent Roman into a delirious haze of lust.

She pressed her hips down against his, the warmth of her

sex teasing his hardened cock through the layers of their breeches. He was not wearing any undergarments. Was she? The notion that he could unbutton her fall and stroke her sex was intoxicating and fast becoming all-consuming.

Roman slid his hand over from her waist and flicked the buttons at the top of her breeches. The fall gapped open, and he tucked his hand inside. She was as bare beneath the breeches as he was.

His hips twitched against hers with need as he worked his hand between them. He was still wearing his blasted glove, but he didn't care. He teased her clitoris and was rewarded when she pulled her mouth from his and let out a long, low whimper. She kissed his jaw and his neck as she moved her hips against his hand.

She suddenly froze against him. "We've stopped."

Roman withdrew his hand from her breeches as she scrambled off him and threw herself into the opposite seat. She quickly re-buttoned her fall, and Roman tossed her hat over.

She caught it easily just before the door opened. Her gaze caught his, smoldering with her lingering desire. Roman's body thrummed as he ached for her.

He stared at her with dark promise, wishing they'd had a much longer journey in the coach. He lifted his hand and licked the finger of his glove, tasting her on the kidskin. Her eyes narrowed at him just before he climbed down from the coach.

Roman thanked the coachman before walking toward the house. He heard Ellis moving behind him. Graham opened the door, and Roman stepped into the entrance hall. He inclined his head at the butler and said he was going upstairs for the evening.

Moving into the staircase hall, Roman slowed, dallying whilst he waited for Ellis. She approached him with a guarded look, and Roman feared they would not continue what they'd started in the coach. They'd had several conversations about why they should not engage in this sort of familiarity.

Familiarity?

That word didn't remotely come close to the primal, explosive connection firing between them.

Ellis came abreast of him at the base of the staircase, and he held his breath. "Come to my room," she whispered. "When you can."

"Soon," he promised.

She gave him a sultry stare, and he assumed her momentary wariness came from wondering if he would want to continue. He most certainly did. In fact, he feared he would expire if they did not.

But they would. As soon as he could dispatch his valet and ensure the servants would not disturb them.

Then, he and Ellis would see this attraction to its natural and thrilling end.

~

*R*oman paced in his chamber after dismissing Graham for the evening. The butler also served as his valet because Roman found he didn't need to pay two salaries when he had such a small household. If anyone knew that he, a marquess, didn't have a dedicated valet, they would surely think him a failure, or at least incredibly strange.

It was after eleven, but Roman wasn't sure all the servants had retired. The footman was typically the last one awake, but Roman had clearly informed Graham that he didn't require anything further.

Why was he so bloody nervous?

He realized his tension had little to do with whether his

retainers were still knocking around and more to do with the fact that he hadn't been with a woman since his wife, and she'd died over two years ago. Furthermore, they hadn't shared a bed for several months before her death, because she'd found reasons to deny him. In fact, Roman had spent that time sleeping in the chamber Ellis now occupied.

When he thought of her in the bed he once slept in, his body heated again. Not that it had fully cooled since they'd left the coach.

It occurred to Roman that he hadn't ever wanted Clarissa this desperately. Perhaps because when he thought back, he could see that she hadn't ever been interested in sharing his bed.

Bloody hell, he did *not* want to think about Clarissa right now.

Roman strode to the door and, opening it, stepped into the narrow hall that adjoined the larger staircase hall via an archway. He would not go that far, however. The door to Ellis's chamber was to the left.

Before he could take a step, he froze. Because Patience, the maid, was just exiting that doorway. She carried a basin and toweling.

His heart thumped as he waited motionless to see if she would notice him. Thankfully, she didn't seem to as she moved toward the archway. Roman slunk backward over the threshold of his chamber just as Patience paused and turned. Did she see that his door was open?

He held his breath until she departed. He closed the door and pressed his head against the wood as he closed his eyes and filled his lungs. This was madness. He ought to go to bed. Alone.

Except his body was still hard and eager, his mind full of Ellis and how badly he wanted to touch her sex with his bare hand. Perhaps if he just waited a little while longer...

He resumed pacing.

A few minutes later, or perhaps much longer since he wasn't actually tracking the time, he heard a light rap on the door from the bathing chamber. Roman crossed to it in two giant steps and threw it open.

Ellis stood just over the threshold. Her face was spectacularly bare, and he drank in her beauty. Her blonde hair was plaited and tied with a light blue ribbon. The plait hung over her shoulder, the curled end grazing her breast.

She wore a light dressing gown that left no doubt as to her true gender. Her curves were easily discernible, and Roman wondered how she was ever able to accomplish hiding herself in the men's costumes.

"You take my breath away," he whispered.

She gave him a tentative look. "May I come in?"

He stepped aside in invitation. "Of course."

"I wasn't sure," she said as he closed the door. "I thought you were coming to *my* chamber."

"I was. That is, I tried. However, I saw Patience leaving and managed to retreat before she saw me. Then I began to doubt the wisdom of this tryst." He wiped his hand over his brow. "I am likely thinking much too hard about this, but, you see, I haven't been with a woman in a very long time and I—"

She took his hand, effectively silencing his blathering, and led him toward the mahogany four-poster bed. The feel of her skin against his made him want to pull her against him, but he let her lead him.

When they reached the bed, she positioned him against it, then pushed him back until he sat on the green coverlet. She stood before him and locked her gaze with his. "How long?"

He blinked at her, trying to determine what she was asking. What had he just said? That he hadn't been with a woman in a very long time. Damn, he was flustered.

"About three years."

Her features didn't change. "Well, at least you aren't a rogue like some of the other gentlemen with whom you associate. Though I suppose most of them—all of them now?—are reformed." She cocked her head. "But you are also a reformed rogue. You mentioned you were a rake before you inherited the title and that you frequented bawdyhouses."

"Just one bawdyhouse," he clarified. "I was a very particular rogue."

She laughed, and the sound was low and seductive. Roman's already hardened cock lengthened.

"How did you go from that rake to a monk?"

He didn't want to tell her that his wife had made him doubt himself. "When I inherited, I dedicated myself to my new duty. You've seen the state the finances used to be in. I had much work to do. When I married, I took those vows very seriously. Since my wife died, I have continued to be busy."

She arched a brow. "You simply have no time for personal gratification?"

"Oh, I make time for that."

"I know. I heard you the other night. I should have explicitly asked if you take time for sex. It seems you do not."

Roman's pulse had never moved more frantically, and his body had never been in such a heightened state of arousal. He could hardly believe how plainly she was speaking or how incredibly erotic it was. "You heard me the other night?" His voice nearly cracked.

She nodded. "I had to go back into the dressing chamber to fetch my hairbrush. I could hear you against the door." She took the smallest step forward—it was all she could do, for her legs now brushed against his.

Her gaze held his, and he was lost in the dizzying desire he saw in the blue depths of her eyes.

He parted his legs. "How did you know what I was doing?"

"I know what men do," she replied matter-of-factly. "I've helped a man do that. Well, he was more boy than man. We were only seventeen."

Her words enflamed him. He was both furious with any man that had touched her and so aroused by her knowledge and experience that he had to work hard not to throw her on the bed and ravish her.

He clasped her waist and could tell she wasn't wearing anything beneath the dressing gown. His lust intensified. He pulled her to stand between his legs. "Tell me, Ellis—that is your true name, isn't it? I do not want to call you anything but your real name when I make you mine."

Her jawline was red where she'd worn her beard, but the color had begun to fade. Now it flushed back, moving up her face in a delicate blush.

"Yes, it's Ellis. That was my mother's maiden name."

"Ellis Dangerfield," he murmured. "Tell me, when was the last time you were with a man?"

"Five years," she replied.

"And how many men have you been with?"

Her brow shot back up. "Will you tell me how many women you've been with?"

He laughed softly. "Ten, perhaps. Or twelve. I'm embarrassed to say I don't know for certain."

"Two men. The boy-man and someone else who was entirely forgettable." She narrowed her eyes at him. "My experience doesn't bother you?"

He shook his head. "On the contrary. I find it oddly provocative. But let me be clear, my goal is to ensure that your past experiences pale in comparison to the present."

"That is an excellent goal. I shall endeavor to do the same."

"You've already done it. Your frank conversation and boldness are absolutely intoxicating. Honestly, I don't know how I haven't already torn your dressing gown away." He moved his hands to the front of her gown and loosened the fastenings. "The other night—did you stay in the bathing chamber and listen until I finished?"

She nodded. "I heard you climax. Then I went back to my room and pleasured myself."

Fuck. Roman didn't think he'd ever been in this state of pure lust before. He wondered if he could actually come listening to her talk.

Her gown now gapped open, and Roman could make out the curve of her breast as well as the flat plane of her stomach. And he glimpsed the golden curls at the apex of her thighs.

Before he could push the garment apart, she opened it and shrugged it from her shoulders, letting it fall to the floor. Her plait still teased her breast, the curls at the end brushing against her right nipple.

Roman reached up and grasped the plait. He leaned forward and smelled her hair, closing his eyes at the deliciously floral and very feminine scent. "I've never smelled this on you before."

"I washed with my regular soap. That's why you saw Patience leaving my chamber. I wanted to smell like a woman."

He pulled her toward him so he could put his mouth on her. Pushing his hand beneath her breast, he cupped her as he drew her nipple into his mouth. She gasped and clutched the back so his head, her fingers digging into his hair. He wanted her hair free too.

Roman released her breast. "You taste like a woman, that's for certain." He plucked the ribbon free from her hair and pulled the plait apart impatiently.

She took over from him and loosened her blonde locks. When the plait was gone, she combed her fingers through her hair and shook it over her shoulders. It caressed her upper arms in gentle, golden waves.

"How in the hell do you get all that under a wig?" He shook his head. "Never mind. I don't care right now. I want to toss you onto my bed and bury myself inside you." He stood and removed his dressing gown, casting it away carelessly. "Do you have any objection to that?"

"Will you be wearing one of your French letters?" she asked.

Shit. "I don't have any. I told you; I haven't done this in ages."

"I don't mind. But you must leave me before you spend." The edge of her mouth ticked up in an alluring half-smile. "And don't worry, I'll help you finish."

"If you don't stop speaking in such an erotic manner, I'm going to finish before we even start."

Ellis closed the small space between them and curled her arms around his neck. "Then we'd best begin."

CHAPTER 11

Ellis wasn't entirely sure where the boldness Keele liked had come from. It wasn't that she was restrained, at least not with those who knew her well. But as companion to the daughter of a duke, she knew her place was to be seen and not heard—because the duchess had driven that into her since the day she'd joined the Henlow household.

Those days were behind her. She could be who she wanted to be, including a seductress taking what she desired most. Right now, that was Keele, this amazing man who'd made her feel something she hadn't in a very long time: wanted.

He looked at her with a primal yearning that made her tremble. There were many reasons she should not surrender to this connection between them, but she didn't care about any of them. Not tonight.

"You are an astonishing woman," Keele whispered just before she lowered her mouth to his.

His lips sealed to hers as he gathered her tightly against the warmth of his body. He pressed one hand to her spine, and the other caressed the curve of her backside. His mouth opened, and she met his tongue with her own as rapture spread through her body.

Though it had been some time since she'd experienced this kind of encounter, this could not compare to anything in her past. Keele aroused her in ways she'd never known and simply couldn't deny.

He cupped her backside as their kisses deepened. She clutched his nape and splayed her hand over his shoulder blade, feeling the ripple of muscle as he moved.

Leaving her mouth, he kissed along her jaw and down her neck as his hand came between them to clasp her breast. He dragged his thumb over her nipple—over and over. She moaned softly just before he sucked her into his mouth. He suckled her flesh as he kneaded her backside. Heat and longing flowed to her sex.

Moving his mouth to her other breast, he kept his hand on the first one and squeezed her nipple—not too hard, but he pinched enough to make her gasp and for another jolt of white-hot passion to tear through her.

He gripped her thigh and lifted her leg. "Straddle me, like in the coach." His demand provoked another surge of lust as she eagerly complied.

Ellis climbed over his thighs, her legs dangling against his. This position opened her sex, which was entirely the point. She quivered with want and, thankfully, he did not make her beg.

He slid his hand along her thigh to her sex, his fingers teasing her sensitive folds. In the coach, she'd been shocked —in the best possible way—when he'd unbuttoned her fall and touched her. The feel of his glove against her had been delightfully erotic, but now she glad for his bare flesh as he teased her clitoris.

"Ellis, you are so wet," he rasped. "I don't know how much

longer I can wait."

She rocked against him, seeking more of his touch. "I don't want you to. I need you inside me."

He drove his finger into her sex, and she moaned as her head fell forward. He pumped into her, and she met his thrusts as she dug her fingernails into his shoulders. Pleasure built and pushed her toward the edge.

But then he was gone, and she was lifted from his lap. In a fluid series of movements, he picked her up and pressed her back on the bed, climbing up beside her. Then he was between her legs, pushing her thighs open.

His mouth crashed down on her sex, licking and devouring her with greedy abandon. Whilst Ellis was aware of this act, she'd never participated in it. She was not at all prepared for the overwhelming rush of sensation and flash of pure ecstasy. Mindless, she clutched at his head as she bent her legs. He was relentless in his assault with his lips and tongue. Her muscles clenched as she barreled toward release.

He slid his fingers into her as he sucked her clitoris, and Ellis couldn't hold on any longer. She flew apart with a loud cry as her orgasm shuddered through her.

"Roman," he growled as he moved up her body. "Call me Roman." He claimed her mouth, and she tasted herself on his tongue.

She must have called his name—Keele—as she'd come. At least, she thought she had. She honestly could not recall.

"Do you need a moment?" he asked, his voice tight with desire.

"For what?" She drew on his lip with her teeth as she wrapped her legs around his waist. Lifting her hips, she pressed her sex against his rigid cock, and lights danced behind her eyes as he rubbed against her clitoris.

"You've answered my question, I think. I wondered if you

needed time to recover before I drive inside you. I did promise you I would do that, didn't I?"

"I don't know if you promised, but I've certainly been hoping you would. I can't stand to be without you another second." She reached between them and stroked the length of his cock, eliciting a deep groan from his lips before he kissed her again.

Ellis worked his shaft, and his hips began to move, then she guided him to her sex. His hand joined hers, and together, they steered him home.

He filled her slowly and completely, claiming every part of her. Ellis closed her eyes and basked in the heady sensations rippling through her. She'd never ridden so high or wanted so much.

She tightened her legs around him, her heels pushing against his backside as he pulled back and then drove forward. Again and again, he thrust into her, sending waves of sensations through her that were going to ruin her completely.

They moved together, faster and deeper, their bodies slick and their desperate sounds of desire filling the air around them. Ellis has never experienced such harmony, such primal beauty, or such delicious pleasure.

Slipping his hand between them, he stroked her clitoris and sent her into another fever of ecstasy. She tumbled into darkness as she cried out his name, drawing him deeper as she became lost in oblivion.

Her orgasm was still moving over her when he grunted and removed himself from her sex.

"Ellis, I'm going to come."

She somehow managed to reach for and find his cock. His hand was already there, but she brushed it aside and took control, stroking him as he climaxed. He shouted, and she worried someone would overhear them.

When he finally slowed, she rose and pushed him down beside her. She didn't release his shaft until he opened his eyes and fixed on her. They were both panting, but she was beginning to catch her breath. Nevertheless, he curled his hand behind her head and pulled her down for a blistering kiss.

They had to break shortly to continue to settle their racing pulses. Ellis backed away and slipped off the bed.

"Where are you going?" Keele sounded alarmed. Rather, Roman. She wasn't sure she ought to use his name for fear she might slip up in front of someone, but she would at least think of him as Roman instead of Keele. It was far more intimate, and they were now, well, intimate.

"Just to wash my hand." She winked at him over her shoulder.

He chuckled. "Would you mind bringing me a cloth?"

She went into the bathing chamber and recalled the night he'd come in as she left the bath. He'd seemed shocked to hear that she'd listened to him pleasure himself, then aroused upon her revelation that she'd done the same. If only they'd done so together… Perhaps another time.

Was she thinking this would happen again? She hoped so.

After washing him from her hand, she took a cloth back to the bed. "Where do you need tidying?"

He gestured to his abdomen. "Just a bit here. And I suppose my cock."

She cleaned his belly first, then carefully dried his shaft. He'd gone slack but began to stir. She arched a brow at him. "You're becoming aroused again?"

"Apparently," he said with a wicked grin. "Ignore it."

"I shall. For now," she added, giving him an openly seductive stare. She tossed the cloth aside, then snuggled against him, laying her palm against his chest. He had a dusting of dark hair between his nipples, and his muscles were taut and well-defined. She could feel his heart thumping madly.

"I hope you didn't alert the servants," she said. "You were quite loud."

He glanced down at her with a wry smile. "So were you. I'm not concerned. With any luck, they are two floors above us and two floors below. In any case, I'm not sure I could have modulated myself. It's been too long."

"Despite that, I'd say you didn't appear to be out of practice," Ellis said. "In fact, I would say your expertise is unparalleled. At least in my experience. But then, no one has ever put their mouth on my sex before. That was extraordinary."

He grinned with equal parts pride and arrogance. "I'm thrilled to be the first."

The notion that someone in the household might have overheard them niggled at the back of Ellis's mind. She rose up and looked down at him. "I truly hope no one heard us. That could be quite bad."

Smiling, he cupped her head, threading his fingers through her hair above and behind her ear. "No one heard us. And my household is incredibly discreet. I would trust them with your secret, but it is not mine to share."

"Thank you. For both those sentiments." She turned her head and pressed a kiss to his upper wrist. "It's too bad my bedchamber doesn't have a door to your dressing chamber."

"It is. However, your bedchamber is supposed to be for guests, and I would not want them barging into my bath. You, on the other hand, are more than welcome to join me whenever you like." He brought his thumb to her mouth and stroked her lower lip.

She licked the tip, and he drew in a breath. "Why have you been celibate since your wife died?"

He moved his thumb back to her hairline. "Why have you

been celibate since your last lover?" His mouth tipped into an adorable smirk, and she couldn't help but laugh.

"The question I expected was, 'why have you had a lover at all?'" She sobered. "If you don't want to answer me, you don't have to. I appreciate you letting me hold onto the things I'm not yet ready to discuss." His trust in her made her feel more important and special than she had in a very long time. Perhaps ever. The moment he'd learned her real identity, he'd continued to believe in her and to show her a profound understanding that shocked her—in the best way.

"I wasn't driven to take a lover," he replied. "I was focused on my marquessate and Lacey and Company."

She knew how hard he worked at both, and his dedication to his father-in-law's business was both surprising and inspiring. It was one of the many things she found so irresistible about him. "You are very involved with that, more than I would have thought from a man of your station."

"I know it's unusual and even derided by many." He held her gaze. "Do you find it odd?"

"Perhaps, but I understand why you've undertaken that level of involvement." Ellis positioned herself partly on top of him and rested her head on his chest. "I think I'm more surprised that Mr. Lacey has included you as a part-owner of the company."

Roman stroked her spine with his fingertips. "Truthfully, that shocked me too. I asked for that as part of the marriage settlement, thinking he would refuse or at least require me to wait some amount of time to see how—or if—I would actually participate. He gave me a very small holding when I married Clarissa, and it has increased annually."

"You could own even more in the future?" Ellis asked.

He nodded. "The maximum I will own is forty-five percent."

"I take it that was her dowry?"

"No, which is why it was so shocking. That was separate from her very generous dowry. Don't judge Josiah harshly, but he very much wanted Clarissa to marry into the peerage. He was willing to pay a good sum, and I was in need."

"Then she died," Ellis said softly, wondering what had happened to her and how deeply her death had affected him. She wasn't going to ask, though. Roman would tell her when he wanted to—or not. "Is that why Mr. and Mrs. Lacey hope you will marry Margot?"

"Yes." He paused, and his hand stilled. "You seemed upset upon learning that Margot and I were to become betrothed. Dare I hope you were jealous?"

Ellis turned her head and buried her smile into his chest, then she kissed him just below his nipple, drawing him to press his palm against her spine. She heard his breath catch.

"Not jealous, for I've no desire to wed, but I was—*I am*—attracted to you, and I had the impression you might feel the same." She feared she really had been jealous, for she had to admit that she was drawn to him in many ways that went beyond the physical.

Pushing that disquieting thought aside, she kissed him again, for longer, using her tongue to taste his flesh. He shivered, and she continued talking. "But then I wondered if I'd imagined that. I didn't think you would engage in a liaison with me whilst becoming betrothed to someone else. And if you did, well, my opinion of you would plummet."

He laughed, and the sound vibrated his chest beneath her. "Your impression was correct. I've been attracted to from the moment I realized you were a woman, and perhaps even slightly before that, much to my shock." She licked his nipple, and he moaned. "Something about you is devastatingly allur-ing." He traced his fingertip up her spine and grasped a lock of her hair, tugging on it gently. "It pains me greatly to think the next time I see you, this gorgeous mass will be hiding under that terrible wig."

She lifted her head. "My wig is terrible?"

"Only because it's not you. I hate it almost as much as the beard."

"You're not the only one." Ellis had so many questions for him—about his rakehell youth, about his wife, about when he would marry again. Surely he must, for he needed an heir.

She settled on one and met his gaze. His eyes looked like quicksilver in the light of the candles beside the bed. "Your marriage was not a love match, then?" A shadow passed over his expression, dimming its intensity. "My apologies. We were talking about the dowry, and I was only curious. Again, you need only tell me to mind my own business."

"It was not a love match," he said, surprising her. "What *is* your business exactly? Do you plan to be my secretary forever?" He ran his hand down her back, to the crease at the top of her backside. His palm skimmed to one cheek where he squeezed her gently.

Ellis brought her body up and straddled him, her sex covering his as she kept one hand on his chest. "Forever is a very long time. I'd like to remain your secretary for the foreseeable future, provided I can maintain my disguise. I confess I've been worried, since you found me out almost immediately, then Margot happened upon us."

"Then we must be careful, for I would very much like you to be my secretary for as long as you like. I'd also like you to be whatever this is." He gestured between them. "If you are amenable."

"Hmm, I'll have to consider that." She rotated her hips against him and felt his cock lengthen against her sex. "Perhaps you could persuade me of the benefits of—" she caressed his chest, then bent over him to kiss his neck, "—*this*." She dragged her tongue along his throat.

Roman pushed her hair back from her ear and grazed his teeth along the lobe. "Allow me to show you."

That is what he spent the rest of the night doing, and by the time she left at dawn, after brief snippets of sleep, Ellis returned to her chamber thoroughly convinced.

~

The following day, Roman couldn't stop smiling. Because he couldn't stop thinking of Ellis and spending most of the night in her arms. He'd been searching for an opportunity to kiss her all day, but none had arisen. Desperate, he'd suggested at one point that they close the door to the study.

She'd reminded him that it hadn't stopped Margot from walking right in and catching them together. Then she'd escaped upstairs to her chamber to work so he couldn't keep distracting her. He didn't know if he was flattered or offended. Nevertheless, after she departed, he was also able to focus on work, albeit begrudgingly.

The Laceys were due soon for the weekly acquisitions meeting. They were having it today instead of Thursday since Pritchard would be arriving tomorrow and they would be busy with him.

Roman went upstairs to the library to wait. Once there, he picked up one of the manuscripts Margot had sent him to read and sat in one of the chairs situated near the bookcases. Before he could finish the first page, Ellis walked in.

"There you are," she said, coming toward him. "I didn't realize you'd already come upstairs to the library."

He smiled at her, and Ellis noticed he did that more now. That made *her* want to smile. "You were looking for me?" He immediately stood and set the manuscript down on the now-vacant chair.

"Not particularly, but the Laceys will be here soon, so I was wondering where you'd gone."

"Well, now I'm disappointed," he said with a mock pout.

She schooled her features into a cool stare. "No flirting. It's hard enough to work so closely together in the study, which is why I felt compelled to leave."

He sighed. "I'm sure we were both able to accomplish more, lonely as it might have been. Since we have a few minutes before the Laceys will be here, let me show you something." He led her to the corner near the windows where a large potted palm stood.

Once there, he turned and noticed she hadn't followed him. "Aren't you coming?"

She narrowed her eyes at him. "Are you trying to maneuver me behind that palm so you can steal a kiss?"

"No, I'm going to show you something you likely haven't noticed. Humor me whilst we await the Laceys?"

"All right." She sounded as though she were granting him a large favor as she joined him. "What have I failed to notice in this corner?"

"Have you perused every book on the shelves?"

"I believe so," she replied.

"So you think." He arched his brow with a smirk as he crouched down and gestured to the books on the lowest shelf. "You've even investigated these?"

"They are crop treatises, if I remember correctly. I confess I passed right over them."

"Precisely what my father hoped." Roman tried to pull one of them out and couldn't. "They're not really books at all, you see." Then he pushed on the spine of the book at the end of the shelf. The fake books swung open, and Ellis gasped.

"A secret compartment?" she asked.

Roman nodded. "My father had it built into the bookcase so he could hide his naughty books."

She stared at him. "Naughty books?"

He pulled one forth and handed it to her. She gave him a dubious glance before flipping it open. Then she gasped again.

"My goodness, these are—" She rotated the book sideways, and Roman stood so he could see what she was looking at. It was a drawing of two people copulating in an unusual position. "The drawings are beautiful. Why do you hide them?"

He shrugged. "I suppose because they've always been there."

She cocked her head with an amused smile. "And when did you find this secret compartment of naughty books?"

"When I was twelve or thirteen, perhaps? I confess I perused them often when I was home from school."

"You were very naughty," she said with a bit of a scold in her tone that, surprisingly, contributed to his arousal.

"I wanted to be."

She laughed. "What a terrible rogue you were." She flipped the page, and the next drawing was of a woman performing oral sex on a man beneath a dining table. He was fully dressed, as was she, and he was drinking port with other gentlemen.

"Now that I've done," she said. "Not like that, of course. I can't imagine the other men at the table aren't aware there's a woman underneath pleasuring their host. Nor can I imagine the host could manage to keep himself collected, particularly when it came to climax. To do so would be a form of torture, would it not?"

When Roman had thought to show her the compartment and its contents, he hadn't considered they would have an in-depth discussion about any of the drawings. Consequently, he hadn't envisioned that he would sport a raging erection when his former in-laws arrived.

"Which part have you done exactly?" he cleared his throat because he suddenly sounded as though he'd swallowed sand.

"The same thing the woman is doing." Her gaze flicked to his groin. "Perhaps I'll demonstrate my skill later."

He groaned softly as he took the book from her and tucked it back onto the shelf, then closed the compartment. When he stood, he pulled her more firmly behind the palm and pressed her against the bookcase.

She looked up at him, her eyes smoldering. "Roman, you said you weren't maneuvering me behind the palm to steal a kiss."

"I hadn't entirely planned to, but you're the one who has me thinking of your mouth on my sex." Roman was going to be in bad shape by that evening. Hell, he was struggling to keep himself from carrying her to his bedchamber right now. "Just one kiss?" he begged.

Her lips were parted, and he could see she was breathing faster. She might not be as aroused as he was, but she was on her way.

"*One*," she said, her eyes narrowing with desire.

He clasped her face between his hands and claimed her mouth. How he wished she wasn't wearing the wig so he could run his fingers through her hair.

He held her tightly as he ravished her mouth. She clutched at his coat and pressed against him.

She pushed at his chest, breaking through his rapturous delirium. "I hear them coming," she said urgently as she took a step back.

He tipped his head down and worked to calm his galloping pulse as he wiped his hand over his mouth. He heard Ellis walk away but didn't look at her. He didn't dare.

But he needed to move out from behind the palm. Taking a long, deep breath, he walked quickly to stand behind a chair that would hide his erection.

Graham entered and announced the Laceys. They exchanged greetings and took their seats. Roman hesitated until their collective attention was not directed at him, then practically threw himself in the chair.

They began to discuss the manuscripts they'd received over the past fortnight. There was one that Margot was keen to discuss, so she launched into her analysis.

Finally, Roman's body had cooled, but he still didn't trust himself to look at Ellis.

"Mama, did you read that book?" Margot asked.

Roman glanced toward Harriet and saw that she was staring at Ellis.

Margot spoke again. "What about you, Papa?"

Josiah was also looking toward Ellis.

Roman turned his gaze to her to see what was drawing their attention. *Oh no.*

The beard on one side of her face, from the top of the sideburn down to her jaw, had fallen away. Did she not notice? She was busy writing notes.

At last, she raised her head, and her eyes met Roman's. He lifted his hand and touched the side of his face, his eyes rounding slightly before he allowed a faint grimace.

Her brow furrowed as she lifted her hand. Her eyes widened. She went pale.

Roman heard Margot gasp.

"I see your beard isn't real," Josiah said, studying her intently. "Why is that?"

Roman wiped his hand across his brow as his heart pounded.

Ellis clutched her pencil and notebook. Her face was a mask of fear and anxiety. Roman worried she might flee.

Josiah nodded as if he'd answered his own question. "I see it now." Roman held his breath, waiting for the man's outrage. "You seem very young. You must wear the beard so that you'll be taken more seriously, so people won't think you're too inexperienced."

Roman exhaled as relief poured through him. But it was exceedingly short-lived.

"No, no, that's not it." Harriet shook her head and then leaned forward, her gaze narrowed on Ellis. "Young, yes, but that's not the reason for the beard." She paused, and Roman once again couldn't breathe. "He's a...*woman.*"

There was no mistaking the horror that captured Ellis's features. And there was no denying that Harriet was correct.

CHAPTER 12

*E*llis was shaking as she tried to press the beard back to her face. It wouldn't stick. She was nearly out of the adhesive and hadn't used as much today in order to preserve what she had left.

Roman had probably dislodged it when he'd kissed her. She cursed her stupidity and weakness for allowing him to do so.

It took every fiber of her being not to jump up and flee the library—or perhaps the house. She was going to have to do that anyway. She could not continue in Roman's employ.

Mr. Lacey eyed Roman. "Did you know your secretary was a woman? Forgive me, but you don't seem surprised."

Roman sent Ellis a look of apology and sympathy. "I did know, and I acknowledge a female secretary is unacceptable to most people. However, she's extremely qualified, and I'm incredibly satisfied with her work. In fact, I would ask that you don't discount her because of her sex."

"Of course, I wouldn't," Mr. Lacey said, sounding slightly insulted, which surprised Ellis. His brow creased as he regarded Roman. "Surely you know me well enough to realize I wouldn't object to your hiring whoever you think is best for the position."

Roman blinked, appearing bewildered. "I do know that you are more forward-thinking than most gentlemen, however the topic of women working in clerical or secretarial positions hasn't ever come up in our conversation before. I suppose I didn't even think to talk to you about it."

"All you need do is see how much I've encouraged Margot to participate with Lacey and Company, and even Harriet." Mr. Lacey smiled at both his daughter and wife.

Now that Josiah pointed that out, Ellis could see how he would not be bothered by Ellis's position. She felt a great relief.

"I say she should just be herself." Mr. Lacey turned his gaze on Ellis. "And who is that exactly?"

Ellis's relief was short-lived as panic overcame that emotion. She wasn't going to tell them who she really was, of course. She glanced toward Roman, who also appeared tense. He watched her expectantly, clearly waiting for her to answer as she wished.

"I am Mrs. Daniel Ellis, a widow," she said far more calmly than she felt. "My husband left me without funds, and I don't have any family, so I needed to find employment. As you know, that's difficult for a woman unless she wants to go into domestic service, which I did not. I'm afraid my skills do not lie in that domain." She summoned a self-deprecating smirk to sell the lie, though in truth, she would not make a very good housemaid. "My husband was a clerk to a barrister. I learned many skills from him, and I had hoped to find that sort of work. However, I was unable to do so as myself, and so I disguised myself as a man, and Lord Keele was kind enough to hire me and allow me to prove myself."

"Which she has done beyond my expectations," Roman said firmly.

Ellis was incredibly grateful for his support. He continued to surprise her with how vehemently he supported her, even championed her. She'd had allies before —Min, Sheff, the duke, her friends—but she hadn't had a partner who not only saw her value but made sure others saw and appreciated it too. All of this kept her from completely losing control.

"Did you know she was a woman disguised as a man when you hired her?" Mrs. Lacey asked. Ellis couldn't tell how the woman felt, but she seemed less enthusiastically supportive than her husband. Then again, Ellis had observed that she was overall more reserved.

"I confess I did not at first," Roman replied. "However, I saw through her disguise relatively quickly. By then, I'd already decided she was too valuable to let go."

Ellis slid her attention to Margot, who'd been quiet through the entire exchange. She met Ellis's gaze and brightened.

"I think Mrs. Ellis is brilliant, and it would be wonderful to have another woman working at Lacey and Company, even though she doesn't actually work *for* Lacey and Company." Margot gave Ellis an encouraging smile. "I like working with her. And thank you, Papa, for giving me the chance to work with Lacey and Company. I can't think of any other fathers who would allow that."

Ellis couldn't either, and she found herself envying Margot Lacey. She had two wonderful, supportive parents. It was no wonder Roman had continued to maintain a close relationship with them after his wife's death. Especially since he didn't have parents of his own.

"I have no issue with Mrs. Ellis's employment," Mr. Lacey said. "In fact, it would be a shame if she were to leave. It's clear she's an exceptional secretary."

"Can she now dress as a woman and simply be Mrs. Ellis?" Margot asked, her brow creased with concern.

"I have no problem with that." Roman slid his attention toward Ellis, his eyes glittering with anticipation.

She could tell he was eager to see her dressed as a woman, and she could not deny the relief that coursed through her at the prospect of no longer having to dress as a man or wear this horrible hair on her face.

However, much as she wanted to dress as a woman, she needed to think about the consequences of doing so. The servants in the house would know she was a woman, and the more people who knew, the higher the risk that some member of the Henlow household would find her. She wasn't worried about facing any of them anymore—she'd already decided she wanted to see Min and Sheff soon. She never wanted to see the duchess again, but since it seemed she was not in London, that was not in danger of happening.

The problem with discovery now was that she was secretary to the Marquess of Keele, and she wasn't a widow. She was a young, unmarried woman, and her position in Roman's household would be viewed as scandalous. Whilst Ellis didn't care about her own reputation, she wouldn't allow this situation to reflect poorly on Roman, or on Min or Sheff if her identity as Min's former companion was revealed.

Ellis realized the others were watching her expectantly, and with kindness and encouragement. She felt surprisingly emotional. Why? Because, like Roman, they wanted her for who she was and what she could offer. "Thank you. I appreciate your support and understanding. I'll have to think about whether I want to give up my disguise." For now, she removed the rest of the beard as it was failing anyway.

"I do understand," Mrs. Lacey said sympathetically. "There will be people who are scandalized by Keele having a female secretary, especially since you live here. I confess I will need to become accustomed to the arrangement."

"But she's a widow," Mr. Lacey argued. "There's no need for her to protect her reputation."

"Not in the same way," Mrs. Lacey pointed out. "However, there will be some who think it's inappropriate, and Mrs. Ellis won't wish to be shunned."

Mrs. Lacey was right. If Ellis was going to be a woman, it might be best if she returned to the boarding house. The thought of leaving Roman's household made her surprisingly sad.

"I like that she lives here," Roman said. "We have a highly professional relationship, and that's all that should matter. Shall we return to business?"

Ellis was grateful to him putting an end to the conversation. They continued with the meeting, and Ellis tried not to think too much about what would happen next. But when the meeting concluded, her anxiety returned.

After the Laceys departed, she stood in front of her chair and put her head in her hands.

Roman came to her and tried to wrap his arms around her. She backed away from his embrace. "You can't do that." She glanced nervously toward the open door of the library. "I need to go to my chamber. I can't have Graham or anyone else seeing me without my beard—not until I determine what to do."

Roman took her forearms and turned her so that her back was to the door. "Now no one can see you if they come in, all right?"

Giving her a caring smile, he clasped her hands and massaged the backs with his thumbs. "Don't fret, Ellis. All will be well. You saw how the Laceys reacted, and I've told you my retainers are discreet. They will not share your secret. Besides, the Widow Ellis story is a good one."

"I shouldn't have used the name Ellis when I came here. If the Laceys or one of your servants mentions the name 'Mrs. Ellis' in reference to your secretary, who happens to *lodge* here, that might draw someone's attention. And if they share that I have blonde hair, it would be easy to make the connection that I am Ellis Dangerfield, former companion to Lady Minerva Halifax. Now, Lady Minerva Pierce."

"Who would know any of these things?" Roman asked with a slight chuckle.

"*You* put it all together," Ellis replied, and Roman grimaced faintly. She took her hands from his and clasped them in front of her. "Presumably, the employees at Lacey and Company will also come to know who I am, as well as those working at the New Bond Street library. The circle grows wider, and so does the risk of my being found."

"What if you continue to wear a wig over your blonde hair?" Roman suggested. "You could be a brunette."

Ellis blinked. "That's a good idea. I don't have one, however."

"Then we'll procure one," he said.

"I also need my clothes from the boarding house."

"We'll go there too."

"And what about the servants?" she asked. "You're just going to tell them I'm a woman?"

"Leave it to me." He held her gaze and looked quite serious. "You said you trusted me."

"I do." The tightness in her chest loosened. Her fear and anxiety diminished, and it was all because of the man in front of her. He'd done so much to give her a safe place. That was it—she felt safe here. With him. She'd never experienced that before.

"This will work," he assured her. "I promise. Now, let's be on our way. I find I'm most eager to see you in feminine clothing."

She shook her head but smiled, for she couldn't completely contain the emotion inside her. "Thank you for supporting me and giving me the security I need right now. Let me reapply the beard one last time before we depart."

"Just one moment," he said before lowering his head and briefly kissing her bare cheek. "I couldn't resist."

"Please go make sure there's no one lingering outside the library and that I can make my way to my chamber without being seen."

"I shall be your lookout," he said with a charming, flirtatious grin that suffused her with an almost absurd joy.

He went to the door and turned his head toward her bedchamber. Then he glanced back and waved her toward him. "It's clear."

She hastened from the room, and as she passed him, he whispered, "I will miss your backside in those breeches, however."

Ellis looked at him over her shoulder. "Who says I'll never wear them again?"

His sensual stare chased her as she dashed to her bedchamber.

~

After they returned from fetching Ellis's clothing and purchasing a very attractive dark brown wig for her to wear, Roman asked Graham to assemble the servants downstairs.

Arriving in the kitchen, Roman inhaled deeply. The cook, Mrs. Long, and the maid, Patience, were clearly in the middle of preparing dinner. "My apologies for interrupting you at this time of day." He fixed his gaze on the cook in particular. "I promise I'll be quick."

Mrs. Long nodded in appreciation.

"I need to tell you something about my secretary," Roman said. "Mr. Ellis is not actually a mister. He is, in fact, Mrs. Ellis, a widow. She disguised her sex because it's unusual for a woman to be hired as a secretary."

Mrs. Long appeared surprised. "It's unheard of."

"For the most part, yes," Roman agreed. "However, Mrs. Ellis is the best secretary I've ever employed, and I don't wish to lose her. Starting this evening, she will be dressing as herself—Mrs. Ellis—and you will address her as such. She will also be taking meals with me in the dining room.

"The Laceys are aware of her true identity, but I would ask that you not go about sharing the fact that I have a female secretary. There are people who will be scandalized, and I'd just as soon avoid that if possible."

"That is perfectly understandable, my lord," Graham said.

Mrs. Long glanced toward the stove. "I need to return to cooking dinner."

"Of course. Thank you, everyone, for your loyalty and discretion." Roman went back upstairs.

He was aware Graham had followed him, and when they reached the ground floor, Roman turned to face the butler. "Is there something else?"

Graham was rarely flustered, but his expression creased and he hesitated the barest moment before speaking. "I wondered if there was anything more you might like to share about Mrs. Ellis." He seemed to be referring to something in particular, and Roman wondered if Graham suspected their liaison.

"Were you already aware that my secretary was a woman?" Roman asked.

"I might have suspected, my lord."

Roman inclined his head. "Well, I have nothing to share, and I expect you to quash gossip of any kind. Is that understood?"

"Quite." Graham hesitated again, but Roman could see he wanted to add more. "May I just say, my lord, that it is very nice to see you smiling more."

Roman wasn't sure what to make of that. He'd been inordinately happy today after last night's activities with Ellis, and he supposed his mood had lightened greatly in the time she'd been there. He was glad that his butler was aware of his mood and disappointed—in himself—that anyone in his household might worry about him. "Thank you, Graham. I appreciate your concern." He smiled at the butler before going upstairs.

Roman went directly to Ellis's chamber to tell her she could join him for dinner, and every other meal, and that the servants were now aware of her secret. He knocked on the door, and when she opened it, his jaw dropped.

She wore a rather simple ivory day gown, but the style—with the very high waistline—accentuated her bosom to great effect. The gown, as opposed to her menswear, made her seem somehow taller, and though the sleeves were long, he appreciated seeing the shape of her arms. How she'd ever managed to pass as a man was astonishing.

She took his breath away.

Roman stepped inside and closed the door.

Ellis gently frowned at him. "This is incredibly inappropriate now that the entire household knows I'm a woman—assuming you told them."

"I did, but I don't care about that for a moment." He continued to stare at her. "Let me just look at you."

She hadn't yet donned the wig, and her blonde hair was still pinned to her head from wearing the men's wig. The elegant column of her throat begged for his kisses, but he restrained himself.

"You are even more beautiful than I imagined," he breathed. His body roared right back into full arousal.

"In this plain gown?" She arched a brow at him. "You've seen me in nothing at all."

"Don't remind me," he groaned.

Her gaze flicked to his cock again, and he resolved right then that he'd need to frig himself before they left, else he'd be in misery for the remainder of the day.

"You appear to be in need of some…help," she noted. She took his hand and led him to the cushioned bench at the foot of her bed. Pushing him down, she carefully knelt before him, adjusting her gown so it pooled around her.

Roman's pulse thrummed in his ears. He wanted to tell her she needn't go to the trouble, but he couldn't form any words as she unbuttoned his fall.

"I will take your silence as consent," she said, slipping her hand into his pantaloons and finding his sex.

Rather than close his eyes as he was tempted to do, he focused on her as she pulled his cock free. She looked up at him, and their eyes met.

"I consent," he rasped, his voice dark and desperate. "With absolute vigor and demand."

She gave him a small, thoroughly wicked smile before she licked the head of his shaft. Roman grunted loudly, then swore quietly. This was not the middle of the night. He could not make such noise.

"Yes, do be quiet," she commanded just before she took him into her mouth.

Sensations he'd never known thundered through him. He lifted his hips toward her, silently begging for more. He watched her movements—the way her hand cupped him, then stroked his flesh, the bob of her head and the flick of her tongue.

Roman worried he wouldn't last long, but damn, he never wanted this to end. She sucked him with a delicious rhythm as he arced into her mouth, his hips coming off the bench with each thrust. He worked to keep control, lest he mindlessly lose himself.

She slipped her other hand into his pantaloons and when he next rose, she caressed his backside, squeezing his flesh. Blood rushed to his cock, and he couldn't help moving faster. She brought her hand around and cupped his balls.

"Ellis, I'm going to come."

Her response was to gently squeeze him and suck him harder as her mouth moved over him with increasing fervor, taking him deeper toward her throat. Ecstasy exploded inside him, and he clamped his jaw closed to keep from shouting. Throwing his head back and closing his eyes, he clutched her head as he climaxed spectacularly.

Roman succumbed to the most blissful darkness as wave after wave of pleasure washed through him. He'd never known such completion, such absolute joy.

Gradually, he slowed, and she finally took her mouth from him. He tipped his head forward, panting as he worked to catch his breath. "Good God, Ellis."

She wiped her mouth in a thoroughly ladylike fashion, as if she'd just finished eating a biscuit, then rose. "Better?"

"Never more." He could hardly think straight. She went to her dressing table and pulled the wig onto her head. At length, Roman came to his senses and refastened his fall. "What about you?"

"What about me?" she asked as she pinned the wig to her hair.

"That was very one-sided," he said.

"Was it?" She glanced at him over her shoulder, her gaze sultry. "I enjoyed that immensely."

He stifled a moan, for she was going to arouse him again. "You can't know how that thrills me. However, I consider myself in your debt, and I plan to repay it in full, with interest."

"I eagerly anticipate that. In the meantime, we should be on our way shortly, shouldn't we?"

He stood. "I suppose so." He was already devising plans of what he would do to her that evening. He could hardly wait.

Now that his head was clearing, he realized he hadn't communicated what he'd meant to—his entire reason for coming to her chamber. "I've spoken to the servants, and they've promised their discretion." He didn't mention Graham suspecting their affair. "I've also informed them that you will be dining with me from now on. At least, I hope you will." He gave her a courtly bow. "Miss Dangerfield, will you do me the honor of accompanying me to dinner this evening?"

She laughed softly. "Yes. But don't call me Miss Danger-field, not even in private. I am Mrs. Ellis."

He nodded. "I will do as you command."

"Now go and wait for me downstairs." She waved him toward the door. "I need to don my stockings and boots and fetch my pelisse and accessories."

"If I must," he replied with a sigh. He grinned as he left the room, then went to fetch his hat and gloves.

It occurred to him that he hadn't been this happy in years. Perhaps he'd *never* been this happy. Certainly not with Clarissa, though he'd hoped to be.

Thinking of her and her betrayal brought a moment of sobriety. Roman would do well to recall his personal vow never to allow himself to be vulnerable again. With the exception of the surviving Laceys, everyone in his life had hurt or abandoned him.

Perhaps Ellis would be different. Except they had no future together. She did not wish to marry, and she was not the sort of wife he needed. She had no fortune and not even any family connections, as far as he knew. Yes, the Duke of Henlow had provided her a recommendation for employment, but it wasn't as if he'd given her money outright.

Roman's good mood was in danger of disappearing completely. Perhaps Ellis *wouldn't* be different. She was harboring secrets, just as Clarissa had. He supposed the difference was that Ellis clearly acknowledged she was withholding things from him and had indicated she may share them at some point.

Wincing inwardly, he entered his chamber and found his hat and gloves. He wanted to recapture his joy of a few minutes ago and stop thinking of obstacles to his current situation, which brought him much-needed happiness.

There was nothing wrong with enjoying this affair with Ellis for as long as it would last. He deserved that much, didn't he?

CHAPTER 13

*E*llis regarded herself in the mirror as she donned her gloves. The dark brown wig was an improvement over the men's wig and facial hair, but Ellis missed her own hair. She looked forward to the day when she could be fully herself again.

How quickly that had changed. When she'd started working for Roman, she'd been happy *not* to be herself.

In her haste to leave the Duchess of Henlow's house, Ellis had brought just two gowns that would be considered appropriate for evening events. She'd donned one of them this evening, a pale blue gown from two years ago with ivory ribbon stitched at the hem and the waist.

Roman's maid, Patience, had offered to assist Ellis with dressing if she needed it. However, Ellis had only taken clothing from her old life that she could manage herself, which, admittedly, comprised most of her wardrobe.

Her allowance for clothing had been minimal, especially when compared with Min, of course, and she'd never been permitted to have anything that was too fashionable. Per the duchess, only the plainest and utilitarian garments would do. No one would care or even note if Ellis wore the same dress multiple times in a Season or over multiple Seasons.

Occasionally, Min's maid had helped Ellis don a ballgown or style her hair. Although "ballgown" was an exaggeration, for Ellis's evening wear was nothing like what other young women wore. Her garments were made of the least expensive materials possible and sported little or no ornamentation. Min fought for her to have more impressive clothing, but Ellis had never particularly cared.

Still, Min often made sure Ellis's costumes were decorated with extra ribbons, like the gown she wore tonight, or flounces, and that she had jewelry to wear. Indeed, every piece of jewelry that belonged to Ellis had been gifted to her by Min. And Ellis hadn't brought a single one with her when she left the household. She now felt regret, for Min must have been upset—and she'd every right to feel that way. Ellis's only defense was that she'd been more distraught than she'd ever been in her life, and she hadn't been thinking clearly. She'd just wanted to leave as quickly as possible.

Gloves in place, Ellis plucked her reticule and cloak from the bed, then made her way downstairs where Roman was waiting. It would just be the two of them traveling to Marylebone for dinner since Oliver Pritchard had not accepted Roman's invitation to stay whilst he was in London. Instead, he would be visiting his uncle, a barrister who resided in Bloomsbury.

Since Mr. Pritchard wasn't staying here, the Laceys had offered to host dinner tonight, which Roman had eagerly agreed to. He didn't like to entertain.

Ellis was relieved Mr. Pritchard was staying elsewhere. For now, she and Roman didn't have to worry about the librarian being in the same house with them whilst they tried to conduct a secret affair. At least she hoped it remained secret. She couldn't tell if anyone in the household suspected the intimacy between her and Roman.

Whilst she tried to keep their interactions purely professional and respectable, Roman sometimes couldn't help his reactions to her, namely every time he saw her dressed in something that wasn't men's clothing. He reacted with giddy excitement, and though it was very sweet, she worried someone would notice.

He waited for her at the bottom of the stairs and behaved as she expected. His eyes were bright with admiration and anticipation as he swept her with an approving perusal.

"Beautiful." He spoke softly, for Graham was surely in the entrance hall waiting to open the door for their departure.

"Thank you," she replied. "Would you mind helping me with my cloak?" she asked, handing it to him.

"I would be delighted." He held the garment for her and wrapped it around her shoulders. She fastened it at her throat.

"Let us depart," he said.

She did not take his arm as she preceded him into the entrance hall. They were employer and employee as far as anyone else was concerned. Outside, Roman helped her into the coach, and they were shortly on their way to Marylebone.

"Have I told you how relieved I am that Pritchard isn't staying with us?" Roman said from beside her. They now shared a seat when traveling in the coach.

"Yes, you might have mentioned that." The edge of her mouth ticked up sardonically in an almost-smirk. "Although without him staying with us, you'll need to find a way to speak with him regarding Margot."

"That's true," Roman said. "I will pull him aside this evening and discuss our plans to walk in the park tomorrow after the meeting at the New Bond Street library. You will serve as chaperone, which they may balk at."

"They may, but I'm afraid we must insist. And yes, I'm aware of how hypocritical this is given our…activities and the fact that I am not actually a widow. However, I'm willing to engage in a bit of deception to protect Margot's reputation. Hopefully, she will soon wed the man she loves, and it will all have been worth it."

Ellis truly hoped this would all work out for Margot. Whilst Ellis didn't necessarily believe in happily ever after, at least not for her, she was wholly in favor of it for others, especially her friends.

Roman tipped his head toward Ellis and nuzzled her cheek.

"What are you doing?" she asked with a smile.

"Basking in your lovely scent. Have I also mentioned how exceedingly glad I am that you now smell like a woman?"

She laughed. "Keep your hands to yourself until later. I don't want you dislodging my wig as you did with the beard."

"Yes, Mrs. Ellis." He clasped his hands in his lap and sat straight, smiling.

Ellis reached over and took one of his hands. "This is acceptable."

He gave her a squeeze. "I'll take what I can get."

They soon arrived at the Laceys' palatial home. Ellis stared at the imposing wide facade. It seemed even larger than the Duke of Henlow's house in Grosvenor Square.

"Their house is spectacular," she whispered. She could only imagine the size of the dowry Roman had received when he married their daughter. Ellis's curiosity was great, but she wasn't going to ask.

"Lacey has done very well for himself," Roman said as they walked toward the door. "In addition to his business interests, he's made keen investments. He could not be more different from my father."

Ellis understood why he was especially close to Josiah Lacey. Roman had even indicated Mr. Lacey was the father he wished he'd had.

The butler greeted them whilst a footman took their accessories. Ellis tried not to gape at the awe-inspiring entrance hall with its soaring ceiling and gleaming marble floor.

"This way," the butler said as he led them up to the drawing room, where Mr. and Mrs. Lacey were waiting. Mr. Pritchard was already there. He stood with Mr. Lacey, whilst Mrs. Lacey was seated.

Again, Ellis tried not to stare at the incredibly large and elegantly appointed room. It spanned the front of the house and clearly adjoined another, likely similarly-sized room at the back. The paintings and décor were astonishing, and the number of seating areas exceeded those at Henlow House by one. It could not, however, compare with the large drawing room—not to be confused with the small or family drawing rooms—at Beacon Park, the Duke of Henlow's country estate.

In her survey of the room, Ellis noted Margot was not yet present. She and Roman exchanged greetings with their hosts and Mr. Pritchard, who was the same age as Ellis. He was affable and handsome in a wholesome way. He had dark red hair and warm, golden-brown eyes to accompany his cheerful demeanor.

Sweeping into the drawing room in a beautiful gown of pink silk decorated with several flounces at the hem and ribbon along the neckline and at the edges of her puffed sleeves, Margot greeted everyone with a smile. She wore a beautiful pearl necklace with matching earbobs, and her hair was intricately styled and adorned with a pearl comb shaped like a flower.

Her smile widened slightly as her gaze landed on Mr. Pritchard. Right away, Ellis saw the love Margot felt for him. It was the way Persey looked at Wellesbourne, Tamsin looked at Droxford, Gwen looked at Somerton, and Jo looked at Sheff. Ellis *hoped* it was the way Min looked at her new husband, Evan. That Ellis hadn't witnessed that with her own eyes made her feel terrible.

Deep emotion pulled at her throat for a moment as Mr. Lacey introduced Mr. Pritchard to his daughter. The two made a good show of pretending to meet for the first time.

Right away, Roman and Mr. Lacey began to talk about the New Bond Street library and the meeting tomorrow with Mr. Inman. Margot joined in the conversation eagerly. Ellis, however, was drawn to a portrait hanging to the left of the magnificent marble fireplace. A similar portrait hung on the right, and Ellis recognized the subject as Margot. She deduced the one on the left to be Clarissa, Roman's wife. She'd never realized he did not have a portrait of her at his house, at least not that she'd seen.

Ellis studied the likeness of the woman Roman had married. She had lighter hair than Margot and a longer face. Her brows were thinner and more arched, her features more aquiline and delicate. She looked a bit like a doll. Something about her provoked a cold sensation in Ellis. Perhaps it was just that the poor woman was deceased.

Mrs. Lacey came up beside Ellis. "That's Clarissa."

"She was very pretty," Ellis said.

Nodding, Mrs. Lacey contemplated the image of her daughter with a sad smile. "Clarissa was a wonderful young woman, so kind and caring. She was very accomplished at the pianoforte and a wonderful singer. Our daughter was also an excellent watercolorist. That is one of her works over there." She gestured to the opposite wall at a painting of what appeared to be Hyde Park.

Ellis admired the watercolor. "It's lovely. She sounds very talented."

"There was almost nothing she couldn't learn to do," Mrs. Lacey said with pride. "All her tutors raved about her talent. She was so eager to try things—and to master them," Mrs. Lacey added with a chuckle.

"Did she also enjoy reading, like Margot?" Ellis asked.

"Yes, though not as much. Clarissa preferred to share her talents, which was why she was so gifted with music and painting."

Ellis sensed Mrs. Lacey's lingering sadness and imagined she would always feel that way. "It must be terribly difficult to lose a child. I'm so sorry."

"It is," Mrs. Lacey agreed. "But we carry on. And we have Margot." Her gaze moved to her surviving daughter, and again she smiled, but with more warmth this time.

The butler entered and announced that it was time for dinner. Roman quickly moved to offer Ellis his arm so Mr. Pritchard could escort Margot. She sent Roman a look of gratitude.

Dinner passed pleasantly, with Margot and Mr. Pritchard doing very well with their roles as brand-new acquaintances. Indeed, Ellis had the impression they were enjoying pretending not to know one another.

Still, there were several moments when Ellis had to quash a smile or a chuckle as she caught them stealing looks at one another. They would have to announce their desire to court soon, because if the Laceys were astute at all, they would notice the two of them had already formed a tendre.

Aware of Roman seated beside her, Ellis wondered if anyone deduced the connection between them. Hopefully not. She worked very hard not to pay too much attention to him when they were around other people.

It was difficult, for she was incredibly drawn to him. Whenever he was near, her body hummed with delight and want. And she was just happy to be in his presence. She enjoyed working and conversing with him.

After seeing Clarissa's portrait and speaking to Mrs. Lacey about her, Ellis wanted to question him about his marriage. However, she sensed there were things about Clarissa that he didn't wish to discuss, which meant Ellis shouldn't speak to him at all about her. They'd agreed to keep their secrets secret, but she began to wonder if she didn't want to share her secrets with him.

He wouldn't think less of her if he learned she was illegitimate, would he? Since she couldn't answer that definitively, she decided she wasn't yet ready to tell him.

She glanced toward him again and saw that he was watching her. His gaze held a hungry glint, despite the fact they'd just finished the final course. She narrowed her eyes at him slightly, trying to communicate that he needed to stop looking at her as if she were a cake in need of being devoured.

Roman picked up his wineglass and gestured toward her in a subtle toast. She shook her head almost imperceptibly. He was incorrigible.

And she didn't want him any other way.

～

The following afternoon, they—Roman, Ellis, all three Laceys, Mr. Inman, and Mr. Pritchard—met at the Lacey and Company subscription library on New Bond Street. They gathered in Mr. Inman's office and discussed Mr. Pritchard's new role as well as his transition from Oxford to London.

They needed to find a suitable replacement for Pritchard at the Oxford branch, and though Roman had a few people in mind, he had not yet decided. In fact, he wanted to travel to a few of their other branches to interview potential replacements. After London, Oxford was perhaps their largest branch, and he preferred to promote another of their librarians currently working at a smaller branch.

They'd taken a break so that Inman could show Pritchard the library, and Harriet wanted to make tea. Margot had joined them on her way to speak with one of the clerks about a new title from Lacey and Company that was not being borrowed as much as she'd anticipated. She was hoping to gain some insight into what they could do to encourage readers to read it.

Josiah had remained in order to review some papers Inman had in his office. He was engrossed in his task several feet away from where Roman and Ellis sat, their chairs next to one another.

Ellis leaned toward him and spoke softly. "Which libraries do you plan to travel to?"

Roman leaned in her direction as well. "Hoping to come with me?" he whispered.

"I actually would be interested in visiting another branch. In fact, I find the position of librarian to be intriguing." She glanced at Josiah. "I wonder if Lacey and Company would ever hire a woman to be a librarian. It seems a reasonable occupation that I could actually do as a woman without raising too many eyebrows."

He gave her a rueful smile. "That is true. Given that Josiah has no issue with you as my secretary and indeed believes you are quite brilliant, I would say the chances of Lacey and Company hiring a female librarian, namely you, are great."

Roman didn't want her to leave London. But she was just musing or perhaps flirting. Or both. "Perhaps you *should* come with me," he suggested.

She cocked her head. "Why don't you have a branch in Bath?"

"We have been interested in opening one there, but we've yet to find an acceptable location. Perhaps I will add Bath to my travels and search again. I believe we're ready for an expansion soon."

"Keele," Josiah called from across the room. "I've found some paperwork that I believe your former secretary left here at the library. Inman set it aside for me to review today. This is his handwriting, isn't it?" He held up a piece of parchment with a rather uneven scrawl.

Roman grimaced. "Yes, that's his abominable handwriting. His samples before I hired him were so much neater." He looked over at Ellis, who'd heard many things about Roman's former secretary, including the fact that he'd overrepresented his skills.

"I'm so pleased you found Mrs. Ellis," Josiah said with a shake of his head. "The last one was incredibly inept."

Roman noted Ellis's quiet pride. He was very glad he'd hired her—for so many reasons.

Harriet returned with the tea tray along with Mr. Inman. "Who would like tea?"

"I would," Inman replied with a smile. "Thank you, Mrs. Lacey."

Ellis leaned toward Roman. "Where are Margot and Mr. Pritchard?"

"Hopefully right behind Inman," Roman said. He hoped they hadn't done anything foolish.

"Here's a file marked Oxford," Josiah said. "I suppose I should have a look at this since Pritchard is here." He pulled out a piece of paper, his brow creasing. "What's this? 'My dearest Margot—'" He stopped reading abruptly.

Roman tensed. He cast a sideways glance toward Ellis, and their eyes met. She appeared to be just as concerned. They returned their attention to Josiah, whose face was turning a rather mottled red. Roman could count the number of times he'd seen the man angry, and it certainly seemed as though this was one of them.

Josiah looked about the room and stood, clutching the single piece of parchment whilst the folder fell to the floor. "Where is Margot, and *where is Pritchard?*"

"What's wrong, dear?" Harriet asked with alarm.

"This bloody letter is wrong!"

Harriet's hand fluttered to her chest. "What is it?"

Josiah thrust the parchment at her. "Read for yourself."

Roman jumped to his feet. Ellis followed, setting her notebook down in her chair.

"We'll go find them," Roman offered, although he feared it was too late to save them from exposure. How had a letter to Margot, presumably from Pritchard, found its way into a file? Clearly, his idiot former secretary had misfiled it, and now Margot would pay the price.

Harriet's gasp filled the room as she clapped her hand to her mouth. She handed the letter back to her husband, her face pale. "You must find them."

"I'll just step out and see if I can locate them," Inman said, his face flushed. He undoubtedly wanted to be anywhere other than his office right now.

A search mission wasn't needed, however, for Inman passed Margot on his way out. She sailed into the office, her features bright and happy, her eyes full of unmistakable ardor. Indeed, her lips were dark pink and slightly puffy, as if she'd been kissing. She glanced about the room and quickly ascertained that something was wrong. Her joyful expression faded, and wariness darkened her gaze.

Josiah handed the letter to his daughter. "Explain this. Where is Pritchard?"

Margot looked down at the parchment, then inhaled sharply. "Papa, I *can* explain—"

"I'm sure you bloody well can, but your behavior is inappropriate at best, and thoroughly ruinous at worst. I can see from the date on this letter that you and Pritchard have been carrying on for months!"

"It's not like that, Papa. We've only met in person once before."

"You've met before?" Harriet asked, aghast.

Margot snapped her attention to her mother. "Just once, Mama, but we've been writing to one another for nearly a year. I had written to him about a library matter, and, well, we began corresponding. We have much in common, and we fell in love."

"That can't be," Josiah said angrily.

Roman stepped forward with a soothing smile. "Let's take a moment. I'm sure you can understand that neither Margot nor Pritchard expected this to happen."

"But they've met before now, and they've lied to us," Harriet said.

Josiah fixed his furious gaze on Roman. "Did you know about this?"

Roman froze.

"Yes, Papa, he knew," Margot said. "I told him because I didn't want to marry him. I explained I was already in love with Oliver."

Pritchard entered just then. His features were taut, indicating he'd heard some of what was being said as he approached the office. Or perhaps Inman had warned him.

Instead of shrinking away or prostrating himself, he went to Margot's side and stood tall as he addressed Josiah.

"Sir, I should have come to you long ago," Pritchard began in a strong, clear tone. "Margot and I were waiting for the right time to tell you about our love. It was my understanding you had hoped she would wed another." He glanced toward Roman. "I'd hoped to find a way to prove myself to you, and I believed this opportunity in London would allow me to do so. It's true we were not honest with you, and I regret that. We pretended to meet for the first time just last evening and planned to court so you could see the depth of our care for one another, but that was wrong of us. We should have been honest from the start. Let me do that now.

"I love Margot with all my heart. As you know, I come from a good family. I work very hard, and I think you'll agree I have a bright future. I will take excellent care of your daughter."

Margot's features softened with happiness as she beamed at Pritchard.

Harriet blinked and sniffed. "They're in love, Josiah."

"We are," Margot said firmly. She looked her father in the eye. "And I want to choose my husband, unlike Clarissa. She didn't get to choose, and she wasn't happy."

The room fell silent. Josiah's color faded so that he almost appeared pale now. Roman grew agitated. How much did Margot know? Clarissa hadn't been happy—with Roman. Presumably, she'd been quite delighted with her paramour. But as soon as Roman had learned of her affair and insisted she end it, she'd sunk into depression until she'd become ill and, eventually, the laudanum had claimed her. Had she expressed her unhappiness to her sister? Roman wasn't sure he wanted to know.

Harriet touched her husband's arm. "Margot is right. We

pushed Clarissa, and you see what happened. She was unhappy, and she became ill. Then she…well, she's not here, is she? We can't make the same mistake twice. We must support Margot. Mr. Pritchard has made an excellent case for himself, hasn't he?"

"He has," Josiah said gruffly. "But he's not a member of Society."

"I could be," Pritchard said. "My grandfather is a baron, and I've already received an invitation to join a club."

"Have you?" Josiah asked with surprise, his brows arching.

Roman knew it was the Phoenix Club, for he'd recommended Pritchard for membership. He thought it would be the perfect way for the young man to establish connections and meet people in London. Roman knew the owner of the club, Lord Lucien, and was pleased when he'd informed Roman that he planned to extend the invitation.

"Does this mean we can marry, Papa?" Margot asked hopefully. "I'm very sorry we lied. You and Mama were so hopeful Keele and I would marry, and the truth is neither of us wants that." She glanced toward Roman, and he gave her a slight nod. "You must realize we are almost like siblings."

Harriet sent both Roman and Margot an apologetic look. "We should have thought of that."

There was a long moment of silence before Josiah voiced his decision. "Yes, I consent to your marriage."

Margot squealed with delight, then hugged her father fiercely. "Thank you, Papa. You've made me so happy." She turned and embraced her mother whilst Pritchard shook Josiah's hand.

Josiah seemed a little perturbed, but there was also relief in his features. The four of them spoke for a few moments. Roman glanced toward Ellis, who arched her brows before turning toward her chair.

Josiah left his wife, daughter, and future son-in-law and

joined Roman, his features grim. "I hope you're not terribly disappointed. We'd all hoped that you and Margot would make a match."

"Margot spoke the truth. We didn't really want to marry. I didn't say anything because I was hoping things might change. But we really do have a rather sibling-like relationship." Roman gave Josiah a regretful smile. "I want her to be happy, and I'm glad she will be, especially with someone who is such a vital asset to Lacey and Company. I see this as a smart move for everyone."

Josiah chuckled. "Of course, you would find the benefit to Lacey and Company in this, but I still feel beholden to you and your future." He sobered. "You must marry, for you need an heir. I know you dislike the Marriage Mart, so marrying Margot was an excellent solution for everyone." He exhaled. "Alas, we'll need to find someone else—someone suitable, with connections and perhaps a decent-sized dowry. Let me help you if I can, please."

Roman was distinctly uncomfortable having this conversation when Ellis could almost certainly overhear them. It felt wrong to be discussing his future marriage, which wouldn't be happening anytime soon, in front of his current lover.

"I appreciate the offer," Roman said. "I'm not in a hurry, but I appreciate your support."

"We'll get you settled, my boy," Josiah said, clapping him on the shoulder. "I mean that. I think of you as my boy."

Josiah returned to the happy couple, and Roman blew out a long breath in an effort to relieve the tension of the last several minutes. He moved his attention to Ellis seated in her chair. She was writing more notes in her book.

Perhaps she hadn't overheard what they were saying. Either way, Roman wasn't going to mention it.

He sat down and leaned toward her. "Well, that wasn't

how any of that was supposed to go. So much for our plans for their secret courtship."

Ellis looked over at him and smiled. "Life often doesn't adhere to our plans, does it?"

Roman felt certain she was referring to her own life, and he had to agree that his hadn't traveled the path he'd planned. If it had, he would be happily wed to Clarissa and hopefully a father.

Instead, he found himself alone once more, abandoned by Clarissa, whom he'd cared for, at least initially. His focus settled on Ellis a moment, though she'd gone back to her notebook. He cared for her too, he realized.

And someday she would also leave him.

CHAPTER 14

*L*ate that night, Ellis sat at her dressing table, brushing her hair. Her gaze was unfocused as she contemplated the many things swirling in her mind. Whilst they'd been at the library that afternoon, a note had been delivered from Jo—via Pandora since Jo did not know where Ellis was living. And Pandora had been kind enough to ensure that it was delivered by someone from Wellesbourne House who was not wearing livery.

Jo had set up a meeting tomorrow with her and Ellis's father, Rowland Harker, at his home in Bloomsbury. Ellis ought to have been excited, or at least nervous, but she couldn't stop thinking about what she'd overheard Mr. Lacey saying to Roman after he'd given his consent for Margot to wed Mr. Pritchard. *You must marry, for you need an heir. We'll need to find someone else—someone suitable, with connections and perhaps a decent-sized dowry.*

Ellis had known from the beginning that her affair with Roman was temporary, that she was indulging her desire to…be desired. Besides, she didn't even want to marry. But hearing Mr. Lacey describe Roman's need for a wife and the inevitability of his marriage had struck her in a way she hadn't expected.

Roman *needed* an heir, and to have one, he required a marchioness—and not one like her. Ellis did not have a fortune, and she was no one. She was worse than no one; she was illegitimate. There would be no benefit to him in their marriage, and that was what he needed. In fact, marriage to her could be a liability.

A soft knock on the door jolted her. She blinked and set her brush down, turning as Roman walked in. Like her, he wore his dressing gown. He smiled at her after closing the door. "There you are. I've been expecting you."

"Perhaps I wanted you to come here for once," she said coyly, trying to improve her mood. She didn't want to be sad about losing Roman. She wanted to enjoy the time they had together.

"I don't mind coming here," he said. "I'll go wherever you are."

His words were bittersweet because of what she'd overheard today, reminding her that this would end. There would come a time when he would *not* go where she was ever again.

She pushed those thoughts from her mind and pivoted back so she was facing the mirror instead of Roman. "I hate to ask for more time away, but I need to go on an errand tomorrow afternoon for personal reasons. Please don't ask me what it is and don't offer to accompany me."

"Of course. Take whatever time you need." He moved toward her, which she could see in the mirror. "Do you require transportation?"

Ellis shook her head. "I'll be with Jo."

Roman stopped behind her chair. "That's good to hear. Will she fetch you from here?"

"No, she doesn't know I live and work here. She'll pick

me up at Green Park across from Devonshire House." She met his gaze in the mirror. "And you don't need to walk me there."

"All right." He sounded disappointed and perhaps a trifle defeated.

She didn't want him to think she wasn't appreciative of his concern. "Thank you for understanding—I'm grateful for your support. And your trust. I know it's difficult for you not to press me for answers."

He held his hands over her shoulders. "May I?" At her answering nod, he massaged her gently. She closed her eyes and sighed, appreciating his touch.

After a moment, Roman made a tsking sound. "I still can't quite believe how things unfolded this afternoon with Margot and Pritchard. If not for my inept former secretary, our plan would have worked."

Ellis opened her eyes. "I would say the end result was what they'd hoped for, even if getting there was a little painful."

"I was concerned they would be found out," Roman said, a faint grimace creasing his features. "I was sure Harriet was catching on to their not-so-subtle looks of longing."

Ellis laughed softly. "I did wonder about that too. I worried they would be caught at some point before the plan could be fully executed. If not, it would have had to have been a very short courtship. They were not at all skilled at masking their affection."

"Very true," he said, falling quiet as he massaged the space between her shoulder blades.

"Do you think anyone here notices the way we regard one another?" Ellis asked.

"I doubt it." He shrugged. "Even if they did, they wouldn't say anything."

"Not to you, but they may talk amongst themselves or tell a family member or a friend."

"They would never," he said confidently.

Ellis turned in her chair to face him, and he took his hands from her. "How can you trust them so implicitly? Everyone has a price or a loyalty."

"They are loyal to me, and they cannot be bought." His brows drew together. "Are you genuinely concerned the servants are going to tell someone that we're having an affair?"

"I'm not *worried* about it, but I accept there is a risk and that could happen." She stood and walked toward the bed. Was she feeling annoyed because he seemed obtuse about the possibility of their being discovered? Or was it the realization that their affair was finite?

"Is everything all right?" He sounded concerned, which was very nice. And only added to her inner torment.

She didn't want to be tormented. Not now. Not when she could spend tonight in his arms and many nights in the days and perhaps weeks to come. She moved to face him, her hip grazing the side of the bed. "I confess I'm thinking about my future a bit. I will likely need to make some decisions about things."

"Is this to do with your errand tomorrow?" he asked.

"Somewhat." Ellis wasn't sure how meeting her father would change things, but it would. And she needed to see Min—and Sheff—soon. Doing that would open up a great many feelings, and perhaps decisions, that she'd been avoiding.

Roman moved to stand at the end of the bed, just a foot or so away from her. "I hope this doesn't mean you're going to be leaving my employ anytime soon. How can I manage without you?" He smiled.

Ellis arched her brow. "As your secretary or your lover?"

"Both. I need you, Ellis. Shall I show you how much?" He reached for her, and she allowed him to clasp her waist and draw her close.

"You don't need me. You *want* me." She didn't mind that distinction. The reason she hated to see this affair end was because she didn't want to lose that feeling. Being wanted was the most wonderful thing she'd ever known. "You could find replacements for both those roles," she suggested saucily, though there was an undercurrent of truth, at least to her. Could he detect it?

His gaze darkened as he unclasped her gown and parted it. "I don't want replacements. I want you."

He slipped his hands into her garment and clasped her bare flesh, his fingers curling into her as he lowered his head and kissed her. This wasn't a gentle seduction, but a claiming —Roman was asserting his passion, and Ellis eagerly accepted every thrust of his tongue and brush of his lips.

She unfastened his dressing gown and pushed her hands up his chest, her palms mapping this now-familiar terrain. Cresting his shoulders, she pushed the garment down, and he shrugged out of it, letting it drop to the floor. They did the same with her gown.

Roman cupped her backside as he plundered her mouth. Ellis curled her hands around his neck, and he lifted her leg, guiding it around his hip, opening her so she could press intimately against his sex. She sprung gently on her feet, and he understood, picking her up as she launched against him and wrapped her legs around him.

He held her easily, clasping her to him and moaning softly as she rotated her hips. Turning, he backed her against the bed and eased her back, crawling over her as they pivoted and straightened across the mattress. It was as if they'd executed this dance countless times. Their bodies were simply becoming attuned to one another. Ellis reveled in their connection and compatibility, the sheer simplicity of how well they fit.

At least physically and mentally. She would not think of the ways in which they were ill-matched. Not yet.

Roman dropped savage kisses along her neck as he licked and nipped at her flesh. Ellis kept him captive within the circle of her legs and twined her fingers in his hair, guiding him lower to her breast. He did not need encouragement, for he quickly found her nipple, pulling on her as she whimpered and prompting her sex to quiver with need.

His mouth replaced his hand, covering and sucking her flesh. She arched up from the bed, desperate for more. Her legs went slack as she focused on the sensations building within her. He took advantage, moving his hand down between them and stroking her sex.

Ellis let her legs fall from him as she opened to his touch, greedy for the thrust of his finger. He toyed with her clitoris, stoking her desire to a fever pitch. Then he thrust his fingers into her, satisfying her craving for completion.

He drove relentlessly as he kissed and suckled her breasts. "Come for me, Ellis. Come hard."

She did not need any urging. Her climax slammed into her with a violent bliss. She cried out, over and over, her body turning limp as a wilted flower.

But he did not allow her any recovery. He turned her to her side and bent her upper leg as he straddled the lower one. Gripping her backside, he drove into her, his cock filling her in the last spasms of her orgasm.

Pleasure sparked anew at the delicious friction of their bodies gliding together. He moved with deep precision, stroking her exactly where she wanted, where she felt the most sensation. Ecstasy built with each thrust until Ellis was on the brink once more. She came harder than the first time, her muscles clenching around him as she pressed her clitoris against his leg.

She felt his hips twitch and vaguely worried that he wasn't going to pull away from her. But he did, which was both a relief and a tragedy as she missed him inside her. She reached for his cock, stroking his flesh as his orgasm claimed him.

"My God, Ellis." He leaned over her and kissed her, gentler than before but still with a searing intensity that made her feel like she was the most important thing in the world.

Smiling, she closed her eyes as he left the bed. She heard him cleaning up, then he came back and tidied her too. He was a very generous and conscientious lover, not like the others she'd known before. But she'd been much younger, and so had they.

Roman pulled the coverlet back, and they slid into the bedclothes together. Ellis lay on her back, and Roman faced her on his side. He stretched his arm over and gave her breast a gentle squeeze.

"Again?" she asked with a light chuckle.

"Certainly, but after some sleep." He nuzzled her neck and kissed her. "You exhaust me. In the best way."

He curled his arm around her possessively, and Ellis exhaled softly with deep contentment. Very quickly, Roman's breathing evened, and she could tell he was asleep.

Slumber did not come quickly for Ellis. She stared at the ceiling for some time, basking in the bliss of these moments and also dreading that they would come to an end in the not-too-distant future.

Tomorrow, her life was going to change yet again when she met her father. Soon, she would need to choose her path —and today had shown her that it wouldn't include Roman.

Should she leave now before losing herself completely?

Or should she stay and cling, even temporarily, to the only true happiness she'd ever known?

~

*E*llis was glad to see Jo again. She missed her friends, especially Min, but right now she was anxious about meeting Rowland Harker. Not *meeting* him since they'd already been introduced, but not as father and daughter. She and Jo had not discussed how they would tell him about having another daughter.

Turning her head toward Jo on the seat beside her, Ellis took a deep breath to calm her anxiety. "Are you going to come inside with me to break this shocking news to him?"

"Of course." Jo gave her an encouraging smile. "I wouldn't send you alone to do that. We sisters must band together. We didn't talk about how we planned to tell him about you, and perhaps we should have. I did think about bringing Sheff along. I hope you know he's a strong ally to us both. He misses you too."

"And I miss him," Ellis said warmly. "Does he know what you're doing today?"

Jo hesitated, then cocked her head. "Yes. We don't keep secrets. Anymore," she added wryly.

Ellis laughed but quickly sobered. "Sometimes it's hard to reveal the complete truth, at least not right away. I find I've had to sit with these revelations about my parents. It isn't that I'm trying to keep a secret—well, perhaps it is since I can't say I'm thrilled at sharing the identity of my mother and my illegitimacy is the least of my embarrassment—I'm just not ready to talk about it too much." Or at all.

"I understand," Jo said gently. "I can only imagine how hurt you've been."

"I appreciate your kindness and support." Ellis tensed.

"Would you mind being the one to tell him? I just don't know how to say it."

"I wondered if you might want me to do that, and no, I don't mind," Jo said, prompting Ellis to let out a relieved breath. "Please understand that I may not be able to control my anger entirely. I am particularly emotional at this point in my pregnancy."

"I do understand. Not about carrying a baby," Ellis added with a brief smile. "Though I can imagine how emotional this would make you feel, baby or not. He was unfaithful to your mother while she was carrying you. That's inexcusable."

They arrived at Rowland Harker's terrace in Bloomsbury.

Jo sent her a mild grimace. "Don't be surprised at how his house is furnished or kept. He employs a butler and a cook. They are a married couple who reside on the top floor. A woman from the neighborhood comes in to do cleaning, but not as often as I think she ought. Whenever I mention that to my father, he waves his hand and says he never entertains, so it doesn't matter."

"And yet here we are, though perhaps we shall not be entertained," she added wryly.

Jo laughed as the coachman opened the door and they stepped to the pavement. When they reached the door, the butler, Peters, welcomed them inside. "Good afternoon, Lady Shefford."

"My father is expecting me," Jo said. "And this is my... friend, Miss Dangerfield."

"Do I hear the esteemed Lady Shefford?" The question floated into the entrance hall as Rowland Harker strode in chuckling from, presumably, the staircase hall. He stopped short and fixed on Ellis. "You've brought a friend. She seems familiar."

"Yes, Papa, you met Miss Dangerfield at my betrothal

ball," Jo replied. "She was Minerva's companion for many years."

"Ah, yes, the companion who may or may not be the daughter of the Duke of Henlow," he noted with a jocular laugh.

Ellis was immediately put off. This wasn't an auspicious beginning.

Jo narrowed her eyes at him. "Papa, don't do that."

"That is a very old and tired rumor," Ellis said coolly, giving him a direct, unflinching stare.

He inclined his head and appeared contrite. "Just so, my dear. It was in poor taste."

Feeling slightly mollified, Ellis continued. "I am not, in fact, Henlow's daughter. Indeed, that is somewhat why we're here today." She couldn't help saying that in response and shot Jo an apologetic grimace—she was going to make the revelation, not Ellis. Jo subtly nodded her head, silently communicating that it was fine.

"I don't understand that at all," Harker said with another laugh. "Do come in and explain."

"Shall we go up to the drawing room?" Jo asked.

"Oh, yes, I suppose so, though it is a bit cluttered at the moment." He sent Ellis an apologetic glance as he gestured toward the staircase hall.

"Just at this moment?" Jo said with an arch of her brow.

Harker laughed again, and Ellis wondered if he laughed all the time. "You know me well, my dear!"

Jo exchanged a wry look with Ellis, then started up the stairs. Ellis followed her, and their father trailed behind.

When they reached the drawing room, Ellis managed to keep from showing a reaction—barely. Cluttered was a vast understatement. There were books and papers on every surface, as well as teacups and glass tumblers. An empty decanter sat on its side on one table. There were even books stacked on the mantel. A collection of drawing supplies, charcoal and pencils, was piled on a table near the windows. Countless pieces of used parchment lay on the table and on the surrounding floor.

Harker seemed to follow Ellis's gaze. "This is my secondary work area," he said. "My studio is upstairs, which I would be delighted to show you, but I'm sure you didn't come to peruse my art. Let us sit." He went to the main seating area and moved some things on the settee so the two of them could sit, whilst he dropped into a chair angled toward them.

"Thank you," Jo said. "I won't prevaricate, for this is a difficult conversation, and there's simply no way to prepare you for its effect."

Harker's light brows pitched over his eyes with alarm. "My goodness, you're giving me a fright, dear girl. Is something wrong with your mother?"

"No. This is about *you*," Jo said, her tone almost stern. "I'm well aware that monogamy is not to your liking. However, I did not realize you'd given up on it so quickly into your marriage to Mama." She paused, and Harker appeared somewhat chastised. "It has recently come to light that you got another woman with child whilst she was carrying me. Today, I'm introducing you to that offspring. May I present Miss Ellis Dangerfield, your second-born daughter."

Harker's brown eyes rounded as he sucked in a breath. He studied Ellis a moment. "Ah, yes, I see it. The color of your hair, of course, and the set of your eyes. Perhaps even your smile, if I could see it." He cocked his head and studied her a moment longer. "And who is your mother? I don't recall anyone named Dangerfield."

"Her mother is the Duchess of Henlow," Jo ground out as if she were trying not to clench her teeth. "My mother-in-law."

Harker pressed his lips together. "Oh, I see. Well, that's a bit awkward, isn't it?"

"*Awkward?*" Ellis hadn't meant to say the word aloud, but it tumbled from her mouth in disbelief.

Jo clasped her hands on her belly and frowned at her father. "Papa, it's far more serious than that, and I think you know it. You had an affair with a *duchess*, and she bore your child."

"I didn't know," he said, holding up his hands as if he couldn't be blamed. "But even if I had, what should I have done?" He blinked. "Why aren't you *Lady* Ellis? Did His Grace not wish to claim you?"

"*Her Grace* did not wish to claim me," Ellis said quietly. "I was given to the Dangerfields for adoption. They were friends of His Grace's family."

Harker clapped his hands on his knees. "Well, this is quite a tale."

Jo scowled at him. "This is not a story to be told for entertainment. This is Ellis's *life*. I brought her here to meet you today. You are her father. Her adopted father and mother died many years ago, and the duke took her into his household as Minerva's companion."

"You say the duke took her in. Why wasn't the duchess eager to have her daughter back?"

Ellis couldn't contain her derisive laugh. "Her Grace has no use for me. She only allowed me to be Min's companion because the duke insisted. However, I don't want to discuss her today. In fact, I'd rather not discuss her ever again. She's not a parent *I* wish to claim. I came here today wondering if you might be that parent, but so far, I'm apprehensive."

His features softened. "I shall do what I can to ease your concern. The reason for your visit is lovely. I'm always delighted to meet one of my children."

One of his children? Ellis turned her head toward Jo to see her reaction.

"Good heavens, Papa, how many by-blows do you have?" Jo's voice rose in consternation, as her brows drew sharply together. She glanced toward Ellis and murmured, "Sorry."

Ellis waved her hand gently. "I'm not offended. I *am* one of his by-blows." She narrowed her eyes slightly at Harker. "I have the same question regarding potential half-siblings."

"Only a few," he replied without even a hint of humility. "This makes three daughters and two sons." He actually sounded proud.

Jo gaped at him. "Why have you never mentioned them to me?"

Harker drummed his fingers against his leg. "I didn't think you'd appreciate hearing about them, and it seems I'm correct. I can see you're upset with me about my liaison with the duchess."

Exhaling, Jo rolled her eyes. "Being angry with you is a futile exercise. You are an infuriating man, but you are also sweet and loving. Perhaps if you could be bothered to tidy your house, you could have a gathering with all your children someday."

"That might be nice," Harker said, appearing as though he'd never considered the idea. "And here we've another to add to our ranks." He beamed at Ellis. "May I say how beautiful you are? More of me in you than your mother, I think, but you do have her stubborn chin," he added with a laugh. "I'd like to paint your portrait. I've painted all my children."

"Have you?" Ellis asked.

Harker nodded.

Ellis was curious to see Jo's, at least. "I should like to see yours."

Jo pursed her lips. "Papa will have to show you. He paints them for himself, not us."

"I see." Ellis had to keep herself from laughing. Jo *had* warned her that he was self-centered, but he was almost comically so.

"Well, this is splendid," Harker said gleefully to Ellis. "You were companion to Min for how long?"

"More than fifteen years."

"Now she is married," Harker noted. "I can't imagine you're still her companion. What are you doing?"

"I'm making my own way," Ellis replied vaguely.

The gold flecks in Harker's brown eyes sparkled. "That sounds intriguing. I'd like to hear all about that. I do love an independent woman. That's what drew me to Jo's mother. She's an astonishing businesswoman." He jumped to his feet. "Come, I'll show you the studio. Jo, will you join us?"

Jo looked at Ellis, and Ellis gave her head a subtle shake. She would be fine alone with Rowland Harker for a few minutes. In fact, she wanted to be.

"I'll wait here if you don't mind," Jo responded. "I'm a bit fatigued this afternoon."

"That's to be expected. I'm looking forward to the birth of my second grandchild, but the first one in line to be a duke." He clapped his hands together with a giddy chuckle.

"You already have a grandchild?" Jo asked, incredulous.

"Just one," he said proudly. "A girl."

Jo and Ellis exchanged glances of disbelief and humor.

"My child may well be a girl too. I hope you won't be disappointed."

He waved his hand. "Bah, I'm sure you'll have plenty of children, or at least until you have an heir. That's your duty now, my dear." He winked at her before he started toward the door. "Come along, Ellis. May I call you Ellis?" he asked. "I would be very happy if you called me Papa."

Ellis didn't think she could do that. Solomon Dangerfield had been her one and only "papa."

"I think I would prefer to call you Rowland, at least for now," she said.

He gave her a solemn nod. "I understand. We mustn't rush things. We should get to know one another." He held his arm out. "Come, take my arm."

She walked to his side and took his arm as he guided her from the room and upstairs to the second floor.

"I apologize, for my studio space is even more cluttered than the drawing room," he said sheepishly.

Ellis wondered to herself how that could possibly be but would soon find out. The studio was very large, as it encompassed the entire front of the house.

"The morning light must be excellent here," she said. That was all she could think to say about her surroundings. There were easels and paints and brushes and buckets and cloths strewn just about everywhere. There were a few empty canvases, but far more that were in various stages of completion. Against the walls, he had stacks of finished work. It looked as though the completed ones were on the far wall. The walls were also covered with his paintings.

"I enjoy painting." Ellis startled as he clapped his hands.

"Splendid! Two of my other children are also talented in the arts. Poor Jo can't even draw a rudimentary flower."

For the next several minutes, he showed her the room and many of his works. They ranged from landscapes to still lifes to portraits. Those of his children adorned the space between the front windows. They included a very pretty Jo from several years ago.

"How old is Jo in this picture?" Ellis asked.

"Seventeen, I believe."

Ellis had to admit he was very talented. "I'm surprised I haven't seen your work before."

He shrugged. "You might have, but sometimes I go many months or even years without painting. I paint for a while, then I write for a while, then I tinker with experiments for a while. My laboratory is back through there." He pointed through a doorway. There was another door near Ellis. It stood ajar, so she poked her head inside. "What's in here?"

"That's my special studio."

A wide, dark-blue velvet-covered chaise longue stood in front of the hearth. There were several silk pillows, both on the chaise and the floor. Various kinds of lighting, including candlesticks, candle branches, and standing torches were scattered about. But none of that compared to the portraits covering these walls. They were not like the ones in the main studio—they were intimate, sensual portraits of women in various states of undress and abandon. There were also a few portraits of men in the same manner.

"I hadn't meant to show you this room," he said with a nervous laugh. "You being an innocent young woman, of course. I'm rather proud of them, though. These are all people for who I cared deeply at some time. A part of me still loves them all." He turned his gaze toward Ellis. "I assume Jo told you of my debauchery. If not, I suppose our conversation downstairs would have informed you."

"Yes, I was aware." Ellis couldn't help scanning the room. Suddenly, her focus fixed on one of the portraits near the hearth. She recognized the subject. In fact, Ellis had seen the likeness at the Laceys' house the other night.

It was Clarissa, Roman's wife.

Ellis walked toward the portrait. "Who is this?"

"That was one of my students," he said. "She was quite talented. With a brush, I mean."

Assuming his last statement alluded to some other skill, Ellis stared at him. "Was she also your mistress?" It seemed likely, given the portrait's presence in this room.

"Oh, yes," he replied nonchalantly. "As was everyone on

the walls in here. Clarissa was one of my longer attachments. I'm proud to say we had a deep and abiding love."

Love? When she'd been married to Roman?

"Was she married, like the duchess?" Ellis asked, though she already knew the answer.

"I'm afraid so." His tone wasn't regretful, at least not for his actions. It seemed more than he regretted having to tell Ellis. "Most of the women in here are. It's less complicated that way. I'm married, they're married…nobody expects anything permanent."

"And were you faithful to any of these people?" Ellis felt certain she knew the answer to that as well. "Or are you not able to be monogamous in any way?"

"I can be faithful for a time, but not long." He leaned toward her with a sly expression. "Usually, there's more than one horse in the stable, if you know what I mean."

Ellis was horrified by her father's overall attitude and behavior as well as by the fact that he'd had an ongoing affair with Roman's wife. Debauched didn't begin to describe him. He lived a life she simply couldn't grasp.

But the worst of it was his liaison with Clarissa. Did Roman know his wife had been unfaithful?

Perhaps that was why he preferred a marriage of convenience—he'd been cuckolded. Except his marriage to Clarissa had been arranged by her parents. It wasn't a love match. Still, to be betrayed, even if you didn't love your spouse, had to hurt.

Ellis couldn't be certain he knew, however. She wanted to ask him, but since she hadn't been keen to share her past, why should she expect him to?

"What happened to your 'deep and abiding love?'" Ellis asked flatly, turning her back on the portrait.

"My love is constant, yet ever-changing," he said with a

sigh. "She became a bit too attached, and I encouraged her to return to her husband—to her duty."

Ellis was growing to dislike this man. "*She* has a duty, but you—a husband to Jo's mother—have none?"

"I suppose I deserve that," he said quietly. "For the most part, I'm very clear with everyone about my expectations regarding love affairs. The only person I truly deceived was Jo's mother, and that was because I didn't realize I was going to. I fell in love with her and didn't think I would ever want anyone else. I was wrong."

"So Clarissa and others like her, they knew your affections would be fleeting?"

"As I said, most of them are married. None of them expected a permanent relationship. Or at least, they shouldn't have. How can they? It's not as if anyone's going to divorce," he scoffed. "Jo's mother and I haven't even divorced, and we've never lived together. Clarissa was perhaps too naïve. She was younger than most of my paramours." He took a deep breath and smiled. "Enough of that. I should like to paint you soon, if you are amenable."

The shift from discussing his former lover to wanting to paint a portrait of Ellis was jarring. Indeed, Ellis felt as if she'd been tossed about in a coach on a terribly rutted road. She wasn't sure she'd be able to forge a relationship with this man. "I'm struggling to understand how you can treat all these people this way, how you can be so callous. And I'm surprised you haven't been challenged to a duel. Or have none of your paramours' spouses learned they were being cuckolded by you?"

"A few of them discovered their wives were having an affair, but none demanded satisfaction." He shrugged. "They may not have known who I was, just that their wife was carrying on a liaison. I imagine it's hard to hide, which is why I typically like to keep the entanglements short. I did wonder if Clarissa's husband knew."

Ellis didn't want to think of Roman discovering this deception. It made her incredibly angry, and it hadn't even happened to her. She needed to escape Harker's presence before she said something she might regret. "I should return to Jo. She's tired, and I don't want to keep her too long."

"Of course." Rowland gestured for her to precede him from his lurid chamber of lovers, and they returned to the drawing room.

"I'm ready to leave," Ellis said, trying to keep her voice from sounding too heavy. She felt as if she were carrying a massive weight.

Jo rose as her father dashed to help her.

"You stood too quickly," he said with a gentle frown. "I would have helped you up." He turned his head toward Ellis. "I hope I didn't shock you overmuch today, my dear. I'm quite thrilled to learn I have a new daughter. Well, not a new daughter, but new to me." He chuckled. "I hope we'll be able to forge a close relationship going forward."

Jo narrowed her eyes at him. "Don't pressure her, Papa. She has much to acclimate herself to, particularly after the way the duchess treated her for so long."

Rowland wrinkled his nose. "I have to confess, when you and Sheff became betrothed, I didn't like her as much as I did all those years ago." He transferred his gaze to Ellis. "I'm sorry for any distress she's caused you. If there is anything I can ever do for you, I hope you'll tell me. I might not have a great deal of money, but I have connections, and I am generally well liked. I think Jo will tell you that I can always put a smile on your face."

Ellis wasn't sure about that. She didn't feel like smiling now.

"Thank you," she said diplomatically.

She and Jo took their leave a moment later. As soon as they were outside, Jo turned to her. "You seem rather shaken after going to the studio. What happened?"

She sent Jo a look of disgust. "I stumbled upon his sordid gallery of mistresses."

Jo frowned. "I'd forgotten that existed. I'm sorry. That can't have made you feel very warm toward him. He's not a horrible person, just incredibly hedonistic. He is unable to control his impulses and has difficulty seeing others' perspectives."

"I gathered that," Ellis said. "How are you now you've learned he has other children and a grandchild?"

Jo made a sound in her throat. "Honestly, I can't even be upset anymore. Just when I think he can't shock me, he does, and the result is that I'm no longer shocked."

Ellis couldn't say she felt the same. The discovery that Roman's wife had been one of her father's mistresses was horrible. She didn't know what to do with that information. She wasn't sure how she was going to be able to look at Roman without him seeing right away that there was something wrong. She would have to find a way to bury her agitation.

When they were settled in the coach, Ellis was eager to cease discussion of their father and speak of something more positive. She turned to Jo. "I'd like to see Min soon. Perhaps we could meet at Wellesbourne House, if Pandora is amenable. I suppose I know she already is."

Jo's eyes flashed with surprise. "I'm so glad! I'll speak with Pandora and Min and arrange it." She grinned at Ellis. "Min will be so happy."

"I am too—or I will be when I see her." For now, Ellis couldn't stop thinking about what she'd learned about Roman's wife.

"Does this mean you'll tell us where you're living and how you're managing right now?"

Ellis shook her head. "Not yet. I've some decisions to make about what to do next. For now, I'd just like to see Min."

Jo nodded but smiled. "I'm sure you know this already, but we'd all love to help and support you with whatever you decide."

"Yes, I know," Ellis said softly. She had truly had wonderful people she could rely on. That included Roman.

But this was an affair not unlike those her father engaged in. Her liaison with Roman would end, and she feared that would happen sooner than she wanted.

CHAPTER 15

The words of the manuscript Roman was reviewing for Lacey and Company blurred before Roman's eyes. He realized he hadn't retained any of the information in the pages he'd read over the last few minutes. Blinking, he leaned back in his chair, then looked toward Ellis's empty desk.

She was working up in the library to avoid temptation. It was for the best, since Roman couldn't keep his hands to himself, nor did he want to. But even alone, he was struggling to concentrate.

Ellis had seemed preoccupied since her errand the other day. He longed to ask her where she'd gone and what had transpired but didn't.

Still, they spent the nights in each other's arms, and the passion between them hadn't dimmed. If anything, it had only grown more intense. Roman ached when he couldn't touch her.

He heard footsteps approaching the door and held his breath, hoping it was Ellis.

It was Graham.

The butler stood at the threshold. "I have a letter for you, my lord."

Roman waved him in.

"This was delivered by one of the lads at Lacey and Company." Graham handed the envelope to Roman.

"Thank you, Graham."

The butler turned and left as Roman's gaze fixed on a single word written across the back of the envelope, beneath the seal: *Confidential.*

He flipped it back over. It had been addressed to him with the address of Lacey and Company in Paternoster Row. The handwriting appeared feminine, but it was not familiar. He opened the envelope and removed the parchment. Opening it, he began to read.

> *Lord Keele,*
>
> *I trust this letter finds you well and prospering in your business endeavors. It has come to my attention that you have recently employed a "Mrs. Ellis" as your secretary. This woman resides, quite unconventionally, in your household. How very modern of you. However, she is not a "Mrs." at all. She is, in fact, Miss Ellis Dangerfield, former companion to my daughter, Lady Minerva. I cannot imagine how Miss Dangerfield came to be in your employ, for she is a rather worthless sort. I can only assume she is living in your household under the guise of secretary but is, in truth, your mistress.*

Roman's hands shook as fury boiled within him. Had someone in his household revealed the nature of his relationship with Ellis? And after all the assurances he'd given her that none of them would say a word. He held his breath as he kept reading.

> *I find myself in difficult financial circumstances, and I am*

*certain you can help. I require £5,000. In exchange, no one will
know that "Mrs. Ellis" is actually Miss Ellis Dangerfield, nor
that she is the disgraced former companion to the daughter of a
duke.*

*Should you refuse, I have prepared a rather detailed
manuscript, which I will submit to various publishers, not
Lacey and Co., of course, as that would be indelicate, which
will detail Miss Dangerfield's indiscretions, of which there are
many. You can't begin to know what scandalous behavior
litters her past, including a most ruinous secret that almost no
one knows. You see, Miss Dangerfield is <u>illegitimate</u>.*

Was that what Ellis had been hiding from him all this
time? He could understand why, but he hated that she hadn't
felt she could tell him. And why would she trust him with
that information? Illegitimacy could ruin someone, especially a young woman with no family or anyone to support
her. Roman finally released his breath and was now nearly
panting, as his pulse was racing.

*If you prefer to let her suffer the indignity of exposure, I
suppose I cannot persuade you otherwise. However, these revelations will also affect you and your business with Lacey and
Co., as well as your personal reputation, which I imagine you
wish to maintain in order to snare your next heiress. I am sure
you would rather avoid another scandal after your father's
profligacy. Indeed, I don't believe you can afford it. The small
sum I require is nothing compared to what you will lose.*

*Please deliver payment to Mivart's. I shall expect it on the
morrow.*

Alice Henlow

The Duchess of fucking Henlow had sent this? Roman's
vision tunneled with a rage he'd never known. Now he knew

why Ellis had been hiding and why she'd cut herself off from her past.

She'd lived in the duchess's household. It was clear the duchess despised her. But why?

Roman glanced upward toward the library where Ellis was working. He wanted nothing more than to run to her and take her in his arms and tell her that he understood why she'd kept secrets from him and why she didn't want to discuss her past.

Part of him was sad that she hadn't confided in him. Had she been afraid that he would think less of her? He could not. She was the finest woman he'd ever known.

He hated that she'd been in pain for who knew how long. God, she'd lived in that household for fifteen years!

Roman vowed to protect her from the duchess and anyone else who would seek to hurt her. Five thousand pounds was a huge sum for him to deliver tomorrow. Hell, it was a massive amount even a fortnight from now. He'd have to liquidate an investment or three, and he'd have to come up with a reason for doing it, because Ellis would notice at some point, since she managed his accounts.

There was no question that he would do it. He couldn't let Ellis be hurt anymore. He would bankrupt himself before he'd allow that.

Would he? His hands shook again, but not from rage. This was from the realization of how much she meant to him.

He also couldn't allow a scandal to taint Josiah—both his reputation and the successful businesses he'd built—nor Harriet and Margot. But damn, it grated to succumb to the duchess's threats. Roman had half a mind to tell Sheff what his mother was doing.

Before he could draft a note to his banker, Ellis walked in. He quickly folded the odious letter and set it on his desk.

Standing, he stepped around the desk and smiled at her. The effort it took not to enfold her in his arms was astounding. "I was hoping you'd come down."

She took a few steps into the office but did not sit. "I came to tell you I'll be having dinner with Pandora at Wellesbourne House again this evening. And I, ah, need transportation. You don't have to accompany me. I really don't want you to wait outside. I've no idea how long I'll be."

"I'm happy to wait—truly. Or I can go to my club while you're there." Perhaps he'd see Sheff and talk to him about his horrid mother. Roman had known that Sheff had difficulty with the duchess, that she nagged him and was demanding, but he'd never had the sense she was as vile as she'd sounded in that letter.

"It truly isn't necessary," Ellis said. Again, he suspected there might be something wrong, that she was troubled. Had the duchess written to her as well, and she was hiding it from him?

"I want to accompany you," he insisted. "I'll go to my club and I'll fetch you on my way home."

"Surely, you'll be out later than I will." She cocked her head. "I think you're just trying to get me alone in your coach."

"Guilty." He gave her a wicked grin as he stepped toward her. He curled his arm around her waist and pulled her against him, lowering his head to kiss her hard and fast.

She pushed at his chest and turned her head sharply toward the door that stood open. "Roman, you can't do that," she whispered urgently.

He shrugged. "I had to, and I'm not sorry."

She set her mouth in a stern frown. "Well, you mustn't do that again. I'm going back upstairs now because you're very naughty."

"I'll show you later just how naughty I can be."

After she crossed the threshold, she tossed him a saucy look. "I already know. And yes, you may accompany me to Wellesbourne House and fetch me on your way home."

"Does that mean you want to be alone in my coach with me?" He gave her a suggestive leer.

She laughed as she walked away from the office. Roman's smile faded faster than it would have because the letter weighed heavy on his mind.

He would take care of it. And tonight, he would hold Ellis in his arms.

~

Though Ellis had flirted with Roman that afternoon about being in the coach together, now that they were on their way, she was nervous. It was becoming increasingly difficult to hide what she knew about his wife. She'd noticed he'd started regarding her with concern, and she sensed he wanted to say something. If he asked whether she was upset and why, she wasn't sure she would be able to keep the truth from him.

Thankfully, it was a short trip to Wellesbourne House. Roman surprised her by taking her hand. She turned her head. She could tell him about Rowland Harker now, but she wouldn't.

She also didn't want the awkwardness that seemed to be growing between them. So, she kissed him.

He cupped her head and returned the kiss eagerly. They spent the duration of the ride locked together, barely breaking apart before the coachman opened the door. As she left the coach, she caught his seductive stare and the promise of continuing what they'd started later.

She walked to the door, which was promptly opened by the butler.

"Good evening, Miss Dangerfield," Ralston said in greeting. "I will show you up to the drawing room."

She followed him to where she'd met Pandora last week. She wondered if Pandora would be there again, or if it would just be Min. She would shortly know.

The butler did not go all the way to the door. Instead, he gestured for her to precede him.

"I was told you would not need to be announced," Ralston said.

"Thank you." Ellis took a deep breath and walked into the drawing room.

Min stood near a seating area, the aristocratic planes of her familiar face tight with anticipation. Her gray eyes fixed on Ellis and didn't waver as she clasped her hands before her. "I was watching for your coach."

Ellis found she couldn't speak, so she nodded.

"May I hug you?" Min asked.

Ellis raced to her, and they embraced fiercely. Several minutes elapsed while they held one another. Ellis couldn't keep from crying, and from the sound of it, Min was doing the same. When they finally broke apart, they began to laugh.

"Aren't we a pair?" Min said. She took Ellis' hand and squeezed it.

"Let's sit, and I'll tell you everything." Ellis tugged her toward a settee. "But first I want to hear how you're enjoying marriage. I'm so sorry I missed your wedding."

They sat together, angled toward each other.

Min kept hold of Ellis's hand. "I understand. I'm so sorry for the way you found out about our mother."

"At least we're actually sisters," Ellis said with a wry smile.

Min began to cry again. "Is it wrong that I'm happy about that?"

Ellis squeezed her hand. "No, I'm happy too. It is the one bright spot in all this."

"The other bright spot is that the duchess has been sent away," Min said. "My father is not renewing the lease on her house in Bath, and she's no longer welcome at the dower house at Beacon Park."

"Where will she go?" Ellis asked.

Min shrugged. "We don't know, and we don't care. I don't think she has much money. She did ask if she could stay with me. I didn't respond. Evan wrote her back and told her not to write to us again."

"Good for Evan," Ellis said firmly. "I don't know what's worse—having a mother and learning these awful things about her or being treated horribly by somebody for so long only to learn that she's your mother."

"Your situation is far worse." Min's eyes shone with kindness and concern. "Our mother never treated me poorly, not in the way she did you. I should have recognized just how terrible her treatment of you was. I should have stood up for you more. Can you ever forgive me?"

"There's nothing to forgive," Ellis said sharply. "You did all you could. You fought for me on countless occasions, and you won some of those battles. Things could have been much worse. I think if you and I had not gotten on so well, she might have been able to convince your father to send me away. Though, I would have gone to live with my cousins, which likely would have been better." Ellis didn't want Min to feel bad about that either. "There's no sense in our talking about things we could have done differently."

"I remember you wanted to live with your cousins," Min said softly. "I also remember telling you that I was glad you didn't, because I liked having you there with me."

Ellis smiled. "You said my presence meant you could pretend we were sisters."

Min nodded. "I craved companionship and affection. Sheff was older and mostly away at school, and my father certainly wasn't paying attention to me." She met Ellis's gaze. "I had the governess, and I had you."

"We had each other." Ellis squeezed Min's hand again. "Which is why I'm so sorry I turned away from you. We must always band together."

"Yes," Min agreed. "Forever."

They released their hands and embraced again, though not for nearly as long as before.

When they parted, Min's expression became wary. "You said you were going to tell me everything. What does that mean?"

Ellis cocked her head. "I wonder if we should invite Pandora and Jo to join us, so that I don't have to repeat everything."

Min laughed. "That probably makes the most sense. You should also know that Iona is here as well. I confess she and I have become close in the last several weeks. I hope you won't take offense."

"Not at all," Ellis said. "I look forward to deepening our acquaintance." But for how long? Ellis had no idea where she would be in a few months. Or perhaps even next week.

"Wait right here." Min jumped up and dashed to a closed door that likely led to a smaller version of this room. In a house of this size, it was common for the two rooms to join together to form a larger space for balls or other gathering.

A moment later, Min led their three friends into the drawing room. How Ellis wished Persey, Tamsin, and Gwen were here too.

"Is all well?" Jo asked tentatively as she entered the seating area.

"Quite," Ellis replied. "Thank you for organizing this." She gave Jo a hug, and their bellies met, Ellis felt a jolt. "Was that the baby?"

Jo laughed. "Yes, she or he is very active in the evening, especially just before dinner."

"We will dine shortly," Pandora said. "After Ellis shares whatever she wishes to share." She sent Ellis a supportive look, which Ellis very much appreciated.

"We need to be closer together," Min announced as she began to move a chair near the settee where she and Ellis had been seated. Iona and Pandora moved two more, and Pandora ushered Jo into one of them.

Ellis retook her position on the settee, as did Min, and Jo was to her left. "I hope you won't think poorly of me," Ellis said nervously.

"We would never think poorly of you," Min assured her. "I noticed the coach you stepped out of was very nice, if a few years old. It definitely wasn't a hackney."

Ellis glanced toward Pandora, who gave her an encouraging nod. "The coach belongs to my employer. Pandora knows who that is, because we happened upon each other one day at her publisher."

Jo snapped her gaze to Pandora. "That's how you found her."

"Yes," Pandora replied. "But I promised Ellis I wouldn't tell you."

"What were you doing at the publisher?" Min asked.

"Working," Ellis replied. "I'm secretary to Lord Keele, and he's a principal in Lacey and Company."

Min's sable brows shot up. "He hired a woman?"

"He hired a *man* named Daniel Ellis. It took him a few days to discover what it was that he found odd about me."

They all laughed.

"He suspected right away that something was off?" Iona asked in her Irish lilt. She had large blue eyes and wavy dark-auburn hair. "Did he suspect you were a woman?"

Ellis lifted a shoulder. "He had inklings, I suppose, but I

made the mistake of bending over in front of him, and apparently he didn't think my backside was at all masculine."

Iona gasped while the others laughed.

"Your curves gave you away," Pandora said through her grin.

"Indeed, but my work was good enough that he didn't want me to leave my post." Ellis held up her hand. "Forgive me, I'm leaving out a very important detail. One of the requirements of my employment was that I reside in Keele's household."

Now, *everyone* gasped.

Pandora's blonde brows drew together. "I thought you were living in a boarding house."

"I was, but Roman—that is, Keele—wanted me to live in his house so I could be available at all times."

Jo narrowed her eyes. "That sounds dubious. What did he want you available for?"

Ellis understood how a marquess insisting a woman secretary live in his house might appear. "He wanted me to work. When he made that demand, he thought I was a man. He had no ulterior motives, I assure you. The secretary before me was atrocious, and there was a great deal of mess to be tidied. He wanted someone who could work long hours."

Min nodded. "So you started working for him dressed as a man, then he learned you were a woman. What did his servants say?"

"I continued as a man until my disguise fell apart one day," Ellis explained, skipping over the incident when Margot had caught them kissing. "I was wearing facial hair, and the beard came unglued in front of Mr. and Mrs. Lacey. Surprisingly, they did not have a problem with my being a woman. In fact, they encouraged me to assume my true identity. That was when Roman—*Keele*—informed the servants that I was actually Mrs. Ellis, a widow. That is also what the Laceys believe. I'm sure you can understand why."

"But you aren't a widow," Min pointed out. "What will happen when that becomes known?"

"It won't, for I don't plan to stay there much longer." Saying that out loud caused Ellis's chest to ache.

"I'm surprised you took this risk at all," Iona said with a slight shake of her head. "I can't imagine it was enjoyable to dress up as a man. And you wore a beard?"

"I did, and I do not recommend it." Ellis wrinkled her nose. "But it was all I could think of to find employment that I wanted to do and that would pay me well enough to save money."

"Save money for what?" Iona asked.

"To make my way." Ellis looked down at her lap. "I don't have a family, and I don't have a means of supporting myself. I have no prospects of marriage, nor do I want any." She lifted her head and regarded her friends, though she didn't focus on anyone in particular. She didn't want to see their reactions—more accurately, their pity. "I'm not in the same situation as any of you. Not even you, Pandora. You've an aunt to take care of you."

"My aunt would take care of you too," Pandora said quietly. "I've told you that."

"My father would take care of you," Min said. "He's offered."

"Sheff would too," Jo put in. "He's told me that many times."

Ellis appreciated their help, but she'd been at everyone's mercy her entire life. She looked to Min and Jo first. "I don't want your father or your brother supporting me. It just doesn't feel right. Anyway, I have no future in this sphere. I'm not going to marry the way either of you have. My future is much more aligned with Pandora. I would much rather live in Bath or some other town that isn't London and perhaps become a librarian."

She thought about the conversation she'd had with Roman about that. It had been an idle thought at the time, but this was a truly feasible option for her and actually made her contemplate the future with something close to anticipation.

If they didn't open a library branch in Bath, there would soon be an opening at a smaller branch when they promoted someone to Oxford. Ellis thought she stood at least a small chance of obtaining that position.

Pandora met Ellis's gaze with a warm smile. She seemed pleased to hear that Ellis wanted to come to Bath.

Jo leaned slightly toward Ellis. "You've called the marquess by his Christian name at least twice now."

"I noticed that too," Min said. "Just as I noticed Ellis's strong reaction to the suggestion of what she might be doing living at his house."

Ellis had planned to tell them about their affair. She just hadn't known how. This saved her the trouble. "While it has never had anything to do with my employment, Roman and I are currently engaged in a liaison."

Iona gaped at her. "Does that mean you're no longer a virgin?"

Ellis laughed. "Not for many years. You will find this shocking, I'm sure, but I never imagined I would marry, and I didn't see the need in preserving some wasted notion of innocence. In retrospect, I think I was seeking whatever affection I could find. I encountered a couple of young men who were rather…affectionate."

"I'm not a virgin either," Pandora declared. "What's the point when I won't be marrying, thanks to Bane."

Iona looked around at them. "So, I'm the only virgin?" She pouted. "I feel left out."

They all laughed.

"Do you plan to wed?" Pandora asked.

"I thought so, but my mother keeps thrusting me at men I don't care for." Iona made a face.

"I thought you were nearly betrothed at one point," Ellis said. "And that you were eager for that. Or did I misunderstand?"

"You did not. He decided not to propose after meeting a young lady with a better pedigree. Most men are not interested in marrying the daughter of an Irish steward." Iona's father had married her mother after she was widowed. He'd been steward on her first husband's estate. That husband's heir, the Earl of Wexford, was Iona's half-brother and married to one of Min's friends.

"If you decide you don't wish to wed, there's no reason to hold on to your innocence," Pandora said.

It was strange to hear her say that. Ellis had known Pandora for several years, and the change she'd undergone as a result of being caught with Bane was both great and unfortunate. Pandora had wanted to marry and have a family, perhaps more than any of them. That one mistake had completely changed her life.

"I'm not sure," Iona replied with an edge of frustration. "I just don't want to suffer my mother's meddling any longer. I do think I'd prefer to avoid the Marriage Mart, but Mama is hoping I'll participate in this upcoming Season. I'm trying to convince her I'm not ready."

"We'll have to come up with a way to help you," Min said with a firm nod. "That is what friends do."

"I keep telling her that Kat did quite well without being on the Marriage Mart." Iona referred to her older sister, Kathleen, who had married Lord Lucien, second son of the Duke of Evesham, and the owner of the Phoenix Club. They had not courted in a typical way at all. But then, perusing the room, only Jo had engaged in a true courtship, and it had been fake.

Iona sent a smile toward Ellis. "And it sounds as though Ellis might be on her way. Perhaps her affair with Keele will turn into something more permanent."

"It won't," Ellis said. "I truly don't wish to marry. Furthermore, Roman was married before. He chose an heiress because of the state of his family's finances. He needs another heiress to continue shoring up the coffers."

Min exhaled. "If you wanted to wed, my father would give you a dowry—I'm sure of it."

Ellis didn't know what to think about that. She wouldn't have wanted that before, for the same reason she hadn't accepted his help when she'd left his household. She didn't want his money, which she acknowledged was rather irrational when she was very soon to be without employment.

A tiny voice in the back of her mind pestered her. *What if she could have Roman forever?* The answer didn't matter because Roman couldn't marry her. Even if she had a dowry, she'd wonder if he was choosing her for that or because he wanted her.

She was also the daughter of the man who'd cuckolded him.

"There is another rather awful reason Roman wouldn't want to marry me." Ellis met Jo's gaze and grimaced. "I didn't tell you about this the other day because I was too upset."

"Tell me about what?" Jo asked, her brow creasing.

Ellis focused on the others as she explained the first part. "When I met Rowland the other day, he showed me his collection of portraits that he'd painted of all his mistresses." Then she returned her attention to Jo. "What I didn't tell you is that I recognized one of the women. She was Roman's wife."

"*No.*" Jo paled. She reached out and clasped Ellis's forearm. "*He didn't.*"

Ellis nodded. "Yes. Our father was Roman's wife's lover. How could Roman ever want a future with me if he knew that? And I wouldn't be able to keep it from him."

"Oh, dear. This is terrible." Min took Ellis's other hand.

Jo's eyes sparked with anger. "I don't think I'll be able to suffer my father's presence for some time. It was one thing for me to accept what he'd done with Sheff's mother. *Your* mother," she said to Min and Ellis. "But this is just more wood on the fire, and it was already a bloody conflagration." She crossed her arms over her belly and scowled.

"Are you going to tell Keele?" Pandora asked Ellis.

"I don't know." Ellis was incredibly conflicted. "I don't know if he was aware of his wife's infidelity—he's never told me about it." Because they'd both kept secrets. "Part of me thinks it's easier to just leave his employ sooner than I'd planned and not tell him. If he didn't know, I'm not sure there's a point in revealing it now."

"What if you *do* have a chance for a future with Keele?" Min's expression brightened with hope. Ellis could see that Min hoped her affair with Roman would turn into something more.

"I think Ellis should tell Keele that she loves him," Iona said matter-of-factly.

Ellis snapped her gaze to the youngest member of their group. "I never said I loved him."

Iona shrugged. "It seems clear to me. But my mother says I can be too romantic, and she's probably right."

"I see it too," Min said. "I noticed something was different about you the moment you walked in. There's a glow about you, but also a weight that you're carrying. Are we wrong? Do you not love Keele?"

Dozens of memories flashed in Ellis's mind. Roman

discovering she was a woman and keeping her on. Roman allowing her to keep secrets despite his own frustration that came entirely from a place of wanting to help and protect her. Roman valuing her work and giving her the opportunity to feel successful and capable. He encouraged and supported her to be the woman she wanted to be. Then, when he'd discovered her true identity, his first words had been to say that he would keep her safe. He'd asked her to trust him, and she did. Completely. With every part of her being, especially her heart.

"I do love him," she whispered. "But I can't tell him that. He needs to marry a well-regarded heiress, not a former companion who just happens to be illegitimate."

Min's gray eyes filled with compassion. "What if he loves you too?"

And what if he didn't? Ellis was afraid to find out.

"You won't know unless you tell him," Jo said. "I speak from experience when I say that sometimes you should take the chance and say something. I wish I'd done so much sooner with Sheff, and he wishes he'd done it with me."

"Do you really think he'd care about your parentage?" Min asked.

"I don't know," Ellis replied quietly, her jaw clenching. She didn't want to think about any of this. It was why she'd ignored the fact that she'd been falling in love with Roman practically since she'd started working for him. Acknowledging that out loud just now made her feel incredibly vulnerable, and she was tired of that. She wanted to feel strong and independent, which was bloody hard when the truth of Ellis's background could thoroughly ruin her. If anyone learned she was a bastard, there would be no hope of a librarian position or any other role in polite society. She may very well have to consider becoming a hermit, as she and Roman had once discussed.

And never mind the awful truth of Rowland Harker having an affair with Roman's wife. How could Ellis continue with Roman knowing what she knew and keeping it from him?

A tiny voice in the back of her mind asked why. Ellis had been keeping secrets from him all along. What was one more?

But this wasn't her secret. It was about Roman's wife. She already felt guilty for keeping things from him. She couldn't add another.

Pandora clasped her hands firmly in her lap. "I don't think you should tell him any of it—about Harker or how you might feel. You've already made your decision that you'd like to come to Bath and be a librarian. I think that's a wonderful idea."

Min sent her a dark look. "Don't try to persuade her based on your own experience. Just because Bane treated you horribly doesn't mean Keele will do the same to Ellis."

Pandora pursed her lips at Min. "Nor should you force your opinion on her just because you managed to reform a rogue, and so did Jo. That doesn't mean that Ellis will."

"Is Keele even a rogue?" Iona asked.

"He was," Ellis said. "When he was younger, before his father died. Then he grew serious and married to save the marquessate."

"So, he's a rogue that reformed himself," Min said. "Splendid. I think you should tell him. What's the worst that could happen?"

That she would be abandoned again. Ellis couldn't face that.

"'Never allow a rogue to see your heart,'" Pandora said loudly. "That is directly from our rules. Ellis will break that if she reveals herself to Keele."

"We've all broken the rules at some point," Jo muttered. "Including you."

Pandora made a sound in her throat. "I'm aware. I'm the reason the bloody rules exist. Forgive me if I'm trying to save one of our own from potential heartache."

"Your points are well made," Ellis said with a grateful nod. She couldn't discount how aligned she was with Pandora above the others. Her advice was, by nature of their similarities, more helpful.

Ellis glanced around the circle and smiled at each of her friends. "I'll think about all you've said. I think we need to take Jo downstairs so she can eat."

"*Thank you,*" Jo said with great relief, prompting them all to laugh.

They stood and made their way from the drawing room. Min and Ellis brought up the rear, and on the way out, Min touched Ellis's arm. They stayed back a moment as the others started toward the stairs.

Min looked at her imploringly. "If you love Keele, you must tell him. If there's even the smallest chance you could find happiness together, don't you think you should take it?"

"What if there's a greater chance that he doesn't want me?" Ellis asked. "I don't wish to suffer that kind of rejection." *Again.*

"I don't want that for you either." Min looped her arm through Ellis's and leaned her head against Ellis's.

They walked downstairs together, and Ellis was just happy to have her sister back.

CHAPTER 16

After dropping Ellis at Wellesbourne House, Roman continued to the Phoenix Club, where he would bide his time while waiting for her. He wasn't in a particularly social mood, but he could sit in a corner of the library and sip one of the club's excellent—and smuggled—Scottish whiskies.

Since it was still early in the evening, he didn't encounter many gentlemen as he made his way upstairs to the library, a quieter space than the larger, more populated members' den, which was on the same floor. Not long after he situated himself in a comfortable chair, a waiter came to deliver a whisky. The employees knew what he liked.

Taking his first sip, he noticed Sheff and his new brother-in-law, Evan Pierce, walk in. They scanned the library, and Sheff's gaze settled on Roman. Sheff leaned toward Evan and said something, then they headed in Roman's direction.

"Evening, Keele. Mind if we join you?" Sheff asked.

"Not at all." Roman held his glass on the arm of his chair.

Sheff moved a third chair to be closer, whilst Pierce sat in the one that was already angled near Roman's. "Whisky?" Roman asked.

"Of course." It seemed Roman almost always encountered Sheff here. At least, that was the case before he'd married. Now, Sheff did not come round as much.

Seeing him now, Roman couldn't help thinking of the letter he'd received from Sheff's mother. But then it hadn't been far from his mind since he'd received it earlier.

While Roman could come up with the money to pay her tomorrow, he wasn't sure he should. He'd considered insisting she sign a document saying she wouldn't request more money, but the more people he involved in the transaction, the more likely the entire sordid situation was to become known.

Furthermore, he couldn't believe the duchess would do what she threatened. Why would she be so cruel? And why was she in need of funds in the first place?

Perhaps Sheff's arrival was fortuitous. Roman considered how to broach the subject of the duchess whilst the footman delivered whisky to Sheff and Pierce.

"This is particularly fine," Pierce noted after taking a drink. He held the glass up and surveyed the amber liquid.

Roman thought he had an idea of how to wrangle a conversation about Sheff's mother. He lifted his glass to the other two men. "I find myself sitting with two newly wedded gentlemen. How are you enjoying being married?"

They outdid each other in their exuberance regarding their wedded state, and, after swallowing his gulp of whisky, Roman had to laugh. "It sounds as though you both made the right choice." He looked to Sheff. "How is it sharing Henlow House with your parents? I confess I might have chosen to live elsewhere with my new bride."

"I'd planned to do just that, but my father has taken up residence in Marylebone with his lady love. He's found love at last and knew he couldn't live with her at Henlow House." Sheff gave his head a faint shake. "It's ironic that my father's reputation is that of a complete libertine and yet people have continued to accept him in Society."

"Because he's a duke," Pierce said with a wry chuckle.

"Yes. But my point is that he's now in a loving, monogamous relationship, and to live openly with her at Henlow House would garner all manner of criticism. He's already been somewhat snubbed since returning to London with Mrs. Welbeck." Sheff frowned. "It's a shame, for she's a lovely woman and the granddaughter of a viscount. Her husband was a naval captain. My father wanted to divorce my mother so he could marry Mrs. Welbeck, however, that would be a difficult war to win." A grimace marred his features briefly.

"It sounds as though you like Mrs. Welbeck," Roman observed as he swirled his whisky.

"I do. Min and I are thrilled to see our father happy at last. *Everyone* is aware that our parents' marriage was disastrous almost from the start—through no fault of his, I'll add."

That was also surprising. "But you just said he was a libertine," Roman said.

"He had his reasons." Sheff leaned forward and spoke in a low tone. "I recently learned that whilst he fell in love with my mother and proposed marriage, she only accepted to become a duchess, then spurned him after she produced an heir." His lip curled before he sipped his whisky.

That version of the duchess seemed more like the woman who'd sent Roman that horrid letter. "I take it your mother is not living at Henlow House either?" Roman asked, glad that his plan for learning about her was working.

Sheff reacted as if he'd just smelled a pile of offal. "God no. None of us wants to see her again. She's not welcome here."

"And she's simply staying away?" Roman knew she was in London, unless she'd lied about being at Marvit's.

"We hope so," Pierce replied. He appeared to share his brother-in-law's disgust regarding the duchess.

Roman fixed his gaze on Sheff. "Your mother has long been a prominent member of London society. How is she taking her banishment?" He glanced toward Pierce. "At least, that's what this sounds like."

"Banishment is the perfect word," Pierce said. "Nobody in the family wants anything to do with her."

Sheff's brow creased. "I'm concerned she'll try to return to London, but it will be difficult for her. My father has cut her off, and she won't have money to support herself here— or in Bath where she's currently living. She'll have to sell her jewels, and I can't see her parting with them. I believe they're dearer to her than family."

Pierce exhaled. "We must sound heartless to you. While we can't explain what the duchess has done to turn us all against her, please be assured it's deserved."

"I know how families can affect one another." Roman thought of his own father, with whom he'd had a terrible relationship, and of his dead wife. Both had hurt him.

Roman wished he knew *what* the duchess had done. "Why not give her a moderate allowance to ensure she stays away? That might be the smarter thing to do."

"I've suggested that to my father," Sheff replied. "But we all agree she can't be trusted. We don't want to encounter her as we go about our lives."

"Perhaps you should buy her a castle in the most remote area of Scotland you can find," Roman suggested.

"I did recommend that at one point," Pierce said. "But I'm new to the family, and I must defer to my wife and her father, as well as Sheff." He glanced toward his brother-in-law.

That wasn't a bad idea. Roman could buy the duchess a home somewhere—not a castle, given the state of his coffers —rather than just give her the money she'd demanded. He could ask his solicitor to draw up a contract. She would receive the property if she swore never to return to London.

Satisfied that he'd learned all he could, Roman finished his whisky and stood. "I must be on my way."

"Already?" Sheff asked in surprise.

"Afraid so. I've business to conduct." He didn't really, of course, but he wanted to be waiting for Ellis when she was finished with dinner. "Evening, lads."

Roman took his leave, glad that he'd decided to go to the club. At least he knew why the duchess was seeking money— because she'd been cut off by her husband and the rest of the family—even if he didn't know the reason for her banishment. He had to think it had something to do with Ellis. The duchess seemed to despise her daughter's former companion, and now the entire family had ostracized her.

What was between the two women?

Roman had his coachman park near Wellesbourne House, though not directly in front. He'd wait a little longer to move into a position where Ellis could see from a window that he was waiting. He didn't want to knock on the door and announce his presence.

An hour or so later, the coachman drove forward, and it wasn't long before Ellis left the house. Roman felt a swell of joy at seeing her, though it had only been a couple of hours since they'd parted.

He stepped from the coach and eagerly helped her inside. She sat on the rear-facing seat, a clear indication—at least to Roman—that she was still agitated about something. He sat down opposite her.

"Did you have a nice time?" he asked as the coach started moving.

"I did. Thank you." She smiled vaguely, but her posture was stiff.

"Then why are you tense?"

She blinked at him. "You think I'm tense?"

He regarded her a moment. "Yes. You've appeared agitated or upset for a couple of days now. I know there are things you're keeping from me, and I don't wish to press you about them, but you can trust me—with *all* your secrets."

She brushed at something on her gown, casting her head down. "Does that include a secret that would almost certainly upset you?"

"Yes," he replied without thinking. "I don't want you to carry something that's troubling you, even if it would trouble me too." Truthfully, he was already agitated knowing she was. "I would share your burden."

She met his gaze unflinchingly. "I don't want you to think less of me. This secret will change things between us."

"I promise you it won't," he vowed.

"You don't know that. This is…unconscionable." She finally looked away, turning her head toward the window. Her features were stoic for the rest of the ride.

Roman sat brooding, tension coiled within him as they approached his house. He didn't wait for the coachman to climb down and open the door. Instead, he departed the coach and held his hand up to assist Ellis.

Though they wore gloves, her touch was electric. Roman had to keep from pulling her toward him. She preceded him into the house, where Graham greeted them.

"I trust you had a pleasant evening," the butler said pleasantly.

"Yes, thank you," Ellis replied with a brief smile. "Good night, Graham." She glanced back over her shoulder as if she were trying to communicate the same to Roman. Then she continued toward the stairs.

Roman removed his hat and gloves as he followed her. She couldn't just go to bed. He needed to make sure she believed him when he said he could never think poorly of her. But he also didn't wish to upset her further.

When she reached the door to her chamber, she turned partially toward him. "I'm going to bed now."

"I don't want to say good night like this," he said. "I can see you're upset."

She hesitated, then ultimately exhaled before opening the door and stepping into her chamber. The fact that she didn't close it behind herself led him to believe he was welcome to go in after her. So, he did and then closed the door firmly.

"The household is still awake," she pointed out as she removed her gloves and tossed them on her dressing table.

"I know. I won't stay long." He watched as she unclasped her cloak, then moved to take it from her shoulders.

She gestured to a hook in the corner, and he went to hang it there. When he turned back around, he saw that she'd stepped out of her slippers. Her gaze was now seductive, surprising him after she'd said she wanted to go to bed. Did she have any idea how alluring she was?

"You said you didn't want to 'say good night like this,'" she said. "How were you hoping to say good night?"

"The way we usually do." Roman crossed to her in two large steps and swept her into his arms.

Their eyes met briefly, and the only thing he saw was a dark desire that matched his own. He kissed her with a heady passion that forced all other thoughts from his mind. She pressed against him as she skimmed her hands up beneath his coat and clasped his shoulders. He could feel her fingertips digging into him through the fabric of his waistcoat and shirt.

He twitched, desperate to remove the coat. She understood and pushed the garment over his shoulders and down his arms. It quickly found the floor. Then her hands were on his cravat, loosening the knotted silk that Graham had so painstakingly tied earlier. Roman clutched her waist as he kissed her again, his tongue thrusting against hers as they fought feverishly to claim the other.

His cravat disappeared, and she began unbuttoning his waistcoat. When it was open, she pulled his shirt from his breeches and unfastened his fall. She tucked her hand inside and stroked his cock. Roman strained against her, his hips rotating mindlessly as she worked him into a desperate state of need.

Roman tore his mouth from hers. "Your gown. Front or back?"

"Front. I don't have a maid." He brought his hands up and pulled at the slender cord holding her neckline taut above her breasts. Damn, but he was woefully out of practice. Though he didn't think he'd ever stripped the garments from a woman in this manner. Indeed, he would tear them from Ellis's body if it wouldn't be too beastly.

He latched his mouth onto her neck, suckling her flesh as she panted. "I want to rip every garment from you."

"You can't ruin my clothing," she rasped. "I don't have much."

"I'll buy you a new wardrobe. Anything you want." He would give her the sun and the moon and every goddamn star in the sky.

She put one hand on his cheek and drew him to look at her. The blue of her eyes shone incandescent in the firelight. "I don't want a wardrobe. I only want you."

Roman groaned before seizing her mouth in another nearly brutal kiss. She clutched at his head as she pumped his cock. If she didn't stop, he was going to come, and that would be a shame. He didn't want to spend in her hand before he could feel the velvet crush of her sex pulsing around him.

Managing to loosen her bodice enough for the front of the gown to fall, he swept the garment up over her head and cast it aside. "Women have too many bloody garments," he muttered as he kissed the tops of her breasts.

She awkwardly pulled his waistcoat away, using her free hand to tug the garment from his back. In the end, she had to take her hand from him long enough to remove it entirely. Roman took advantage and turned her about, pressing her back against her bed.

"Not fair," she whispered as he worked to unlace her corset.

He struggled to pull the ties loose. "For the love of God, help me," he begged as his fingers continued to fail.

Pushing his hands aside, she finished his work, quickly loosening the garment until she could thrust it down her body. Roman watched greedily as her breasts were freed from their cage. While she worked to remove the corset completely, he cupped her through her chemise.

Ellis arched her back, offering more of herself. Then she untied the lace at the top of the chemise that cinched the neck and tugged the thin garment down, baring her to his hunger. She put one hand over his and used the other to guide his head to her breast, urging him to taste her. He grunted as he closed his mouth over her nipple. She cried out softly, scoring his scalp with her nails.

He licked and suckled her, ravishing first one breast, then the other. She pushed the straps of petticoat from her shoulders and somehow kicked the garment away. Her hands came up under his shirt, skimming his abdomen. He straightened briefly to whisk the shirt off. As he did so, she lifted herself onto the bed, her legs dangling between them.

She wore only the chemise, with her breasts bared, and her stockings, held up by simple ribbon garters.

But Roman was out of patience, and it seemed, so was she. Ellis grabbed at his waist as she spread her legs and wrapped them around him. He put his hand between them and stroked her clitoris. Thrusting his fingers lower, he found her wet sheath. She arched her back, then moved her pelvis, grinding her sex against him.

"Come into me, Roman. *Now.*" She reached for his cock, and their hands met as they guided him into her body.

He drove hard and fast, and her muscles immediately clenched around him. She fell back on the bed as he thrust into her, working hard against his own impending orgasm. He would not come, not until she had fully climaxed.

Over and over, he filled her. By now, he recognized the signs of her body as she neared release. Her sex spasmed around him, squeezing him relentlessly. She stiffened, and he rubbed her clitoris with a firm, intense speed until she cried out his name and shattered into pieces. He didn't stop moving as he saw her through the climax, somehow managing to keep his own completion at bay.

Her body slackened, and her whimpers quieted. That was when Roman let go. He drove into her several more times and her sex contracted around him once more. He nearly forgot to pull away, but he did, pivoting his body so he would not spill himself on her.

She typically joined her hand with his, but not tonight. He didn't think about it. Not now, as his body shuddered with an overwhelming orgasm. He gripped the bedpost with his free hand as he finished.

When he finally fell from the height of ecstasy, he opened his eyes. Ellis was no longer on the bed. He blinked, and she was suddenly at his side, pressing a cloth into his hand. Then, she was gone.

He tidied himself, then re-buttoned his fall. When he straightened, he saw that Ellis was back on the bed, sitting up against the headboard. She wore a night rail, that was, disappointingly, opaque.

"Are you going to bed now?" she asked.

He usually stayed. Or she stayed with him, depending on where they were on any given night. But it was early, and she'd been right—the household was still awake. In fact, he worried they might have been heard, especially since Graham had likely come up to see if he required assistance. *Damn.*

"I would like to talk, if you're amenable." He perched on the edge of the bed. "It's important to me that you know I wouldn't ever think badly of you. I asked you to trust me, and you said you did. I hope you always will." He could see she was torn. Her features were creased, and her eyes were dark and troubled.

Roman didn't want to tell her about the duchess's letter. It was too horrible. It seemed obvious that Ellis had left the Henlow household because of the duchess. But was it just because she'd been treated poorly? That would certainly be enough, especially now that Lady Minerva was married and she no longer needed Ellis as a companion. Why would Ellis remain?

"It is it to do with the Duchess of Henlow?" he asked softly.

Her eyes widened as she sat up straight from the headboard. "What do you know?" she asked in alarm.

"Only that her family has banished her for some reason. I wondered if it might have something to do with you, since you left the household. Did she drive you away?"

Ellis put her hand to her mouth and looked away from him. "Yes, it's to do with her. She has always hated me—since the day I went to live with them after my parents died. It never made sense to me. It still doesn't."

She met his gaze once more, and her eyes were now bright with emotion. "I recently learned the duchess is my mother, that I'm the illegitimate offspring of an affair. It's ironic, since so many people assumed I was Henlow's by-blow. But *she* is my parent, not him."

Roman stared at her, shocked by this revelation. What-ever he'd anticipated, it had never been this. "You had no idea?"

She shook her head. "Why would I think a woman who loathed me could be my mother? I didn't even realize I'd been adopted until recently, though perhaps I should have known since I don't particularly resemble either of my parents."

Roman ached for her, and more than ever he wanted to strike out at the duchess. There was no way he would pay her extortion now. Neither was he going to reveal the letter to Ellis. She need never know just *how* cruel her mother was. "That must have been devastating to discover." He stood and moved around the bed to sit nearer to her.

"That isn't everything." Ellis scooted away from him, and he didn't understand why she wouldn't want comfort. "The rest is even worse. Her lover was Rowland Harker."

"Lady Shefford's father? He's your father too?" Roman was again shocked, but he didn't see how that worsened anything.

"He's the most abysmal rogue." Ellis shook her head, her disgust evident. "I went to his house the other day so we could be introduced as father and daughter. Jo took me."

That was her errand, and the reason for her strange behavior the past few days. "What happened?" Roman prepared himself for something terrible. Though how could anything be worse than what she'd already revealed?

A truly abhorrent thought stole into his mind. God, Harker hadn't tried to seduce her before he'd learned the truth, had he? Before he could voice the fear, Ellis spoke.

"I saw a collection of portraits Harker has painted over the years—of his mistresses." Ellis hesitated, her features growing apprehensive. "I don't know if I should tell you this."

Roman had a very bad feeling. A chill swept over him, icing his veins. "Tell me."

"One of them was Clarissa."

The room went black for a moment as Roman's vision tunneled. He stood and stalked to the fireplace, his heart crashing about his chest.

"I'm sorry, Roman." Ellis's voice somehow broke through his haze of rage. "I didn't want to tell you. But I can't continue to be with you and not reveal the truth. You said you wanted to share my burden. I was glad to hear you say that because I'm afraid I can't carry it alone and look at you every day. I can only imagine how angry you feel."

"Angry isn't a big enough emotion," he growled. For so long, he'd wanted to know the identity of the man who'd broken Clarissa's heart and caused her death. Now he did. And he could finally seek vengeance for the tragic loss of a young woman with her entire life before her.

Except the blackguard was Ellis's father.

"Did you know she'd been unfaithful?" Ellis asked softly.

"Yes, but I didn't know with whom."

"I had no idea," she said. "I'm so sorry."

He turned to face her. She now stood next to the bed, watching him with anguish—and trepidation. "I didn't tell you because, just as you didn't want to share parts of your past, I preferred not to disclose some of mine."

She nodded in understanding, her expression sympathetic, and it nearly broke his heart. "I think it's best if I leave your employment."

"You are far more than my bloody employee," he ground out.

"I'm not sure that matters. There's no future for us, Roman. Even if there wasn't this horrible tangle with my father and your wife, there is *me*. I'm penniless and illegitimate. You need an heiress of good standing who will help you reclaim your family's place in Society. You know what I say is true. We've had our time, and it was wonderful. But it's time we moved on."

Wonderful? No, it had been perfect.

But she'd laid it all out quite clearly—and accurately. There was no future for them. He did need an heiress, and he was going to demand satisfaction from her father. Just thinking of him having a portrait of Clarissa, like some kind of trophy, made him sick. He would hate for Josiah or Harriet to ever learn the truth.

What made him feel worse, however, was the thought of losing Ellis and what they shared. "I don't want it to be over," he rasped, his throat tight with emotions that ranged from fury to despair.

And love.

He knew in that moment that he loved Ellis. Far more than he'd ever imagined he might care for Clarissa. Ellis had transformed him from a bitter widow to a man who looked forward to every day. His household was warmer and brighter with her in it.

"There has to be a way," he croaked. But right now, his thoughts and emotions were completely jumbled.

Ellis shook her head.

Shaking, Roman went about picking up his strewn garments. "I need to think."

"There's no thinking required," she said simply. Without emotion.

Roman's heart blistered as he walked to the door. He

stopped to look back at her. "Your father—" He blew out a breath and made a frustrated sound. "His behavior cannot go unanswered. You will hate me, Ellis, for what I want to do."

"I suspect you want to call him out, and that if you do, you'll likely kill him. I can't stop you. I won't stop you." She took a breath, her voice lowering. "I hardly know him, and I've no affinity toward him. In fact, I found him rather repellent overall. Still, he is my father. And he's Jo's father. I cannot wish for his death. I beg you to reconsider."

"I cannot. He's despicable. He devastated the Laceys." Roman couldn't breathe. "He drove Clarissa to her death. When I learned of the affair, I demanded she end it. But she said her lover had already pushed her away. She was despondent, saying that she would never love anyone as she loved him and that she'd made a huge mistake in marrying me. She began taking laudanum. One night, she drank too much of it and didn't wake the following morning. I will never know if she'd intended to die or not, but I'm not sure it matters since the result was the same."

Ellis pressed her hand to her mouth and looked as if she might cry.

Roman wished he could hold her, but he needed time to determine what he would do.

He opened the door and turned away from her. "I'm sorry, Ellis."

As he stepped over the threshold, he pulled the door closed. Just before it snapped shut, he swore he heard her say, "I love you."

But he could not have. How could she love him now?

CHAPTER 17

Ellis barely slept after Roman left her room. She had dozed fitfully, then given up before the sun rose. It didn't take long to pack her things, for she didn't bother with the men's wardrobe. She felt a little guilty leaving it behind, however, she wasn't able to manage carrying everything on her own, and she wasn't going to ask for help.

Then she'd taken on the painful task of writing her letter of resignation. That had taken far longer than packing her things and was perhaps the most difficult thing she'd ever done. Anguish tightened every muscle in her body as she left the letter on Roman's desk in the study where they had come to know each other so well and where they had shared their first kiss.

Fighting back tears, she quietly departed just after the sun rose. She walked to Grosvenor Square as quickly as she could whilst carrying two valises. Where else could she go but Henlow House? She supposed she could have gone to Wellesbourne House. Pandora certainly would have welcomed her there.

But Ellis needed to go home. It was time.

Nervously, she knocked on the door at Henlow House. Percy, the butler, greeted her warmly.

"Good morning, Miss Dangerfield. It's wonderful to see you." He glanced at the lightening sky but said nothing about the shocking earliness of the hour. His gaze dipped to her valises. "Dare I hope you've come to stay, at least for a while?"

She nodded. "If I may, Percy. I doubt Lady Shefford is yet awake, but I don't think she will object, nor will his lordship."

"*No one* here would object, Miss Dangerfield. In fact, I imagine there will be unanimous delight."

Emotion swelled in Ellis's chest. These people wanted her, whereas her own blood, her mother, did not. Ellis would never be able to reconcile those things. She just had to accept that was the way it was.

"I'll just go up to my old room, then," she said.

Percy took her valises from her as she stepped inside and moved them to the corner of the entrance hall. "Jack will take these up for you, but not to your old room," the butler said, referring to one of the footmen. "Lady Shefford made it clear to me that if you returned, you were to have Lady Minerva's former suite."

Ellis wasn't sure how she felt about that. It was Min's, not hers. It was also far larger than her room on the third floor.

Jo had expected her to come? How, when Ellis hadn't even decided until late last night?

"Are you certain that's what I should do?" Ellis asked. "It doesn't seem right."

"Everyone is in agreement, Miss Dangerfield, including Lady Minerva. It's not as if she needs that chamber any longer."

Ellis quashed a smile. "No, she does not." Apparently, her sisters had been plotting behind her back. She didn't mind one bit. It was, she decided, quite nice to have sisters.

"Would you like breakfast sent up?" Percy asked as Ellis removed her gloves.

"Not yet. I think I'll rest for a while. Thank you, Percy. It's absolutely lovely to see you."

He inclined his head, and his eyes gleamed with warmth.

Ellis moved into the staircase hall and slowly made her way upstairs. This was home, or one of them, anyway. But this was the place where she'd spent the most time over the past seventeen years of her life. There was also Beacon Park and the Grove, the beloved home near Weston, where she and Min spent every August and where their little club of friends had been formed. It was also where Pandora had been ruined and the Rogue Rules had been born.

Ellis yawned as she finally made her way into Min's chamber. It was pink and rose and almost unbearably floral. It had been designed by their mother and wasn't particularly to Min's taste. Strangely, Ellis liked it, though she'd never said so. The busy flower patterns appealed to her for some reason, and she liked the pink with the small accents of ivory and green.

Did that mean she had at least something in common with her mother? Ellis didn't like to think so, but again, she had to accept what was and not what she hoped for.

Jack delivered her valises, and like the butler, he welcomed her effusively before departing. Ellis couldn't help but smile through her exhaustion. It felt good to be home.

～

*E*llis woke late that morning and took the breakfast that Percy had offered earlier. The cook had included her favorite apricot jam, and again, Ellis couldn't help smiling. It was remarkable, given how heavy her heart felt after how things had ended with Roman last night.

Perhaps it was time to let the past—even the most recent—go.

Her breakfast had come with a note from Jo asking Ellis to join her in the drawing room whenever she finished, if she wanted to.

After pinning up her hair and donning a simple day dress, Ellis regarded herself in the glass and was pleased with what she saw. No more facial hair or wigs. She wasn't Lady Minerva's companion, nor was she the Marquess of Keele's secretary. She was also no longer his lover. She was just simple Miss Dangerfield, and she liked that.

She went downstairs to the drawing room on the first floor. Jo and Sheff were there together, and as soon as she stepped over the threshold, Sheff shot to his feet. He grinned. "Ellis, you're back. I'm so happy to see you."

He came toward her and embraced her tightly. She closed her eyes for a moment and welcomed his comfort.

"Thank you. I'm glad to be back."

He guided her to the seating area, and she sat down on the settee next to Jo, who took her hand and smiled. "Is it all right that you're in Min's room?"

"It's strange," Ellis admitted. "But it's comfortable."

"You can redecorate it however you like," Sheff said. "You're also welcome to an entirely new wardrobe."

Ellis pressed her lips together. "That is most generous of you, but I cannot accept."

Sheff's brow furrowed briefly. "Why not? You're a member of this family."

"I suppose I am, but I don't see a life for myself here in London. What would I do? Be a governess to your child?" She glanced at Jo's belly.

"We would never ask you to do that." Jo hesitated. "Unless… Is that what you want to do?"

"No," Ellis said. "I would prefer to be a loving aunt."

Sheff grinned. "So, you shall be. You are welcome here for as long as you like. Forever."

Ellis hoped she wasn't going to hurt their feelings. "I deeply appreciate that, Sheff—more than you can know. However, I would like to make my own way. I thought I might try to become a librarian, though not here in London."

"You would make an excellent librarian," Jo said.

"Won't you miss it here?" Sheff asked with genuine concern.

Ellis realized she would. This *was* her home, and they were offering her the opportunity to keep it. But she didn't want to be the spinster aunt, at least not in the same household.

Sheff gestured toward her. "If you'd rather live somewhere else, we can arrange for that too. Or you could go live with Father in Marylebone. He said he'd be delighted to have you. He's always loved you, you know."

Again, Ellis felt too much emotion welling within her. "Thank you. I will consider your kind suggestions."

Jo rested her hand on her belly. "Well, if you chose to stay with us until I have the baby, I wouldn't mind the support. I am thrilled to have a sister."

Ellis couldn't deny she felt the same. She now had *two* sisters *and* a brother. She also had a living mother and a living father, neither of whom she wanted anything to do with. She was incredibly troubled about Rowland Harker and the conversation she'd had with Roman last night. She couldn't fault him for his anger but hoped he wouldn't act on it.

Hurting his wife's lover wouldn't make him feel better, but Roman had to determine that for himself. Ellis could not make his problems hers. Not after he'd so clearly turned away from her after she'd done precisely what he'd asked of her—to share her burden with him.

"We're so happy you're here," Jo said. "Can I ask why?" she added tentatively.

Ellis exhaled. "Did you tell Sheff about Rowland Harker and Roman's wife?"

Jo grimaced faintly. "I did. We don't keep secrets from one another. I had to tell him. It affects you, and you're our family."

"I'm not angry," Ellis assured her. "I would expect you to share it with him. You're married, and you *shouldn't* have secrets. Secrets are what brought us here."

"So true," Sheff agreed. "I confess I don't know that I can be civil to Harker next time I see him."

Jo scowled. "I'm even angrier now than I was when you told us last night. Which is silly because I've known he had affairs with married people. I'm embarrassed to say his behavior didn't trouble me as much as it does now, because I didn't have a personal relationship with anyone who was affected. I thought I could express my distaste for his activities and still maintain a relationship with him, but I can no longer do that. He needs to stop philandering, or I will not associate with him."

Ellis squeezed her hand before letting her go. "I never meant to cause heartache for you or to divide you and your father."

"You did nothing," Jo said quickly. "It's his fault. How did Roman take the news?"

"Quite poorly." Ellis wasn't going to detail just *how* poorly nor would she share the particulars of Clarissa's death. She wasn't keeping secrets; she was preserving a poor woman's dignity, she hoped. "He has long been angry with whoever it was that seduced his wife, and I think he was resigned to never knowing the man's identity. Now that he does, I worry he'll demand satisfaction."

"He's not going to call Harker out, is he?" Sheff asked sharply.

Ellis tried not to reveal the depth of her agitation. "He might. I asked him not to, but I don't think I persuaded him. I should have told him that it would be more damaging to him than to Rowland."

Sheff's features had darkened. "I'll speak to him."

"I don't know if you should," Ellis warned, thinking of how furious Roman had been. "But I won't tell you what to do."

"I've known Keele a long time," Sheff said. "I'll dispatch a note asking him to meet later." He nodded at them both before quickly departing.

Jo sent a hopeful look toward Ellis. "Did you tell Roman how you felt?"

"No." Ellis tipped her head down briefly. "I wanted to, but I just…didn't. He was angry about Rowland, and rightfully so. Furthermore, he didn't argue with me about what he needs, which is an heiress." She returned her gaze to Jo. "Please don't suggest the dowry options again. Even if I *were* an heiress, it wouldn't work. How can he marry the illegitimate daughter of a man he despises? And what if he does call Rowland out? I have to imagine he'd wound him, if not kill him. While I don't particularly hold our father with affection, I certainly don't want him to die. I don't think I could be with Roman if he dueled with him."

Jo's face was creased with concern. "Perhaps Keele just needs time to let his anger cool. What did he say when you left?"

"I don't know," Ellis replied. "I left a note this morning. I didn't tell him where I went, and I asked him not to try to reach me."

Jo scooted forward, which took slightly more effort than normal. "Ellis, why do you keep doing this? You cut yourself off from the people who care about you. Do you think that you deserve to be unhappy? You *don't,*" she said forcefully. "Nothing that has happened is your fault, regardless of what the duchess might have told you."

Did Ellis believe that she didn't deserve happiness? She didn't think so, but after years and years of hearing how unworthy she was and how she was lucky to be a companion in their household, she truly didn't think she deserved more.

Ellis stared but saw nothing as her thoughts tumbled over themselves.

"You may be right," she said softly. "Will you excuse me? I think I need to be alone for a little while."

"Certainly," Jo said, "but I'm here for you as your friend and your sister. I love you."

This time, the emotion welling within Ellis reached her eyes, and she feared she would cry. She didn't want to do that in front of Jo. "Thank you," she croaked before she turned and fled.

CHAPTER 18

*E*llis's note to Roman had been devastatingly short and flat.

> *Dear Roman,*
> *I am grateful for the opportunity to be your secretary. It has been an invaluable experience. I deeply appreciate your keeping my secrets and hiding me. Now it's time for me to face things and decide my future.*
> *I think it's best if you don't know where I've gone, and I would ask that you not try to find me. We both know that we must travel separate paths.*
> *Fondly,*
> *Ellis.*

Fondly? There had been no mention of their affair, nor of the wondrous joy they'd shared. And not a word about love.

Perhaps he'd misheard her last night as he'd left the room. He should have gone right back inside and questioned her. He regretted not doing so.

However, her letter didn't sound like something a woman

in love would write. Not that it mattered whether she loved him or not. She believed they had no future, and he couldn't disagree with her.

When he wasn't thinking of Ellis, which was nearly every moment, he stewed about Rowland Harker. He'd stolen a happy future from a naïve young woman.

Though if Clarissa were still here, Roman would not have come to know Ellis in the way that he did. And now, he simply couldn't imagine his life without what they'd shared.

Because his study now reminded him of Ellis, Roman had spent the day working at Lacey and Company in Paternoster Row. Josiah had remarked upon his quiet and almost surly demeanor. Roman had briefly explained he hadn't slept well, then spent the rest of the day avoiding everyone.

Returning home at dinnertime, he noted a coach parked in front of his house. Roman thought it might belong to Sheff.

Graham welcomed him into the house.

"Is Lord Shefford here?" Roman asked.

"He is," Graham confirmed. "Upstairs in the library. I told him I didn't know when you would return, but he insisted on waiting. He sent a note this afternoon, then arrived here a short while ago."

"I see." Roman grew concerned. It was entirely possible that Sheff knew where Ellis had gone. Was something wrong?

Roman handed his hat and gloves to Graham and dashed up the stairs, ascending two at a time. He walked into the library.

Sheff stood at the window and turned as Roman entered. "I saw your coach drive up."

"Why are you here?" Roman strode toward him as his concern bloomed to full anxiety. "Graham said you sent a note earlier. Is something wrong? Is it Ellis?"

"In a way." Sheff gestured to the main seating area. "May we sit?"

"I'd rather not," Roman said.

Sheff shrugged. "Have it your way. I came to speak with you about my father-in-law, Rowland Harker."

"I know who your father-in-law is," Roman grumbled. Though he wasn't as angry as he'd been last night, mention of the man still raised his hackles. "I can guess why you want to speak to me about him, but I would prefer not to discuss it."

"I imagine not, so let us ignore the details. You can't call him out," Sheff said plainly. "I realize he's a blackguard and deserves some sort of comeuppance, but is there another way you can gain satisfaction? Does it help you to know that Jo and I are prepared to cut ties with him entirely? In fact, Jo is going to give him an ultimatum that he must stop philandering."

"You really think he'll do that?" Roman scoffed.

"I don't know," Sheff said, and he sounded genuine. "If he won't agree to it, we shall wash our hands of him. Still, we'd rather you didn't cause him physical harm."

Roman dearly wanted to at least hit the man in the face. "How else am I to have satisfaction?"

"I understand you're angry." Sheff raised a placating hand. "Perhaps it would help to confront him."

Roman blew out a breath and stalked across the room. For years he'd thought about what he wanted to do to the man who'd caused so much devastation with his careless behavior. He turned halfway and glanced over at Sheff, who was fixed on Roman expectantly.

"I was very angry last night when Ellis told me that Harker had been my wife's lover, but I don't want to hurt him." Roman felt some of the tension leave his shoulders. "I blame the man for corrupting an innocent young woman and causing her family untold grief." Roman explained how Clarissa had died.

"*Bloody hell,*" Sheff breathed. "I didn't realize."

Roman faced him. "Would you tell someone if that had happened to your wife?"

"No." Sheff's brows drew together. "I'm sorry, Roman. I'll go with you to confront Harker. We'll inform him it's time he retired from his debauchery. If he doesn't, he will never meet our child, and I'll ensure he's completely cut from Society. No more social engagements, no painting anyone or providing lessons."

Roman felt as if he'd been hit in the gut. "I hadn't put that together. I believe Harker was Clarissa's tutor. He can't be allowed to teach any young women ever again."

Sheff's eyes darkened with fury. "Agreed. We'll extract that promise from him too—and I'll make sure he keeps it. Let's go see him now."

Roman was torn. Part of him never wanted to see Rowland Harker, but perhaps a larger part of him wanted the man to know what his behavior had wrought. Perhaps that would even convince him to stop. "Yes, let's go and put an end to his depravity."

~

A short while later, they arrived at the Bedford, a chop-house near where Harker lived and where Sheff said he would likely be at this hour. They found Harker upstairs in a small, private dining room just as he'd sat down to eat. It was perfect for confronting the man, particularly if Roman decided after all that he simply couldn't avoid punching him in the face.

Roman didn't think he'd met Harker before. The man was attractive, which wasn't surprising since he was Ellis's father, with blond hair and golden-brown eyes. He grinned broadly as they entered, and his features revealed him to be a man who smiled often. "Good evening, Sheff. You've brought a friend! How charming. Would you care to join me? The lamb is excellent."

"This is Lord Keele," Sheff said ominously.

Harker's expression dimmed. Roman couldn't tell if he knew who he was—at least relative to one of his past lovers. It was entirely possible he'd heard the name Keele in another context.

"I don't believe we're acquainted, my lord," Harker said, his tone still affable if a bit uncertain. "I'm pleased to meet you."

"Whereas, I would sooner meet vermin," Roman replied with a faint sneer.

Harker blinked. All the good nature that had lit his features evaporated. "There's no call to be rude."

"You'll find he has every reason to be rude or even downright insulting." Sheff glanced at Roman. "Will you tell him, or shall I?"

"I'll tell him." Roman's pulse sped as he fixed a glower on Harker. "While we haven't met, you knew my wife, Clarissa, very well."

"That's right." Harker grimaced, and Roman almost gave the man credit for not trying to hide the fact that he'd known Clarissa. "I was just speaking of her the other day, in fact. Life is funny, isn't it? How you can think of someone and then they appear, although, in this case, she can't appear. But someone else *is* here…talking about her…" his voice trailed off awkwardly.

"And why *isn't* she here?" Roman asked with soft menace.

"I believe she died, my lord." Harker's voice had climbed then caught. He coughed. "I'm very sorry to hear that happened."

"Do you know how?" Roman asked. "Of course you don't. I made sure no one knew because it was horrible and would have ruined her. I can't say for sure that she intended to die on purpose." Roman took satisfaction from Harker's soft gasp. "She became ill after you pushed her away. At the time, I didn't know you were her lover, but it has recently come to my attention that you are the reason my wife withered and died."

Harker blanched. "You're saying she killed herself?"

"As I said, I don't know and I never will. What I can tell you is that she died a melancholic and broken woman. You deprived her parents of their beloved daughter and me of my wife. She loved you more than anything. She even regretted marrying me, though it wasn't as if she could wed you for you already have a wife, don't you?"

Harker put his hand to his brow and fidgeted with his hair, appearing most anxious. "She asked me quite insistently to run away with her, and I declined. I told her that she needed to return to you and that our affair was simply a passing fancy. I assured her she would move past it and likely forget me entirely."

Roman blinked. Harker had encouraged her to go back to Roman after she'd begged him to flee London together? Some of the rage he'd carried dissipated. He would never forgive Harker, but perhaps he didn't hate him quite as much. It was better to try to do the right thing, even if it was late in coming.

"You're despicable," Sheff said with disdain. "You must stop this behavior. You believe your actions have no consequences, but they do. This is just one instance that you now know of, but there are almost certainly more. Not to mention the countless children you've fathered illegitimately."

"They aren't *countless*," Harker argued, still pale and agitated.

Sheff stared at him coldly. "You weren't aware of one of your offspring until a short while ago, so I'd say that's a reasonable description. You'll either stop behaving in this manner, or you will finally suffer for your behavior."

"How?" Harker croaked as he sent a fearful glance toward Roman.

"To start, Jo and I will be finished with you. Then, I will make sure no one in Society engages with you—*ever*. And you will never teach anyone again. That is non-negotiable."

Harker's gaze turned pleading. "But teaching is how I earn money. How will I survive?"

"Perhaps you should try living within your means," Sheff sneered. "You receive plenty from Jo's mother to live a comfortable life. Although I'm sure I could persuade her to rescind that allowance. When she hears the true depth of your debauchery, she may do far worse to you than I've threatened. I'm also confident Jo can talk her half-siblings into turning against you too. You will be alone and destitute."

Harker stared at them with wide, panicked eyes. "Fine—no more teaching. But I don't know if I can stop the other. I've tried to be monogamous or even refrain from physical pleasures, but it's as though I'm incapable. I loved Jo's mother. I hated that I had betrayed her, but I couldn't seem to help myself."

"You must try harder," Roman growled.

"I will." Harker nodded eagerly. "I promise."

Sheff inclined his head. "If you fail, the consequences I've laid out will be yours."

Harker blanched. "I understand." He looked at Roman. "I did love Clarissa, if that means anything. I loved them all, just not as much as they loved me or for as long." He appeared regretful, but it didn't matter to Roman.

He stalked toward the man and leaned down, setting his hand on the table next to Harker's plate. Roman met his gaze and snarled. "I've wanted to call you out and demand satisfaction for years, but I'm not going to because I'm in love with your daughter. Killing her father, even one she doesn't know and likely doesn't care to, would not change anything that's happened in the past." *It could, however, make her hate me.* Thinking of that possibility filled Roman with a deep and horrible torment.

"You're in love with Ellis?" Harker asked in surprise.

Roman straightened and turned away. He was not going to satisfy the man with an answer. He did note, however, that Sheff was stifling a gleeful smile.

As Roman strode toward the door, he heard Sheff deliver a parting warning to Harker.

"We'll know if you don't keep your word. Do not disappoint any of us, especially your children. They deserve better."

Roman opened the door and stalked out of the dining room toward the stairs. He didn't stop until he was outside the chop-house. He took several deep breaths and felt a weight lift from his body. Was that because he'd finally confronted the man who'd cuckolded him, or did he feel lighter because he'd finally declared his love for Ellis?

Sheff joined him on the pavement. "You're in love with her, eh?"

How long had Roman loved Ellis? For some time. Perhaps even from the moment he'd discovered she was a woman. His immediate reaction hadn't been anger or disgust. Even then, when he'd barely known her, he'd felt an overwhelming urge to protect and support her.

He'd known he was falling in love with her after he'd received that vile letter from the duchess. Again, he'd been overcome with the absolute need to keep Ellis safe. He would pay any price, risk everything he had for her.

"Yes." Roman walked toward the coach.

"You don't appear to be filled with joy," Sheff noted wryly as he kept up beside him.

No, but he ached to be. "I completely botched things."

"So I gathered." Sheff shrugged. "I don't know what happened, but Jo told me enough. Ellis is ready to leave London and strike out on her own, something about becoming a librarian. I offered her a dowry, but she won't take it."

Again, she didn't sound like a woman interested in marriage, but then she'd never claimed to be.

"She thinks you need an heiress. Is that true?" Sheff cut his hand through the air. "It doesn't matter. If you love her, you must tell her." He grabbed Roman's arm, pulling him to stop just before they reached the coach. "Don't wait. You'll regret it." Releasing Roman, he gave him a dark stare. "I regret not running to Jo the moment I suspected I loved her."

"I don't know where Ellis is." Did that mean Roman would run to her? He wanted to but wasn't sure he should.

"Shall we go to my house next?" Sheff asked blandly.

Roman understood he was implicitly saying Ellis was at Henlow House. The urge to go to her was overwhelming, but he needed to approach her in the right way. In the best way. "Not tonight. I've some things to arrange."

"Tomorrow?"

Roman nodded. And all would be revealed—for better or worse.

CHAPTER 19

*E*llis was surprisingly happy waking up in Min's old bedchamber the following morning. It probably helped that she'd spent a lovely evening with Jo and Min. They'd dined and laughed and hadn't spoken much of Rowland Harker or the duchess, and Ellis hadn't let them speak at all about Roman. Thinking of him made her sad, but that would lessen with time. She rather doubted the emotion would ever go away entirely.

One of the maids had come in to wake her up and had also brought breakfast. Then she'd returned to help Ellis dress, not that Ellis really needed her. However, Ellis hadn't wanted to refuse her enthusiastic assistance. The entire household was exceptionally pleased to have her back. Ellis had to acknowledge that it felt wonderful.

She just wished she had something to do. She missed her work. And Roman. Did he miss her too?

Pushing him from her mind, she went to the door and planned to go to the library to read a book. That was the way she'd always cured her boredom. There had been many occasions when the duchess had taken Min shopping or to make calls and hadn't brought Ellis along. Ellis hadn't minded, for she much preferred the books.

As soon as she swung open the door, Ellis stopped short. The duchess was standing just over the threshold, her piercing blue eyes regarding Ellis the way she always did—with judgment and disdain.

"What are you doing here?" Ellis asked loudly, her heart pounding with distress.

The duchess's face was angular, her lips, which were currently pursed, narrow and her nose slender. She'd always been very thin, which made her features seem more extreme, at least to Ellis. Despite that, Ellis now saw the similarity between them, and it made her angry.

"I've come to see you," the duchess replied crisply. She brushed past Ellis into Min's bedchamber.

Ellis faced the duchess. She couldn't think of what to say and fought to calm her racing pulse.

"I shouldn't be surprised that you usurped Minerva's room," the duchess announced crossly as she glanced about the chamber. "I imagine you'll try to rise above your station as much as you can."

"What station is that, exactly?" Ellis asked, giving in to her anger in front of the duchess for the first time. "My *station* is the only thing you've ever given me. I'm a bastard because of *your* behavior. It's a mark against you, not me."

"Me?" The duchess narrowed her eyes. "Society does not look at it that way. You should close the door. I can't imagine you want the entire household hearing what I have to say."

Ellis hesitated. On the one hand, she didn't particularly care if the household heard anything, but on the other, she'd always been a private person, or at least a person used to clinging to the shadows. In the end, she moved away from the door without closing it and glared at the duchess in open mutiny.

"I don't particularly want to hear what you have to say. How did you even infiltrate the house? It's my understanding you've been banished."

The duchess pursed her lips again and strode past Ellis to close the door firmly. She turned back and moved to stand in the center of the room, once more clasping her hands in a ladylike fashion before her waist. "If you think I have no way to enter the house I called home for more than two decades, you are even more foolish than I thought. I've come to discuss something with you. I informed your employer—rather, your lover—that you are illegitimate."

Ellis paused. Had Roman known that already when she'd told him?

She crossed her arms over her chest. "What did you do? And when?"

"Does any of that really matter?" the duchess asked in annoyance.

"I'm merely curious, because I've already told him that I'm illegitimate," Ellis explained.

"I see," the duchess murmured. "Well, as you pointed out, I've been pushed out of the family, and I find myself in need of funds. I had hoped that Keele would pay for my silence regarding your unfortunate background, but he refused."

She'd tried to extort Roman? Ellis couldn't believe the woman's gall. She was overjoyed that Roman had denied the duchess, but why hadn't he told her?

The duchess continued, interrupting Ellis's thoughts. "I'm afraid my only option now is to find a way to earn money for myself. The only means I can think of is to publish a memoir in which I will detail your father's affairs, as well as my own indiscretion—and I may as well include the story of your brother's fake betrothal and how he never really intended to marry that strumpet, but then she trapped him with a child.

You must agree it's a riveting tale of one of Society's most prominent families."

Ellis gaped at the duchess, unable to believe what she was hearing. "You would ruin the entire family, including your-self...*for money?*"

The duchess shrugged. "What else am I to do? Henlow will no longer pay for my house in Bath, nor will he allow me to stay at the dower house at Beacon Park, nor will he pay for me to live anywhere in London. What am I to do?"

"Why is that any of our responsibility, especially your children? We don't owe you anything."

"You owe me life." The duchess snarled.

Ellis could do nothing but laugh. "After the way you've treated me the past seventeen years, the only thing I owe you is my eternal loathing. You are the worst person I have ever known, and this threat you've just made only proves my point."

Breathing deep to calm her rage, Ellis took a moment to contemplate the woman before her, with whom she shared blood and nothing else. Still, she had memories of the duchess laughing and spending time with her children, just not with Ellis. She'd always thought the duchess loved Min and Sheff, if no one else. "Why do you want to torture every-one, including yourself as well as Sheff and Min? I expect you to torture me—you've always done so. But why? What did I ever do? It wasn't *my* fault you had an affair with Rowland Harker."

The duchess's jaw was tight. Her lips had gone white, and she'd let her hands fall to her sides. "I despised having you in my household," she spat. "I couldn't wait to get rid of you the moment you were born. Henlow wanted to raise you as his own, but I wouldn't allow that. He insisted on placing you with the Dangerfields, who had so desperately wanted a child and didn't have one."

Ellis's heart swelled at the mention of her adoptive parents. She missed them so very much.

"Every time I looked at you, I saw Rowland Harker," the duchess went on. "You were—you *are*—a constant reminder of the abhorrent mistake I made, and I know that's why Henlow wanted you in this household. His cruelty was unparalleled. It wasn't enough that he paraded his mistresses around and behaved like an utter reprobate."

The duchess seemed to have no idea of her hypocrisy in saying her husband's cruelty was unmatched. She could give lessons. But Ellis didn't have a chance to point this out as the duchess pressed on.

"When I publish the book, I daresay no one will blame me, considering how Henlow has always treated me. They'll understand that I went elsewhere for affection. The duke is the clear villain of this tale."

Ellis shook her head. She was beginning to wonder if the duchess might be a little mad. "You can't do this."

"You're not going to stop me. And it's not as if you can give me any money," she said with a light, humorless laugh.

Ellis wondered if she could convince Sheff to use the money he would have offered as Ellis's dowry to pay the duchess off. It would be worth it to remove her from their lives forever.

Her door flew open, and Sheff was there along with Jo and Min. He stalked into the chamber, his dark blue eyes dark with fury. "How the bloody hell did you get in here?"

Jo and Min followed him in. Min appeared equally irate, and Jo only a bit less so.

The duchess lifted her chin. "This was my home until you so cruelly threw me out."

"When I find who let you in, I will dismiss them immediately," Sheff growled. "Nobody wants you here. I'll escort you out."

"She needs money," Ellis said. "She tried to extort Roman, but he refused."

"Did he?" Sheff asked in surprise. "He said nothing about that."

"You've seen him?" Ellis was momentarily distracted by the mention of the man she loved and missed more than anything.

"Forget about your sordid little affair," the duchess snapped at Ellis. She directed her cool gaze at her son. "Yes, I require money to live since your father refuses to provide me with a residence."

"She's going to publish a book about the family," Ellis explained. "She plans to include every sordid detail, including the fact that your betrothal was fake."

Jo moved to sit on a chair. Sheff rushed to help her as Min stepped toward their mother.

"I think you might be evil," Min said, her expression a mix of anger and sadness.

After settling Jo, Sheff spun on his mother. "Father didn't cut you off entirely. He just isn't giving you enough to live as you have been. You don't deserve to. You have enough to remove yourself to a pleasant country village where you can try to manage everyone and repel a whole new group of people." He advanced on her, joining Min. "We will *never* let you publish lies—or anything else—about our family."

Min glowered at the duchess. "I don't even know why you'd want to do that. You'd expose yourself as the horrible person you are."

"No, I wouldn't," the duchess replied calmly. "As I explained to Ellis, your father is the villain. He's treated me horribly all these years. I sought affection elsewhere with Rowland Harker, then your father made me live with the consequences of my actions. It was most cruel. People will be sympathetic to me, you'll see."

"How evil to have to suffer the consequences of your actions," Jo muttered.

"How about we publish a book explaining the real story before yours is published?" Ellis suggested. "As it happens, I know a publisher."

"Excellent idea, Ellis," Sheff said, glancing at her with a faint nod before directing a glare toward the duchess. "Of course, the real story is that *you* were being unfaithful to Father long before he sought comfort in the arms of others. He loved you, and he married you thinking you loved him too."

Ellis took satisfaction in the duchess turning scarlet.

"He lied to you," the duchess sputtered.

"Don't even try to make us believe that," Sheff said with disgust. "He told me personally, and if you think I couldn't see the hurt he felt when you betrayed him—you're even colder than I thought. You married him for the title but made him think that you loved him. Then, as soon as you provided an heir, you found a lover. Honestly, I'm glad you did. Giving us Ellis as our sister was probably the nicest thing you've done for us."

Ellis's heart expanded. She looked toward Sheff and Min. He was too focused on their mother, but Min smiled at Ellis and nodded.

"I couldn't agree more," Min said defiantly. She narrowed her eyes at the duchess. "I will sell everything I own to ensure you leave London and never return, nor can you go to Bath or Weston or anywhere else we might be. Have you considered Australia?"

"You don't need to do that," Sheff said to Min. "I'll give her the money to leave. But just once, then never again."

"I don't want your money," the duchess in a near-whine. "I want only your love and respect. I deserve it."

"But you're never going to have those things." Min's lip

curled. "I will never forgive you for the way you've treated Ellis or the way you treated Papa." She moved to stand beside Ellis, their arms touching.

Sheff crossed to Ellis's other side. "I feel the same."

Ellis was incredibly humbled by her siblings' support. Summoning a brief smile, she regarded their mother with a glorious sense of victory. "You've lost. Nobody here wants you. They're my family now. They've chosen me, and now I have the family I've always wanted."

Min took Ellis's hand. "The family *she* deserves."

"Despite your efforts, I'm here and I'm happy," Ellis said, clutching Min fiercely. "You have nothing, and I'm fairly certain I can ensure no one in the publishing world will buy your lies. They won't want to be sued for libel, and I'm sure you'd rather not participate in a very public lawsuit."

The duchess sucked in a breath, her cheeks hollowing, making her appear almost skeletal. "You are all a disappointment to me." She glowered at Sheff. "I'm at Mivart's. You can send money there."

"Only if you promise never to bother us again," he said. "I'll have my solicitor draw up a contract."

"You would do that to your own mother?" she asked, aghast.

"I actually don't have a mother anymore," Sheff said, almost cheerfully. "Shall I show you out, ma'am?"

The duchess gasped, and her eyes narrowed. She turned on her heel and stomped from the room.

Min and Ellis looked at each other again and began to laugh. They quickly embraced, and Sheff joined in. Then they all flopped down in the seating area with Jo, who regarded them with warmth and encouragement.

Sheff stretched out his legs as he settled into his chair. "That was almost fun."

"Almost," Min said. "It was also rather harrowing." She looked at Ellis. "Are you all right?"

"I am, surprisingly. I can't thank you all enough for your generosity and your support. And your love," Ellis added softly.

"We do love you," Sheff said.

"And you *are* part of this family." Min smiled widely. "I loved what you said to her."

"Oh yes, that was brilliant," Sheff agreed. "I only wish you all could have seen Keele and me when we confronted Harker."

Ellis snapped her gaze to her brother. "What are you talking about?"

"Last night, Keele told him he knew Harker had been his wife's lover."

Ellis's joy faded beneath a heavy weight of apprehension. "Did he call him out?"

"No, Keele decided he didn't need to do that anymore," Sheff replied. "If it helps to know, I think he'd already mostly decided that before I arrived to talk sense into him."

"I'm so relieved," Ellis said, slumping back against the settee next to Min. "How did Harker react?"

"He was surprisingly contrite and said he would make an effort not to continue his philandering. He knows that if he does, his life will be over as he knows it. He will be cut off from you and Jo and from our child." He glanced at Jo, who nodded. "I also might have mentioned that your other half-siblings would be inclined to no longer speak with him if they learned the true depth of his debauchery. We also made it clear that he would be shunned by Society, and we made him promise never to teach painting again."

Ellis stared at him in awe. "You didn't hold back."

"Nor should we have," Sheff said.

Noting Sheff said "we," she realized he meant himself and Roman. "How was Roman?" She was still worried about him.

"I will let him tell you."

"He doesn't even know where I am," Ellis said. "Unless you told him?"

Sheff shrugged. "I didn't tell him you were here, but Roman is a smart man."

"I should see him." Ellis needed to tell him how she felt. She should have done it the other night instead of hiding behind a rogue rule. It was time to let him see her heart. He wasn't truly a rogue at all, and even if he were, she would love him anyway.

"I think you'll find that if you stay around the house today, you might have a chance to speak with him." Sheff stood. "And that's all I'm going to say about that. Bye for now, sisters. And wife," he added with a special smile toward Jo before leaving.

"That sounds as though he's going to call today," Min said, her eyes sparkling with anticipation.

"It does," Ellis replied, suddenly feeling nervous.

"Are you ready for that?" Jo asked.

Ellis shook her head. "But I will be."

CHAPTER 20

Naturally, it was the one day when Roman was eager to speak with Josiah that his former father-in-law was late coming into the office on Paternoster Row.

Roman acknowledged it was strange being around Josiah and Harriet knowing what he did now about Clarissa. It wasn't that she'd been unfaithful—that wasn't new, of course—but Roman now knew the identity of the man she'd loved and who had treated her so callously. He felt sorry for her wonderful parents, who had been nothing but kind and generous to him, and who had loved Clarissa so fiercely. Harriet especially carried grief, but there was nothing Roman could do to alleviate her pain except show her the appreciation and love that he had for some time.

At last, Josiah came upstairs near noon. Roman had been working at the table in Josiah's office so he could capture his former father-in-law's attention as soon as he arrived.

"You're finally here," Roman said, jumping to his feet.

Josiah's brow furrowed slightly. "Did I miss an appointment in my diary?"

"No. I have something to speak to you about."

Nodding, Josiah set the leather case that he used to take papers to and from the office on his desk, then hung his greatcoat on a stand in the corner by the door.

Roman wasn't sure how to begin. He supposed he felt awkward discussing his plans for a future with another woman who wasn't Josiah's daughter. But it wasn't as if the man didn't expect Roman to remarry. In fact, he'd been encouraging him to wed his other daughter. Perhaps that was another reason Roman was uncomfortable.

"Before you get started, Harriet wanted me to ask if you were all right," Josiah said as he crossed back to his desk. "She remarked yesterday that you seemed upset, and I confess I noticed you were not quite yourself. Dare I say you're…brooding?"

"That would be a fair characterization," Roman replied. "That's what I want to talk to you about."

Harriet bustled in just then. "There you are, Roman. Would you care for tea?"

"Yes, thank you."

She looked expectantly at her husband.

Josiah held up a hand. "I'm speaking with him now, in fact."

Roman stifled a smile. She hadn't even asked a question, just sent her husband a glance, but Josiah had known exactly what she was trying to communicate. Roman realized he wanted that kind of intimate connection with a person—with *his* person. With Ellis.

"Shall I leave you to it, then?" Harriet asked.

"No, stay. Please," Roman said. "I was upset yesterday because Ellis left my employ and my household."

"That's a tragedy!" Josiah exclaimed, his forehead creasing with grave concern. "What happened?"

Harriet walked over to Roman and put her hand on his arm. Giving him a sympathetic, motherly look, she guided him toward the seating area. "I understand now why you were so bothered yesterday. You must miss her very much."

"Of course he does," Josiah said. "She's the best secretary he's ever had."

Harriet snapped another look toward her husband, but Roman couldn't see Josiah's reaction. She then returned her gaze to him, and her expression softened. "Does Ellis know you love her?"

Roman managed to keep his jaw from dropping. "How did you know?"

Harriet shook her head faintly. "Men are so silly. I've known for some time. I think I might have puzzled it out right after we discovered she was a woman."

"*I* didn't even know I loved her then," Roman said.

"As I said, men are silly." Harriet's eyes gleamed with mirth.

"Is that true?" Josiah asked, sounding shocked. "Not about men, about you being in love with Ellis." He came to join them in the seating area, though no one had sat.

Harriet laughed, and Roman couldn't help smiling. "Yes, it's true." Roman quickly sobered. "However, there are reasons we can't marry."

"I hope it isn't money," Josiah said. "I don't want you to worry about that. Your future here is quite secure. Who else am I to leave the company to, in addition to Margot and her betrothed? You're a part of this business now and part of this family."

Roman didn't trust himself to speak. Whilst he knew they considered him family, to hear them say that now, when he wanted to marry someone other than their daughter, meant everything to him.

"Why is it you think you can't marry?" Harriet asked with a pleasant expression. She didn't seem concerned in the slightest.

Roman couldn't tell them about Harker, but the man was no longer an obstacle. At least, not for Roman. However, perhaps Ellis wouldn't be able to move past what Harker had done. It might be that she felt guilt on her father's behalf, which was, of course, completely unnecessary.

And apparently, money wasn't a reason for them not to wed either. Not just because Josiah had just told him he needn't worry about it, but for the reason that Sheff had stated—Roman would want to marry Ellis even if he hadn't a farthing to his name. He only needed to know whether she wanted to marry him too.

The last issue was that of her birth. Roman didn't give a fig that she was illegitimate, but he knew many would. However, that was still a secret, and he hoped it would remain so. If not, they would weather the scandal. Hopefully, the fact that she was already a marchioness would mitigate any damage.

"I suppose there really isn't a reason," Roman said.

Now Harriet's forehead gently creased. "My dear boy, you can't think *we* would take any issue with your marrying—Ellis or anyone else. Aside from the fact that we know you need an heir, I think Josiah would agree with me that we want you to find love and companionship, as we have." She sent a loving glance toward her husband, which he returned.

Roman had long envied their closeness. It was now clear to him that he would never have had that with Clarissa. She'd been pushed into their marriage against her wishes, and, in truth, he'd been lured into the arrangement too. But whilst he'd hoped that affection would bloom between them, it seemed she either hadn't given them the chance or decided it would never happen, at least for her.

"I'm very glad to have your blessing," Roman said. "I think of you as my family too. Indeed, you're the mother and father I always wished I'd had."

"That makes me very happy," Harriet said. "May I?" She held her arms out to Roman.

"Of course." Roman embraced her, and when they parted, Josiah surprised him by embracing him too.

"I could not have asked for a better son," Josiah said, sounding as though he had a rock stuck in his throat.

When Josiah stood back, Harriet quickly squeezed his hand before fixing on Roman once more. "Now, what are your plans?"

Josiah regarded him intently. "You wanted to speak with me about something. Is this about Ellis? *Mrs.* Ellis, I mean. I should not refer to her by her surname as if she's your secretary any longer. She's to be the Marchioness of Keele."

Ellis was, of course, not *Mrs.* and revealing her as an unmarried miss might upset them, especially Harriet. Still, Roman couldn't lie. They would soon find out who she was. Not that she was the Duchess of Henlow's illegitimate daughter. Roman would do whatever necessary to protect that secret.

Roman grimaced as he anticipated their reaction. "Ellis is her Christian name. She is actually Miss Ellis Dangerfield, former companion to Lady Minerva, daughter of the Duke of Henlow. She is not a widow."

Appearing discomfited, Harriet gently wrung her hands. "Did you know that?"

He nodded. "We lied to you about Ellis being a widow. It seemed prudent."

Harriet gasped softly. "That was very dangerous to your reputations."

Josiah eyed Roman. "It was indeed. I suppose I see now why you supported Margot and her secret courtship. You are all very lucky that your scandalous behavior wasn't discovered and made public. For all of our sakes."

Roman felt quite like a son being admonished by his parents. It made him surprisingly happy. "I never meant to risk anyone's reputation. But you are right that we behaved foolishly. I'm sorry."

"What's done is done," Josiah said with a slight grunt and a wave of his hand. "It's all worked out for the best, and now we're to have two happy marriages."

Roman certainly hoped so. "I don't know if Ellis will say yes, which is why I need your help. I have a plan, and you will be part of it."

Josiah rubbed his hands together. "Let us sit and plot." His eyes glowed with mischief.

Harriet gave Roman a reproachful look. "As long as there is no deception involved, I'm eager to assist."

Putting his hand on his heart, Roman met Harriet's gaze. "I promise there is no deception, just a plan to show Ellis how much I love her."

"Then I can most heartily endorse that." Harriet took her seat. "How can we help?"

~

It was now mid-afternoon, and Ellis had been reading in the library for nearly an hour. She began to think Roman wasn't actually going to call, that she'd misunderstood Sheff's hints.

Blinking rapidly, she flipped the pages back because she hadn't retained anything she'd read.

Why was she even sitting here waiting when she knew what she wanted? She snapped the book closed. She didn't need to wait on other people anymore. She was going to make her own future and might as well start now.

She stood and set the book on a table as she eagerly faced the main doorway. What would be the fastest way to reach Bolton Street? Waiting for a vehicle from the mews or walking?

Percy stepped inside, interrupting her plans. "Miss Dangerfield, you've a caller. Lord Keele."

Ellis's heart pounded. Anticipation surged through her. "Please show him in, Percy. Thank you."

The butler turned and had barely stepped over the threshold before stopping short. "My lord, did you follow me? I see you did. Very well." He pivoted back toward Ellis. "Here is Lord Keele." Percy quickly took himself off.

Roman glanced behind him, then stepped into the library and immediately closed the door. He took a few steps toward her before stopping. "Aren't you going to admonish me for closing the door?"

"I should, but I don't want to." The other door to the library was already closed. "Are you planning on ravishing me?" she asked.

"Don't tempt me." He closed his eyes briefly, then smiled. Then, he immediately sobered. "I came here to apologize. And please don't flirt with me."

She pressed her lips together to keep from smiling. "I will not flirt with you."

Roman groaned softly. "Just the way you say that is flirtatious."

What was happening? Weren't they at odds? Wasn't he angry?

Ellis managed to take a deep breath. "Please make your apology, though I don't think you owe me one."

"The hell I don't," he said harshly. "I walked out on you the other night, and I should not have. I'm apologizing for that, *and* because I should have told you that your mother sent me a letter."

"I know about that," she said.

He blinked at her in surprise. "You do?"

She nodded. "The duchess was here earlier. She informed me of her desperate attempt to extort you. I greatly appreciate your denying her demands."

His shoulders sagged. "You're not angry that I refused her?"

"Of course not," Ellis said with fast conviction. "I wouldn't want you to give her a shilling."

"Good." He sounded relieved. "I didn't see a point in paying her. I didn't think she could be trusted to leave, and Sheff agreed with me."

"I agree with both of you." She hesitated as she searched his familiar face, her gaze lovingly appreciating the hawk-like sharpness of his nose, the masculine angles of his jaw and cheekbones, the deep gray of his eyes fringed in gorgeous black lashes. "Sheff told me you called on Rowland Harker. That must have been difficult for you."

Roman's jaw tightened briefly. "It had to be done. I'm also sorry for making you think I was going to call your father out." His expression softened, and she resisted the urge to embrace him. There was still more to say.

"I don't think of him as my father any more than I think of the duchess as my mother." Ellis shuddered in revulsion. "I hope the meeting with him gave you some sort of satisfaction, if not peace."

"It did. But I will have no problem never seeing him again, and I realize that could create some difficulty for you. Though if you don't think of him as a father—"

"I do *not*," Ellis confirmed vehemently. "You shall never have to see him again. I honestly don't know if I will either. It's sad, really, because I suspect he actually has a decent heart. He seems almost…compelled to behave in the manner in which he does. It reminds me of someone consumed with drink." She shook her head. In truth, she pitied Rowland Harker, for he prevented himself from forming deep and meaningful connections with people, including his own family.

"I don't want you to keep yourself from him on my account," Roman said. "But it doesn't sound as though that will be a hardship."

"It will not," she agreed. "Does this mean he isn't going to come between us?"

"Not as far as I'm concerned. Which leads me to the other reason for my visit. I've come to offer you a proposal," Roman stated rather matter-of-factly.

Whilst it wasn't the manner in which she might have expected him to make a marriage proposal, Ellis was too glad to care. "And what is that?" She smiled expectantly.

"I've just come from Lacey and Company, and Josiah agrees it's past time we have a branch of the library in Bath," Roman replied. "We would very much like you to be the librarian at that branch."

Ellis's heart sank. He didn't mean to propose marriage to her at all. But he'd behaved in a flirtatious manner. This didn't make sense.

"Or," he continued, and Ellis held her breath. "You could accept a different position, one that I would prefer to see you take." He moved toward her and dropped to his knee in front of her, taking her hand. "I think I heard you say 'I love you' the other night, but I don't know if I imagined it—because I wanted it so badly to be true—or if it really happened. Either way, I am here to tell you that *I* love *you*, and nothing would make me happier than if you would be my wife. Will you marry me?"

"Yes," Ellis replied without hesitation. "I *did* say that the other night."

He smiled, but only briefly. "And what about marrying me? Is that a yes too?"

"Resoundingly." Ellis grinned. "As much as I would love to be the librarian in Bath, I believe it would interfere with my duties here in London as your wife."

Roman closed his eyes briefly and bent his head. Turning her hand, he pressed a kiss to her wrist.

He looked up at her. "You're sure this is what you want? Because I want you to have a choice. I want *you* to choose your future."

"I know," she said. "Why did you propose the library first? Did you think that was what I wanted most?"

Roman grimaced faintly. "I feared it might be. You have always been clear that you didn't wish to marry, and I can't say I blame you, considering how your life has been managed for so long. However, I am never going to do that to you. As my wife, you will be my equal partner at Lacey and Company. We will share the stake in the company together."

Ellis realized this was very close to Pandora's book, *A Season in Shadow*, where Dinah was able to make her own choice. But while Dinah chose herself, Ellis was choosing Roman. However, she realized in choosing him, she was also choosing herself—and a chance for happiness she had never expected.

Ellis knelt down in front of him.

"What are you doing?" Roman asked.

"You weren't standing, and I want to kiss you."

Roman cupped her face in his hands as he grinned. "Not if I kiss you first."

He pulled back several moments later. "What made you change your mind? About marrying."

Ellis felt embarrassed telling him, but she didn't want there to be any secrets between them ever again. "I realized I thought I didn't deserve to be happy. The duchess had quite convinced me that I wasn't worthy of love and that I wasn't at all wanted. Coming back to Henlow House, I see how everyone here loves me. And no one has ever made me feel as wanted as you do."

"*Ellis*, nothing is truer than the endless want I have for you." He kissed her again, hard and fast, then looked into her eyes as he cupped her face. "I felt much the same—that I was unlovable. Love and a family of my own are all I've ever wanted. Then Clarissa chose someone else. But I do have a family—the Laceys."

"And me," Ellis said quickly, aching for how lonely they'd felt until finding each other.

"And you." He smiled gain. "You are my family. As well as my love."

She pressed her lips to his and was immediately consumed with insatiable need she now knew was driven by the deep love they shared. Would they ever tire of one another? She couldn't imagine it, especially not now. They kissed eagerly, feverishly, and she soon pushed his coat off. Ellis pushed him backward, but he clasped her waist and pulled away.

"We can't do this on the floor in the middle of the library at Henlow House. Now, if we were at Bolton Street—"

Ellis kissed him again to smother his complaints before rising and pulling him up along with her. "The settee is right there. Will that be acceptable instead of the floor?"

Groaning, Roman stood. "I should not let you seduce me, Miss Dangerfield. It's highly improper."

"It's a bit late for propriety, don't you agree?" She arched a brow at him as she guided him to the settee and pushed him down.

Roman chuckled. "I suppose. Do as you will, my love."

"Thank you for your consent." She hiked up her skirts and straddled him.

"I don't suppose the door locks?" Roman asked.

"We'll be quick," she replied instead of telling him they did not. She slid her hands between them and stroked him through his breeches. This truly was madness. Anyone could interrupt them.

His gray eyes smoldered with want as she stared up at him. "I am powerless to deny you, even when common sense begs me to." He cupped her head and pulled her down to him for a searing kiss.

Ellis shuddered with desire, desperate to feel him inside her. Would he remove himself from her body as they'd always done? They didn't really need to, unless they preferred to avoid having a child just yet.

She snagged his lip with her teeth before lifting her head slightly to look at him. His lids rose, and she nearly lost herself in the haze of passion darkening his gaze. "Will you pull away from me when you climax?"

"Do you want me to?" he asked softly, and she couldn't tell what he might prefer.

"No," she said tentatively. "Is that all right?"

"That is more than all right, for too many reasons to count." He kissed her again with something akin to possession, and Ellis felt she might burst with joy.

She continued to stroke him, and his hips moved with her, seeking her body. As she began to unbutton his fall, she heard the door open.

Damn.

Jerking away from him, she scrambled off Roman and adjusted her skirts. He worked to refasten his breeches, but his poor body was in a rather advanced—and unmistakable —state of arousal.

Thankfully, it was only Jo. Still, Ellis gave Roman a look that told him to stay where he was.

"Oh!" Jo immediately turned her back. "I did not mean to interrupt."

"It's quite all right." Ellis found Roman's coat and thrust it at him.

"I take it the two of you have made up?" Jo asked.

"We're to be married," Ellis replied.

Jo gasped and glanced over her shoulder at them. "Is it all right if I turn back around?"

"Yes, we're decent." Ellis smirked at Roman's groin. "Mostly."

He gave her a roguish smile as he donned his coat.

"Then I'm going to hug you." Jo rushed over and embraced Ellis, and they both laughed.

Jo stepped back and beamed at them. "When will you wed?"

Ellis watched Roman as he finally stood. He appeared to have recovered himself, which was unfortunate. However, Ellis was certain she could return him to his former state with little effort.

He lifted his shoulder. "As soon as possible. I'll obtain a special license."

"Thank goodness," Ellis said, causing Jo to laugh again.

"This is wonderful news," Jo said. "I'm going to plan a dinner to celebrate. And a wedding breakfast."

"That is very kind of you," Roman said.

"Ellis is my sister," Jo replied simply, as if that explained her generosity, but Ellis knew that blood ties did not guarantee love or affection. "I love her very much, and I'm beside myself with joy."

"One thing we did not discuss was the Duchess." Roman looked at Ellis. "What are we going to do about her threats?"

"We got carried away before I could explain that," Ellis said. "When she was here earlier, Sheff said he would pay for her to leave us alone. He's asked his solicitor to draw up a contract so she can't ask for more money. After that, he will give her a set sum, and we will be rid of her at last."

Roman appeared relieved. "An excellent plan."

Ellis went on. "I do think we should put it out through Mr. Lacey that publishers should not take any inquiries from the Duchess of Henlow about a memoir or from anyone claiming to write an exposing tale about the Henlow family. We must warn them that such a manuscript is riddled with lies, and that anyone who publishes it will be sued for libel."

"What an excellent solution," Roman remarked with an admiring glint in his eyes. "I'm sorry I missed that confrontation earlier today."

"We're sorry we missed your confrontation with my father," Jo replied. "I still can't quite believe he said he's going to try not to philander, but I suppose we'll see if that actually happens."

"He did say it would be very hard." Roman frowned slightly. "It sounds as if he has true difficulty in denying his baser needs."

Jo clapped her hands together. "I'm going to go tell Sheff the news, if you don't mind."

"Please do," Ellis replied with a smile.

"I'll make sure no one comes in here for the next hour or so," Jo said as she went to the door.

"Ten or fifteen minutes is probably fine," Roman called after her. As the door closed, he pulled Ellis into his arms, and she laughed softly.

"How quickly can you get that special license?" she asked.

"Tomorrow. We can marry the following day."

"That doesn't give us much time to plan the wedding breakfast."

He raised a brow at her. "Do you want more time?"

"I don't want to wait a single second to be your wife, but I can be patient." She narrowed her eyes and looked at him in sensual invitation. "Somewhat."

"I much prefer your impatience, dear almost-wife." He swept her into his arms again. "Would you mind showing me?"

"Every minute of every day." She kissed him, and it happened that ten minutes was more than enough.

Still, they managed to fill the entire hour.

CHAPTER 21

*E*verything worked out exactly as Roman had planned. He'd obtained the special license the day after becoming betrothed to Ellis, and they'd married the following day at St. George's in Hanover Square.

It was very different from his first wedding at the St. Marylebone parish church, and that wasn't because there were more people in attendance, but because of the joy and love filling his heart. He would be forever grateful that Ellis had been driven from her family and found safety and comfort in his employment, in his household, and most importantly, in his arms.

Roman had been particularly happy to have Josiah standing beside him as he took Ellis's hand in marriage. Ellis was equally thrilled to have her sister Min with her. Indeed, Roman marveled at the bond of friendship not just between the two of them, but within their larger circle.

Now, five days later, they were gathered for dinner at Henlow House, as organized by Lady Shefford. The ladies were all in attendance—eight of them, he realized. Even the

Duchess of Wellesbourne had returned to town, though she hadn't been able to arrive in time for the wedding.

The friends were seated together on one side of the drawing room. Roman walked over to where their husbands had collected on the opposite side. He glanced toward the lot of them—Sheff, Evan Pierce, the Viscount Somerton, the Duke of Wellesbourne, and Baron Droxford. "What are they doing over there? Should we be worried?"

They all laughed, even Droxford, who was generally rather stoic.

"I want to say they're harmless," Wellesbourne said. "However, the truth is, if they put their minds to it, they could likely set London, and perhaps all of England, on its axis."

Somerton coughed. "I think you meant to say the world. Do not underestimate their power."

"Hear, hear," Droxford said, lifting his glass of wine. They'd finished dinner, and the gentlemen had only taken port for a short while before joining the ladies in the drawing room.

Aside from the group of friends, they'd also invited family, which included the Duke of Henlow and his love. Ordinarily, it would be scandalous for a nobleman to bring his mistress to an event and expect people to interact with her, however, no one here stood on that kind of nonsense. It was clear that no one in the family or their close circle referred to her or thought of Mrs. Welbeck as simply his mistress. It was also obvious to anyone with eyes that she and the duke were absolutely smitten with one another. This was not a fleeting affair.

The Laceys were there, of course, including Margot and her betrothed, Oliver Pritchard. They would be married after the new year in Marylebone.

Pierce inclined his head toward the ladies. "I'm sure

they're presenting your wife with her copy of the Rogue Rules. It's a tradition they have when one of them marries."

Roman had heard about those. In fact, he knew precisely which rule Ellis had broken, though it seemed there were several. "It doesn't appear those rules have worked out well for them. Haven't they all broken one or more and are now married to—well, I suppose former—rogues?"

"*Former* is the key," Wellesbourne said with a faint smirk. "I think we'd all agree that we've been exceptionally fortunate to gain our wives." He lifted his glass, and everyone followed suit.

After swallowing a sip of port, Roman shot a glance toward the circle of ladies. "Will it be a problem if I go over there and interrupt?"

The men regarded him with a mix of wariness, apprehension, and pity.

Somerton arched his blond brows. "If you dare."

"Not sure I would," Droxford said. His had been the expression of pity.

"Wish me luck, then." Roman started toward that side of the room but was intercepted by Margot.

She gave him a tentative look. "Are you going to speak to the ladies?"

"I had planned to, yes. Do you plan to warn me against doing so as the men did?"

"Oh, no," Margot said. "I would like to join you. I felt nervous walking over there by myself. It's a rather intimidating group—a duchess, a countess, a viscountess, a baroness, the daughter of a duke, and your marchioness."

"You needn't feel intimidated," Roman said. "They're just people, and you know Ellis well enough. They're all her friends. They will be your friends too, I'm sure."

"Come." He walked with her to the group of ladies as Ellis

finished unwrapping a package. She smiled at the framed item on her lap.

"I can't say I'm surprised," Ellis said. "To receive it, I mean. I'm still rather shocked that I'm in a position to do so. I never imagined I would be married." She glanced warmly at Roman before shifting her gaze to Pandora. "You've outdone yourself. I love all the personal touches." Pandora had personalized each set of rules for the bride with decorative details along with the text. "Thank you."

"Your Rogue Rules had to have books, and I couldn't resist stitching the beard and mustache up in the corner." She winked at Ellis, who laughed again.

"May I see this?" Roman moved to stand next to his wife's chair. She held it up to him.

"Pandora always embroiders a copy of the Rogue Rules for the bride," Ellis explained.

"I'll never wed, so I'm delighted to be the one to make them," Pandora said with a mischievous grin

"Never say never," Roman advised. "I think Ellis and I can both tell you that the best intentions don't always happen."

"Agreed," the Duchess of Wellesbourne said. "I'm certain plenty of others here would say the same."

Several of the ladies nodded.

Roman gestured to Margot. "I believe you've all met Miss Lacey."

Min smiled warmly at Margot. "Yes, of course. We were remiss in not inviting you to join us."

"It's all right," Margot said. "Mama and I did not come directly to the drawing room after dinner."

"You must sit with us," Lady Somerton, who was Pierce's sister, insisted. "There's always room for more. Just ask Iona. She's the newest to our group and the only one besides Pandora who is left unmarried."

Though Miss Shaughnessy smiled, Roman detected a hint

of nervousness in her features. Margot sat down beside her. They appeared to be of a similar age.

Miss Shaughnessy turned to Margot. "Is it true you and your betrothed fell in love writing letters?"

"Yes, over several months, though I knew after the first letter he was special." Margot beamed.

"And no one knew this was happening?" Miss Shaughnessy seemed most intrigued.

Margot blushed faintly. "No, but it did come out, of course, now that we're betrothed."

"It's a splendid idea," Miss Shaughnessy said, sounding almost contemplative.

"Well, I don't think we planned it as an *idea*, exactly." Margot's brow briefly pleated before she smiled. "But it did work out rather wonderfully."

Roman looked down at Ellis. "Would you join me for a moment?" He held out his hand to her.

"Of course." She set the Rogue Rules down on her chair as she stood. "Pardon me, ladies."

"And there she goes," Pandora said with a sigh. "Choosing her husband over us."

"Not entirely," Ellis said. "You're all of very great importance to me, and I'm sorry I didn't rely on you sooner."

"We understand." Min gave her a caring smile. "And we love you."

Ellis took Roman's arm, and he led her to where Josiah and Harriet were speaking with Henlow and Mrs. Welbeck.

Mrs. Welbeck was a delightful woman and was, in fact, the granddaughter of an earl.

Josiah turned to Roman. "Ready?"

Roman nodded before addressing Ellis softly. "We're going to make an announcement now."

"What is this about?" she asked, appearing concerned.

"I've already said I don't want to be the librarian in Bath. I can't do that."

Josiah chuckled. "No, no, but you will be instrumental in helping us choose a location, if you agree to what we'd like to announce."

Harriet beamed at her. "We'd like you to be secretary of Lacey and Company. You will have your own stake in the company and be an integral part of its operation and success."

Ellis sucked in a breath, her eyes glowing with surprise and joy. Roman delighted in how happy she was.

"I don't know what to say." Ellis beamed at the Laceys, then at Roman.

"I say it's well deserved," Henlow replied proudly.

Ellis met Henlow's gaze. "Thank you for believing in me and supporting me when others would not."

Roman knew she thought of the duke as a surrogate father in ways that she would never consider Rowland Harker. They had not invited Harker to the wedding but had glimpsed him loitering outside the church when they'd left. Time would tell if he lived up to his promise, and, truthfully, they weren't paying close attention, nor did they plan to.

"Are you ready for me to make the announcement?" Roman asked.

Ellis nodded. "Though, you needn't make a fuss."

Henlow looked at her with mock admonishment. "My dear, you must become accustomed to fuss. You are the Marchioness of Keele now, and there will be much fuss over you from now on."

Ellis laughed. "I will try."

Roman took her hand and gave it a squeeze, then turned to address the room. "I have an announcement to make," he said loudly. "Lacey and Company is proud to announce the appointment of our new secretary, Lady Keele. May we all lift our glasses and toast to the extreme good fortune of Lacey and Company to have such an amazing woman in this role."

He lifted his glass, and there was a round of huzzahs.

"We didn't all have drinks," Ellis said.

Roman quickly handed her his port. She met his eyes over the rim of the glass as she took a sip. There was something seductive about the way her lips pressed against the glass, and Roman had to steel himself against becoming aroused. Now was not the time.

"When can we leave?" he whispered.

She laughed at him as she handed the port back. "Not for a while yet. You'll have your time alone with me, my lord." Her eyes gleamed with promise. "All the time you could ever want."

He shook his head and gazed at her with overwhelming love and gratitude. "Forever wouldn't be enough."

EPILOGUE

Westlands, June, 1817

Ellis and Roman were thrilled to become an aunt and uncle in early January when Jo and Sheff welcomed their daughter, Elinor. They'd all spent the holidays at Beacon Park together, including Min and Evan, so they'd been present for Elinor's arrival on Epiphany. To a one, they were completely enamored.

Then they were delighted to journey to Winterstoke, the Somerton family seat, in Wiltshire in early June to meet Gwen and Lazarus's new son, who'd been born in April. Felix, named for Lazarus's beloved father, was as much of a charmer as his own father.

They'd stayed a week, not wishing to overstay their welcome and knowing they would all be together soon in August when everyone planned to be in Weston for their annual summer holiday. The Grove, the Duke of Henlow's house there, would be overflowing with Ellis and Roman, Min and Evan, and of course Jo and Sheff and sweet Elinor, whom they all called Ellie. Her name was a nod to Ellis, which made her heart even fuller, if that was possible. Then, just when she thought she could not be happier, something happened to prove she absolutely could be.

Today was another such day.

Ellis practically skipped down the wide staircase at Westlands, the Keele family seat. Located between Birmingham and Manchester, the manor house was a large rectangle with a central courtyard, originally built in the late seventeenth century and improved twice. The most recent renovation had set the family on its path to ruin as Roman's grandfather had incurred great debt to modernize the house. Ellis still couldn't quite believe she was mistress there.

They'd been at Westlands a fortnight, and Ellis was already in love with the retainers and the tenants on the estate. She'd never imagined a life like this, and every day had to remind herself that this was real.

Roman also did his part to ensure she never forgot.

Smiling, she went in search of him, for today's exceptionally wonderful news was entirely for him. As expected, she found him in the large study, which was set in the corner of the ground floor overlooking a magnificent garden currently bursting with color from dozens of roses in full bloom.

When they'd first arrived, Ellis had been surprised—and touched—to see that the study had been refurbished to include two desks so they could continue to work together. The desks were pushed together so that they faced each other. It could be quite distracting, but thankfully the study was also furnished with a large chaise longue and a lock on the door.

Ellis leaned against the doorjamb as she watched Roman work. His quill scratched over the parchment as he focused intently on whatever he was doing. She would never tire of just observing him. She'd never known anyone more dedicated or committed to his work and to the purpose he'd set himself—to leave his family's legacy in far better condition than in which he'd inherited it.

A large part of that, he said, was marrying Ellis. He told her repeatedly that she had already improved the family to a level not before seen. He was incorrigibly and unapologetically romantic. Ellis could not have asked for a better husband.

At last, he glanced up. "How long have you been standing there?"

"Long enough to wonder if I'd lost the ability to distract you."

He grinned as he set his quill in the stand and rose. "Never."

Ellis's pulse leapt as she met him in the center of the room. "What are you working on?"

"Just writing a response to Josiah. We need to print more copies of *A Season in Shadow* again. It has become our best-selling novel."

"Pandora will be thrilled." Ellis smiled. "I'll write to her and let her know, if that's all right."

"I think Josiah might have beaten you to it," Roman said with a chuckle. "I can hear his excitement in his letter. Have you come to work or perhaps for some other reason?" He gave her a seductive look.

"Actually, I came to tell you something important." Ellis tamped down her giddiness lest she spoil the surprise.

"Did you?" He put his arm around her waist and pulled her toward him. "Here, I hoped you'd planned to distract me as you implied."

"I fear this will be a major distraction, but it can't be helped."

Roman flinched. "Has something happened? The duchess hasn't emerged from the rock she crawled under, has she?"

Ellis laughed softly. "No, this is something pleasant. Something wonderful. I've waited to tell you until I was absolutely certain, and now I am." She took his free hand and pressed his palm to her lower abdomen. "We are to be parents."

His eyes rounded with wonder, then a grin nearly split his face as he swept her up and spun her around. But he quickly set her down. "That didn't make you ill, did it?" He kept his hands on her waist as his brow furrowed.

She shook her head. "I have not been ill at all, actually, but Mrs. Gentry said that is not uncommon. She said her sisters were not ill when they were carrying."

Mrs. Gentry was Westlands's housekeeper and had quickly become a confidante and mother-like figure to Ellis, just as Harriet Lacey had. She and Josiah would be thrilled to learn they would be grandparents, for that was the role that Ellis wanted them to assume.

"You feel completely fine?" he asked, sounding puzzled.

"More than." She smiled. "You're happy?"

He grinned again. "I'm bloody ecstatic. When is this happening? Do you know?"

"Based on when my courses stopped, I would guess around Christmas, perhaps a bit sooner."

"What a lovely gift he or she will be." He touched her abdomen again, his features alight with wonder. "I can't wait to meet you," he whispered. Then he gazed into Ellis's eyes. "Thank you for making all my dreams come true."

She curled her arms around his neck. "And thank you for making mine come true. Especially coming to Weston in August. I know you'd rather work, not that you won't work while we're there."

"I plan to be anywhere you are, unless you tell me otherwise. I can't bear to be away from you." He kissed her soundly.

When they parted, Ellis sighed. "How did we become so lucky?"

"I'm not sure, but I will never stop being grateful. What is unlucky, however, is the fact that you did not shut or lock the door. How can we properly celebrate this magnificent news?"

Ellis gave him a saucy look. "I didn't think of it as I was too eager to tell you."

"As you should have been. Allow me." He sprinted to close and secure the door, then returned to her as quickly as he'd left.

"Where would you like to *celebrate*?" Ellis asked, glancing about the room. "I don't believe there's a piece of furniture in this room that we haven't, er, celebrated."

"The desks hold a certain nostalgia for me since we met with you working as my secretary." He shook his head. "I should be eternally ashamed for allowing our relationship to progress as it did, but I'm afraid I was completely unable to resist you."

"It took the both of us to flaunt propriety so flagrantly, and I've no regrets." She loosened his cravat, knowing she would have to knot it again later. Redressing each other had become one of their favorite intimacies.

"Then allow us to flaunt it once more as flagrantly as possible." Roman leered at her before capturing her mouth in a kiss full of unrestrained passion and boundless love.

Ellis had no regrets about anything anymore. Her life had led her here—to this joyous moment in this incredible man's arms and a future she was eager to experience with him.

Nothing could be more perfect.

Don't miss the next Rogue Rules, WHAT THE SCOUNDREL DESIRES:
When a jilted young lady claims a letter-writing courtship with a viscount, his cousin pretends to be her invented beau. But when he falls for her, he faces an impossible choice: walk away or confess his deception and risk losing her forever.

Would you like to know when my next book is available and to hear about sales and deals? **Sign up for my VIP newsletter** which is the only place you can get bonus books and material such as the short prequel to the Phoenix Club series, INVITATION, and the exciting prequel to Legendary Rogues, THE LEGEND OF A ROGUE.

Join me on social media!

Facebook: https://facebook.com/DarcyBurkeFans
Instagram at darcyburkeauthor
Pinterest at darcyburkewrite

And follow me on Bookbub to receive updates on pre-orders, new releases, and deals!

Need more Regency romance? Visit my website and check out my other historical series:

The Phoenix Club
Society's most exclusive invitation...

Welcome to the Phoenix Club, where London's most

audacious, disreputable, and intriguing ladies and gentlemen find scandal, redemption, and second chances.

Matchmaking Chronicles

The course of true love never runs smooth. Sometimes a little matchmaking is required. When couples meet at a house party, provocative flirtation, secret rendezvous, and falling in love abound!

The Untouchables

Swoon over twelve of Society's most eligible and elusive bachelor peers and the bluestockings, wallflowers, and outcasts who bring them to their knees!

The Untouchables: The Spitfire Society

Meet the smart, independent women who've decided they don't need Society's rules, their families' expectations, or, most importantly, a husband. But just because they don't need a man doesn't mean they might not *want* one...

The Untouchables: The Pretenders

Set in the captivating world of The Untouchables, follow the saga of a trio of siblings who excel at being something they're not. Can a dauntless Bow Street Runner, a devastated viscount, and a disillusioned Society miss unravel their secrets?

Marrywell Brides

Come to Marrywell, England where the annual May Day Matchmaking Festival has been bringing hopeful romantics together for hundreds of years. The dukes and rogues of the Regency will meet their matches with spirited and captivating ladies who may very well steal their hearts.

Wicked Dukes Club
Six books written by me and my BFF, NYT Bestselling
Author Erica Ridley. Meet the unforgettable men of
London's most notorious tavern, The Wicked Duke.
Seductively handsome, with charm and wit to spare, one
night with these rakes and rogues will never be enough...

Love is All Around
Heartwarming Regency-set retellings of classic Christmas
stories (written after the Regency!) featuring a cozy village,
three siblings, and the best gift of all: love.

Secrets and Scandals
Six epic stories set in London's glittering ballrooms and
England's lush countryside.

Legendary Rogues
Five intrepid heroines and adventurous heroes embark on
exciting quests across the Georgian Highlands and Regency
England and Wales!

If you enjoy mysteries and a slow-burn romance, you may
like my Victorian mystery series, Raven & Wren, beginning
with **A WHISPER OF DEATH**.

When an earl is stabbed and left for dead, he acquires a
mysterious power to see things he can't explain. His new
ability leads him to the house of a dead man, where he meets
a clever and intriguing woman who, with her particular set
of investigative skills, may be able to help him. But can she
trust the enigmatic gentleman who is clearly hiding
something?

Like contemporary romance? I hope you'll check out my

Ribbon Ridge series, a ten-book family saga set in a small town in Oregon wine country.

I hope you'll consider leaving a review at your favorite online vendor or networking site!

I appreciate my readers so much. Thank you, thank you, *thank you*.

ALSO BY DARCY BURKE

Historical Romance

<u>*Rogue Rules*</u>

If the Duke Dares

Because the Baron Broods

When the Viscount Seduces

As the Earl Likes

Until the Rake Surrenders

Since the Marquess Demands

What the Scoundrel Desires

How the Devil Sins

The Phoenix Club

Improper

Impassioned

Intolerable

Indecent

Impossible

Irresistible

Impeccable

Insatiable

Marrywell Brides

Beguiling the Duke

Romancing the Heiress

Matching the Marquess

The Matchmaking Chronicles
Yule Be My Duke
The Rigid Duke
The Bachelor Earl (also prequel to *The Untouchables*)
The Runaway Viscount
The Make-Believe Widow

The Untouchables
The Bachelor Earl (prequel)
The Forbidden Duke
The Duke of Daring
The Duke of Deception
The Duke of Desire
The Duke of Defiance
The Duke of Danger
The Duke of Ice
The Duke of Ruin
The Duke of Lies
The Duke of Seduction
The Duke of Kisses
The Duke of Distraction

The Untouchables: The Spitfire Society
Never Have I Ever with a Duke
A Duke is Never Enough
A Duke Will Never Do

The Untouchables: The Pretenders
A Secret Surrender
A Scandalous Bargain

A Rogue to Ruin

Love is All Around
(*A Regency Holiday Trilogy*)
The Red Hot Earl
The Gift of the Marquess
Joy to the Duke

Wicked Dukes Club
One Night for Seduction by Erica Ridley
One Night of Surrender by Darcy Burke
One Night of Passion by Erica Ridley
One Night of Scandal by Darcy Burke
One Night to Remember by Erica Ridley
One Night of Temptation by Darcy Burke

Secrets and Scandals
Her Wicked Ways
His Wicked Heart
To Seduce a Scoundrel
To Love a Thief (a novella)
Never Love a Scoundrel
Scoundrel Ever After

Legendary Rogues
Lady of Desire
Romancing the Earl
Lord of Fortune
Captivating the Scoundrel

Historical Mystery

<u>*Raven & Wren*</u>

A Whisper of Death

A Whisper at Midnight

A Whisper and a Curse

A Whisper in the Shadows

A Whisper of Secrecy

Contemporary Romance

Ribbon Ridge

Where the Heart Is (a prequel novella)

Only in My Dreams

Yours to Hold

When Love Happens

The Idea of You

When We Kiss

You're Still the One

Ribbon Ridge: So Hot

So Good

So Right

So Wrong

ABOUT THE AUTHOR

Darcy Burke is the USA Today Bestselling Author of sexy, emotional historical and contemporary romance. Darcy wrote her first book at age 11, a happily ever after about a swan addicted to magic and the female swan who loved him, with exceedingly poor illustrations. Join her Reader Club newsletter for the latest updates from Darcy.

A native Oregonian, Darcy lives on the edge of wine country with her guitar-strumming husband, incredibly talented artist daughter, and imaginative, Japanese-speaking son who will almost certainly out-write her one day (that may be tomorrow). They're a crazy cat family with two Bengal cats, a small, fame-seeking cat named after a fruit, an older rescue Maine Coon with attitude to spare, an adorable former stray who wandered onto their deck and into their hearts, and two bonded boys who used to belong to (separate) neighbors but chose them instead. You can find Darcy in her comfy writing chair balancing her laptop and a cat or three, attempting yoga, folding laundry (which she loves), or wildlife spotting and playing games with her family. She loves traveling to the UK and visiting her cousins in Denmark. Visit Darcy online at www.darcyburke.com and follow her on social media.

facebook.com/DarcyBurkeFans

instagram.com/darcyburkeauthor

pinterest.com/darcyburkewrites

goodreads.com/darcyburke

bookbub.com/authors/darcy-burke

amazon.com/author/darcyburke

threads.com/@darcyburkeauthor

tiktok.com/@darcyburkeauthor

www.ingramcontent.com/pod-product-compliance
Lightning Source LLC
Chambersburg PA
CBHW022012120726
47898CB00006BA/1829